Francesca

Woman From Many Stories

Lois Collins

Author's note: This is a work of fiction. Names, characters, places, and incidents are the product of the author's imagination or are used ficti-tiously. Any resemblance to reality is by coincidence.

DEDICATION

To the Creator of All Things

To the Characters in the Book

To the Reader

To My Ancestors

To My Children and Grandchildren

To All Future Generations

To My Friends

To My Former Patients and Students

To Mother Earth

TABLE OF CONTENTS

ACKNOWLEDGMENTS

To the joy, guidance, and expertise brought to me by my editor, Holly Chapman, a deep thanks. Holly, your trust in me and my work was my balm in Gilead. For the careful read and fantastic suggestions from my daughter Machell Cusek, a deep thanks. For the encouragement from both my daughter and son Charles Collins, a deep thanks. I love you both. For the read and powerful encouragement from my sister, Luann Spraker, a deep thanks. For the wisdom of pipe carrier Jack Chambers, a deep thanks. Lastly for the support of my village of friends and muses: Sandra Bernal, Evamarie Bill, Frank Bleyer, Tanya Briggs, Benjamin Brock, Maynor Brooks, Noreen Calvin, Carole Cantrell, Linda Chambers, Symmone Chavez, Ellen Friedman, Syrennia Henshaw, Kathleen Hosner, Julie Hotchkiss, Kaya Kotzen, Laura Llardo, Etiole Libbett, Marion Livingston, Marietta McDuffy, Keyonda McQuarters, Carmen Mercado, Erin Mitchell, Johnnie Moore, Lorna Mullings, Kim O'Connor, Teresa Ontiveras, Chavella Perez, Tracie Reithman, Kenny Rooth, mentor: Julie Sass, Andrea Shamoon, Jay Smith, Hal Snyder, Lucia Spears, Sarah Steele, Ardita Thaci, Avni Thaci, Victor Virzi, Heather Wen, and, of course, my parents, siblings, extended family, the family of my children's father, and my many wonderful friends.

AUTHOR'S PREFACE

As I began in the early 21st century to contemplate the future world of my great-grandchildren in the mid 21st century, the imagined Francesca entered my thoughts. She began to relate to me stories about her family and about the generations that led to her birth. I was intrigued by the fascination held by Francesca with her transcultural family and their stories.

As Francesca related more and more of these stories, I began to see many threads of strength woven through the transcultural and transgenerational relationships. Francesca found herself with an inheritance of emotional gems created by her ancestors from both the beauty and the alchemy of their struggles.

Francesca's fascination with the family stories was nourished by her family. When two or more family members were together, stories would often be told. For Francesca and her family, their stories were a tool by which they could encounter their profound truths and use them for their transcendence.

Francesca's family owned their stories. They used their stories to connect themselves to the divine place of their origin, their present, and their future. They used them to connect with each other, the world at large, and to strengthen their confidence in themselves. They accepted the power of their stories and of the people in them. It was the power of generosity of heart of their family members that gave them the good stories.

Every story had a life of its own. They were a fluid and organic part of the changes encountered by her family. All of the changes of life were embraced by this family. They accepted their relationship changes, life cycle changes, economic changes, political changes, and the shifts of mother earth that caused the destruction of their environment as they knew it. As they continued as a family, their voices rang out their marvelous tales. And their marvelous tales gave this family's energy a presence for eternity.

For Francesca personally, these stories were the rock that guided her through the mundane, blissful, scary, and profound moments of her life. They were her voice.

FRANCESCA'S FAMILY TREE — MATERNAL SIDE

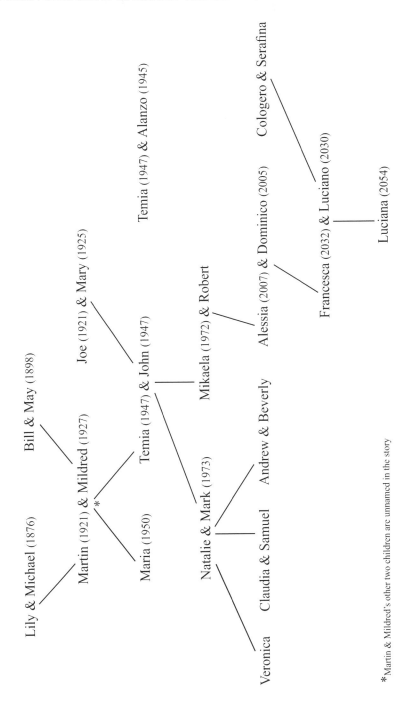

*Martin & Mildred's other two children are unnamed in the story

FRANCESCA'S FAMILY TREE — PATERNAL SIDE

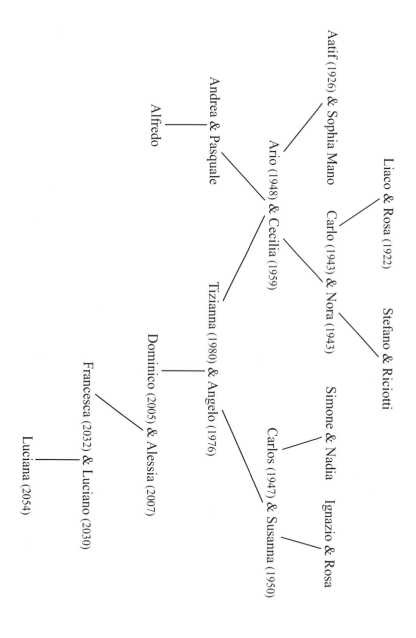

RELATIONS AND FRIENDSHIPS NOT IN FAMILY TREE

Allegrettis: Alessia's host family as a high school student in Genoa.

Bersanis: Cousins on Naples family farm. Margarita and Josefa Bersani with Maximillian and Laura as birth children and Luciano as adopted son. Julianna is Maximillian's girlfriend and Mariano is Laura's boyfriend.

Duccinio and son Tommy: Cousins in Genoa.

Gusbiertis: Ignacio and Rosa, the parents of Susanna Martoni, Carlos's wife.

Jake: Grandfather of John, Temia's first husband.

Marellis: Family friends Liliana, Gilberto, and Marcella of Orvieto.

Martonis: Flavio, Luciano's best friend, and Patricia, his mother.

Perla: Alessia's best friend in America.

Vallis: Susanna, Francesca's best friend, and Daniele, her father. Catrina is Daniele's girlfriend.

Vallis (not related to Susanna): Vincenzo, best friend of Carlos Martoni, Angelo's father.

Ventos: Luciano's Sicilian relations, Cousin Girolermo and wife Teresa.

ITALIAN WORD DEFINITIONS

Ciao! = Hi!

Godere! = Good fortune!

Grazie = Thanks

Mangia! = Eat!

piazza = square, market

Signora = Mrs.

Signore = Mr.

Signorina = Miss

cugina, cugino, cugini = girl cousin, boy cousin, cousins

famiglia = family

figlia, figlio = daughter, son

fratello, fratelli = brother, brothers

mamma, mamme = mom, moms

marito = husband

moglie = wife

nipote = granddaughter, niece

nonna, nonno = grandmother, grandfather

nonni, nonne = grandfathers/grandparents, grandmothers

papà = dad(s)

patrigno = stepfather

sorella = sister

zia, zie = aunt, aunts

zio, zii = uncle, uncles

Chapter One

PREGNANT!

My name is Francesca. I was born in 2032, January 26th to be exact, in Turino, Italy. How I came to be born in this incredible place near the river and in the foreground of the Alps is a beautiful love story I'd like to share with you. But before I do, I must tell you some news that is new to me too. I just did a pregnancy test and, yes, it seems that I am pre… pre… PREGNANT. A walk down to the river will surely help me get my head around this. It's not that my pregnancy isn't wanted. Quite the opposite, in fact. It's just that when Luciano and I decided to have a child, our immediate environment was not quite so precarious. Granted, it wasn't exactly a trip to the beach either.

Global warming is a big issue now, in 2053. We in Italy, unlike some of the big countries, began to pay attention to our changing environment some time ago. After all, the glaciers in the Alps were receding before our very eyes. And we felt the increased tremors under our feet from the offshore fracking.

Our diminishing water resources and the instability of our land was a wake-up call for us as a people. We began to keep our waters clean, changed our energy to solar and wind, and started a huge trash-recycling project. Our scooters and cars now have solar powered batteries, as do our stoves, heaters, and water heaters. And we discontinued the fracking. Much to our amazement, even those who profited from the old ways eventually got on board with our new priorities. They realized the need to save our environment for future generations was more important than further increasing their profits.

I am proud to say that we Italians organized ourselves. Yes, I did use the word 'organized' to describe us. Maybe we tapped into the consciousness of our organized military and government-obsessed ancestors. I don't know. But the bottom line is we have gotten ourselves focused on the sustainable basics for human life.

So to Luciano and myself it seemed okay to have a child. Now, however, just recently, our tremors have increased in frequency and intensity. And the government just notified us that Mt. Vesuvius is showing signs of agitation. We are to be prepared for a possible eruption.

I am sure that you can understand why I am a little concerned about bringing a child into the world right now. Ah, well, it helps me to walk towards the river, and it helps me to tell you, the reader, my thoughts.

My feelings are a real jumble of excitement and worry. I can't wait to tell Luciano this evening about our pregnancy, and I can't wait for his comfort. One thing about my Luciano, he is a rock of kindness and wisdom.

You, the reader, will meet him this evening.

Now, back to my walk to the river. This is my favorite walk. I do it often with Luciano, and when my best friend, Susanna, lived in Turino, I walked with her. Every Sunday my mamma and Nonna Tizianna take this walk after the cleanup from the family meal. You can imagine the beauty of it with the green rolling hills at our side and the curvy river about two miles ahead. In the background stand the mountains that poke up into God's living room.

So, as I make my way to the river, this is a good time to tell you how my parents met and settled in Turino. My mamma was from America and is a bundle of energy, talent, intelligence, and love. I know you can tell that I love my mamma a lot. Her name is Alessia. So, onward with how she and my papà met, married, and settled in Turino.

ALESSIA'S BIG CHANGE

Alessia sat at the kitchen window in the apartment she shared with her best friend, Perla. She held her steamy hot cup of mint tea and looked out onto the fire escape. The sky was its usual early spring gray. In two hours Alessia had to report for curtain call in a musical that had opened in Chicago three months ago. She had two more weeks left on her contract.

"Hmmm, my friend is thinking about something really deep. I can tell," said Perla as she entered the room, one hand rubbing a towel around her big wet head of hair and the other clutching a bottle of conditioner.

Perla was an artist. The dining room of their large, rambling, two-bedroom, inner city flat served as an art studio for Perla and a music room for Alessia.

"I heard from the Allegrettis, my exchange family in Italy, this week," Alessia explained. "They said that there's a big music bonanza in Genoa in two months. It will be a presentation of some Broadway tunes and some opera works. Artists are invited to audition. They said I could stay with them for the audition and the performances. Performances! Wow!

They're so positive!"

"Whoa, Alessia, are you considering it?" asked Perla half excited and half surprised at the news.

"Yes, I think I am. I loved Italy. And the experience would be great for my resume. I might even be able to stay and work there for a while. It would be a welcome break from these gray skies."

"Oh my gosh, Alessia, this might really happen! But wait, your dad. His baby so far away? Really?"

"I know, Perla. I need to have a conversation with my folks. If there is distance involved, my dad would be uncertain at first, but both he and my mom would want the best for me. Everything will work out. I just need to think it over a little bit more."

"My contract with the show is almost over," Alessia continued, "and our lease is up in one month. Say, can I convince you to a life in Italy?"

"Wait, how did we get to a life in Italy from a music bonanza try-out?" Perla said with a twinkle in her eye.

"But, I mean, who knows? I should probably plan to go for six months and then take it from there," said Alessia.

"Good thing you live below your means, my friend, with your spirit for adventure."

"But Perla, seriously, what about Barcelona for your art? Barcelona is so near to Italy. Rico would love it over there!" Alessia encouraged.

Rico and Perla had been in love since sometime midway through college. Rico now had his master's in city planning and worked for a well-funded, nonprofit organization that developed plans for inner city neighborhoods. They then presented these plans to the city and negotiated for their implementation. That way, the plans incorporated the needs of the citizens and earth sustainability as opposed to the needs of the wealthiest backer of the politicians. Rico loved his work almost as much as he loved Perla. Alessia knew her proposal was a long shot.

"If it's not a major metropolis in the United States, then it's Puerto Rico, Alessia. Not Espana for Rico!"

"Oh well, I was just hoping! When are you guys getting married, anyway? Or is it just your favorite conversation?"

"Well, if you must know, we thought sometime this next month at the justice of the peace. Will you witness for us?"

"You're kidding, right? Justice of the peace?"

"Yes, we want it small and meaningful."

"Okay, okay, Perla. Listen. I know a minister who will marry you guys. We can use my folks' house. There's room in the rec area downstairs. I'm sure my folks will agree. You know they love both you and Rico. How many people will it be?"

"Alessia, you are such a dear. And bossy, too. Did you know that?" Perla said with a smile. "Hmm, let's see," she continued, "There's Rico's mother and stepfather, my sister and parents, you, your folks, and Alonzo, Rico's best friend. So, about ten people."

"Great. We'll do it before I leave for Italy. Hey, how about a honeymoon in Italy?"

"Alessia, enough of Italy already!" Perla retorted.

"Whoa! I need to catch the blue line downtown to the theatre. Love you, my dear, at-last-engaged Perla! Ciao! Ciao!" And after grabbing her jacket, scarf, and backpack, Alessia was out the door.

That weekend Alessia went to see her parents. They lived in a comfortable Chicago bungalow an hour by public transportation from her apartment. It was about six o'clock on Saturday evening when she arrived. Her mom, Mikaela, sat with her feet up on the coffee table. Also on the table was a plate with some Ruben sandwich crumbs left on it.

"Hi, Mom. I see that you had one of your favorite sandwiches."

"Hey, my love. And yes, I did, Alessia. Do you want one?" her mom offered in a cheerful but a bit tired voice.

"Hmm, I think I do," said Alessia as she bent down to kiss her mom's cheek. "Sit still. I'll make it," Alessia said as she took her mom's plate and put it in the dishwasher.

Mikaela was an actor in a locally produced TV series. In it she portrayed a very serious businesswoman. She was a friend of her handsome neighbor who was a save-the-planet-oriented lawyer. The hint of romance was initially impeded by their strong viewpoints. Yet as the story progressed a romance began to bloom as they both began to hear each other under their dogmatic masks.

Mikaela loved her work. But for the past week, the make-up calls had been at six in the morning. Not Mikaela's preferred hour.

"You look tired, Mom. Early calls, huh?"

"Yes, for just one more week. Then they're going to shift to ten o'clock. They want to do some afternoon and early evening work along the lake. I love the outside work. But enough of work. Come, Alessia, and relax. Enjoy your sandwich and tell me how things are going," her mom continued as she patted the seat on the couch next to her.

"Well, really well. That's why I came by. Where's Dad?"

"He's on a bike ride. He'll be back soon."

"Oh, okay. Well, I heard from the Allegrettis last week," Alessia began.

"Really? How are they? I always liked them and they were the best to you."

"I know. And they still are. They called to tell me about a singing bonanza in Genoa of both Broadway and opera songs," Alessia informed her mom.

"Alessia, what are you thinking? Oh my, I see that look of fascination in your eyes. You'd be great, of course. But, are you really going to do it? Could it work with your contract and everything? Sorry. Let me be quiet so you can tell me," said her mom as she took a breath.

"Yes, my contract is up next month. The timing is good for me in that way, and I'm ready for a change. I'd hate to leave you guys, but I really want to do this!"

"Well, how about the apartment lease with Perla?" Mikaela asked Alessia in her usual cover-all-the-bases approach.

"Our lease is just about up. But there is something in regards to Perla that I want to talk to you and Dad about. She and Rico plan to marry. They were just going to go down to city hall. I thought that was such a sad idea. So, I suggested that they have the wedding here!"

"Alessia, maybe they liked the city hall idea," responded her mom, not one to infringe on another's desires.

"Oh, no, Mom. Perla loved the idea of having their wedding here," Alessia quickly replied.

"I would love for it to work out, then. Let me think through the schedule of the shoots. In two weeks we're off for Sunday only. But, wait. We finish filming early the day before, like by eleven in the morning. I could call Reverend Jim to see if he could come that afternoon. How about a four o'clock wedding? By the way, Alessia, how many people are we talking?"

"Around ten," Alessia answered.

"Okay, then. Usually numbers grow, so we'll plan for twenty. Tell Perla to order their cake. You young ladies can decorate the basement.

Your dad will help with the set-up. He's great at all that. Also, ask your dad if he'll grill some chicken and corn. He can warm the tortillas on the grill and toast some buns. We can order guacamole, green salad, fruit trays, and salsa from the grocery store. I'll cook rice and beans. If the bride and groom agree with the menu, we're straight."

"Mom. Stop. When are you going to cook the rice and beans? I'll take care of the rice and beans. You've taught me well. The beans are cooked in the slow cooker overnight, rice on top of the stove cooked in vegetable broth with all the spices and colored with annatto."

"Sometimes I forget how grown you are. All right. Deal. I'll pick up the sides from the grocery store on my way home from the shoot."

Bang goes the back door. "Well, your dad's home. The wedding is an easy sell, but good luck on Italy," her mom added as she rose from the couch.

"Mom, where are you going?" Alessia asked, not too calmly.

"You can manage your father. You always do. I'm going to put a load of laundry in the washer while you two pow-wow."

"Hey, baby," her dad shouted to Alessia as he headed to the refrigerator and planted a kiss on Mikaela's cheek as she passed by on her way to the laundry room.

He blew a kiss to Alessia and grabbed some water. At last, not the pop! It had taken Alessia years to convince him to switch to water. He also grabbed some dark bread, shredded cabbage, and a few shreds of meat for a sandwich.

"So, what's new?" he asked, ready for Alessia's latest news.

"Well, a lot of good stuff, Dad," Alessia said and took a bite of her sandwich.

Her dad brought his sandwich over to the couch and sat by his energetic daughter. They munched their food amicably together for a moment.

Then Alessia said, "Well, Dad, I heard from the Allegrettis last week."

"Oh, really, how are they?" her dad interrupted.

"Fine, Dad. They called to tell me there's an opera and Broadway song extravaganza in Genoa in two months. They asked if I wanted to participate. They thought that I could earn a spot in it. The try-outs are in four weeks. Dad, I'm seriously thinking about doing it."

"Italy, huh? I think you'd make it, Alessia."

Her dad was always straight with Alessia. He knew she was talented and bright. To him, she was the brightest of rays of the sun. But he was also able to remain clear on any area that could benefit from improvement. Alessia trusted his evaluation completely.

"Wow, Dad. That's big encouragement from you."

"Well, my dear Alessia, you would do well, but it would be hard for me to have you so far away. You know that. But, is this really in your heart to do?"

"It really is, Dad," Alessia answered.

"Then go for it, Alessia. With your talent, I knew it was only a matter of time until you left this big old city," her dad said as he looked at Alessia with resignation and then at his sandwich to avoid any communication of his intense sadness.

"Oh, Dad, you're the greatest!" said Alessia as she threw her arms around his neck. Robert smiled and glowed with pride.

Then Alessia jumped up and shouted, "Mom! Dad's okay with it!"

"Great, honey," her mom responded from the laundry room. "I knew you guys would work it out!"

Alessia completed her contract the week of the wedding. She also continued her work on the paperwork for her travels and the competition. The Allegrettis were thrilled that she would be there soon.

The Friday before the wedding, Alessia and Perla went to Alessia's parents to decorate the lower level. As they passed through the gate of the back yard, they discovered that Alessia's dad had mowed the lawn, and cleaned the grill from the winter snows. He had also moved the grill close to the outdoor table for easy transfer of the grilled meats, corn, and tortillas onto the covered platters in the chilly, spring weather.

It was about six o'clock in the evening. Alessia shouted as she entered her childhood home, "Hello, anyone home?"

"I'm down here," responded her dad from the lower level.

Alessia and Perla bounded down the few stairs to the lower level from the back door. They each toted paper bags filled with colorful paper items.

"Wow, Uncle Robert, I love this set up!" exclaimed Perla. Alessia's dad had placed the tables in the center to form one big table that could easily seat fifteen. A large bouquet of spring flowers adorned the center of the table. The bouquet was filled with daisies of all sizes, shapes, and colors.

"The flowers are from Mikaela and myself for the wedding," Robert said.

"The flowers are beautiful! I wonder how you knew my favorites," Perla said while she flashed a smile at Alessia and then at Uncle Robert.

"Where's Mom?" asked Alessia.

"Her shoot was later today. She'll be here by seven-thirty or so," responded her dad. Then he asked, "Anyone for a pizza? I'll pop one in the oven."

"Yes!" they responded simultaneously.

Then, with the swift moves of dancers and the eyes of artists, Alessia and Perla rapidly transformed the room into a joyous, festive site worthy to embrace the declaration of love between Perla and Rico. They unfolded two large gold paper tablecloths and covered the tables, then returned the gorgeous daisy bouquet to the center of the table. Next, Alessia and Perla ran streamers across the ceiling in red and gold twists that gave the room the illusion of a magical place. They twisted the streamers into a semicircle on the carpet at the far end of the room. Above that they hung white and gold streamers in a semicircular pattern. They then covered the food table along the side wall with a red paper tablecloth. Pleased with their progress, the best of friends sat down at the table and made about thirty sparkly white and twenty gold tissue flowers. They spread them over the table and in the special semicircle space at the end of the room.

The last thing they did was a sound check with Perla's favorite TV music station that would play during the dinner party. In that sweet, youthful blend of excitement and fatigue, they high-fived each other at the sound of the music in the beautiful room. After a couple of celebratory dance moves, they flopped onto the couch to rest. Alessia broke the silence and said, "Well, Perla, are you ready for tomorrow?"

"I've been ready for a long time," Perla responded as she smiled at her best friend.

Alessia barely got, "This is good," out when her dad shouted from upstairs, "Pizza's ready!"

"Coming!" shouted the young ladies in unison. As they mounted the stairs, Mikaela, came through the back door onto the stair landing. Alessia hugged her and grabbed her hand.

"Mom, come and see the room," Alessia said as she pulled her mother down to the lower level. Her dad came down to greet Mikaela and to admire the room.

"Nice, really nice," Mikaela said. "Both the fresh and the tissue flowers work well with the colors," she added. "Good job, everyone!"

"Let's go eat," said Alessia's dad as he gave Mikaela a gentle hug.

All four enthusiastically made their way up the stairs with anticipation of the warm, aromatic, thin crust pizza accompanied by lemonade. Then Alessia and Perla left to get some rest for the big day tomorrow.

The wedding was a beautiful celebration of love, family, and friendship. The air vibrated with positive emotions, music, dance, and savory food. People had a very good time. Perla and Rico were obviously deeply happy.

The week after the wedding, Alessia and Perla helped each other move out of their apartment. Perla moved into Rico's flat and Alessia moved back with her folks. Rico brought a friend and his small truck to make the job easier.

"Hey, how about some Thai food after we finish?" Perla offered.

"Sounds like a plan!" Alessia agreed.

The four young people sat in Rico and Perla's apartment with their Thai food. Thus, the two best friends began the next leg of their life journeys. The two would have spatial separation, but a strong soul connection would always remain between them.

A few days later, Alessia sat on her parents' front porch to rest a moment from her trip preparations. It was a sunny day with a tease of warm air that would probably disappear into clouds and chilly temperatures the next day. But today this northern city was sunny. All of Alessia's papers were in order for the trip. She had appropriate clothing packed and enough money for the trip. Alessia always spent less than her earnings. She loved the security of savings. Thus, her finances were in order for her to travel.

In about an hour, she would drive over to her nearby grandparents to pick them up. They were her father's parents. They were now in their upper eighties. Today she would take them out to dinner to one of their favorite neighborhood restaurants. During her childhood they had taken her to the most wonderful restaurants. Alessia felt honored that she could now take them out from time to time. She loved their company. Her grandpa was always such a tease and taught Alessia how to not take people so seriously. And her grandma was always full of love and patience. She taught Alessia the ever presence of love available in one's life. As excited as she was to take them to dinner, Alessia knew it would be hard for her to tell them about Italy and her plans, and hard for them to hear she was leaving.

Her grandma and grandpa never missed a new musical she was in, just like they had never missed a school production during her childhood. Now, for the first time they would miss her performance, as it would be in Italy. But Alessia would reassure them that she would envision them in the audience and feel their love as she sang every song. She would tell them that their steady presence in her life as a child and young adult gave her the strength to continue with her dreams wherever they might lead her. Alessia would simply tell them that she loved them and always would. She would promise to call, FaceTime, and e-mail. They would stay in close contact. She knew that to celebrate her life was also to celebrate them.

This was the first of the possible last good-byes that resulted from her decision to go to the extravaganza in Genoa. She wondered if she would see them again. But she believed what her mom and Abuelita Temia had taught her—that the spirits of those we love are always close to us. Thus, Alessia always thought about, talked about, sang about, danced about, and wrote about, those she loved, whether they were on this earth or in the next place.

You can understand, dear reader, how I can love my Mamma Alessia so much!

The dinner with her grandparents was lovely. They were so proud of her. They hugged her a little longer than usual at the end of the evening.

For a couple of days the next week, Alessia went to her mom's set to be with her and watch her work. She loved her mom's ability to convey to the camera the most subtle of emotions. For Mikaela, the camera was a part of herself. She made sure the camera knew intimately every nuance of her character's essence.

"Thanks for being here, Alessia," Mikaela said. "I love it when you visit the set."

"Me too, Mom. I love to hang out with you, and I learn when I watch you work!"

"So, are you ready for Italy?" Mikaela asked as she sipped her hot mint tea.

"Yup! It has the feeling of both a new adventure and going home at the same time," Alessia responded.

"I understand. When we love a place, it is home," Mikaela concurred. "I am so happy for you, Alessia. I will miss you very much. It has been a blessing to have you close to us for this long. But now, I also feel deep down that this is the right thing for you to do," Mikaela concluded as she looked softly into Alessia's eyes.

"Thanks, Mom!"

"Come on," Mikaela said as she stood up and grabbed Alessia's hand. "Let's go! The break's almost up. I need to get a quick make-up touch-up and do a costume change."

"Yes, let's go," Alessia said as Mikaela pulled her out of her chair. They walked arm in arm towards the dressing rooms.

That evening Alessia Skyped with Temia and Alanzo as they had arranged the day before by text message. Temia still hiked Arizona's mountains with her husband, Alanzo. Alessia looked forward to Skyping with them. Her perpetually young and adventuresome abuelita cracked her up. And she knew that her abuelita understood her artistic drive and love for Italy.

"Hola, Abuelita," Alessia said, looking at her abuelita's face on the screen.

"Hola, mi amor," Temia responded.

Alanzo popped his head into the screen and said, "Hola, Alessia, what's new?"

"Well, mis Abuelitos, I'm heading off to Italy. There's a singing extravaganza in Genoa and I'm in the try-outs for it next week."

"This is so exciting!" they both crooned.

"You will do great!" Alanzo added.

"Let us know how it goes," said her abuelita. "Are you staying with the Allegrettis?"

"Yes, I am. Actually I found out about the extravaganza from them."

"Well, take our blessings with you and have a good time. Your voice—and its beauty—stays in my head always. Remember that. We can probably Skype when you are in Italy, right?" asked her abuelita.

"Absolutely, and I will remember, Abuelita," Alessia assured her.

"We love you," said Alanzo.

"I love you both so much! Ciao!"

"Ciao, mi amor," said her abuelita with moistened eyes as they disconnected.

So the next week Alessia's parents, grandparents, and best friend, Perla, dropped Alessia off at the airport. Alessia would never set foot in the city of her birth again and only once in the country of her birth the rest of her life. Italy was on!

Dear reader, Dominico is my future papà. This is how he got to the same spot in Italy as Alessia, my future mamma, so they could meet!

DOMINICO PREPARES FOR GENOA

Dominico stared out his bedroom window over his desk past the vineyards to the sky. The paperwork was completed for the try-outs. He had contacted a cugino from the Naples family branch who lived in Genoa.

"Dominico! I am so glad that you will be in Genoa. Please, you are welcome to stay here. It will be quiet as it is only my figlio and myself," said his cousin Duccinio.

Dominico was grateful for Duccinio's welcome. His family planned to pack themselves into his Zio Pasquale's flat. Pasquale was his mamma's only sibling. His family believed he would be accepted in the extravaganza and thus they made it a big family event at Zio Pasquale's large flat. Despite the size, his family would fill up the flat and Dominico needed quiet.

Duccinio continued, "You were incredible in Rome. I look forward to the extravaganza. Plan to stay with us."

"Thanks, Duccinio. I will," concluded Dominico.

Duccinio was a generous and gentle man. As many of Dominico's family members, Duccinio attended Dominico's performances whenever possible.

It had been a special opportunity for Dominico to perform in Rome as a baritone stand-in for the role of Dancaire in the opera *Carmen*. His reviews were very good. But, Dominico relied on his own standards of excellence to discipline his artistic growth. He also continued to apply for opportunities to sing to build a solid professional foundation for himself. The extravaganza was the next step.

Dominico went downstairs and out to the patio. His parents, Angelo and Tizianna, were there with their coffee and some figs.

"Hey, my two favorite people! What's going on this beautiful afternoon?" said Dominico to his parents.

"Come sit down and join us, figlio," said Angelo.

"I think I will. The coffee smells great! I'll bring mine out and join you," said Dominico as he returned to the kitchen to make his hot cup of coffee.

"Have you finished your arrangements for Genoa?" inquired his mamma.

"Yes, I'm all set," Dominico said as he placed his cup on the table and took a fig.

"It will all go well, Dominico," Angelo said.

"I agree," said Tizianna. "So, Angelo," she continued with a twinkle in her eye, "should we go to Genoa and check out this baritone?"

"Well maybe, Tizianna, we should!" responded his papà as they all laughed.

As they finished their coffee, Angelo said, "Dominico, come and walk with me out to the vineyard. There are a couple of vines I want your opinion about." Angelo knew his figlio grew serious before an audition. He wanted to offer Dominico a diversion the afternoon before his travels to Genoa.

"Great, Papà, let's go!" responded Dominico. "Mamma do you want to walk with us?" Dominico added.

"No, figlio, I want to find my accordion and sit with it for a while."

As the two men walked in tandem up the vineyard path they heard Tizianna's lively accordion notes bouncing off her agile fingers. Their beautiful sounds, the bright warm sun, the hum of the little bees in the vines, and their papà-figlio camaraderie combined made it a most pleasant walk.

Dear reader, I think it is sooo romantic how Alessia and Dominico met. But, they weren't thinking romance at the time.

DOMINICO AND ALESSIA IN GENOA

Dominico arrived a day before his try-outs at Duccinio's. He settled into his room and joined Duccinio and his ten-year-old son for oysters and pasta supper. Dominico loved the hint of salt in the air as they sat on the family's balcony with the pasta. Duccinio was a safety inspector of the ferries that ran between Genoa and Barcelona. Duccinio spoke with great admiration of the efficiency and safety of the solar powered ferries. He said that it was safer and much more efficient to run frequent smaller ferries than the larger, less manageable structures.

"I hope to ride a ferry one day to Barcelona. Cugino Alfredo is in Barcelona, as you may have heard. He's an energy engineer there," said Dominico.

"Let me know when so I can get you a discount ticket," offered Duccinio.

"Thanks, Duccinio," said Dominico. "By the way, who was the chef for this delicious pasta?"

"Well, it was a joint effort," clarified Duccinio.

"Yes!" exclaimed Tommaso. "I carefully poured the oysters into the hot water."

"Well done!" Dominico exclaimed. "I guess that means I'm the kitchen cleanup man."

"I'll help," said Tommaso.

"Glad to have your help, Tommaso. Maybe you can tell me about your favorite class in school."

"Sure! It's the soccer league after school."

"Well, I was thinking more about which class in school. But your answer was good. Do you want to kick the ball around a little in the square after we finish here?" offered Dominico.

"Papà, can I?"

"Are you up to this tonight, Dominico?" questioned Duccinio.

"Yes, it will help keep me loose for tomorrow."

Dominico liked Tommaso, and he was in admiration of his cousin Duccinio's dedication as a single father since the death of Tommaso's mother four years ago.

"Okay," affirmed Duccinio.

The next morning Dominico rose early and did a few vocal warm-ups after his coffee, corn porridge with ham, and fruit. He went for a brisk walk and then reported to the try-outs. The opera house was within walking distance.

Dominico signed in and then waited for his name to be called. He was after an Alessia. She was given the first slot since she had traveled from overseas. He was given the second slot because he was well known locally.

The stage door opened and a fast-moving blur of full, intensely curly, long, golden hair passed him. Suddenly she stopped when she saw him in the "next up" chair. He could hardly hear his name called as this shapely woman turned to him and cast her large blue eyes on him. She clutched her violin, smiled a full gorgeous smile, and said, "Godere!"

He was surprised at her perfect Italian, and then responded, "Grazie!" as he rose and regained his focus on the try-out.

His two songs went well. Actually, very well. He was then asked to wait for just a few minutes.

All of the contestants were allowed to sit in the last three rows of the lower level if they wanted to listen to the other contestants' voices. Alessia sat there. She wanted to drink in as much as she could while there. Alessia especially wanted to hear the voice of the handsome man that went after her. She closed her eyes and let his tones envelop her. She was impressed with how he phrased the song's message and with the strength and sheer beauty of his baritone voice. Alessia was in contemplation on his tones when she heard one of the clerks whisper in her ear.

"Please, Signorina Alessia, will you come with me?"

Alessia followed her backstage where she was introduced to the baritone, Dominico. The clerk informed them that the committee definitely wanted them to perform individually in the extravaganza, but also thought they might make a good duet. If they were interested, the committee wanted to hear them perform together.

Alessia and Dominico both agreed to the idea, so the clerk gave them the music of a short duet and an hour to work on it. They gave each other a look of determination and went off to a practice room.

Dominico was impressed with Alessia's disciplined exactness, power, and beauty of her voice work. Their focus was, at least for the time being, only on their artistry. They both listened as they worked and then their faces broke out into large smiles. The moment they stopped singing, Dominico said, "Our voices really complement each other."

"I agree. Let's work this. It sounds good!" added Alessia.

For the next forty minutes their voices spiraled around each other as if they had been created from the same source.

During the duet audition, the committee was caught up in the beauty and power of their blend. Their performance was a magic that exceeded the imagination of the directors. They inserted several duets for them throughout the extravaganza, both Broadway tunes and opera works.

Rehearsals were to begin the day after tomorrow. Alessia and Dominico returned to their hostess families for the evening and the next day.

Alessia told the Allegrettis that she was paired with a baritone from Turino for a number of songs. She said that his voice was amazing and his eyes gave her a sense of reassurance inside.

Signora Allegretti could sense an appreciation for this man beyond his artistry, but would dare not say it to Alessia. Instead she said, "It's great that your partner's voice blends so well with yours!"

"Yes, it is!" said Alessia as she bounded off to her room to call her folks, shoot an e-mail off to Perla, and review the music they had been given for the extravaganza.

The next day when Alessia took a break from her practice, Signora Allegretti took her down to the wharves.

They found a little café near some of the fishing boats. Signora Allegretti ordered a fresh caught snapper for them. They both sat with their mineral water and took in the sea air while the chef did his wizardry with the fresh catch.

"Signora Allegretti, I love this place so much. It feels good to be back. Thank you so much for a place to stay once again."

"Alessia, you and your parents are always welcome in our home. You are famiglia to us!" Signora Allegretti said. She raised her mineral water to Alessia and Alessia raised hers also for a toast to family.

The next day the rehearsals began. Alessia and Dominico worked hard together and individually. When they were on stage during the rehearsals, all present held themselves in absolute stillness to absorb within their visual and musical beauty. The woman who would become my mamma stood on stage erect and graceful at almost 5'6". Her thick, tightly curled, blond hair expanded around her to below her shoulders like a strong, gold light of transcendental energy. She had the gentle strength, shapely hips, and chest like my Nonna Mikaela. Her skin was of a light olive with a slight gold undertone. Her large blue eyes were kind, yet bottomless with their energy. Her voice was a full contralto with a huge range that swept up the audience into the song. Her violin was at her side as if it was a natural part of her body. Then, in a graceful swerve, it was on her chest singing the notes of dreams beyond the composer's.

The man who was to become my papà, Dominico, stood a tall, handsome 5'10". His hair was black with many tight waves. His complexion was dark olive and his smile was full, wide, and joyous. Dominico's voice was warm and flooded one's heart, which was unusual for an Italian baritone. His favorite instrument other than voice was piano. One of the duets that my parents performed at the extravaganza incorporated voice, piano, and violin. The audience loved it.

The presence of this dynamic couple changed the extravaganza event overnight. People filled both the opera house and the piazza during the performances. A large screen TV was set up in the piazza for the people on the streets of Genoa. Genoa was in an embrace of love and beauty. And there were my future parents as huge contributors to this age-old Genoan blessing.

Dear reader, does this all sound too amazing? Well, all I can say is that it was.

The Allegrettis videoed Alessia's performances and forwarded them to Mikaela and Robert. This was a lot of video as Alessia performed every night of the extravaganza, as was Dominico. There were six performances. In the audience for the last two nights were also Dominico's Papà Angelo and Mamma Tizianna as well as his Nonno Ario and Nonna Cecilia. In addition, there was Cugino Duccinio, Zio Pasquale, Zia Angela, their figlio, Cugino Alfredo, now from Barcelona, and my mamma's American cousin, now from Barcelona, Samuel, and his wife, Claudia. How amazing that both Dominico and Alessia now had cugini in Barcelona!

Tizianna and Cecilia observed Dominico closely. Tizianna and Cecilia observed Alessia closely. They both looked at each other and whispered, "I hope they each see what is obvious beyond their incredible blend of voices."

But any soft whispers in the hearts of Alessia and Dominico about each other were quietly ignored by both of them. After closing night, Dominico introduced Alessia to his family. Alessia introduced him to the Allegrettis and her cousins. Pasquale invited everyone over to their flat for a late supper and some wine.

So, off they went to Pasquale's spacious flat. Alessia totally charmed

Dominico's famiglia. She was interested in all of their activities from solar vehicles, green engineering, and farm life to education, hiking, dance, and music. Alessia found them gracious people. Thus, they won each other's hearts.

Dominico's famiglia also embraced Alessia's tall, dynamic cousin, Samuel, and his petite, energetic, Puerto Rican wife, Claudia. Samuel entertained them with some tall tales from America in a mix of English, Spanish, and Italian. Cousin Samuel was always outgoing like that. He enjoyed himself and people enjoyed him. It was a lively group. They parted at the end of the evening with promises to visit each other in Barcelona and Turino.

The next day Alessia awakened early to meet Samuel and Claudia at a nearby café. They had an early ferry ride to Barcelona. It meant so much to Alessia to have this time with Samuel and Claudia. Samuel and Alessia grew up close. They saw each other at least bi-weekly. After Samuel met Claudia in high school, she was at all the family gatherings and became close with Alessia. When Samuel went to Grambling, then MIT for his master's, and Claudia to Grambling, then Boston University for her master's, Alessia still saw them every holiday. Now, however, she hadn't seen him since his move to Barcelona two years ago. It was a permanent move; he was an engineer for a Spanish renewal energy business.

Over breakfast at the café, Alessia learned that Claudia was pregnant. Alessia found it hard to contain her excitement and bounded out of her chair to hug both of them. After fresh fruit juice, tasty rice porridge, and great coffee, they began their good-byes. With many hugs and many promises from Alessia to come to Barcelona before she returned to the States, they parted ways. Alessia returned to the Allegrettis and crawled into bed where she slept and slept and slept.

When she awakened, she found Signora Allegretti in the kitchen. The air was filled with the fragrant aroma of vegetable soup with bite-sized bits of fresh fish.

"Mmm, that smells good!" Alessia said.

"Here, sit down and have a bowl. Are you feeling more rested?"

"Definitely. Mmm, this is just what my body needed!"

Alessia continued, "Dominico and I have been invited to sing in a few Italian and other European cities for their summer and fall festivals. So we've decided to take them up on it. It will also give us a chance to write some songs together, which we want to do as well. After I finish this delicious soup, I'm going to call my folks to tell them the news. Dominico is the best to work with and I want to take advantage of this opportunity."

"Sounds great to me," Signora Allegretti said assuredly as she smiled inside herself.

Dominico went over to his Zio Pasquale's to bid good-bye to his family. He also told them that he and Alessia had accepted invitations to tour a few festivals in Europe over the next few months. Eight stops were lined up so far, and the festivals' committees were sending them funds for travel expenses. Dominico added that he and Alessia wanted to take advantage of the opportunity and use the extra time they'd have to write a few songs together.

Out of earshot of Dominico, once again Cecilia and Tizianna conspired. "I doubt Alessia will go back to the other side of the globe," said Cecilia to Tizianna.

"I agree, Mamma," Tizianna responded. "I think that Dominico will work towards that! I would wager that Dominico is smitten. Well, these young people have their own way to work things out. It will be fun to see how they do it!"

"Yes, it will be fun to watch," said Cecilia as she put her arm through her daughter's.

Across the room, Dominico admitted softly to his heart that he was smitten. He couldn't keep his mind off this beautiful, kind, and talented woman. At some point, he reasoned, he would know if she had romantic inclinations towards him. But for now, he did not want to get lost in his own feelings. He had an obligation to himself and to her to do well on this four-month tour.

"Alfredo!" Dominico said as he caught Alfredo's eye. "Let's go grab a coffee before you head back to Barcelona."

The two cousins said their good-byes and went to a café near the ferry dock. Alfredo had to catch the ferry to Barcelona late that afternoon as he had to work early on Monday. Thus, he could not stay for the post-extravaganza street fiesta that evening.

So with great anticipation to share a personal time, the two cousins who were raised close as brothers strode with their arms on each other's shoulders down the street towards the café.

After they pulled out a couple of chairs and sat at a small table with their coffees, Dominico asked, "How is it in Barcelona?"

"It's a good spot, Dominico. I like the city and the work. The research on the job is focused to enhance the advancement and efficiency of green power. My dream job. The politics on the job are manageable and I like most of the people. A division of my company actually meets with a division of Papà's company in Turino. A few months back he made a presentation at our company. He stayed with me and saw my flat for the first time. He liked it and I felt proud to entertain my papà in my adopted city.

"Now, thanks to the extravaganza, I have met another connection with our family. Samuel. He's in another division of my company. But, we've made plans to meet for coffee next week. Good people, Dominico. Speaking of good people, when are you coming to visit? There is a spare bedroom."

"Well, now that you mention it—the festival tour that Alessia and I are doing actually ends in four months in Barcelona. Maybe…"

"Say no more, cugino. Please stay with me. You both are more than welcome," said Alfredo.

"Thanks so much," responded Dominico. "Samuel invited us, but they are a little farther from the festival site. So we've arranged to go there for a couple of days afterwards. Your invitation works out perfectly."

"And if you are moving at your usual snail's pace, Dominico, the couch is a pullout for you," said Alfredo with a twinkle in his eye.

"What do you mean, cugino? We're working hard! There's no time."

"I'll wager that the two of you will find time sooner or later," offered Alfredo. "She's a great person and you two are smooth together."

"I know. I know. We'll see. But to change the subject, how is it really for you in Barcelona?" asked Dominico. He had hoped that it would be less complicated for him in Barcelona than other locations. Dominico remembered well when, at the time of their university exams, Alfredo confided in Dominico that he was gay. Dominico had been supportive of him from that time onward.

"I have met some good people, both gay and straight. I'm happy. I'm interested in someone. But we'll see."

"Whoa!" exclaimed Dominico. The two cousins then laughed as they realized that both their paths were filled with eminent love. They then relaxed in their chairs and companionably watched the crowd in the piazza for a short time. Dominico walked with Alfredo to the ferry dock. The cousins embraced and then Dominico continued on to Duccinio's flat. He was to meet Alessia in four hours to go over the two songs and possible encores for tonight's street festival. Dominico looked forward to the street festival. It would be a relaxed venue. Then, he and Alessia would have only one day to rest before they left for the European tour.

On her day of rest, Alessia phoned her parents to give them her European tour itinerary. Her father was filled with questions, once again, about this Dominico. These questions had been fielded previously during her initial phone call about her tour plans. In addition, Signora Allegretti had called Alessia's parents to speak highly of Dominico and his family. But, Alessia was patient with her father. She understood him. This was how he said, "I love you." Of course, after a few minutes of conversation, he gave his blessing. His trust in Alessia's judgment was strong, he just had to extend his father's protection as best he could across the waters.

"Well, Mom, I think that Dad is okay with the tour," said Alessia.

"Oh, yes. He'll be fine," said her mom. "Do you need us to send you anything? Do you have enough hair products?"

"I think I'm straight with hair products. I needed a couple of dresses for the performances, but I found a shop here with styles that I think will work well on stage. They also have a good tailor for alterations. In fact, I'm going to pick them up now.

"I'll text you as we arrive safely in each town. Most of the travel is going to be by train. The trains are fast, safe, and the height of comfort. They will give us a good place to rest and write our ballads."

"Well, take care. I love you very much," her mom said.

"By the way," her mom continued. "Our house is filled with one relative after another coming to view the video. I love to have your music fill the house. I do understand what people mean when they speak of the beauty in the blend of your voices."

"Thanks, Mom. I love you."

"I love you too. Be well."

"I will. Talk soon."

"Yes, talk soon," her mom said as she hung up.

On the tour there were moments over a meal and a glass of wine when Alessia and Dominico had the opportunity to deepen their friendship. They shared glimpses of their past and desires for their future. And they shared many laughs over silly incidences that happened to them on their travels.

They also got into a rhythm on how they intertwined when one or the other had an idea for lyrics or a tune. They went into a sixth sense back and forth with each other until the song was done. They also discovered that they both loved to exercise. They walked everywhere when they arrived at a new location.

Somewhere between the music notes and the cities, their feelings grew for each other. By the time they hit Barcelona, they knew they were in love. Upon their return to Italy, they were dedicated to both a personal and a musical life together. They decided to marry in a month's time.

ENGAGEMENT OF DOMINICO AND ALESSIA

Alessia had communicated frequently by e-mail and phone to her parents while on tour. She was open about her deepening relationship with Dominico. Mikaela and Robert had spoken to Dominico on several occasions by phone. It was clear to Mikaela and somewhat clear to Robert that they were serious. So it was no surprise to Mikaela when Alessia called to invite them over for the wedding. Her father, of course, had concerns.

"Yes, Alessia, I am sure that Dominico has your best interests at heart. But, Italy… it's so far…"

In a couple of days Robert came around, even though the distance was a little hard for him to swallow. He knew that frequent travel would be financially and environmentally prohibitory. But, they would stay connected, he reasoned. So he focused on his daughter's joy and planned enthusiastically with Mikaela for their voyage to their daughter's wedding in the Piedmont countryside of Italy!

Thus, my maternal Nonno Robert and Nonna Mikaela arrived at the Morelli family farm three miles outside of Turino two weeks before the October 5, 2030, wedding date. Angelo and Tizianna welcomed them graciously, and the blend of two families began. There were long evenings spent over pasta, polenta, and rice, rich with vegetable and meat sauces. Mmm, the aromas were reported to be fresh and rich with herbs like basil and cilantro, as well as curry, coriander, turmeric, black pepper, and cayenne. These people, now my family, wove their connection with stories that arose from their memories amidst the rich scents that bubbled out of the sauces on the kitchen stove. Mikaela and Alessia were at home in a kitchen of well-blended spices and offered a few tasty sauces of their own to the mix. Robert was intrigued with Angelo's sun grill. Robert and Angelo discovered that they both had a fascination with new sun energy technology and had long discussions on the topic. Robert also loved the solar scooters, so with Robert on his own scooter, Angelo escorted him on another scooter through the rolling countryside. Robert loved it!

As the days went on, this intimate group told many family stories. They were fueled as the evenings advanced with a little more wine and fresh fruit after the succulent meals. The stories' languages were a blend of Italian and English. Everyone knew enough of each to keep the excitement up. Almost every evening, Nonna Tizianna pulled out her accordion and the stories transformed into song. Thus my family spun together with sauces, stories, and song.

Alessia and Dominico had a simple country wedding. It took place on the patio along the rear side of Angelo and Tizianna's farmhouse. It was a beautiful, flower-lined patio with tables and chairs to accommodate the extended family.

Alessia's best friend, Perla, arrived the day before with Cousin Samuel and Claudia (looking quite pregnant), along with Dominico's Cugino Alfredo. With the help of Samuel, Perla arranged a showing of her smaller works to pay for her trip to Barcelona and Turino. Fortunately, it was very successful.

WEDDING OF DOMINICO AND ALESSIA

Alessia was beside herself with joy to see her cousins and her best friend from America. It had been so long since she had seen Perla! They greeted each other with great emotion.

Alessia introduced Perla all around and then guided her to the patio off the kitchen for a cool drink.

"It is so good to have you here!" said Alessia as she handed her a glass of cold lemonade. "I miss Rico," Alessia continued.

"Yeah, I wish he could be here too," responded Perla. "But you know the expense of travel now."

"I do. I'm just so glad you're here. Thanks so much, my dear friend."

"And thanks for your help, cous," she said to Samuel as he sat with his cold lemonade glass against his forehead with one hand and the hand of Claudia in the other. "By the way, cous," added Alessia. "You'll never cool down holding Claudia's hand like that! And you've already got one baby on the way!" she teased.

Samuel flashed one of his engaging smiles.

That afternoon the six young people sat at a patio table and chatted away. They flew over many topics and laughed and laughed and laughed. Soon Carlos and Salvaturi, two of Dominico's closest school friends, arrived. Now there were eight, and a lone soccer ball not too far from the table seemed to draw Samuel's and Dominico's attention at the same time.

Samuel and Dominico rose from the table. Dominico kicked the ball up on his knee and then to Samuel. Samuel returned the pass. Then Dominico said, "Let's go to the courtyard and kick the ball around."

"Great!" said Samuel. "The Barcelonians against the Turinesi."

All eight got up and declared their loyalty to one side or the other. They had two teams of four quickly.

Despite the heat, they all enjoyed a vigorous game. When they had laughed and run themselves into a sufficient sweat, they sought the reprieve of the well water. When their thirsts were quenched, they began to throw the water on each other. Their laughter rang out over the fields.

Dominico grabbed Alessia and swung her around. They then hugged each other with abandon. How sweet it must have felt to be in love and to be surrounded by friends and family!

The next day the wedding was the best of celebrations! A distant cousin who was a magistrate in Turino performed the ceremony. There was plenty of food! The tables were laden with fruits, pastas, sauces, wines, and fine lemon cake. The marital couple was serenaded on the dance floor by Nonna Tizianna on her accordion, Samuel on a drum, and Claudia with a flute. Soon Dominico relieved Tizianna on the accordion and Alessia accompanied him on the violin. Everyone danced, toasted with wine, and shouted excitedly at this surprise duet. My grandparents and great-grandparents danced and danced and fell in love for the billionth of times. The children spun around until they lay on the patio bricks with their dizziness. It was a great time for all.

As the stars twinkled the midnight hour, many of the guests began to drift away. Our cousins and mamma's friend, Perla, found their guest beds. The parents and grandparents found their rooms and were soon fast asleep.

But, the newlyweds went to their bed and found each other with an energy that overwhelmed the billions of stars' light.

Somehow by the time that Dominico and Alessia awakened, Tizianna, Mikaela, Angelo, and Robert had the kitchen in order and sat with their coffee or tea and bread or polenta. They had planned an excursion to the mountain park and were preparing for the adventure.

Dominico and Alessia were to accompany their cousins and Perla to Genoa and see them off at the ferry to Barcelona. Then they would stay at a romantic seaside cottage near Genoa for a couple of days.

When Dominico and Alessia returned from Genoa to the farm, they found that Mikaela and Robert had extended their stay. Both Dominico and Alessia had surmised that they enjoyed the area tremendously. They were right. Upon Tizianna and Angelo's invitation, they planned to stay on another week to look around Turino and Genoa for a possible relocation in five to ten years. Tizianna and Angelo were ecstatic about Mikaela and Robert's plan, as they enjoyed their company greatly. In addition, they knew that would be best for Alessia, whom they loved deeply. Alessia and Dominico were also hopeful that it would work out for her parents to relocate to Italy.

In a week's time, Dominico and Alessia had to leave for Milan and then back up into Europe. Their concerts that included both classic and pop ballads were a great success and their following had grown over the past few months. They traveled for about another year with occasional rests at the farm.

When Alessia became pregnant with me, they chose to slow down their travel. From then forward, they accepted only two travel engagements a year, and they were usually in regional locations. They focused their professional life on their music students that they taught in their home. In addition, they continued to write and record new ballads that they sold on the internet.

During their pregnancy, Dominico and Alessia continued to live on the farm while Dominico and Angelo, with some help from local men, converted the small home and mechanic shop built by Aatif to Dominico and Alessia's new home. They added rooms in back, which became three modest bedrooms. They laid tile floor and cleaned out the old work shed. They repaired the house's tile roof and added new roof tile over the bedroom extensions. They took off the old shed roof and created a garden patio with that space. The front wall windows and door of the shed had long been filled in with stone and remained as such. Angelo converted the old hearth to a sun energy heat source and a solar kitchen was put in place along the front wall. After five months of work it was ready for Dominico and Alessia to move in.

It was in that home that I was born, and it was there that I grew up surrounded by expansive love, energy, strong opinions, musical sounds, and savory spices bubbling on the stove. When Papà cooked, the sauces were hot, pungent, and sweet, as he loved to use cayenne. My mamma's sauces were earthy, rounded, and smooth, as she preferred cumin and black pepper as her dominant spices. My sauces were somewhere in between, as I used all their spices. We all were passionate about oregano, cilantro, basil, and lots and lots of garlic. Now that's a well-flavored life!

Chapter Two

So that's my story of how I landed here in Turino. And I must say that despite all the tremors and uneasiness of Vesuvius, I'm glad I'm here. The river with its movement onward always moves my spirit. The continual presence of a breeze along the river blows away my worries. That constitutes a good vision for me to transmit inward to the baby.

Well, I'm ready to head back to the farm where Luciano and I live with Nonno Alfredo and Nonna Tizianna. Actually since the grape harvest just finished they are in Genoa to visit my Nonno Robert and Nonna Mikaela. They will return tomorrow. So, the farm will be quiet for a couple more hours until Luciano gets home. This will give me time to put on a white bean red sauce and to make the polenta. That will be a good supper for me to share with Luciano the news of our baby and to discuss our future, don't you think, dear reader?

LUCIANO AND I GROOVE INTO OUR PREGNANCY

Luciano parked his scooter in the shed and then came in through the kitchen door. As usual he came directly to me and gave me a kiss. Luciano never gave an unfocused kiss. He is always present in his kisses and I love it. How did I luck out?

He asked, "How was your day?" Then he looked at me kind of funny and said, "What's going on, mi amore? You look like a cat that's swallowed a bird."

"Is it that obvious? Well, yes, there is something new inside, but ..."

I didn't get the rest of the sentence out when Luciano grabbed me and swung me around (you can guess that our farmhouse kitchen is big).

"Are you, I mean we, pregnant???"

I could only nod my head up and down because he had me in his arms in one of his great focused kisses. I melted and felt a lot less anxious about motherhood.

Later on, after our polenta and sauce supper, Luciano and I sat in the quiet of the evening on the patio. I held in my hands a cup of warm mint tea and Luciano held in his hand a glass of wine. The stars began to sparkle and the earth smelled rich and moist. Luciano began, "Francesca, this child is going to be just fine. Whatever happens with Vesuvius or whatever else, we will be able to manage, somehow. Ah, just a minute!

Wait right here!"

Luciano bounded out of his chair and ran into the house. Soon I heard a beautiful tango coming out of the windows.

Luciano returned and stood by my chair with his hand extended to me. I rose up and folded myself into his arms. We glided, swiveled, and read each other's bodies as we moved over the patio bricks.

Luciano whispered into my ear, "This child wants to come here. We have just been together a short time and bam! Here comes the baby. Some things we just can't fight, my beautiful Francesca!"

I laughed. Which was Luciano's goal.

Luciano continued, "Did you ever think during all those years as kids on the Naples farm that we would have a kid of our own?"

"Nope," I replied.

"I didn't either," responded Luciano. "But, I would be lying if I said I didn't notice your beauty as you became a young woman. I didn't let myself go much further than that because you were dating that guy Marco, right?"

I laughed and replied, "Yes, I was. He was a good life lesson for me."

"Well, I'm sure glad that lesson is finished!" Luciano said as he held me close and kissed deeply my ready lips.

Then, as we gently released our embrace, Luciano said, "I'm going to check on the hens and goats. I know Angelo loves to do it, but they're not back until tomorrow, right?"

"Yes, tomorrow," I responded as I sat back down with my warm tea.

Then, dear reader, I began to muse under the warm stars about my Luciano. Things are usually simple, straightforward, and less complicated for Luciano than for myself. Even as a child I felt secure around Luciano and was comforted by his perspective on things. No wonder I fell in love with this generous man.

Before I tell you how I fell in love with Luciano, I will tell you about the man that was my "lesson" that Luciano is glad I'm over. My lesson's name is Marco.

ALWAYS TOGETHER

Somehow I felt that Marco and I would always be together. Marco appeared on our doorstep at age twelve. My papà answered the door.

Marco introduced himself and said that he wanted to learn to play the violin. He said that he heard the sound of the instrument often as he passed by the house. Marco said it was the most beautiful sound he had ever heard.

"I want to learn how to play that sound," Marco said as he looked up at my papà.

Marco stood there with wiry black hair, a tall but very thin frame, and a warm but no-nonsense look in his eyes. He fixed his gaze up at Dominico with intense anticipation.

Dominico invited Marco inside and said, "Well, let us see what we can work out. Signora Alessia is the violin instructor. Let me speak with her."

Mamma Alessia came to the vestibule in a couple of moments and invited Marco in. She had seen Marco in the fields of a nearby vegetable farm. She saw the fresh dirt on his sturdy brown lace-up shoes. There was no sound of a motorbike at his arrival. Alessia knew that he had walked. She placed a violin in Marco's hands after an illustration of the proper position of one hand on the violin strings, and the other hand on the bow. Mamma Alessia picked up her violin and pulled across the strings. Marco did the same with amazing fullness. Then Signora Alessia said, "Speak to your parents, Marco. If they agree, some produce would finance the lessons."

Marco smiled widely and marched home with his loaned violin.

So Marco showed up every week at our house. I had seen him at school, but we had never spoken before he came to the house. Now we chatted frequently at school. He would often stay for dinner after his lesson and my dad would ride him home on the scooter.

If he came early for his lesson, we would often play duets, with me on the piano. We shared the common language of music, which bridged us out of that twelve-year-old's awkwardness with the opposite sex. And since we were both expected to help out with after-dinner cleanup, this fostered a brother-sister tone to our relationship.

After a few months we relished our time together and added more activities to the relationship. We would arrange to gaze together at the stars if a comet was due to pass by. I'd go to his family farm to help with a busy harvest as he did at my nonna's farm. At school we collaborated on how to complete our homework in a timely fashion.

By age sixteen, we became aware of an energy between us that seemed to compel us to hug good-bye just a little longer and just a little closer. Also, once I noticed his greeting kiss on the cheeks included a slight lip graze. I remember the surge it gave me down to my hips and onward to my toes.

So by the time we took the exams for the university at age seventeen we knew that we were in love. At the university Marco focused on art rather than music. His watercolors and oils were highly regarded by the professors. He became a prolific artist and began to have showings. I focused on dance and literature. We continued to play our instruments, but more as a hobby for relaxation. With the energy of youth we were able to study, have time with our friends at the cafes, and time to take walks on our family farms or along the river. On these walks we spoke of our latest art creations. We also spoke of our dreams for our art in the future. However, by the middle of our second year at the university, Marco had less and less time for our walks and talks. He said it was just the demands of his art work, and he continued to profess his love for me.

Soon, I dreamed of our life after our university years. We casually spoke of marriage during the little time we did have together. Then, during the last year at the university, Marco's art career catapulted him out from our now infrequent encounters. Marco had produced a huge amount of work. He engaged in it with the same confidence as he had the violin in his past. To him, if he heard it in his mind, he could reproduce it on the violin. Likewise, if he saw it in his mind, he could create it with his hands. Marco's talent was obvious to fellow students and his professors, as well as some of the art dealers.

A few months before our exit exams from the university, the professors asked him and another art student, Margarita from Barcelona, to show their work at an exhibition in Berlin. I was very excited for him, and for Margarita as well. I had met Margarita and her friends at local cafes during the years at the university. She was great fun and always had a smile. Marco, I recalled, enjoyed her company too. The exhibition was a great success. Marco was only home two weeks when he was asked to exhibit in Paris, also with Margarita. It was after that trip that I noticed an obvious change in Marco. Our time together was rare and for short times.

We were now near the end of the semester and would sit for our graduation exams in the next week. Marco came by late one evening and asked if we could walk. I agreed, but I felt a sense of dread in my heart. We set off down the familiar stone street and headed towards the country. He looked up and then at me and looked up again. He was so handsome to me. Tall, with an elegant carriage of his height. His tousled hair and full lips made him unmanageably attractive to me. He smiled at me but with pain in the energy of it. Marco then said, "I love you, but I don't think we're to be with each other for the long haul."

"What!" I burst out in the shock of the reality of my premonition.

"What do you mean not to be with each other? We've spent most of our lives as close companions… we've had support and love between us… what happened? Let me in on this!" I demanded.

Marco continued, "We have been great. But after this recent travel, I realize that I want to travel with abandon! Maybe even live somewhere else."

"With Margarita???" I shot back at him.

"Francesca, please understand. I have not had an affair with her, but I want to be free. I guess I want to be free from everything. The reaction of people about my art has changed something inside me. I am not sure who I am now, and I want to find out. Please understand, Francesca. I am so sorry!"

I turned around and headed up the slight incline back towards home. I marched on as the streets narrowed and the fields gave way to stone house walls. My mind struggled to compute what my lover and friend had said. Hmmm. He needed explorations. My brain could not equate that need with the need to let go of our relationship. Marco was at my side, but only to be sure that I would arrive home safely. There was no reconciliation in the bend of concern of his body at my heels. I could say nothing more. Nothing made sense to think, say, or feel at this moment.

All I wanted to do was focus on the feel of my feet on the stone road and my hand along the stone wall. When I arrived at the large wooden door of my family house, I said good night to Marco, stepped through the doorway, and closed the door behind me.

I went directly to the courtyard and lit the candles for our ancestors. I sat with my head on the table and wept silently. The sound of the door closing had awakened my mamma. She didn't hear my steps go towards my room, so followed her intuition to check on me. She found me on the patio and pulled a nearby chair next to me and sat down. I felt her gentle hand on my head. We reached our arms towards each other and held each other. Thus my healing began.

Mamma gave me a gentle squeeze and then rose and went to the kitchen to make hot tea. She returned to the table with two cups of steaming fresh mint tea. We sat in the garden with the lit candles, sipped the tea, and inhaled the fragrant herbs in large pots and in the earth along the small courtyard garden paths. I softly told her of Marco's decision. Mamma listened and listened to my descriptions of my injured heart, confused soul, and unsure mind. Gradually I began to feel that I could sleep. When Mamma saw me a little more peaceful she suggested that in a few days, as I had only one exam left, we could take a road trip. Perhaps we could take Sophia's route, she offered.

I was sure this was a great idea. We women in the family call the road between Naples and Turino, Sophia's route, while the men call it Aatif's route. Both Sophia and Aatif took this route up from Naples, though Aatif earlier than Sophia. Aatif did the journey with the Allied troops at the end of World War II and Sophia did the journey up to Aatif six months later. Aatif had made many enduring friendships along the road. His open heart, despite the rawness of war all around them, welcomed people to trust him. He took the time to repair many of the farmers' vehicles after completion of his work on the Allied vehicles. This endeared many of the farm people to him. Thus members of Aatif's family for four generations now have been welcome on these farms. Over the years my parents had developed a deep friendship with Liliana and Gilberto Marelli on one of these farms at the outskirts of Orvieto. Their daughter, Marcela, and I had also become close. So Mamma said she would contact them and see if a visit from us would be convenient for them. With that happy thought I headed to my bedroom.

Sleep came easily after my nocturnal time on the patio with my mamma. Dreams came in a very vivid, colorful form. I dreamed of orchards in the sun with the view of the old fortress city Orvieto. In the dream Marco ran with outstretched arms between the rows of grape vines. It seemed a bizarre thing for him to do, even in my dream state. But then, after a few more passes, he seemed to have taken flight from the vineyards. Marco simply disappeared. His presence in the vineyards was replaced with Marcela and myself. We danced along the paths between the grape vines. We laughed and lifted our heads to the blue sky. Then I realized that the bright sky was the sun that hit my eyes from the window in my own bedroom. Before I opened my eyes, I smelled the sweet earthy scent of fresh polenta. Its sumptuous corn porridge smell filled my nostrils where it vied with the scent waves from Papà's roasted coffee. This morning life felt a little less empty compared to last night.

The clear blue sky seen at the latched window gave me energy to face the day and to plant my feet on the tile floor. After a quick face and teeth wash, I made my way to the kitchen. Papà loved the morning chef duties. Mamma was on her daily speed walk. Papà and I were just about to sit down to our morning feast when Mamma passed through the big wooden door that just a few hours ago had seemed so arduous for me to find.

"Mmm, smells good!" Mamma said as she headed off to the shower.

Papà served us both plates of steaming corn porridge. He made mint tea for me and he poured coffee for himself. We settled onto the tall stools on the living room side of the long kitchen counter. Papà and I talked about the coming trip and my exam in two days. Then, when his plate was empty, he looked at me with a softness in his brown eyes. It was as if he knew what was going on inside me, which he did. He then said, "It only means he was not the partner for you. Trust me, Francesca."

"Papà, I trust you. But, I feel so betrayed to have trusted Marco."

Papà went on. "Your mamma was not my first love. Nor was I hers. She is my best and deepest love, however. All other relationships pale in comparison to the love with your mamma. But, my first love was a young woman at the university. I met her my second year there. She was vivacious, smart, and wore short skirts. I think it was the short skirts that awakened my far too serious mind. Anyway, she was the first woman I let myself become involved with. We were together for over a year. But then it became clear to her that she could capture the attention of some of the wealthy students from the corporate families. One in particular, with a red Fiat, literally whisked her away. I thought she meant all those words of her love for me and her admiration for my dedication to music and family. I think she thought she meant them. But, she discovered that the driver of the red Fiat was much more to her taste. So off she sped. My ego was devastated more than my heart, and I healed."

"My self-confidence returned as time went on. Your Nonna Tizianna encouraged me with these words, 'Avoid doubt in your decisions just because another changes theirs.' That thought didn't take my sadness away instantly. But, it did keep me in the reality of what had happened," Papà concluded.

"Over the next couple of years, I focused on my friends and my music. My inner self strengthened. When I met your mamma, I tried to keep the brakes on my emotions. But who can resist your mamma? We did pretty well to keep our attraction under wraps until after the extravaganza in Genoa. But then as we toured and spent more time together, all the brakes were off. We were unabashedly in love. We wanted to always be with each other. Our train rides between festivals were filled with not only song writing, but conversations on how our life would look for us as life partners."

Papà couldn't help but smile as he remembered. He then turned to me and said, "Be gentle with yourself, Francesca. You will heal in a strong way."

"Thanks, Papà," I said as I gathered up my empty plate and silverware. "I love you." I hugged my papà, washed our dishes, and headed to the patio. My papà was so cute with his heartfelt attempt to comfort me. I was shocked that he told me about that woman at university. This endeared my reserved papà to me even more.

That morning the empty space inside left by Marco's absence had begun to shrink. I then sat on the patio by my favorite rosemary bush, closed my eyes in the warmth of the morning sun, and began to focus on the movements of my breath as I inhaled and imagined it entering my rose colored heart. I sat until I felt more intact. Then I went to prepare for my exam. To give myself a break, I met my best friend, Suzanne, briefly at a café at the piazza. We are always there for each other when we hit bumps in our lives. After a warm embrace, we parted, I picked up some fresh bread for dinner, and went home. That evening, with Mamma's curried squash soup and the fresh bread with olive oil warm in my belly, I continued to study. In the morning after a brief sit on the patio and after my papà's breakfast, I hopped on my scooter to the university. The exam went well. Yes! The road trip was upon us!

SHORT TRIP WITH A BIG TRANSFORMATION

Early in the morning on the fourth day after my "news" from Marco, Mamma and I were ready to set off. I had checked out the tires and the charge of the solar battery the afternoon prior to our day of departure. We left at seven in the morning after hot polenta with sour cream, tea, and oranges. Our breakfast was made by our famous morning chef, Dominico, of course. The small gray car was packed with bread, cheese, grapes, tea, and water for our consumption on the road. We also brought some of our northern cheeses, Asiago "dulce" and ricotta, wines, rice, and hazelnuts for our friends and cousins farther south. We kissed and hugged Papà and headed out.

It was spring and the sun was bright and warm but not intense. This gave me the ideal nurturance light to heal my emotional state. As we drove over the small road and then onto the main highway, we enjoyed the sights of the green fields from newly emerged plants. Beyond them rolled the multicolored hills of wildflower blossoms. The bold beauty of the foothills and the high mountains stood strong in the distance. I let this beauty sweep into my soul and brighten it up. Mamma turned to me with those very kind large blue eyes and smiled when we passed a particularly spectacular view of the hills or mountains.

After she drove around a bend that revealed a lime green field next to a golden wheat field, she said, "You will feel better than ever, soon."

"I know, Mamma. I don't like this anger that I feel towards myself. I don't like that I trusted Marco even when he began to pull away," I said with a sigh.

"Francesca, issues about trust and our judgment can put us into unsolvable tailspins. Things happen in life. We cannot know what will happen next with anyone or anything. We can only know that we will be all right and that we will continue to love ourselves. That is what keeps our heart open and that is what keeps positive possibilities available to us."

"Hmmm. Makes sense. Mamma, Papà said something similar in his roundabout way a couple of mornings ago." We both laughed at memories of Papà's "roundabout ways."

"You know, Mamma, what I have noticed in the past few days is that Marco became for me a big source of my feeling good. I lost track of how to first be kind to my own heart. To be honest, though, to be with just me right now feels a little lonely," I observed.

"That's okay. Give yourself time to grieve, Francesca," Mamma said kindly.

I smiled and comfortably resettled myself into the passenger's seat for the rest of the drive.

To lessen my grief, I decided to enjoy the love that was in my life now and, for that matter, the love that was in this car. So, every time my mamma's large soft eyes met mine, I mirrored that love deep into my heart. Whenever she turned her smile to me, I let that compassion fill my soul. Gradually over the hours and the miles I could feel this love in me warmly spiral around. Little piece by little piece, my grief and self-pity began to spin out. I was able to reflect compassion and even love for myself. Wow! How great that felt!

After a couple more hours, we arrived at our friends the Marcellis in the surrounding countryside of Orvieto. Mamma disappeared into the kitchen with Liliana, Marcela's mamma. Marcela and I took off for the vineyards. It was our favorite place to walk. We had been friends since our youth. Our parents welcomed each other to their homes whenever they traveled to or through each other's province. These friendships had developed out of an intergenerational respect between the families. My great-great-nonno, Aatif, fixed their family's tractor and also helped rebuild their courtyard wall towards the end of World War II.

Marcela was always more reserved than me. She carried her small stature with a warm gentleness. Marcela's straight dark brown hair was usually worn in a long thick braid. She had light complexioned skin and round brown eyes framed with thick dark brown lashes. Today Marcela wore a light blue sundress and walked with ease over her beloved vineyard paths. She was in her final year at the university in Genoa with a major in public health nursing. Her plan was to return to her province to work. So, arm in arm we walked and basked in the camaraderie of many years. We shared stories of our lives since our last visit four months ago at my home in Turino.

"I'm sorry to hear about Marco, but I am not surprised. I thought he was a bit distracted during my last visit to Turino," comforted Marcela.

"I missed it at the time, Marcela. But I see it now and agree with you."

"I am really sorry," Marcela said as she gave my arm a gentle squeeze. "I have not met anyone to even be sad over!" she exclaimed with a twinkle in her eye.

"In time, my dear friend."

"Yes, Francesca, you are right. In time and hopefully with no sadness!"

"Let's make a pact to trust our futures to bring wonderful men to us," I offered to Marcela.

"Perfect!" said Marcela as we clasped our hands together in solidarity.

As the latest news for each other waned and our appetites rose, we returned to the farmhouse. Our mamme were on the veranda. They had set out Liliana's sumptuous mid-day meal. It was embellished by the cheese we brought. At the table we feasted on a delicious luncheon of greens and truffle pasta. Their white wine was, of course, excellent. Upon our departure, I insisted that Marcela stop by to spend some days at our house before her return to Genoa. She agreed and thus we parted with many hugs, kisses, and promises to see each other soon.

After a few more hours that encompassed two rest stops, we entered the countryside around Naples. We exited the highway and drove along the country road a few miles. Then, there it was on the right side of the road, the family farm of my ancestor Sophia. The long stone single-story farmhouse stood at the perimeter of a low stone-wall courtyard. A small stone shed stood to its right. The farm was set among many rocky fields on which the sheep grazed and a couple of smaller, less rocky fields that were cultivated with corn and beans. Directly behind the farmhouse stood the fig and orange trees with a large patio and vegetable garden between the fruit trees and the house. I loved this simple, rustic farm. The house had been carefully constructed long ago with stones from the fields.

Probably by now you, dear reader, have heard so many times about the Naples family farm and about how important the road between the Naples family farm and Turino is for us as a family. Before we actually arrive at the farm, I would like to tell you why I say it is important. My family has been connected to this farm since the arrival of Aatif to Naples during the Second World War. Aatif was our family patriarch on my papà's Mamma Tizianna's side. Let me tell you about Aatif as he was a quiet but strong man whose actions I benefit from to this day.

ORDER IN CHAOS

Some people have the gift to create order in chaos. My great-great-nonno, Aatif, was such a person. He was born in Tunisia in 1926. His mind was the sort that understood how tools and machines were organized and how they work. Barely in his teens, the youth of his Tunisian neighbor-hood sought him out to help construct or fix their wooden carts. The carts enabled these man-children to make some money for their families. On market day they helped the vendors haul fruits and vegetables to market. And if they were lucky, they would be hired to also haul the olives from the farms to the local presses. Thus, Aatif's skill was crucial for his friends' and acquaintances' economic welfare.

Aatif's father was a machinist who worked in the French infrastructure development of the Tunisian railways. Aatif's father drew diagrams for his son of the machines that comprised his day's work. Aatif studied his father's drawings of the engines and of the even smaller machines used to make the engine parts. He was able to apply the concepts of these machines to repair the popular motorbikes and later to repair larger motored vehicles. He was clever with his adaptations to use few tools and to be efficient with his time. Despite this economic benefit to the family, his father made sure that Aatif dedicated a couple of hours a day to his studies and that he observed his prayer time. But other than that, Aatif was free to fill his day with his mechanical repairs. He was able to contribute substantially to the finances of the family. Then in 1942, when Aatif was sixteen, World War II arrived in Tunisia. There in Tunisia the Allied forces successfully defeated the Italians and Germans. Aatif made himself useful with some technical repairs needed by the Allied forces' vehicles. Aatif's skill was unusual and his reputation spread widely among the Allied military. Their vehicles were challenged in this drier terrain. Aatif became their resource for all complicated issues with their vehicles in this new environment.

Aatif saw his relationship with the American Allies as more than a temporary economic boost. He saw it also as an opportunity to get out of his beloved, but colonized, Tunisia. Therefore, when asked by the Allied forces to remain with them as a mechanic, he agreed. In 1943 when the Allied troops invaded Sicily, with the blessing of his father and mother, Aatif went with them. He worked on their vehicles' mechanical repairs during the fast domination of Sicily. He then arrived onto the Italian mainland in his role as mechanic in the Allied invasion of Naples.

Aatif was raised with great respect for the positive potential of every human being. It was this respect that allowed him to continue to live amidst people at war and keep some sense of personal peace. The faith he carried with him out of Tunisia was a faith that emphasized good deeds and frequent prayer. He kept this faith close to him and followed it daily with prayer and kind interactions.

Aatif missed his family greatly. But, he reasoned, it had been his destiny to leave. He was grateful for his family's support at his departure. He carried their faces in his heart always. Aatif aspired to emulate his father's wisdom and also create a family filled with courage and compassion. He knew that he would one day find a woman of his mother's dignity and strength.

As fate would have it, Aatif met such a woman amidst an exhausted, war-torn people. Aatif had been in Naples only a couple of weeks when he met Sophia. She was as beautiful and peaceful as her name implies.

WHEN KINDNESS TRUMPS FATIGUE

Sophia tied the three kilo bags of coarsely ground wheat on the back of her bike. She then carefully tied the goatskin bag filled with goat milk under her cloak. With her small cutting knife covered and in place in her boot, she took off on her peddle bike towards the outskirts of Naples. There she and a few other younger women cared for the children of the couples involved with the reconstruction of their war damaged homes and shops. It was only a two-kilometer bike ride from the family farm to Naples.

Today Sophia felt beyond tired. There was little sleep and little time to eat over the past few weeks. But, she felt energized by the strength of her Naples to prevail over the Germans. Now the Allied forces were here as of five days ago. Although held in some suspect, they gave a bit more security to the area. However, the hard work to rebuild was up to the people of Naples.

As Sophia pedaled her bike, her round brown eyes focused on the rocky green hills that extended from the road. Their steadfastness gave her strength. She pushed on.

The last couple of days she had noticed an Allied camp along the road just ahead. A handsome young man was always there crouched over a truck or a cycle motor. He would look up with a warm smile and nod as she passed. Sophia would nod and continue on. She liked his smile and she liked his intelligent eyes. But then her thoughts moved on. She had little energy to give to handsome young men.

Today, however, he hailed her down as she passed.

As she got off her bike and walked it up to him, he said, "My name is Aatif. I have constructed a small platform for the back of your bike to carry the wheat. Would you like me to attach it?"

Sophia was surprised, but welcomed the kindness. "Yes, thank you," she responded. "My name is Sophia."

Even though they were both physically and emotionally worn, in this time of excessive human madness, they, as some others, were able to express and appreciate kindness. Thus, in this place, in this war, on this road, a love was kindled that lasted generations.

Aatif remained in Naples with the Allied troops until 1945 when the war ended. During that time he and Sophia had married. Sophia's family embraced Aatif. Her family consisted of her widowed mother, Elena, and three brothers. Her brothers had fought in the monarch brigades but now were able to be back at the farm and repair the war damages. Sophia's mother and brothers were quietly but deeply impressed with Aatif's hard work to assist them. They were also impressed with his kind ways. During his time off from the Allies, Aatif assisted Sophia's family with the crops and the reconstruction of the stone fences. He repaired their two motorbikes and small farm truck. Fortunately, the farmhouse was not damaged and they still had most of their goat herd intact.

Aatif found solace in the love of Sophia and her family. Aatif had fallen deeply in love with Elena's Sophia. So after some months of work on the farm during every spare minute and after long conversations with Sophia, Aatif said to Elena with a bit of caution and much respect, "Signora Elena, I would like the honor of your daughter Sophia's hand in marriage. I will work hard and care for her well. Your family will be as my family and always welcome in our home."

Elena was silent for a moment and Aatif's heart stopped. Her eyes looked at Aatif with an expression of welcome, but she said, "I must consult my sons and, of course, Sophia before I give you my blessing."

This shocked Aatif. He had expected a quick yes!

But instead she left him and went out into the courtyard where her sons had gathered with Sophia. They leaned against the wall by the large tree and rested in the cool early evening breeze after their day in the field.

Aatif followed. Beads of sweat appeared on Aatif's forehead and at the back of his neck. He wasn't prepared for a whole family confrontation.

I must give you, dear reader, a little inside information and say that my family is always ready for a little joke. Okay, so now back to poor Aatif!

Of course, at the news from their mother, Sophia's brothers could not resist torturing Sophia and Aatif with somber faces and shoulder shrugs. When they felt Aatif and Sophia had suffered enough, which was only a few moments because Aatif and Sophia looked so anguished, everyone burst out laughing. Sophia was hugged and spun around. They then grabbed Aatif and hugged him with many slaps on the cheek. They all quickly washed up and sat down to the mutton stew with polenta. Sophia's family shouted toasts of blessings for Aatif and Sophia while they opened the wine that accompanied their stew. Aatif and Sophia married within two weeks. They got their papers from the magistrate. In this seaport town it was not unheard of for foreigners to marry a Napolean. However, by law it was taboo. But now it was also wartime. The magistrate gladly provided the marital documents for Aatif and Sophia in exchange for bountiful produce from the farm and Aatif's repair of the magistrate's vehicle.

Aatif was proud, happy, and full of plans for their future. During his time in the Naples area, Aatif enjoyed the combination of mechanic work with the Allied forces and the farm work with Sophia and her family. But, this changed in 1945 when he was obligated to continue his work for the Allied forces during their push up to northern Italy. He decided to use this to his advantage and with Sophia's agreement, to establish his work in the more industrial north after his arrival there with the Allied troops. Thus, before his departure he, Sophia, and her family arranged the plan for her travel north to join him once he was settled.

Upon arrival up north and the completion of his obligation to the Allied troops, Aatif located an abandoned animal shelter on the outskirts of Turino. He rebuilt it to create a machinist shop. Attached to the shop Aatif built a two-room dwelling of stone and mortar. He completed the shutters just in time to protect the rooms from the fall rains.

Whether in his shop or on people's farms, the skill of Aatif consistently turned mechanical disasters into efficient motorbikes, cars, and farmer's trucks. Aatif's reputation grew as an excellent, honest mechanic with reasonable prices. He had secured himself economically in the community. That enabled him to soon receive his beloved Sophia.

After about eight months Aatif sent word to Sophia.

SOPHIA'S VOYAGE TO AATIF

Sophia sat at the sturdy wooden table and looked into her mamma's kind large brown eyes. The meal was finished, the dishes washed and put away. And so they sat together. The men smoked outside. They leaned against the house or perched themselves on the short wall that marked the farmhouse courtyard. They talked of the crops, and of the neighbors who had fled to America. They did not speak of Sophia and Mario's voyage tomorrow. It had been spoken of enough. Neither did the women at the kitchen table speak of it.

Sophia loved this woman with all her heart. Her mother had always supported Sophia's headstrong ways. Elena called it courage.

Elena knew that Sophia would do well with her new husband. Aatif had won Elena's confidence with his hard work around the farm over the past couple of years. He treated Sophia and everyone with great respect. Yes, he would be a good husband for Sophia.

And now Aatif was up north. Elena loved Aatif like a son and missed him since he had left. Elena had never noticed Sophia to let sadness touch her like it did when Aatif left. She was her energetic self but just a little slow on the usual fast smile. Elena knew that her daughter's quick smile would soon return.

Now, as planned, with the war over and Aatif settled as a mechanic in Turino, Sophia would journey to him. Mario, Elena's second oldest son would journey with Sophia and work a while there on railroad construction before returning home.

So, peacefully, the two women sat together. Sophia knew that the kind of love Elena had shown her was rare and a forever gift. It had a depth that could never be repaid. It could only be accepted.

Sophia went over the list of food for the journey.

"Mamma, we have corn meal, water, fish packed in rosemary, oil, and cheese. Is there anything else that we may need?"

"I have an herb bundle, in case there are any injuries and some more rosemary for tea to keep you well. Drink it daily. Here is the blessed medallion for your journey. Keep it close to your heart," Elena said. "Everything will be fine," she concluded as she gently patted Sophia's cheek.

The next day Sophia and Mario climbed aboard the back of a farm truck. A neighbor had business in Rome. He agreed to drive Sophia, Mario, and two others in the Naples area to Rome. Sophia and Mario paid a large fee to their neighbor for the petro. The roads were difficult to navigate. They had huge holes. For miles they drove in the fields because long stretches of the roads were impassable. Sophia's back and hips ached with the jostles of the truck. At night one of them stood guard, as the country was still unsafe for travelers. Fortunately they passed the night without incident. In Rome, Sophia and Mario had a cousin in a convent who put them up for the night. The shower felt wonderful on Sophia's tired skin. The next day, with fresh provisions provided by the convent, Sophia and Mario continued on the next leg of their journey. Their cousin was able to connect Sophia and Mario with a clever man who, for a fee, provided transport to clergy and others. Thus they continued on to Genoa on the back of his truck.

Aatif had left a large portion of his salary from the troops for Sophia's family and for Sophia and Mario's journey north. So Sophia and Mario were prepared for the transport fee. But the driver's truck did not have the capability for such a long trip. They made it as far as a town called Orvieto when it broke down. There they stayed overnight while a local mechanic and the driver worked on the truck. Sophia had the name of a farmer whom Aatif had befriended during the Allied troops' northern march. Word was sent to him that Aatif's wife was nearby in passage to Turino. His name was Raimondo Marcelli. He brought water and polenta wrapped in paper with cured olives. Sophia and the others were most grateful.

By the next afternoon the truck had been repaired and they were on their way. However, about twenty miles outside of Genoa it broke down again. Neither the driver nor any of the passengers could motivate the vehicle to move one more inch. It was mid-day and the passengers had no recourse but to begin to walk to Genoa. The driver stayed with the truck. All of the water, as well as the food, had been shared and finished. Sophia and Mario walked slowly, as did the others. Their mouths became dry and their bodies exhausted. Fortunately, their bags were light over their shoulders as they were empty of provisions. Sophia still had some money. She had it cleverly hidden in cloth folds next to private areas of her anatomy. But the money did not serve them on this road. They arrived

after sunset in Genoa. Sophia and Mario found the tavern as described by
the truck driver. The tavern owner offered them water as they described
to him the predicament of their truck driver. As promised, they gave the
truck's location to the tavern owner. He was a friend of their driver and
right away sent a mechanic out to the truck on a motorbike. He carried
with him a lamp, some tools, water, bread, cheese, and some gasoline.

The tavern owner offered them a cup of fish soup and welcomed
them to pass the night in the tavern for a small fee.

Sophia and Mario quietly slept with their heads down on a back table.
In the morning they made their way to the trains. They washed their faces
and drank the cold water from the fountain in the piazza. Their spirits had
greatly improved. As they walked on they gained energy from bread and
cheese bought from a street vendor. They were relieved to find out that
the train tracks were open into Turino. They boarded the train and within
two hours they were in Turino.

Once off the train, Aatif had directed by letter that they hire a motorbike ride to his mechanic shop and house. Anyone with a motorbike
would know him. He was right. They quickly found a young fellow on
a bike who immediately hailed a friend over when he heard that they
were Aatif's family. So they each climbed behind one of Aatif's clients
and sped on to the shop. They arrived within minutes. When Aatif heard
them, he jumped up from his crouched position by a motorbike. He ran to
his fatigued but relieved family. Aatif swung Sophia around in his arms
and strongly embraced Mario. He quickly poured them hot coffee, and
ladled out two steaming bowls of goat and vegetable soup, and placed a
large plate of flat cornbread on the table. He just sat there and looked at
them with such joy.

Then he prepared hot baths and laid out clean clothes for them. He
had bartered with a client for newly sewn simple nightshirt for each of
them as well as new day shirts. His wife smiled at him in her new nightshirt. She then lay down in his bed and fell fast asleep under the warm
wool-filled, cotton-covered quilt. Sophia dreamed of a ride on soft clouds
with lots of water to drink.

Mario managed to stay awake long enough to tell Aatif of the journey.
He then began with news from the farm but was shortly stopped as his
eyes closed into a heavy sleep. Aatif led him to his warm quilt covered
bed in the small room adjacent to the living area. Mario slept a hard

sleep. He dreamt of bumps and long walks.

Aatif placed the food in the sealed ice chest. He washed up the dishes, bathed, and crawled into bed by his wife. Ahhh, to have her smell fill his nostrils once again. Aatif dreamt of heaven.

Within a year after that, Aatif was able to secure seven acres about three kilometers out of town. It proved to be good farmland.

That land, dear reader, is our family land to this day. I live on that land now with my Luciano and nonni.

But now back to the story of my one of many journeys to our Naples farm, as my mamma and I have arrived. We drove into the courtyard and parked.

MORE OF THE SHORT TRIP WITH A BIG TRANSFORMATION

There was Cugino Luciano at the end of the courtyard by the shed with his arms around a damaged tractor tire. He flashed one of his great, wide smiles at us and shouted, "Hey, Zia Alessia and Cugina Francesca!" as he put the tire down and attempted to clean off his hands and shirtfront with a slightly cleaner rag. He hurried over to greet us. By the time we finished big hugs with Luciano, Cugina Laura, Zia Margarita and Cugino Maximillian were upon us with warm embraces. Zio Josefa, the only one not there to greet us, was still out with the sheep.

"I'll be right back out to help you with the tire, Luciano, as soon as I splash some cool water on my face," I said. He knew to expect as much. We both loved to tinker with vehicles. We had always enjoyed each other's company. He was only a little older than me. We both loved not only mechanics but also the rural lifestyle. In addition, we shared a love of music, literature, and art. Needless to say our conversations flowed easily. So I rushed away quickly to freshen up and return to assist him.

Luciano had completed his university work in agriculture a year ago. He now had a job in the region with the department of agriculture. It was his job to coordinate the market produce from all the co-op farms.

While we repaired the tire and replaced it, Luciano chatted away about one of his favorite projects at work. He was very excited about the support he was able to give farmers to grow organic and heirloom crops in a profitable way. He had completed a 25-page pamphlet on the process.

The pamphlet explained how to balance the production to meet local consumption needs and to also meet export demand. It would be shared with all the Italian provinces. We sat and leaned against the tractor with the tire now in its place. He laughed and said that some of the northern provinces had requested his pamphlet. He smiled at me with his smoky green eyes.

"So, dear Francesca, you northerners have requested intellectual property from us southerners. Will wonders ever cease?"

We smiled warmly at each other over this age-old Italian rivalry. I thought he might have shown a slight sign of awkwardness during the eye contact, but it passed.

I was fascinated with the agricultural progress around Naples and asked Luciano to elaborate.

"What is really great," Luciano continued, "is that the income of the Naples area has increased since the province's support of the small farmer. We provide assistance with irrigation techniques, heirloom plants, and natural pesticides. Production has increased and this has attracted agriculture students and government officials from around the globe. So we have become somewhat of a teaching laboratory on profitable sustainable agriculture.

"But, the arm of the project that I love the most is the evaluation process. What I mean is, we evaluate if there is sufficient food in all the districts. If there is a shortage in any of the districts, we then create a plan in coordination with the local authorities and farmers to eliminate the shortage. I feel this practical benefit for the families of the province is the best outcome of our overall program."

"I know all this is a lot of work—great work, but a lot of work. Do you still have time for your art?" I asked Luciano.

"I make time, Francesca, because I love it too much. It's a little easier now to find time that Marta is on work assignment in Sicily for her law firm. She'll be back within a couple of weeks for a brief visit," Luciano added.

"Well, dear Luciano, are wedding bells in the near future?" I teased.

Luciano laughed. "I don't know. Maybe in a couple of years."

I thought I saw a hint of sadness in Luciano's eyes as he looked at me and said, "Marta's career is important to her. She wants it well established before marriage." Luciano shrugged and ran his large hand through his thick, wavy, dark brown hair.

"Come on, let's see this latest painting," I said as I half-danced over to the shed.

His artwork was in the shed on the side by a large window. Tools and space for a vehicle were on the other far side that had two smaller windows. On the easel was a painting of a sunrise over the hill that was in the near distance behind the house. The capture of the oranges and browns on the softly darkened sky above the green field was stunning. "I really like it, Luciano. It's really good."

"Thanks," he said. "Before we go in, do you want to stretch your legs and find Josefa and his sheep?"

"I would love to," I responded. We marched out of the shed and up the hill, spotting Josefa as he came down the ridge to our right. We waved at Josefa.

As we walked toward Josefa, Luciano asked, "So, how's Marco?"

I told him. Luciano's eyes widened and his mouth opened in shock as his strong shoulders raised his arms upwards. There Luciano stood against the sky. His tall, firmly framed body with his deep olive-toned skin stood against the glow of the sun. To me, that was a beautiful sight. His body posture messaged surprise with a bit of exasperation.

But he was without words for only a split second. He lowered his arms and burst out, "Why? How? I thought he was a grounded guy. He was always friendly and a great artist. Wow. Well, I'm so sorry, Francesca." Then he added, I thought a little sadly, "Sometimes people change their priorities."

"Yeah, they do, Luciano. Life goes on, right?"

"Right."

By then Josefa had guided the sheep below us into the pen guarded by two dogs. Josefa came up to us and I was able to give my kind zio a big hug. He said, "Come on, let's go in and get some of Zia Margarita's good rice balls and greens."

"Sounds great!" Luciano and I chimed together.

Everyone sat and joked around the dinner table until sunset. Laura and I began to help Mamma and Zia Margarita with the meal clean up.

I hugged my cugina and said "Go enjoy yourself with Natalie. I got you covered in the kitchen."

Laura and her friend Natalie had recently passed the exams that qualified them for the university. So a little special treatment was in order for my younger cugina.

Luciano went off to assist Maximillian with some of his calculus. Maximillian was in second year of university. Maximillian and Laura were younger than Luciano. Luciano was a doting big brother and loved them both. They had been raised as brothers and sister; however, Luciano was not their blood brother. He was taken in as their own by Margarita and Josefa when he was two.

How that happened was pretty sad. Margarita and Josefa were recently married. They had plenty of food from this intergenerational, well-managed farm. They also had generous hearts. Thus, when their lead farm workers Cologero and Serafina Vento were killed as they walked along the roadside by a car that made a fast turn, Margarita and Josefa took in their son, Luciano. The tragedy was announced in a major Sicilian newspaper. No relatives from Sicily contacted the Bersanis. There had been no family that Luciano's parents had spoken of during their four years on Margarita and Josefa Bersani's farm. So, with no one to contact and no response from the newspaper announcement, they adopted Luciano as one of their own.

But that was over twenty years ago. Right now, the day after my arrival at the farm, Luciano has grabbed my hands in an attempt to pull me up from the patio chair where I sat in quiet contemplation with my lemonade.

Luciano said, "Francesca, come with me to Flavio's. We're going to hike along the Positano ridge."

"Luciano, you know I'm always ready for the Positano ridge!" I exclaimed.

Laura and Natalie also wanted to come, so we made it a two-motorbike adventure. It was only about a thirty-minute ride on the country roads to Flavio's house.

Maximillian decided to spend the afternoon studying so he'd have enough work done to be able to go to his girlfriend Juliana's that evening.

"Well, have a good time this evening my little fratello," said Luciano with a gentle slap to Maximillian's cheek and a look of brother-to-brother understanding in his eyes.

Thus with water, fruit, and leftover rice balls we took off for Flavio's house. The roads were smoother than I remembered from a few years ago. The speed and the wind felt good on my cheeks. I felt secure with my arms around Luciano. My eyes searched ahead for that first glimpse of the aqua Mediterranean.

Then, there it was. The gradual appearance of turquoise blue between the trees and rocks as we rode up the gentle rise of the bluff to Flavio's. We parked the bikes in the dirt drive of the small, stone house as Flavio opened the wooden door and came out to greet us.

"Francesca! This is great! It's been too long!" shouted Flavio.

Then out came Patricia, Flavio's mother, with a bundle of breads, wine, and dried fish for our hike. We all shared hugs and kisses. While the men arranged the food in backpacks, we ladies went with Patricia inside to freshen up. Patricia was short and a little round. I'd always loved her. She was consistently relaxed and always welcomed Flavio's friends. Thus with a beautiful lunch on our backs, we set off along the bluff's trail with full view of the expansive Mediterranean.

We often stopped on our hike to inhale the splendor of the dramatic cliff coastline as it met the sea. We celebrated the boldness of nature's display with our loud voices in song. We sang old and new love ballads. We even belted out a couple of my parents' popular ballads.

Perhaps our most fun was the entertainment of Flavio's antics. He made any gathering a lighthearted venture. As we headed south on the trail we met a young married couple from Sweden. They were very friendly, so we chatted briefly. They had one more day in the area so we told them of some not-to-miss local sites. Of course Flavio offered to escort the young lady around, but she would have to leave her husband behind. Everyone laughed and we parted company.

"Hey, Flavio," I said. "Do you think their Italian was good enough to get your joke?"

"Yes, my flirtatious friend. I don't know if they could understand you well enough. We might all be in big trouble!" added Luciano.

Flavio just waved off our teases. The laughter at Flavio's expense triggered our appetites and we decided to stop and rest. We settled down on the ground a short distance off the trail. We stretched out on the blanket and ate the scrumptious lunch. Then we lay on our backs, with our bellies full, and watched the few clouds scoot across the sky. The younger women talked of their anticipated course of study and of their romantic interests. Flavio and Luciano talked of their jobs briefly and then fell asleep in the soft sun and cool sea breeze.

Me, I relished being with myself in the presence of folks that I love and in a place that I love. My life had begun to form without Marco as my partner. I laid my hand on my stomach and felt my strong center. Then I fell into a deep peaceful sleep. I awakened when I sensed a large shadow over my face. I looked up and there was Luciano grinning at me.

"Let's go, sleeping beauty. Time to head back to the farm!" Luciano said.

As the sun lowered towards the sea's horizon we trekked back to Flavio's. Still with the sun, although very low, we hopped on the bikes to the farm. We dropped off Natalie at her small country house to change her clothes. That evening, she and Laura planned to attend a mutual friend's celebration of his successful exam completion.

As the sun set, we arrived at the farmhouse courtyard. We propped the bikes in the shed and went into the farmhouse to relate our story of the beautiful hike to the rest of the family.

After hot lamb stew, wine, and fruit, Luciano excused himself and went out to the shed. Josefa went out to check the animals. Mamma said to me, "Francesca, you look tired. Go ahead and get some rest. We'll straighten up the kitchen."

"Thanks, Mamma. I think I will." I kissed my mamma, Laura, and Zia Margarita goodnight and off I went upstairs to our room. I washed up, put on my long cotton nightgown, and got under the sheets and quilt. As my eyelids closed, I noticed a ray of soft moonlight on the wall joined with a faint light cast from the shed. Soon I was fast asleep.

Sunday, after tea and cornmeal porridge with sour cream, I sat out on the veranda and wrote and wrote and wrote in my notebook. I decided to celebrate all the good memories with Marco. I wrote down all the good times we had. I wrote of the conversations that gave me comfort, the fun walks, the long study sessions, and the musical duets on piano and violin. The more I wrote, the more I saw his half presence with our physical touch, our talks, and our long walks. During the time with him, I had rationalized that it was the artist's mind. True, I had never noticed this distraction with my parents who were also artists. Nor did I feel it with myself and wasn't I an artist? Maybe it was the painters who are particularly distracted, I had erroneously reasoned. How off from reality my past thoughts seemed now as I revisited our relationship through my written recollections.

Then I heard a blast of music that broke my thoughts from the past. It was a tango that flowed out of the portable player in the window of the shed. Luciano emerged from the shed with a smile on his face and his arms in dance form. He knew that dance always made my heart sing.

"May I have this dance, Francesca?" he queried.

"But of course, Luciano," I responded with a twinkle in my eye, as I rose to engage his embrace. After a short initial rock, we glided over the stone veranda with an intense and consistent sense of the other's movement. As it finished I felt only sunshine.

"Thanks, Luciano, that was great," I said softly.

"My thanks to you, Francesca. It's not every day a guy gets to dance with a real dancer," he said as he bowed.

We both laughed. Then he disappeared once again into the shed. I went in to help with dinner.

After dinner my papà called. He spoke with my mamma for a while and then with Luciano.

When I got on the phone, he asked, "How are you?"

"Really good, Papà." I told him of the visit with Marcela Marelli and of the hike on the bluff near Flavio's. I could hear the relief in his voice at my happiness. "I love you and miss you, Papà. See you soon."

"Same here."

"Do you need Mamma on the phone?"

"Well, just for a minute."

"Hold on. Big hug!"

He and Mamma spoke for a couple more minutes. Mamma kissed into the phone with a "Ciao, Ciao."

The evening was now warm and dark. Mamma and Zia Margarita settled on the back terrace with their wine. Luciano asked me, "Do you want to see my latest project in the shed?"

"Yes!" I responded as I caught his pace and moved towards the shed. "So, Luciano, you've begun a new project already? Was the paint dry on your sunset, yet?" I asked as I looked up into his warm eyes.

When I entered the shed, I was not prepared for what I saw.

"Wow, Luciano! It's fantastic!" I said with an obvious blush!

There was a painting of me asleep in the grass on the bluff. It was as if my presence had cuddled into the hillside. My expression was one of deep peace. I was shocked by the beauty of his work and what I noticed about my essence. There was no grief in my frame. There was only life with its endless supply of energy. I really liked that!

I gave Luciano a big hug. "I'm glad you like it," he said. "It was a vision in my memory from the hike that had to be put to canvas. This is a present for you, Francesca, to honor your university graduation."

"Oh, my, Luciano. What a treasure this is. Thank you. But I still have to complete my thesis."

"I know. You will."

He went off to assist Maximillian with his business economics. I went to the back terrace to escort Mamma and Zia Margarita to the shed to see my fantastic portrait.

The next day Laura, Mamma, Zia Margarita, and I put in Zia Margarita's late spring plantings in her vegetable garden. The physical labor in the soil felt good, and their fellowship, the plants, sun, and smell of the dark brown dirt centered me.

"The garden looks beautiful. Thanks so much, all of you," said Zia Margarita. "Let's go and have some coffee before we begin dinner preparations."

"Zia Margarita, I'm going to pass on the coffee. I think I'll walk a little. Do you want to come, Laura?"

"No," said Laura, "because I know what your little walks entail. That's a little more energy than I have today." She then flashed her beautiful, playful smile towards me.

"Ah, a good party last night, eh? Okay, I'm off then. Back soon."

So, my mamma, Laura, and Zia Margarita went in to clean themselves up and begin dinner preparations, and I hiked out to the far fields to help Zio Josefa bring in the sheep.

Zio Josefa greeted me with a warm smile. "Well, my little Francesca, who is not so little anymore, I see you still love the fields."

"Yes, I do, Zio. After graduation, I may move in with my Nonna Tizianna on the family farm. It is close to my parents, but definitely in the country."

"That sounds good for you, Francesca." He said. "You are happiest when you have your hands in the dirt." He then laughed a big belly laugh.

We traipsed over the hills companionably and arrived at the pen. There was Luciano at the pen gate unchanged from his clean work attire.

Evidently he had spotted us from his scooter as we passed over the ridge. He laughed at the dirt on my hands, face, and blouse.

"Look out, Luciano, or I'll touch your pristine white shirt!"

He shouted, "Oh, no you won't!" and took off in a run to the house.

I took off after him. He was up in his room changing by the time I arrived at the kitchen door. The women in the kitchen laughed heartily at my reddened, dirt-streaked face and my bent over frame that panted for breath.

My mamma said, "Did you catch him?"

"No, but I will next time!" I said with conviction.

The next day was our last day at the farm. I found some excuse or other to get out to the fields and to oil up a tiller. I also found some of Luciano's CDs in the shed and danced around the courtyard with an imaginary partner. As I moved around, I began to plan my dance demonstration that would accompany my thesis. My thesis was on the influence of African dance movements on dance around the world. I would begin with African drums accompanied by West and North African dance moves. Then the music would transform but keep its same complex rhythm. The music would alter to accompany the moves of classical ballet, flamenco, tango, tap, swing, mambo, rumba, cha-cha, bachata, meringue, salsa, cumbia, two-step, and Charleston. The African dance moves from each dance type would flow into each other as one choreographed piece. I was excited that I now knew exactly how I wanted the presentation to go. To celebrate I began to dance an intense salsa.

When I caught a glimpse of Luciano's scooter on the road, I stopped. My work was too young and tender to share.

"Why did you stop, Francesca?" asked Luciano as he entered the courtyard. "Your moves were great! Very distracting! I almost hit a pothole!" he teased.

"Well, I hope that the professor panel thinks they're great," I replied.

"They will," he replied as he pushed his scooter into the shed.

Mamma and I were to leave the next day, which was Wednesday. But, we were not alone in the car. As coincidence would have it, Luciano was booked to give a consultation in the department of agriculture in Turino for Thursday and Friday. Of course, he would stay with us. The ride back home would be easier and faster with him as a driver. We would drive straight through with only short rest stops. We would be home by suppertime. Papà would have one of his creations ready for supper. He was excited about Luciano's visit and had asked him to stay until Sunday.

Since in his pre-teen years, Luciano would come up to hike the mountains with Papà. The two of them had always enjoyed each other's company. They both shared a seriousness, but were also spontaneous and loved the challenge of mountain hikes. They avoided dangerous areas, but did strenuous inclines and distances. Neither had family members that loved their intense style on the trails. Thus, their mountain excursions were exclusively their own. They occurred at the very least bi-annually for many years now. Mamma and I share their love for the mountains. But we roam or walk briskly, as the mood strikes us, the gentler inclines.

By seven o'clock Wednesday morning we had the car trunk packed with our luggage and my precious painting. The small painting was well cushioned and placed in an old piece of luggage of Zia Margarita's. After breakfast we packed in the food for the trip as well as some frozen lamb chops. After many kisses and hugs for Zia Margarita, Zio Josefa, Maximillian, and Laura we took off.

We stopped about every two hours to stretch and for restroom visits. We decided to eat in the car. Once again I opened to the beautiful scenery. We were all relaxed and spoke often of our beautiful Italian countryside. We arrived home in the late afternoon with Papà's welcome face at the door. We unloaded the car and settled on the patio. We discussed the trip and I showed Papà my portrait. His eyes got big and he raised his eyebrows very high.

"I didn't realize, Luciano, how talented you were!"

"I really love to paint. For me, it is relaxing, but it's a hobby." Luciano answered. "I'm very passionate about the agricultural work at my job."

"Good luck on your consultation here, Luciano," Papà said. "And, how is Marta? Does she like the law firm?" Papà continued.

"She is well and loves her work. This special assignment in Polermo, Sicily, has kept her very busy. But I did speak with her ten days ago. She said she'll be home next week, actually," said Luciano.

IS SOMETHING GOING ON BETWEEN LUCIANO AND ME?

That evening we ate Papà's great red sauce on spaghetti pasta with a little grated cheese on top. In addition, he made a huge mixed green salad. It was perfect food for our car-fatigued bodies. The wine, full stomachs, and warm evening air on the patio sent our tired bodies to bed early that night.

When I awakened in the morning, my folks were busy working on a rearrangement of a song they had written years ago. They wanted to adapt it for the local festival in two weeks. It would be a duet with my papà on the keyboards. To me this ballad sounded magical.

"Hey, good morning," they said together as if their duet continued into conversation.

"Good morning," I chimed back and headed for the kitchen. "Luciano at work?"

"Yes," my papà said.

After my usual breakfast I called my closest friend, Susanna, to meet for coffee at the nearby café. We had been close since early childhood and now were about to complete our university studies together. We both focused on dance in our studies. Since the completion of our course work, we had procured part-time jobs teaching dance at the Ignacio Studio. She was to teach four ballet classes per week. I was to teach two tap, one salsa, and one hip-hop class per week. We both worked with pre-teen and teenage groups.

My friend Susanna was very tall with long, straight, wheat-colored hair. Her entire presence floated as she moved. Even her blouses seemed to flow around her. Susanna was very kind. She tended to be a little serious. My papà often teased her about this. Susanna enjoyed his antics and often relaxed around my parents. Mamma always invited her to stay for supper when we studied or visited together. Susanna always accepted.

As friends we had a confidence that was unbreakable. This morning at the cafe we sipped our coffee and I told Susanna about the trip to the Naples farm.

"My time on the farm grounded me, Susanna," I explained. "I have said good-bye to all the sadness, anger, and pride that bound my thoughts to Marco. I wrote many pages about my feelings, both good and bad, about my relationship with Marco. Will you come to the river with me while I burn those pages and throw them in the river?"

"Let's go!" Susanna replied enthusiastically.

So we went to my house. Susanna waved to my folks at the piano. I grabbed the papers from my room and some matches by the candle on the side table.

"We need a bowl of some sort," Susanna suggested.

"Oh, right!" I answered.

I grabbed a large conch shell from the patio and Mamma's tobacco pouch from the kitchen drawer. Mamma often used the shell for smudges and the tobacco for offerings of thanks.

So loaded with the papers, matches, tobacco pouch, a sage bundle, and the conch shell, I somehow managed to free a hand that waved to my folks and said, "We're off to the river!"

Papà looked a little confused, but Mamma smiled and nodded, and they went back to their work.

I put the supplies in a small satchel on the back of the scooter. We hopped on and sped towards the river. In a few minutes we stopped and walked the scooter down the gentle bank alongside the river. The river had a good current today. I depended on it to move, without hesitation, some things from my life.

When we arrived on its bank, I put down the tobacco on the earth in the way of my ancestors that my mamma taught me, and her mamma, Mikaela, before her. Mamma's voice rang in my head with these words, "The Creator is in all of life. It helps us on our journey if we give thanks to all of life, to honor the Creator and ourselves."

So now I give thanks to the river. It will help me to release all pain from my past. After the tobacco was put down, I lit a bundle of sage and smudged Susanna and myself.

When I placed the conch on the ground and crumpled up my writings into it, Susanna knelt down opposite me to help shelter the small flame from the slight breeze. We wanted the burn to confine itself to the shell. I lit the paper. Soon all my written travail of Marco was in ashes.

"Okay," I said to Susanna. "I'm ready." We walked to the river. I dumped the ashes into it. Just like that, they were gone!

"Wow!" Susanna exclaimed. "The river really took care of that!"

"Yes, it did!" I responded as I watched the ashes totally disappear in the gray-blue flow of the great river.

With a lighter spirit than I had felt in many days, I turned and said to Susanna, "Thanks for your friendship. It meant a lot to me that you were here."

Susanna smiled and we pushed the bike up to the road.

I drove Susanna home and then returned to mine. We both had work to do on our theses. We agreed to meet at the library the next day.

When I arrived home, Papà was with a piano student and Mamma was in the patio garden on her knees cutting some basil, rosemary, and mint to dry. When I returned the conch she asked, "How'd it go?"

"It went well, Mamma," I responded.

I made Mamma and myself a cup of rosemary tea. Then as I brought her the tea, I announced, "I had a great idea on the farm how to do my dance presentation to enhance my written thesis."

"Tell me," she said as she leaned back, sat on her feet, and took a sip of mint tea.

I explained to her what I had worked out in the farm's courtyard.

"That is a dynamic idea. I think it will go over well," she encouraged.

"My work today is to check over the thesis outline for completion. Also I want to check that I have all the references that I need."

"You're an organized woman, Francesca," said Mamma fondly as she placed her tea on the brick path at her side and once again bent back over her herbal patch. "Thanks for the tea."

"You're welcome, Mamma. I'm off to my room to work!"

Later that afternoon I needed a break from the paperwork and went into the kitchen to help with supper. As I washed the greens and vegetables for the salad, Mamma set up the table on the patio. Papà had marinated the lamb chops since early afternoon in garlic, olive oil, salt, pepper, and basmati vinegar. He placed the chops on the solar grill as Luciano came in the door.

"Hey, everyone," he greeted. "Let me quickly change, and then I'll help." Luciano washed up and put on a casual shirt and jeans. He promptly joined us in the kitchen.

"Reporting for duty!" Luciano exclaimed.

Papà laughed and shoved the bread and cutting board towards him. "Thick slices for the grill, please, sir," Papà instructed. Then he went to the grill to check its heat. He soon had the chops sizzling on the grate. Luciano brought the bread out and Papà placed the slices on the grill to toast. He asked Luciano to open the wine.

Luciano poured the wine and passed a glass to everyone. The bread was toasted to a golden brown, the salad dressed in garden herbs, fresh lemon, and olive oil, and the sizzling lamb chops done to perfection. Luciano was moved to make a toast.

"I wish to toast this generous family with their fine culinary arts skills! And, I wish to toast the scholar's successful completion of her thesis."

Everyone said, "Here, here!" I blushed and the meal began.

We talked of the spring festival in two weeks. Luciano said, "I'd love to return for the festival. It would mean a lot to me to hear both of you, Dominico and Alessia, sing together once again in a public venue."

"Of course, you must come!" my papà chimed in. "Bring Marta, too," Papà concluded.

It was settled. Luciano would return for the festival.

After the kitchen cleanup, Luciano said, "I could use a good walk after a day of meetings. Do your legs need a stretch after all those hours at your desk, Francesca?"

Luciano knew very well that I tolerated only short intervals sitting without movement. He had a one hundred percent chance of a 'yes' to his request.

"Give me just a second to change my top, Luciano. I have a new planting to show you at the farm. Let's head out to Nonna Tizianna's," I suggested.

Mamma gave us a bundle of some of the frozen lamb chops to take to her mother-in-law and we hit the road in the cooler evening air.

As we walked the three kilometers to the farm, Luciano told me about the plans in our Piedmont province to assure adequate food production for our population here and to provide a surplus to sell to the other provinces and abroad. He added with emotion that there also had begun a respectful discussion between healthy food and industrial development interests in the province. They discussed multiple ways they can co-exist and benefit each other.

"I love the challenges here in Piedmont," he added. "But, Francesca, I would like to hear more of what you are up to and what you plan to do after your thesis is finished."

"Well, I thought that I would always teach. Teaching dance was a logical choice due to my passion for dance. And I do enjoying working with my students at the dance school. But over the past year, my interest in writing seems to have burst forth, sharing the spotlight with the dance classroom. Our family stories fascinate me, and I've begun to write them down. I balance the time I spend at my desk writing with working in the fields or teaching a dance class or two." I said with a big smile.

"Speaking of families, Luciano," I continued, "what do you know about your birth parents' families?"

"Not a lot," answered Luciano. "Margarita and Josefa said that my parents were clever farmers, hardworking, and good people. They were from Sicily. They arrived at the farm and asked for work. Margarita and Josefa liked them immediately and were even more pleased when they saw the skill and speed of their farm work. I would like to know more, but for now that's all I know because that's all Margarita and Josefa know."

"Sounds like a mystery that would be fun to solve," I said.

As we arrived at the farm, I pointed out the okra plot to Luciano. "I think that little knoll is high enough to grow it. What do you think?"

"I think you've got a good chance. It looks good so far!"

We knocked on the big wooden door that faced the courtyard. My nonni Angelo and Tizianna were still awake. They had washed up and had settled in front of the fireplace in their nightclothes with their books.

Nonno Angelo opened the door. "Francesca! Luciano! Good to see you!" Angelo exclaimed.

Nonna Tizianna was right behind him with a wide smile on her face. I hugged and kissed my nonni with abandon. We have always had a deep bond. I gave my nonna the lamb chops. "Thank your mamma and Margarita for us," she said.

We spoke of the car trip to the farm and about my thesis work. They also caught up on Luciano's latest career developments. In turn, my nonni told us the latest news on the farm. We learned which workers were here for this season and which ones had moved on. "Luciano, would you be able to stop by before you leave and make suggestions as to our crop choices?" asked Nonno Angelo.

"Absolutely! Is Sunday morning good, before my afternoon train?"

"We will wait for you then, Luciano," replied Nonno Angelo.

Luciano and I, after departure hugs and kisses, set out into the night. There was some mist towards the river, but the overhead sky was filled with stars and a sliver of a new moon. I took Luciano's arm as we ambled along. He reached over and covered my hand with his. We talked of the beauty of the sky, the beauty of our hike last week at Positano, the beauty of the fields here in Piedmont, and of the grandiosity of the mountains that loomed in the distance.

Luciano asked, "What do you want for yourself, Francesca, beyond the writing and dance?"

There was no hesitation on my answer. "I want to be able to enjoy the beauty we live in. I want to have good friends and family around me and to be able to dig in the dirt and fix broken things."

Luciano laughed and then said, "Hmmm. Nice."

"And yourself, Luciano?" I queried.

"A lot of the same, Francesca, but also time with my paints and time in the mountains. And speaking of the mountains, Francesca, your papà and I have scheduled a hike up into the mountains Saturday," concluded Luciano.

"Oh, I know Papà will love that. He looks forward to the mountain ritual that you two have developed," I commented.

"So do I," Luciano responded.

By then, we had reached the house. I noticed that what Luciano did not talk about in his future was Marta.

We joined Mamma and Papà briefly on the patio before we all headed to bed.

Susanna and I met at the library the next day. I brought her home for dinner. She hadn't seen Luciano in a while and my folks always liked her company.

Susanna often avoided her home in the evenings. Her mamma had died when Susanna was fifteen due to a cardiac anomaly. Her papà kept his job at the factory, but would pass his evenings with the wine bottle. After supper he remained at the kitchen table of their small apartment and drank quietly. He remained non-communicative and somber until his early bedtime. However, he always reported on time to the early shift at the factory. For a little more money, he cleaned the small three-story apartment building's cement stairs, the small courtyard at the building's entrance, and the stone walk by the street. Due to her papà's hard work, Susanna never had to worry about food or shelter. And her high exam scores assured her university fee payment.

Susanna loved Daniele, her papà, but his non-communication during his alcohol-filled evenings offended Susanna's sensibilities. When she was not with Francesca, Susanna would return home from the library in the late afternoon to see her father briefly before he was drunk. She would then eat quickly and depart to her room, or to a friend's house.

But today she came straight to my house from the library after a brief call to her papà. He always said yes to her visits with me.

While we feasted on my mamma's fish stew with rice, Luciano kept us entertained at dinner. He performed the funniest renditions of his work colleagues' facial expressions while they fought sleep at a consultant's long and tiresome presentation.

After we cleaned up the kitchen, we all took off for a walk in the early evening air down to our neighborhood piazza to see who was there and to enjoy the fountain. My folks soon encountered some friends and settled into a café table. Susanna, Luciano, and I waved good-bye and decided to head off to an evening movie.

Early the next morning, or so I was told, as I was asleep, Luciano and Papà headed up to the mountains. Mamma and I headed off to the market for some fresh meats, vegetables, and fruits. The market was a supplement to Mamma's patio garden and Nonna Tizianna's farm produce. Nonna Tizianna always kept a stand at the market supplied with their farm produce. Nonna Tizianna used to work the stand herself, but she'd hired two women to run the stand in recent years, and now only occasionally worked it. So, before we left the market, Mamma and I always checked the stand to see if they needed anything.

Upon our return home we put the produce in the cooler. I then worked on my dance presentation for the practicum part of my thesis. Mamma, meanwhile, sat at the small table to complete the month's household budget tabulations.

"Francesca, how is your music supply for your music excerpts?" Mamma asked.

"Well, I think that I have most of them… oh yes, do you have any Charleston or mambo music in your collection?" I asked.

"I think so, no wait, mambo yes, but the Charleston is lost."

"Thanks, Mamma. I'll ask Luciano when they get back. He has a big collection of dance music."

So, there I sat on the floor with my electronics. I matched the musical phrases with the sequence of dance steps. For some of my movement choices, it took a little more time to find the perfect musical phrase.

"Mamma, what do you think of this phrase compared to that phrase for the cha-cha?" I asked as I played the separate segments for her.

"Well, I like the first because it's more intense and it connects better to the prior musical piece."

"Hmmm. I see what you mean. Okay. The first one it is!"

I continued to work as Mamma completed the budget work, read, fussed over her indoor ferns, and set dough for fresh bread. About mid-afternoon she put on a hearty vegetable chicken stew to simmer until Papà and Luciano returned.

It was a little after sunset when they appeared ravenous with hunger and greatly energized by their day up in the mountains. They bore fresh goat cheese as well as our cherished chocolate with Piedmont hazelnuts!

"I see you guys stopped at the mountainside farm!" Mamma exclaimed.

We feasted and they told us lies about the cliffs they scaled. It was a great evening.

Early Sunday morning Luciano packed his bag for home. Mamma arranged a small satchel of food for his train ride. She also sent some of the goat cheese that Margarita favored so well, and some of the chocolate with hazelnuts.

"Luciano, this is the chocolate for your trip and this is the chocolate for your mamma and family," said my mamma playfully as she displayed two separate little packages.

"Okay, okay, I get it. You don't want to hear about any lost chocolate on the train," retorted Luciano.

"Right!" exclaimed my mamma.

He was to leave his bags there at the house, as Mamma and Papà would take him to the train after his promised return to my nonni's farm. So, Luciano and I headed out for the farm with me on the back of the scooter. I was to spend the day on the farm with my grandparents. My parents would join us after they took Luciano to the train.

"Hold on, Francesca! We're off to the country!"

So I held my arms around his chest firmly and shouted, "Let's go!"

His body felt secure to me, and his energy was fantastic! I let the breeze move over my face, the warm sun embrace my back, and the green fields fill my vision. I felt happy.

At the farm Angelo and Luciano went off to walk the farm and talk. I went to roll out the pasta with my dear Nonna Tizianna.

In a couple of hours the men returned. Luciano declined some of Nonna Tizianna's rich coffee so as to not be late for the train. Luciano hugged my nonni and kissed their cheeks. He hugged me and held my face while he kissed my forehead.

"Take care of yourself, Francesca," he said. "I'll e-mail you a big band recording of the Charleston as soon as I get home."

"Thanks, Luciano. You take care, too."

Off he rode. I felt a little sad to see him go. But, I turned to Nonna Tizianna and we walked arm in arm back to the house. We drank the rich coffee and talked briefly about my dance presentation. Then our conversation turned to the way she prefers to season her red sauce. Nonna Tizianna looked at me in a way that made me think she might know something that I don't. I didn't figure out where that look came from, but she did share all the secret ingredients of her red sauce with me during that conversation!

Immediately I forgot about her look when Nonno Angelo poked his face in the back kitchen door.

"Francesca," he said in his hearty voice, "Come out to the fields with me and I will show you what Luciano suggested."

Nonno Angelo knew I would be up and at his side in a flash. I loved any excuse to be outdoors. As I exited the door, he turned and winked to Nonna.

Onward we trudged over the fields.

"What Luciano suggested," Nonno said as we moved along the fields, "is to keep the vineyards and fig grove as they are. He also said that the vineyards still have good support from the soil and the amount is perfect for the current wine market. He did say that it would be possible to increase the corn space and decrease the tomato space. Luciano's rationale is that the heirloom corn that we have is in demand on the world market. He suggested that we grow the tomatoes for local market only, as the southern provinces cover well the world market."

"So, what do you think, Nonno, of his suggestions?"

"They make sense to me, Francesca. The changes are minor, but will give us a big result."

"It seems they are," I stated.

"Let's head back to the house. Your folks should be here soon," Nonno said.

"Get ready for some tall tales from my papà," I warned.

"Oh, he's been to the mountains again," Nonno answered knowingly.

"Right!" I confirmed.

My parents' scooters were in the courtyard when we arrived back at the farmhouse. They sat with Nonna Tizianna at the kitchen table with a cup of Nonna's great coffee in their hands. Even Mamma, who is mostly a tea drinker, loves Nonna Tizianna's coffee. Today, as always, was a great day at the farm. We ate and sipped on wine. Then we drank coffee and ate fruit with cheese. Now, however, Mamma deferred to her tea.

Angelo and Dominico were passionate about bocce ball. So off they went to challenge each other in the special area constructed by Nonno in the courtyard. Nonna put on music and she, Mamma, and I danced on the smooth area of the courtyard by the house. We then waved good-bye to the men who hardly noticed our departure and began our weekly and by now ritualistic walk to the river. We knew the back roads that guided us to the river. I don't remember a time when we didn't do this walk together.

"When did we start this walk?" I asked my mamma and nonna.

Nonna replied, "When I first met your mamma, we decided to go for a walk to get to know each other. We just naturally started towards the river."

"Yes," Mamma added, "it was such a memorable time, we continued to have it as our walk. When you came along, you became a part of our women's walk. Over the years it has remained special each time."

I understood the ancient water goddess's pull. It has been strong for me, too. So, we walked three abreast on the old back road flanked by fertile fields on this quiet Sunday afternoon. When we arrived at the river we sat on its bank until we were sufficiently mesmerized by the water's movement before we headed back to the farm.

We encountered the papà and figlio bocce competitors relaxing in the courtyard under the large tree. All five of us were now ready for the week ahead. After many hugs and kisses we loaded our supplies and ourselves on the bikes. Papà, Mamma, and I then left these dear elders for the short ride home.

At the first of the week, I received the music from Luciano by e-mail. I downloaded it onto my small device for the performance. Susanna and I met frequently at the library to support each other as we worked hard on our theses. We also worked hard on our preparations for our dance studio jobs. They were to begin the next week. Mamma and Papà were busy with students and their festival preparations. So, as usual, our household was very active. We made time to catch up with each other during the evening meal at which Susanna often joined us.

Early Sunday evening Papà received a call from Luciano. They spoke for a while. I noticed this because Papà is characteristically not a phone person. "Hmmm, must be important," I thought to myself.

MORE VISITS OF LUCIANO TO TURINO

"Well, Luciano will still be here for the festival. But, as Marta can't make it, he asked if Flavio could be our guest instead," Papà said after he finished the phone call.

"Of course," Mamma said.

Soon, Friday arrived. By late morning the excitement for Saturday's festival was palpable in the streets. As Mamma, Papà, and I enjoyed some hot vegetable soup with focaccia bread, Mamma said, "Susanna can use my scooter to accompany you to the train. What time is Luciano and Flavio's train due in?" Mamma queried.

"At eight this evening," I answered. "Thanks, Mamma, for the use of your scooter."

"By the way, Susanna and I will cook the supper for tonight. That way you and Papà can be free to focus on your festival performance. And there will be plenty for when Luciano and Flavio arrive," I added as I beamed at them.

I felt a little excited about the weekend. That was probably in anticipation of a rest from my thesis defense preparations.

Susanna and I made a huge pot of lamb stew. We washed some greens and put together a large salad. We then stirred up a big tray of polenta and, voila! A feast! There was enough for tonight and for Mamma and Papà tomorrow before their festival performance. We young folks would eat from the vendors and the pizzeria tomorrow!

As the four of us gathered at the patio table to eat, Mamma exclaimed, "This smells great! I think I'll retire my lamb stew recipe, ladies!"

We all ate heartily. Susanna and I chatted enthusiastically about the exhibitions, vendors, and performances we would see tomorrow. We were mindful of the time, as we wanted to leave by seven o'clock to pick up Luciano and Flavio.

"It'll be good to see Flavio," stated Papà. "It's been a couple of years since I've seen him. Have you met him as yet, Susanna?"

"No, not yet. But Francesca told me that he has a great sense of humor, so I'm sure we'll all have a good time," answered Susanna.

After dinner, Mamma settled herself with a cup of tea and her current book, Papà with coffee and his piano. Susanna and I cleaned up the kitchen and took off on the scooters to the train station to pick up Luciano and Flavio.

Luciano called me on my cell as they arrived and I told him in which scooter park outside the station we were located. When they emerged from the exit near us, I made a big wave with my arm and almost jumped up with the excitement. They made a striking image of manhood at the top of the stairs. Both well built, though Luciano taller. Both with dark curly hair, though Flavio's darker. They quickly descended the wide stairs to us. I hugged Luciano and Flavio. Susanna introduced herself to Flavio at the same time that Flavio introduced himself to Susanna. They laughed and hugged as they stumbled over their words. Luciano and I raised our eyebrows at each other but said nothing of this obvious first impression of compatibility between Susanna and Flavio.

Luciano and Flavio attached their satchels to the rear of the scooters and offered to drive us home. We thanked them, hopped on behind them, and off we went. For me it was reminiscent of the bike ride to Flavio's a few weeks ago. Once again it felt secure to rest against Luciano's back. On the scooter behind us, I'd hear Flavio's voice and then a long phrase of laughter from my usually serious and quiet friend. I'd never heard her laugh so much in all our years of friendship as during that bike ride home. By the time they arrived at the house they were both in such intense laughter that they could hardly swing themselves off the scooter. Luciano and I shrugged our shoulders and parked the scooter.

"Luciano! Flavio!" my papà shouted as we entered the house. Mamma, who had just lit sage on the patio, entered the house and hugged them both.

"Come in and have some hot food. The girls made a great stew!" Mamma said.

While Luciano and Flavio ate, we all sat around the table on the patio, as it was such a beautiful late spring evening. We enjoyed some wine and fruit with cheese together at the end of their meal. Flavio kept us entertained with his latest escapade on the sea, as he had fished with his cousin the week before. Flavio had a talent for telling an ordinary event with great flair. Susanna continued to smile, laugh, and enjoy herself. After about an hour, Mamma and Papà went on to bed. Susanna, Luciano, Flavio, and I played a short game of mancala and then went off to bed ourselves.

The next day at the festival Luciano and I had seated ourselves by the fountain edge while Flavio and Susanna lingered at the vendor area. They appeared to be in a lengthy discourse with a pottery vendor about his artistry. Flavio and Susanna made quite a pair. Susanna was about an inch taller than Flavio. She was as lithe as he was muscular. Susanna's hair was at the lightest end of brown as his was at the darkest end of brown. Their eyes twinkled when they looked at each other.

"I never would have guessed that Flavio and Susanna would hit it off so well," I said to Luciano. "But, it makes sense. They are both practical people. Flavio makes Susanna laugh and Susanna makes Flavio proud. How perfect!"

"Yeah, it seems effortless for them," said Luciano. "Would you like to get some pizza? Hungry?"

"I'm always ready for pizza. Shall we see if we can pull Flavio and Susanna away from the artist?"

We approached the vendor at the moment Flavio and Susanna turned to look for us. They introduced us to the artist. His work was beautiful. As we began to leave the booth, a cup caught my eye.

"Look, Luciano, this is the type of cup that Marta likes. It has an ultra-modern bold design with bold colors."

"Maybe so," Luciano said in a lowered tone as he shrugged while he glanced at the cup. He didn't notice the look his good friend gave him. Rather, Luciano looked me in the eye and said, "Let's see how you north-erners make pizza!" He grabbed my hand and, with full smiles, all four of us headed off to the brick ovens.

That evening we danced in the square while Mamma, Papà, and other artists serenaded us. Mamma and Papà, if we include the encores, sang five ballads. One was their arrangement of a classic ballad and the other four were their own compositions. One was new and three were made famous years back. Most of the people stopped or greatly slowed their dancing just to listen. My parents' subtle harmony and full warm tones rang out over us all in the night air. As always their energy spread outward and then upward to warm the stars. We four, as did the crowd, jumped, shouted, clapped, and whistled at the end of every song. When they finished the crowd settled back into dancing.

Some other friends of Susanna and myself from the university were there, so we all mixed up our dance partners. It was great fun. Then, at about midnight, as the last dance was announced, Luciano and Flavio grabbed me and Susanna respectively, spun us around, bowed and asked for the last dance.

I loved it. That same feeling of security from the scooter rides came over me as Luciano held me. I was really respectful of Marta in how I held Luciano. I glanced at Flavio and Susanna. They were just lost in each other.

We all walked Susanna home first. Luciano and I discreetly walked a little further ahead while they said goodnight. Then the three of us, the former hikers of the Positano ridge, walked on to my house.

In the morning when I awakened, Mamma was out for one of her speed walks, Flavio had used Mamma's scooter to pick up Susanna for a morning ride, and Luciano was deep in discussion with my papà on the patio.

"Hey, gentlemen!" I shouted as I went to the kitchen adjacent to the patio to prepare some tea, warm the cornmeal porridge, and fry an egg for breakfast.

Papà smiled and Luciano said loudly, "Well, good morning, sleeping beauty!"

"Luciano, how about a hike to the river before your train?" I invited.

"Yes, a hike would be good." Luciano answered. "Flavio and I don't need to leave for the train until one o'clock, so we have time."

"Okay, then. We'll take some picnic lunch and be back by one," I answered."

"I'll pack the lunch while you finish your breakfast," said Luciano.

"Okay. The picnic backpack is right where you are in the lower cabinet. We could take some water, wine, bread, cheese, olives, fruit and whatever else you think of."

Papà chimed in, "You know where things are in the kitchen. Help yourself."

Luciano did. I completed my breakfast and went off to get dressed. When I returned to the kitchen, he had the food backpack organized. I put the water and the outdoor blanket in my backpack. Luciano carried the food backpack. We headed west along our brick road towards the back dirt roads to the river.

We passed the road that led to Nonno Angelo and Nonna Tizianna's farm. "Nonno Angelo has already begun to implement your suggestions," I said.

"It's hard for me to believe that he wasn't raised on a farm. He loves it so much," Luciano added.

"Yeah, he does."

"To change the subject a little, how is your thesis work coming along, Francesca?" Luciano asked.

"Well," I answered, "there's only one month left before my thesis defense with my dance presentation. I'll turn in the thesis in two weeks so they have time to look it over for their questions during my defense."

"You don't seem nervous. Are you?"

"Not really."

"I've seen you dance around all the years we grew up together. And I've seen how serious you've been about your studies. It will go well," Luciano assured me. "By the way," he added, "I would love to see your dance presentation."

"Well, maybe when you come back north. Do you have any meetings up here soon?" I queried.

"I have another work conference here in three weeks. Your papà invited me to stay with your family for those four days. Those dates are about one week before your dance presentation. Would you feel relaxed enough to give a family dance presentation then?" Luciano asked.

"Of course! It will help me to have an audience before I present in front of the professors."

Then Luciano pulled his eyes away from mine and looked up and around. He waved his right arm and shoulders and said, "Look at this Francesca! The fields, the trees, the river, and the grand mountains behind it all. I just love this."

"I'm with you on that, Luciano."

We walked for a while in companionable silence. Then Luciano said, "It looks comfortable over there by that tree. Shall we sit and eat there?"

"Only if you can get there first," I exclaimed as I took off at my fastest pace.

"Watch this!" he retorted as his long legs moved fast beneath him. I laughed as I came up and tagged the tree last. Luciano just grinned at me. His smile sent sunshine to my soul. I patted his cheek gently and then opened my backpack to spread out the blanket. I gave him one of the water jugs and I took one as we guzzled down some water on this warm late spring day. Luciano then set out the food and we settled in on the blanket under the tree by the river. He broke the loaf and handed me the first piece, which I ate with a piece of my favorite raw sheep cheese and some Nebiolo grapes. Luciano poured our wine. We toasted to health and family and nature. Then I laid on my back and did my favorite childhood thing: stared at the sky and watched the dance of the clouds.

"This is really good, Luciano. What a perfect day. Tell me what shapes you see up there in the clouds," I said without moving my eyes from the sky.

"Yes, it is a perfect day," Luciano said.

I turned to look at him and there he was on his side grinning at me.

"Don't cheat!" I exclaimed. "You're supposed to focus on the clouds, signore artist," I informed him as I pushed his back to the ground with a gentle nudge on his chest with my right hand.

I then grabbed some grapes and walked towards the river. Luciano followed me.

While we watched the current move down towards the rice patties, I asked, "How is Marta? Did she like Sicily?"

"Marta is fine, and she loved Sicily. In fact, she plans to move there within two weeks' time."

"Really! What brought that on? I thought she loved Naples."

"Me too," Luciano answered. "And she does, but she loves Sicily more."

"Oh."

"Francesca, she found someone there and she fell in love. Also, the firm there where she did the consultant work has hired her. She's happy. It's over between us. Our relationship had been weak for a good while."

"I am so sorry, Luciano," I comforted.

"Well, I've had time to prepare myself. I think I knew that this was where we were headed for quite some time. My sense of loyalty kept the relationship energized far too long. It will take a little time to adjust, but in a way, I am relieved that it's over."

"Yeah, fortunately, you've always been strong, Luciano," I said as I put my arm around his waist and gave him a hug.

"Whoa," he said as he glanced at his watch. "Look at the time. It's after twelve o'clock already."

We rushed back to the blanket under the tree, packed up our picnic, and trotted at a good pace back to the house.

We made it by five after one. Flavio and Susanna had just arrived on the scooter with their joyous selves.

Luciano took the backpacks inside and emptied them. He and Flavio picked up their satchels in the guest bedroom. Then they gave thanks and good-bye hugs and kisses to my folks and jumped on the scooters with Susanna and myself seated behind them with our arms around their strong torsos. We wove down the streets to the train station. At the station there were hugs, kisses, and promises to call soon. Susanna and Flavio seemed to linger a little more on the kisses. Oh well, it is spring, and they were in love.

For the next few days, Susanna and I worked hard on the final drafts of our theses. They were completed and proofread two days before the due date. We handed them in early. That evening, since my parents had each proofread our documents, we took them out to the pizzeria.

We also invited Susanna's papà for pizza, but he said that he had more work to do at the apartment building. So just the four of us sat at a small table outside in the piazza with the aroma of fresh pizza all around us. The pizza had just the right amount of onion, peppers, kale, and ham on a thin layer of well-seasoned tomato sauce. The crust was thin, but airy, with a perfect crunch and pull texture. It had a slightly wood charred flavor. We drank red wine and ate the pizza with the gusto that goes with celebration of a task well done.

"So, Susanna, what do you hear from Flavio?" said my papà with a twinkle in his eye.

"Leave the young woman alone, Dominico," my mamma lightly pleaded.

"Alessia, you know we all love Flavio and love to hear Flavio stories," my papà answered while he quickly kissed the hand of this woman he adored.

My mamma laughed and Susanna responded, "Okay. If you insist, I will tell you."

I thought that Susanna's voice was more animated, grounded, and steady since Flavio had entered her life. This felt good to my ears. I smiled as my dear friend continued.

"Flavio plans to come up for a visit soon so he can meet my papà."

"Susanna, he can stay with us," my mamma offered.

"Absolutely," assured my papà.

"Thanks, I'll tell him," said Susanna happily.

We ordered some pizza to take to Susanna's papà.

Papà gazed at my mamma with the look of well-tested love as he ran his hand gently over my mamma's gorgeous full hair and landed it lovingly on her shoulder. Then he leaned back in his chair and said, "This was so beautiful of you girls. Thanks so much. If it's all right with you ladies, we just want to sit here a little longer together and enjoy the people, the night air, and the wine."

"Great, Papà," I said. "We'll run this pizza to Susanna's papà and take a little walk around the piazza. Thanks again for all the help, both of you."

"Yes, thanks so much," Susanna agreed.

We both hugged them around the neck as they happily sat there. We then took off towards Susanna's apartment with pizza in tow.

"It is fantastic how they are so into each other," said Susanna.

"We'll have that for ourselves, too. Trust me," I said assuredly.

When we arrived at Susanna's building, Susanna's papà, Daniele, was on the bench with his pipe. He waved and smiled as we approached. Seated next to him was middle-aged Catrina who lived on the ground floor. In fact, they sat under her partially grilled flower boxed window. Her flower box was filled with red blooms. They seemed comfortable in each other's company.

Susanna and I kissed her papà on both cheeks and then Susanna offered him the pizza. "This smells wonderful," Daniele said. Susanna kissed Catrina on the cheek and introduced her to me. As I greeted Catrina, Daniele simultaneously tore off a piece of pizza for her and offered it in some of the paper that had been included with the pizza.

"I'll be back a little later, Papà," Susanna told her papà, "Enjoy the pizza, both of you!"

We took off down the street arm in arm. "Look at that. Papà has become friends with Catrina," commented Susanna.

"It looks like life seems a little better for him," I responded. "Your papà looks brighter in his face. The circles under his eyes are less deep and less dark."

"Yes, he mentioned to me a few weeks ago that he wanted to stop drinking. Evidently a friend at work had told him about an AA group that meets in the Community Center every Tuesday evening. He went once, and then in a week, he went again. Since that time he's attended regularly. It's now over three weeks since he's had any wine. I can only hope it continues. He told me about al-anon, a support group for family members. I may go sometime," said Susanna.

"If you need me, I'll be glad to go with you," I offered.

"Thanks, Francesca," said Susanna as she hugged me, and I her. "But I really feel strong. I'll be fine to go alone."

After a couple of meetings, Susanna realized that she was not alone in her situation. She then easily found the fortitude to explain to Flavio about her father. He understood, as his cugino's husband also suffered from alcoholism and he too attended AA. For Flavio, it was a non-issue to give Susanna his full support. Period.

Later in the week, after dinner one evening, Susanna and I went to the fountain in the piazza to enjoy its sound and the people that surrounded it.

As the fountain splashed behind us, Susanna said, "What do you think if I suggest to Flavio that he come up next weekend since Luciano will be here. That way they can travel together and room together at your house. Also, the four of us can have some time together."

"Sounds good to me! We would still have a week to look over our notes for our theses defense after their visit," I concurred.

After a short time we headed back to our homes to rest and prepare lesson plans for our dance classes for the next couple of weeks. By the next afternoon we had three weeks of lesson plans completed. Thus, we were ready for our weekend adventure with the gentlemen from Naples.

Luciano arrived early Thursday morning and went straight to his meetings from the train station. Mamma and Papà were busy with students all day. So after I moved through my dance presentation a couple of times, I made a simple pasta and red sauce with meatballs for supper. I invited Susanna to join us. Luciano arrived around six o'clock. Papà welcomed him at the door. It was so good to see him. He looked a little tired, but maintained his handsome smile and the beautiful glow to his deep olive complexion.

We all ate enthusiastically and shared memories of our last mountain hike. After we cleared the table, Papà, Susanna, and Luciano enjoyed

Papà's rich, well-brewed coffee while Mamma and I enjoyed a steaming cup of mint tea.

It was Susanna's al-anon evening so after a few minutes with our hot drinks she said her goodnights. Papà also had an infrequent local night soccer game nearby that led to his departure soon after Susanna's. Mamma had a rare evening student tonight. This particular student was extremely talented, Mamma had explained, and since she had to work long hours after school and on weekends to help support her mother, Mamma had agreed to evening lessons every two weeks. Amita was always punctual, prepared, and so grateful to study with Mamma. It was a pleasure to hear her lesson.

However, I did not hear her lesson tonight. Luciano needed to do some research at the university library for work the next day. I said I would accompany him and review my thesis while we were at the library. With his help it was short work to tidy up the kitchen. Soon we were off on the scooter to the library.

As before, I enjoyed the security of his back against my chest. The ride to the library was short and the traffic easy. Within a couple of hours he had completed his work. We packed our work in the satchel at the back of the bike and took off towards home. The river gave off minute water droplets into the cool evening air to create a mist. It provided an intimacy to our journey. However, our visibility was fine on the streets to home. Upon arrival at home, I joined Mamma on the patio. We began to discuss my plans after university completion. Papà and Luciano sat at the counter table in the kitchen with their last cup of coffee for the day. They had decided to hike the mountains on Saturday and were going over their plans.

They soon joined us on the patio. Papà said, "Flavio arrives on the seven o'clock train Friday night. I guess Susanna will pick him up?"

"Yes, that's the plan. They are going to go to Susanna's apartment for a late dinner so Flavio and Daniele can meet. Then Flavio will drive himself here after dinner," I responded.

"Do they have any special plans for Saturday?" Papà queried.

"Not that I know of, why?" I responded.

"Luciano and I wondered if we might all want to go up to the mountains for the day. We could pack up some food and make it a great day of adventure."

"Okay, Papà, but you and Luciano have a little different idea of adventure then the rest of us. Unless, Luciano, does Flavio like to hike the more challenging trails?" I questioned as I turned my gaze on Luciano.

"Hmmm, maybe the more gradual elevations with circular trails are his favorite," Luciano said.

"Well, how about this," Mamma offered, "Dominico, you and Luciano go up the steeper trails for the morning. While you're on the steeper trails Francesca, Susanna, Flavio, and I will roam the more gradual trails. We'll meet at a designated spot for our picnic lunch. After lunch we can nap, walk around the streams, or whatever we decide."

Everyone agreed to the plan. We sent texts to Flavio and to Susanna. They both loved the idea of the mountain excursion. So with our Saturday organized, we toddled our tired selves off to bed.

Friday after dinner I began to open up a floor space bordered by our patio, the piano, and the kitchen counter. I pushed back the inside dinner table to the wall where our patio met our indoor space. I moved its chairs out into a row in front of the kitchen counter that divided the kitchen from the rest of the living space. Thus I set the stage for my family presentation of my thesis's accompanied dance demonstration. This was the same floor area that we had used for childhood theatrical performances. During my cugini's visits, that included Luciano, we all let our imaginations run in this space. But tonight, it was my solo.

Mamma, Papà, and Luciano sat on the chairs as I plugged in my music and quickly left to change. I arrived on my makeshift stage in my leotards and a flashy, short, orange skirt. Luciano stood up and clapped and shouted, "Bravo, bravo."

"Luciano," I laughed. "Sit down. And behave."

I felt at ease now. My performance was familiar to my mamma as she had been my best support and critique during its formation. Papà, however, had not seen it in its entirety. And it was all new to Luciano. They sat in supportive expectation. I gently exhaled, then inhaled, turned on the music, and began.

The performance was a gracious flow that felt organic to my body. I loved to be in my body and soar in my spirit at the same time. This was my personal space of ecstasy. At the end, I deeply bowed. I knew that I had nailed it and that I would do well in the presence of the professors as well.

My family stood up, applauded, shouted repeated bravos, and eventually hugged me. I felt a little linger in Luciano's hug. Or maybe it just felt that way because I was on my performance high. One thing I felt for sure was that I would get this degree!

Flavio arrived around nine o'clock. Susanna was with him and all packed for the next day. I had called her earlier to suggest she spend the night with us so we could get an earlier start to the mountain.

It was quite a sight to see my friend in such an easygoing relationship. Flavio and Susanna just beamed around each other.

"Eh, famiglia!" Flavio blurted out as they came in the door.

"Come in, come in," said my papà eagerly as he embraced Flavio and Susanna. In fact, we all embraced them. They carried a celebratory aura of their new love. It was great to be around them!

We moved onto the patio for a little mineral water before early bed.

"How was the meeting of Susanna's papà?" I asked Flavio.

"Great. I liked him. He is a very kind man. I met Catrina also. Susanna had invited her for dinner, as well. Catrina told us of her embroidery work. She had some interesting stories of the items people hire her to embroider."

"Everyone enjoyed each other," Susanna chimed in. "I think the dinner was a success!"

"And can Susanna cook! Fantastic!" said Flavio while he beamed at Susanna.

"Okay, Flavio, your turn to cook next!" said his good buddy.

"Luciano, I wouldn't make people suffer like that. Need some lessons from you, first."

"Okay. Deal. When we get back to Naples."

"My kitchen is yours, Flavio, on your next visit," said Mamma with a twinkle in her eye as she patted Flavio's cheek.

Mamma then rose and said goodnight. It had been a full day for all of us and tomorrow would be another. We all followed Mamma's lead and said goodnight.

As soon as the sun was up we were in the kitchen. I made the cornmeal porridge with cheese. Susanna set out the focaccia and boiled the water for tea. Papà made the coffee. Mamma set out the water, wine, and food for the mountain excursion while Luciano and Flavio carefully packed everything into insulated backpacks. They were able to divide it into four moderately heavy backpacks and two lightweight ones.

There was a bang at the door and I ran to find Nonno Angelo with his arms laden with fresh eggs and cheese. I kissed him on the cheek and took the eggs to assist him. Nonno Angelo then said with his strong voice, "Morning, famiglia! It is a beautiful day for the mountains. Enjoy the eggs and cheese, and Nonna sends her love."

We introduced him to Flavio. He of course knew Susanna. Then, joined by Nonno Angelo, we all sat down to my cornmeal breakfast. We ate heartily to prepare for the mountains. After some of his figlio's good coffee, Angelo said, "Well, run me back up to the farm, Dominico, so you folks can take off."

We thanked Nonno for the loan of his car. "Don't worry, you will pay well come harvest time," he said with a wink.

We all laughed, as we knew that he was right.

By the time the kitchen was cleaned up and the car packed up, Papà was back from the farm. He drove Mamma in Nonno's car. Luciano, Susanna, Flavio, and I went in our family car.

"Luciano, would you drive?" I asked. He agreed eagerly. He loved to drive cars, much unlike myself. I just liked to fix them.

It was a little under two hours to our favorite mountain entrance. We agreed to stop in an hour for a brief rest and then continue. My papà drove the lead car in our little caravan. Luciano felt comfortable with my papà in the lead, though I knew he preferred just a little more speed. I liked that about Luciano. He favored respect over his ego.

As we drove along, I patted Luciano's cheek and said, "You're a good guy."

He just smiled. Luciano was accustomed to my little outbursts of affection.

At that moment it seemed that the angle of the sun deepened the golden olive tone of his cheek. "How handsome," I thought to myself.

On the ride Luciano and Flavio entertained us with renditions of their childhood escapades. First they told a story about a time when they rode a mule to try to escape from a bull. It didn't make much sense to us. Then they told tales of their swim adventures into the caves along the sea. Susanna and I could not tell which was stronger in these adventures— their courage or their imagination. As we wiped the tears from our eyes from the laughter of Flavio's last story, he said, "We must all meet in the

Naples countryside for our next excursion. Besides, Susanna, I want you to meet my family. That way you will know that they are not all crazy like me."

"That's right, Susanna. Flavio is one of a kind," said Luciano.

We all laughed, but immediately in her laughter, Susanna said, "I'd love to," as she smiled at Flavio.

"Well then, it's settled," said Flavio puffing out his chest. "The next gathering is in Naples."

"Hold up," Luciano said. "We haven't heard yet from Signorina Francesca."

"Luciano, you know that I am always ready for a trip to Naples," I answered.

The day was warm as summer was near. The fields and trees were filled with blossoms and new growth in the vineyards. And there they loomed before us, the great mountains, awaiting our arrival. The four of us felt relaxed in each other's company and contentedly traveled along.

We entered the park and pulled up next to Papà and Mamma. As we emerged from the car I could smell that clean, energized, fresh scent of the mountains. I breathed deeply. Ahhh, how I loved this.

We distributed the backpacks with lighter ones for Luciano and Papà, as they were about to embark on some serious climbing. They took off on their incline path. Mamma, Susanna, Flavio, and I engaged a path with a gentle incline for about a mile and then followed a horizontal tract around the west side of the mountain. A stream entered the valley about four miles down our path. The path gently turned downward into the valley by the stream for the last mile. Mamma, Papà, Luciano, and I knew the location. Papà and Luciano had embarked on a trail that was an upside down V between their starting point and the valley by the stream. We all had agreed that we would arrive at the valley by about one o'clock.

The four of us had great fun on our trail. Susanna and I danced along the path once we passed a little rocky incline. We mimicked each other's dance moves and laughed until our sides hurt. Then we calmed down and just walked arm in arm. We took in the sweet air of pine trees and the lively melodies of birds.

Flavio and Mamma dropped back a bit as they were in deep conversation.

"What do you think they're talking about?" asked Susanna.

"Probably you," I answered with laughter in my eyes, but my voice was serious.

"You're right," said Susanna. "Flavio is full of fun, but he is careful with his life. I can feel a seriousness about the relationship between us. He's probably running some ideas past your mamma before he presents them to me. Your mamma is as close as I've had for a mamma for many years."

"You're famiglia, Susanna. She's most likely told Flavio to leave you alone and go back to his leaky fish boat in Naples," I teased as I ran off.

"What!" Susanna shouted as she quickly raced her long legs in my direction.

Susanna caught up and we continued to amble arm in arm until the next bend that revealed the stream that would, in a short mile, lead us to the valley. We slowed for Flavio and Mamma to catch up as we walked the gentle descent to the valley.

There, in the valley, were Luciano and Papà perched on blankets under a shade tree near the stream. With our pace, we were about twenty minutes late. In reality, they were about ten minutes late, but didn't impart that fact to us until later. They had to first tease us incessantly about our slow pace.

We ate the bread, cheese, sautéed truffles, grapes, and olives, and drank the wine and water. As we ate we shared stories of the beautiful sights on our separate journeys. Papà, Luciano, and Flavio also shared the breathtaking photos taken along their paths.

"It is so beautiful here," said Flavio. "I think, though, I will stick to the lower trails. The highest mountain summit I want to approach is our excitable Vesuvius. The height of the mountains here definitely poke into heaven," Flavio said as he looked up to the snowcapped peaks.

We all laughed. "I'm with you on that, Flavio," I said.

The men went off to toss a Frisbee while Mamma, Susanna, and I gazed at the clouds and dozed in and out of light sleep.

"Mamma," I asked, "are you awake?" I knew she was but just wanted to alert her to give me attention.

Susanna turned and rolled her eyes at me. "Of course, she's awake," said Susanna. "You called her."

"I know. I know. It's that I really want to know something," I explained.

"What is it?" Mamma asked.

"How did you know that the love you felt for Papà was the kind of love that would last?"

"Whoa, quite a question for a lazy afternoon. Hmmm, let me see. Let me remember. Well, I felt real secure and relaxed with him from the moment we met. There were aspects of him that I admired and respected, like his musical knowledge and talent. And, to me he was so very handsome. Fortunately, I had trained myself to really focus on my work. This skill came in handy to be able to perform my best in his gorgeous presence."

We all giggled. Mamma went on. "As I got to know him I realized that family relationships were a priority to him. He treated his family members kindly." She sighed and said, "I guess what I am saying is that my gut trusted him as a person, and my intellect saw respectable behavior, and my young womanly body tingled around him. So there you have it!" We all giggled again.

We put on our innocent faces as we saw the men approach. "We better start back so we are out of the mountains by nightfall, besides, I just felt a small quake," Papà said.

We packed up the backpacks. They were all lighter now. We women took turns behind the big rock and washed our hands in the stream. We all headed up the easier path to the cars. Mamma and Papà set the pace with Luciano and myself in second. Flavio and Susanna brought up the rear. It took them longer because their oxygen was compromised by frequent kisses. At least that's what Luciano and I theorized in jest as we teased them with our theory. Flavio and Susanna could not care less about our theories and continued to partake in the joy of each other's kisses.

Luciano and I walked amicably along, arm in arm.

"Luciano, at last I have a chance to ask you how the consultations in the Piedmont office went."

"Actually," he responded, "they have requested another consultation. They also have a coordination project with all the other regions of Italy. They would like me to be a part of that project. With that conversation came a hint that they may offer me a contract to direct the department here in Piedmont. Their director will move soon to a government post in Roma. So, we'll see," Luciano concluded as he cast his warm brown eyes on me.

"Luciano! That's really incredible! How great it would be to have you permanently up north!" I blurted out. "That is, if you would want to," I quickly added.

"Yeah, I do! We'll see," he said again as he raised his shoulders in a sign of hope.

I couldn't say anything for a while. Frankly, I was focused on keeping my heart and mind from bounding too far forward. I focused on the beautiful walk. The lowering sun cut rays through the pines. They flashed hope to anyone's soul able to receive it.

In well under two hours, we were at the cars. The valley had begun to darken. Both Papà and Luciano said they would do the drive home. We headed out, but Mamma, myself, Flavio, and Susanna insisted that the drivers change in an hour to give them a break. Both Papà and Luciano said, "We'll see!"

The break came and went and Papà and Luciano continued to drive. Flavio and Susanna fell asleep. Luciano and I joked with each other that their exhaustion was from the frequent kisses on the trail. I was tired, as well. But, it was more fun to converse with Luciano than to sleep.

We arrived at the house about nine o'clock. Flavio and Luciano quickly wiped down Nonno Angelo's car while I checked the tires and the solar charge. Mamma, Papà, and Susanna unpacked the cars.

I drove the car back to Nonno Angelo with a couple of pieces of his favorite hazelnut chocolate. Luciano followed me on my scooter.

At the farm, we drank a small cup of Nonno Angelo's good coffee, while we described to them some of the beautiful mountain trail sights. We also showed them the photos on Luciano's phone. With many thanks for the car, we hugged and said goodnight to Nonno Angelo and Nonna Tizianna.

Later I heard that Nonno Angelo said to Nonna Tizianna, "I'm sure we'll see a lot more of that boy."

"I think so too, old man," she answered, as they headed off to bed.

We soon arrived home to find everyone in bed. We hugged goodnight and Luciano seemed to linger in our embrace. But I was exhausted, so I wasn't sure.

Susanna was asleep when I got to the bedroom. I bathed, changed into my nightgown, and fell fast asleep.

The next morning we were all slow to get moving after our mountain escapade the day before. We finished breakfast by mid-morning.

Papà, as if to take advantage of the last hours of male companionship in the household, offered a friendly soccer competition between the men and the women at the nearby soccer field. Although, we were no match for the guys in this category, Mamma, Susanna, and I were pretty decent at the game. So, we all headed off to the field with our heads up high, each team convinced they would be victor.

The field was dry, the sky clear, and the day not yet hot. It was a perfect setting to move the ball. Mamma was our goalie and Flavio was the men's. Mamma's intuition was great as to the direction of the ball. She was able to block more balls than penetrated. The men began to get frustrated which made their kicks all the more predictable. Eventually Susanna and I were laughing so hard at the men's frustration that we also became ineffectual at the game. Susanna, myself, and thus by default, Mamma, dismissed ourselves to the sidelines to fall on the grass and laugh heartily. The men shook their heads and continued to pass the ball for a few more minutes.

Soon we all headed back to the house for some lemonade, bread, and cheese before we took Luciano and Flavio to the station. Flavio and Susanna left early for the station because Flavio wanted to stop by Susanna's to say good-bye to Daniele and Catrina. Luciano, Mamma, Papà, and I packed up food items for Zio Josefa and Zia Margarita and for Luciano and Flavio to have during their train ride.

With the satchels packed, Luciano and I took off on the scooter. The sun was now warm, and as I leaned against Luciano's back I could smell his earthy Luciano scent. Once again I felt a comfort and security with my arms around his chest. We first rode the short distance to Susanna's. We met Susanna and Flavio there, and then departed together for the train station.

"Wish the visit wasn't so short," I found myself saying to Luciano as we parted at the station.

"It was far too short for me," Luciano responded. "Best on your presentation and thesis defense this week. It will go well," he assured.

"I think so, too. Take care of yourself, Luciano," I responded.

"You, too," he said as he touched my hair and then departed.

MARCO REVISITED

Susanna and I returned the scooters to my house. I then walked Susanna partway home. She went on to spend the rest of the day with her papà. As I walked back home, I thought that the spring air seemed a little sweeter after the weekend.

That evening at supper, my mamma queried, "How are you feeling about your defense and presentation this week?"

"I'm ready, Mamma. What I would love to do is spend Tuesday and Wednesday at the farm with Nonna Tizianna and Nonno Angelo. I can reread my thesis, review my presentation, and walk around the country-side. My dance classes aren't far by scooter. Thursday I plan to wait for Susanna at her defense to give support. Then mine is on Friday and she will meet me also."

"Sounds like a great plan," Mamma assured.

On Tuesday morning I packed up my papers, electronics, my over-night things, and a couple changes of clothing. Mamma and Papà were about to begin with their morning students. I hugged them good-bye and walked towards the door. A couple of strides from the door, I heard a loud knock. I shouted to my folks, "I'll get it."

I opened the large wooden door for not one of my parent's students, but for Marco.

"Hi, Francesca," Marco said. "Do you have a minute to talk?"

"Mamma, it's Marco. We're going to take a little walk. I'll be right back," I said almost mechanically as I kept my stare of disbelief on Marco. Then I looked towards my parents as I set my bags down inside the door.

"Okay," Mamma said with a look of surprise, wow, and take care all in the same eye glance. Dad looked up from his music, with his protective but reassuring look.

Marco and I headed down our usual direction towards the country. "So, Marco, how are you?"

"Well, fine, really. My thesis was approved so I now have officially completed my degree."

"Congratulations, Marco," I said sincerely. But, I was not sure how I felt walking at his side at the moment. It felt both familiar and out of place. I had gotten to appreciate myself without his connection. At this moment, he almost felt like an extra weight around me. How strange, but that's how it felt.

"I plan to head for Barcelona this next week. It seems like a place where I can work and make a living at my art. I love the excitement of the city."

"That sounds great, Marco."

"Francesca, I feel that I might have cut us off too soon. Maybe you can come and visit me?"

I wiped the sweat from my forehead with my hand and said, "Marco, you are a longtime friend and we were lovers for a short time. For me it is better to remain friends and not lovers. I missed you a lot, but have moved on."

We continued on a few more paces and then I continued, "Marco, take care of yourself in Barcelona. You will do well. And Marco, by the way, discernment with the women!"

We both laughed. Then I added, "Now come and say good-bye to my mamma and papà before their first students arrive," I said as I grabbed his hand and pulled him back up the street towards our house.

I rushed into the house with Marco. Their sessions had not yet begun. "Mamma, Papà, Marco leaves for Barcelona this week to live and work. Isn't that great!"

"Why, yes," they responded a little softly for two robust songsters.

"I want to thank you both for everything over the years. I will keep in touch," said the all-of-a-sudden-thoughtful-of-others Marco while he strode over towards them.

"You are certainly welcome, Marco" said my papà.

"Yes," my mamma said. "Let us know how you are doing."

"Well, good-bye for now," Marco said as his hugged and kissed all of us. I saw him to the door and he was off.

I turned, raised my hands high, and exclaimed, "That's all settled!" My anger towards him had long drifted away. My peace inside was far more valuable than a renewal of his intimacy.

ONWARD WITH MY LIFE

"Well, I'm off for Nonna Tizianna's," I said joyously as I hugged my parents. I grabbed my bags and enthusiastically hopped on my scooter and headed towards the country.

I fell into a relaxed routine at the farm. In the morning I would review information for my thesis defense for an hour and then help my nonni with the morning chores. I particularly loved collecting eggs from the seven hens. After the chores, I still had a couple of hours to review the moves of my presentation before noon. After a noon meal and rest I would walk and walk in the country air. Then, by three o'clock, I took off to teach and check in with my folks at home. In the evening, I would help my nonni with the kitchen chores and then read some more. By the end of the second day, I was ready.

Two evenings before my thesis defense, Nonno stood out in the courtyard with his pipe while he conversed with two of the farm workers. Nonna and I were in the kitchen. I was at the kitchen counter preparing fresh fig leaf tea for Nonna and myself. My cell phone on the table near Nonna rang out.

"Do you want me to answer it for, you?" Nonna asked.

"Yes, thanks, Nonna. It's probably Mamma."

I heard Nonna say, "Oh, Luciano, how are you, dear?" She listened for a moment, and then said, "That's good. Oh, of course, it's no imposition. Yes, she's right here. Francesca, it's Luciano on the phone for you." I placed the two cups of tea on the table and Nonna handed the phone to me.

"Hey, Francesca, how are you?" Luciano asked.

"Good. How are things in Naples?"

"Everything is good here. I don't want to keep you, but did want to wish you well on Friday. It will be great, I am sure!"

"Thanks, Luciano. I feel ready and look forward to its completion."

"I can understand that! By the way, I know you have a lot going on, but have you and Susanna decided when you might come this way for the weekend?"

"We had talked about the weekend after this one. We thought that we might have our minds relaxed, as we would know if we passed or not," I answered.

"Of course you both will pass. That weekend will work out for me and, as far as I can tell, for Flavio too. But I'll check with him to be sure. We'll plan lots of adventures!"

"Yes! I'll be ready for adventures! Thanks for calling, Luciano."

"Of course. Let me know when you get the final word from the university so I can let out a big holler down here!" Luciano said.

"Promise. Ciao."

"Ciao."

Nonna and I enjoyed our tea together. I just love Nonna Tizianna. Her heart is light and that has always encouraged me.

With her cup still half full, Nonna Tizianna went over to her accordion case, opened it, and pulled out her accordion. Nonna sang and played her heart out. What I heard felt so good to me that I had to move my body. I stood up and danced more joy into that stone floor that already held a good amount. When Nonno Angelo came through the door I grabbed his hands and we spun around like a spiral of angel dust.

The next day, after many hugs and kisses, I left for home with fresh produce in my satchel and more courage in my heart.

When I arrived home Mamma and Papà were in session with their students. I waved to them and went directly to the kitchen to put away the produce. I unpacked my bag in my room and went out to the patio for a meditation.

I sat calmly by Mamma's basil and across from the candles lit earlier by Mamma to remember our ancestors. I thanked all the ancestors for the opportunity that I faced tomorrow. I put down tobacco and thanked the creator specifically for all the blessings of my family, friends, food, house, education, career, health, success with my degree, and a good husband in my future. Then, I just sat and observed my breath enter and exit my heart with gratefulness. After about twenty minutes I felt ready for the defense tomorrow.

When Mamma's student's session finished I said, "It's about time for Susanna's presentation and her defense."

"Carry good vibes for Susanna from us with you. See you when you get back," Mamma responded with a smile and a hug as she began to prepare herself some hot tea.

"Sure thing, Mamma."

"By the way," Mamma continued, "how were Nonna and Nonno?"

"Very well. Nonna played the accordion last night and was up early to pick the produce for us. Nonno danced with me and was up early to check on the animals."

"They are amazing. I'll call them after the students and thank them for the produce," Mamma replied.

"Okay, Mamma. I'm off," I said as I kissed her cheek.

Susanna and I sat quietly in the hall and awaited her summons. The summons came for her only ten minutes late. Susanna gathered her music and papers and entered the large classroom.

After little more than an hour she exited with a smile on her face. She explained that she had completed her presentation and had answered all their questions about fifteen minutes ago. The professors then went into private deliberation. They emerged with a unanimous decision to grant her degree. Susanna was to pick up her completion papers next week at the department office. We jumped and hugged and took off juggling all her presentation items as we marched down the hall to the outdoor courtyard.

We packed her items on the back of her scooter and were about to take off for her house, when Susanna put her finger up to halt a minute. She took out her cell phone and dialed Flavio's number with the explanation that he had requested to know right away.

"Of course," I said.

"Flavio, Flavio, Flavio, I passed!" Susanna exclaimed into the cell phone.

I could hear Flavio's responses of joy from a foot away. My, my, I thought. Those two are a quite a pair.

I dropped Susanna off at her house to celebrate with her papà and headed to the dance school. After my class I went home for a restful evening.

My session was in the morning of the next day. I did a short meditation to reinforce my calmness and left shortly after breakfast. Susanna insisted on being there also. I picked up a happy Susanna at her house and we went on to my fate at the university. When they called me in, I saw that my three professors—two women and a man—were seated in a large semi-circle behind small wooden tables. There was a six-inch raised platform in front of them. The platform was quite expansive, actually, to accommodate the performances.

I had given them each copies of my thesis previously for review. However, I had fresh copies for them if they desired. I set up my music, introduced my performance, and then danced. It went off without a hitch. At the end of it I wrapped a long piece of fabric around my waist to act as a skirt, sat down, folded my hands, and readied for their questions. The professors asked questions of me based on my material. They were almost entirely opinion questions. They then stated that they found my sources well documented and appropriately cited. They inquired how I would use the material in the future.

"Professors, I began, I intend to teach and write about dance and other subjects that I love. I will incorporate the material of my thesis and the other information that I have gained at the university in my future oral, dance, and written works whether it is with my students or the general public," I concluded.

As they did with Susanna, they then went off and discussed my work. They returned in a few minutes with a unanimous pass.

With a huge smile and a suppressed urge to dance with joy, I said, "Thank all of you so much. It has been an honor to be your student." Respectfully I shook their hands and left the room.

Susanna could tell by the look on my face that I was triumphant! The two of us were beside ourselves. We hugged and jumped and at last got ourselves onto the scooter. Soon we arrived at my house to help with the celebration dinner later that day!

It felt so good to give the news to Mamma and Papà. They had not scheduled students for that afternoon and jumped up from their paperwork as we came in. They were emotional rocks of strength in my life and I knew I was fortunate to have that. Mamma and Papà were ecstatic! After congratulatory hugs all around I called Nonna Tizianna and Nonno Angelo, and Nonna Mikaela and Nonno Robert. They were all thrilled.

While Mamma, Papà, and Susanna were in the kitchen chopping vegetables for Mamma's red sauce, I stepped out onto the patio to call Luciano as promised.

"Luciano! I have good news!" I blurted out when I heard his voice.

"Fabulous!" he declared. "So, now this is Francesca, the university graduate?"

"It seems so!" I laughed. "A university graduate that is about to feast tonight on my mamma's oysters and pasta in red sauce."

"Yum. Sounds great! Thanks for the great news. We will continue to celebrate next weekend. Let us know which train you and Susanna decide to take," Luciano concluded.

"Absolutely. Ciao."

"Ciao, Francesca."

I then returned to Mamma and Susanna in the kitchen.

"Was that Luciano?" Susanna asked.

"Yes, he said to let him and Flavio know which train we will be on next Friday. He sounded excited to celebrate our successes! It will be so much fun!" I added.

Mamma and Susanna looked at my shining face. Papà discreetly kept chopping. But, Mamma and Susanna just stood there with their full attention on me. They perceived more excitement in my face than from my academic success! I felt it, too. But, what exactly did I feel? That I would have to sort out later, when I was alone. Not now in the presence of two insightful women who know me better than I know myself, and who, by the way, have a gaze on me at the moment that reached my soul.

"Francesca," said Mamma, to break my discomfort, "Would you and Susanna like to go to market and pick up some fresh oysters for my red sauce? Also, Susanna, would you like to invite your papà and Catrina to join us for the celebration dinner?"

"I think they would love it! Okay. Let's go, Francesca!"

We went to Susanna's and the market, and were home with the oysters by late afternoon. We set up the table, and then later, at the appointed time, Daniele and Catrina arrived while Mamma popped the pasta into the salted, boiling water. What a great day! Good academic news! Time in the warm sun at the market, time with family, and a good talk with Luciano. Life couldn't get much better in my way of thinking!

Out of respect for Daniele, Papà served effervescent mineral water for all. Susanna and I placed the olives, salad, and bread on the table. Mamma brought over the steaming platter of fresh pasta with oysters in a red sauce. We toasted each other. Then Papà did a special toast to our guests. Mamma followed with a special toast to the next generation of university graduates. Then at last we dove in to our incredible dinner.

Our animated conversation flew over and between bites of the succulent dinner. Susanna spoke of her plans to hopefully perform and I spoke of my plans to teach and write. Then we talked of the mushroom season this past spring. To our surprise, both Daniele and Catrina had special secret sites for the mushrooms. Mamma and Papà have had theirs for years, as well. So, we all made a pact to go on the hunt together next year and hit all of our sites. At the end of the meal as we sat with our coffee and tea in the warm evening air, Papà raised his coffee cup to Mamma and said, "Thanks for the great sauce! In return I'll do the kitchen cleanup."

"Thanks, mi amore," Mamma exclaimed as she raised her teacup to him.

"Well, I've been known to scrub a pot in my day," said Daniele. "I'll help." So the men chattered away about the local and national soccer teams while they scrubbed, wiped, and dried kitchen items and counters.

Meanwhile, Mamma, Susanna, Catrina, and I, safe under the bright stars above the patio, nestled into our feminine discourse. Catarina spoke of the loss of her husband a few years ago. Their marriage had been without children for an unknown reason. They both accepted it and enjoyed nephews, nieces, and neighborhood children.

"How have you managed since your husband's death?" my mamma asked. Somehow my mamma is able to ask the most personal of questions. I figure because she asks out of concern.

"Oh, I am just fine on my husband's small pension, with its occasional embellishment from my alteration and embroidery work." Catrina smiled easily, and we could see that she was just fine.

"Well, I'm glad you could come tonight, and we will see more of you and Daniele, I am sure," Mamma said.

"It has been a lovely evening," said Catrina. "I've enjoyed it very much."

"I'll probably see you at market tomorrow," Mamma said.

"Yes, I'm sure," said Catrina.

"I'll walk with you partway," I offered to Susanna, Daniele, and Catrina.

Daniele and Catrina walked ahead arm in arm.

Then Susanna said, "Maybe after a good night's sleep, you can tell me tomorrow about that odd look on your face after your phone call."

"Odd? What do you mean, odd?" I said. Then I looked at my best friend and we both laughed.

"Yes, I think by tomorrow I will be ready to," I said as I smiled at my friend.

After a few more feet we parted. When I arrived home, my folks had music on and were on the patio in contemplative absorption of the day. I showered them with thanks, hugs, and kisses. I knew that I worked hard, but it was their emotional and physical support that sustained me during my university years.

I went to my room, quickly showered, put on my nightgown, got in bed under the sheet, and fell fast asleep as the lazy ceiling fan gently moved the warm early summer air over me.

I slept deeply until the morning sun and birds called to open my eyes. Market day! I always enjoy the market, but this market day there would be no pressure of a paper or an exam to weigh on my mind. I felt free! The morning birds were the only sound that danced around the air in the house that morning. Mamma was off on an early morning speed walk and Papà was off to his over-fifty soccer league game. So, I had the quiet to myself.

I took a cup of tea to the patio. Mamma had the family candles lit. I sat in my favorite chair at the table, took a sip of tea, put it down, and closed my eyes. I could feel the gentle early morning sun on my shoulders. I could feel the slight breeze with the fragrant summer smells of ripened fruit and bright flowers at their height of bloom. The song of the birds became less frequent as the morning sun warmed. In my imagination, I saw my breath move in and out of my heart. Gently I focused on it. My thoughts turned to Luciano. I just watched my thoughts. Then, I put my attention back to my breath. That is where it remained for a while. When I was ready, I gently opened my eyes.

So, it was clear to me that I was unequivocally and profoundly in love with a man raised as my cousin. I felt no unease, as we were not blood relatives. For me it was more a sense of surprise. But, would my family see it as I did? I would gently break my feelings to my parents.

And as far as Luciano went? Well, I felt he was attracted to me, but beyond that I wasn't sure. He has always treated me well, as he does everyone. With my studies now behind me, I decided to be more observant of our interactions and see what happens.

I got a fresh cup of hot mint tea as Mamma came in through the door.

"Ready for market, Francesca?" she shouted. "I'll jump in and out of the shower and be right there."

"Perfect," I said. "I'll have some hot tea ready for you."

There my mamma was, fifty years old with joy and health that glowed all about her. Her curvaceous, fit form with her beautiful face that was widely framed by her full head of tightly curled, golden wheat colored hair. To me she had a great beauty.

She taught me to appreciate my beauty as well. We bonded over the care of our hair as we had the same texture and intense curl. Mine was a chestnut brown. I had inherited her shape as she had from her mother. My skin was a deep olive like my papà's and my eyes a soft brown with some green. I liked how I was alike and how I was different from my mamma.

Invariably at the weekly Saturday market, there would be a fan, new to the market, who would recognize her. Mamma would always be gracious and provide an autograph, wish them well, and then proceed to shop. These interchanges were never an imposition for her and thus not for me either. We just considered it a part of our market experience.

Within moments she appeared, showered and ready for market, with her hair up in a high ponytail that expanded like a crown.

"Great. Hot mint tea. My abuelita loved it, as well," she said as some memory of her abuelita occurred to her.

She sat across from me at the patio table. Then she looked me directly in the eye and asked, "How are you with everything that has happened this week?"

"Mamma, I feel so happy and relieved. I know a good career will develop."

"Yes, it will, Francesca. Also, about Marco, I was impressed how you managed his visit."

"I didn't know if I would ever see him again. So, it was a little shocking to see him. But, I had become clear that I no longer had any romantic feelings for Marco. It felt awkward between us after I told him. But, our friendship may return. We did have more years as friends than as lovers, after all. I think the fact that I had moved on caught him a little by surprise. He still has romantic feelings towards me. But now he knows I am not a romantic option. I'm sure he'll work things out for himself. And hopefully it will be with less impulsivity."

"You're a wise woman, Francesca. Ready for market?"

"Let's go, Mamma."

We grabbed our baskets and I dragged the small collapsible cart. We walked arm in arm the few blocks to the market. We shopped in the following order: vegetables, fish or chicken, fruits, bread, and flowers. At home we always have plenty of cheese and eggs from Nonna Tizianna, so we don't stop at those stands. And we always modify our vegetable and fruit purchases according to what is in abundant supply at the farm. As usual, we checked in at Nonna Tizianna's stand. All was well. We met a fan at the fruit stand, and we met Susanna and Catrina at the bakers. We decided to have a coffee with Susanna and Catrina, and then go to the flower stand before we headed home.

The four of us got into a discussion of the merits of focaccia bread as both families had purchased it. Before we parted, Susanna and I decided to meet later, in the cooler later afternoon, and take the market items that Nonna Tizianna needed out to the farm. After our good-byes, Mamma and I hurried to the flower stand and then home, as the ice we bought to keep the fish and meats fresh had begun to melt.

Mamma and I unpacked the food items as Papà returned from his soccer game.

"What a great game!" he exclaimed. "We narrowly lost by only one point." Mamma quickly shooed him off to the shower with promises to hear the rest of the game stories after the shower.

In a little while, Papà popped back into the kitchen with, thank goodness, a fresh smell. He spoke animatedly about his team's great plays.

Papà said, "We are sure to win in two weeks, which is our next scheduled game. We have two Wednesday practices and one Saturday practice before that. We will definitely be ready to win in two weeks."

"I'm sure you guys will win. Any chance it's in the afternoon so I can watch it?" Mamma asked.

"Yes, I think it's at three o'clock," Papà answered.

"Perfect," said Mamma.

Mamma and I quickly put on a big pot of chicken stew with potato, carrots, garbanzo beans, onions, garlic, tomatoes, and swiss chard. It had plenty of oregano, cumin, fennel, turmeric, coriander, and a sprinkle of cayenne. It smelled heavenly. In about an hour we all sat down to the fresh focaccia from market and a bowl of chicken stew. We were all ravenous from our energetic mornings.

"So have you and Susanna decided which train to Naples this Friday?" Mamma asked.

"We'll get the tickets on Monday, but it will probably be the one that gets in at six o'clock. Neither Susanna nor I teach on Friday, so we can travel during the day," I answered.

"I'll send some cheese, ground corn, rice, wine, and hazelnut chocolates for Zia Margarita," Mamma said.

"It seems that with work and all, Luciano will be spending more time up by us," Papà casually offered.

"I'm glad," I responded. "I like his company."

"As I am sure he likes yours, Francesca," Papà continued.

I blushed and said softly, "I know, but I am not sure in what way he likes my company. He's positive around everyone."

"Well, I guess you'll sort that out this trip, then," Papà concluded.

"I guess I, or rather, we will," I said softly, a little surprised how on target Papà was with the topic. I continued, "Marco's break-up taught me to take nothing for granted. It also taught me how to take care of myself no matter what. So, we'll see how the weekend goes."

Wow! I sure surprised myself with that mouthful. Then, Papà responded with a shout, "That's my girl!" as he patted my cheek.

With light feet and heart I then began to get the market items ready for Nonna Tizianna.

Soon Susanna arrived and we loaded the items in the carry case on the back of the bike. Away we sped for an afternoon in the country.

Nonna Tizianna was on the patio shucking beans for supper. We shouted at her from the kitchen door and said we'd be right out after we put up the market items.

As we settled at the patio table in front of the pile of beans, I said, "The focaccia is great this week, as always, Nonna."

"It'll be perfect with the bean soup for dinner," Nonna responded as she smiled at us both.

We took the beans in our hands as well, and the three of us quickly finished the job. We then peeled the early potatoes, onions, carrots, and early turnips for the soup and washed the greens. I picked the fresh garden herbs I know Nonna loved to use for her soups, cut them up, and dropped them into the soup as well. We put it on low and went back out for a short walk among the vineyards.

"Do you still plan to move out here now that you have completed the university?" Nonna Tizianna asked.

"Yes, I do, if it's still good with you."

"Absolutely it is," responded Nonna quickly. "And what are your plans, Susanna?"

"Well, in three weeks there are auditions in Genoa for a mixed venue dance company. The company's focus is mostly on ballet movements. It would be great to perform. Hopefully in the future I'll teach dance, as well."

"Sounds grand. Both Angelo and I would love to attend a performance. I am sure you'll make the company. I've seen you dance and you
are very talented, my dear."

"Thanks, Nonna Tizianna," Susanna responded as she sighed and
shrugged her shoulders. "The way you and all of your family dance has
always inspired me."

"Me too!" laughed Nonna Tizianna. "Well, let's see how our soup is
doing," Nonna added as she turned with her light feet towards the house.

We checked the soup, made a large pitcher of lemonade, and settled
ourselves on the patio. The later afternoon was warm with a slight breeze.
We sat in the shade and mellowed out on this gentle afternoon.

We then felt one of those small quakes. We both looked towards
Nonna Tizianna. She said, "Yes, I felt it. They are more frequent now,
than I remember over the past years of my life. But we still don't have
any word if it has disturbed anything. So, unless we get other signs, and
even if we do, let's keep on living! And you young ladies have a weekend
in Naples soon, right?"

"Yes, we do!" we said, sort of in unison.

"Well, be sure to let me know how the trip goes," she said with a
twinkle in her eye as she danced—yes, danced—towards the kitchen
door to check on the soup.

Soon the sun began to set and Nonno Angelo made his way towards
the house from his precious vineyards and cornfields. Angelo spent most
of his time in the fields. Even though he came by the farm through Nonna
Tizianna's family, he loved it as if it were his own flesh. From time to
time during his retirement, he would be called into the research corpora-
tion for a brief consultation, as he kept himself well read. But his love
was to be on the farm.

Susanna, Tizianna, Angelo, and I gathered around the table on the
patio and enjoyed an evening meal of wine, focaccia, and the slow-cooked
bean soup. The soup was seasoned with only herbs and spices and other
vegetables. Its simplicity and fresh garden aroma was intoxicating.

Susanna and I cleaned up the kitchen and left for home early. Don't
know why so early, really. Maybe it was to give Nonna Tizianna and
Nonno Angelo peaceful time together. For tomorrow the family would
descend on them for their Sunday visit. Or maybe it was because
both Susanna and I were each heavy with the potential of an intimate

relationship. Or maybe we were exhausted from our recent academic accomplishments. Whatever the source, we both desperately needed our rest and sped home to get just that.

ANOTHER WEEKEND ON THE NAPLES FARM

The next week the students at the dance school seemed to mirror my positive energy. They were confident and had joy in their learned moves. For me the week passed quickly.

Friday morning I was up early. Mamma was on the patio, quiet in her morning meditation. I entered the patio and stood by the lit candles a moment and then sat beside her. After a little while, she asked me quietly while she slowly opened her eyes, "Hungry?"

"Not yet, Mamma," I answered. "I'll cook something while you're on your speed walk."

"Thanks, Francesca. Your Papà will drive you ladies to the station as he has a break with students around noon."

"Perfect, Mamma. I love you," I said and kissed her on the cheek as I rose to begin my chef duties in the kitchen.

Mamma left on her speed walk and Papà appeared to make his great coffee.

Around noon, Papà drove Susanna and myself to the train station. So he would not have to park, when he pulled up next to the train station curb, Susanna and I jumped out of the car as we grabbed our satchels.

"Bye, Papà," I shouted as I blew him a kiss.

"Bye, Signore Dominico," shouted Susanna as she blew him a kiss.

Papà smiled a wide smile, waved, and drove off.

The train ride was beautiful and comfortable, as always, on the fast train to Naples.

Both Luciano and Flavio were there to meet us at the station outside Naples nearest to the farm. Susanna and I would separate for a brief time. Susanna was going to stay in the spare room at Flavio's house. I was to stay, as usual, at my cousin's family farm where Luciano lived. Then later, Luciano and I would go to Flavio's for dinner.

It felt so good to once again lean against Luciano's back as we sped along towards the farm. The strong sense of security came back, just as it had before. It was also great to see Zia Margarita and Zio Josefa once again. I sat with Zia Margarita with some tea for a few minutes while

Luciano took a call about a work project that was to start Monday. I gave my kind zia the cheese that my mamma had sent as well as some rice, ground corn, wine, and hazelnut chocolates. She was so happy with the gifts. We caught up on family news as we sipped the tea.

"Yes," I said to her questions, "Nonna Tizianna and Nonno Angelo are well. We still gather at the farm most Sundays. Mamma and Papà still enjoy their students and occasional public appearances."

Maximillian came through the kitchen on his way to check something out in the field before he headed to his girlfriend's house.

"Hey, cugina!" Maximillian called as he approached me to enfold me into a big hug and kiss on the cheek.

"Hey, Maximillian!" I said as he released me. "See you are about to take care of business as usual."

"Don't let my appearances fool you!" he said as he kissed his mamma on the cheek and darted out the door.

Laura was not yet home from the library. She had begun her review for her fall studies. Laura always kept high standards for herself. To study ahead for her courses was one of her tried and true techniques to do well with her studies.

"Glad you came," said Zia Margarita as she patted my hand.

"Me too," I responded. "It's always a special weekend when I get to come here. This weekend is doubly emotional. My friend Susanna has met Flavio's mamma for the first time. This evening, Flavio's mamma is cooking a special dinner for her. Luciano and I are invited. I am so excited to see how their first meeting has progressed."

"I'm sure that everything is just fine. Luciano mentioned to us how happy Flavio is in his relationship with Susanna. He didn't have to say anything, however. It has been obvious to all of us that Flavio is very happy. His conversation has been filled with Susanna, Susanna, Susanna!"

I laughed and said, "I can just hear him! Wait until you see Susanna and Flavio together. They really weave strong, magical energy strands."

"What a funny description, my dear Francesca, but it paints the picture! I can't wait to see them together!" exclaimed Zia Margarita.

"Hopefully after the market tomorrow," I added.

"That would be great. But when you are there this evening, would you and Luciano invite Flavio, Susanna, and Flavio's mamma here tomorrow for dinner?"

"Absolutely. That would be great!"

Luciano finished his call and came to the kitchen to inquire if I wanted to go out to the fields to meet Josefa and his sheep.

"Yes!" I said enthusiastically.

We headed out to the fields. As we ascended the ridge to spot Josefa, Luciano grabbed my hand as if to help me on the ascent. Then when we reached the top of the ridge he just held it. I held his hand as well. As Josefa came over the next ridge we broke our hands and waved to him. We eased ourselves down the slope to Josefa's side. We talked about the sheep and this year's hard wheat crop. We talked about Maximillian's love for the farm.

"He really wants to take over as manager of the farm and I think he would be great," offered Luciano.

"You have trained him well, Luciano," Josefa said fondly while he looked into Luciano's eyes.

"So, now that you are a university graduate, what have you been up to?" Josefa teased as he turned his gaze towards me.

"Well, I haven't shaken up the world too much," I began.

"I wouldn't be so sure," Josefa interrupted with a twinkle in his eye as he opened the sheep pen gate. Luciano hurried in to check if there was sufficient water in their trough and averted his eyes away from our faces for the next few moments.

Back at the farmhouse, I readied myself for the dinner at Flavio's. I put on a fresh pair of capris, bright orange tank top, added my magenta scarf and gold walking sandals. I was ready!

"You look beautiful," Luciano said.

"Thanks. That sea blue shirt is great on you," I replied.

And off we went on that beautiful ride to Flavio's house near Positano. I breathed in the scent of Luciano and of the countryside's moist evening soil. What a great scent combination for my country girl spirit!

When we arrived at Flavio's we found Susanna in the kitchen with Flavio's mamma, Patricia. Flavio was there as well, active in his new role as student chef. He stirred the sauce with a large wooden spoon with one hand and sprinkled in fresh chopped herbs with the other. That morning he had bought a lovely ocean snapper and gently cooked it over the solar grill in the courtyard. It stood steaming on the counter. Patricia had dropped the fresh pasta in the water when she heard our bike.

"Hey, Francesca!" shouted Susanna. "I now know the secrets of good fresh pasta. I'm so excited!"

"Incredible!" I said as I kissed her and then Patricia and Flavio on the cheek.

"So now you are a true woman of the south," teased Luciano.

"At your service, sir," Susanna said as she curtsied.

"Luciano!" exclaimed Patricia. "Serve up the wine please. Susanna has done just fine," defended Patricia.

"Yes, ma'am," Luciano said as he kissed Patricia on the cheek. He then approached Flavio and as he inhaled the aromatic pot said, "Flavio you have taken this new chef role seriously. I think you can now show me a thing or two!" He smiled at his best friend.

I mixed up an olive oil and lemon dressing while Susanna placed the green salad on the table. Flavio settled the still hot fish in the center of the table while Luciano poured the wine. Susanna and I carried the plates with the fresh pasta and red sauce to each place. Patricia arrived at the table with her fresh, perfectly baked, crusty bread. The spicy aroma of the sauce and the herbed grilled fish spiraled in the warm salty evening Positano air that gently passed through the windows. The vision on the table of the red, green, and white colors added to my delight. Hardly able to contain myself, I tore off a piece of bread and dipped it into the olive oil to begin my feast when Luciano stood, took his wine, and said, "I toast my great friend Flavio who has always stood by me since our youth, even sometimes when he should not have. And I toast Mamma Patricia who has always welcomed me here as a son. And I toast Susanna who is not only a recent graduate, but has brought joy to my grumpy friend sitting next to her."

Luciano had to stop because we were all laughing so hard and because we were all anxious to delve into the delicious food.

"Wait, wait, wait," Luciano said. "I have to toast Francesca next." Then Luciano quietly said, "But her presence overwhelms me, so the only words I can get out are, to you Francesca!"

"Bravo, my friend! Mangia, everyone!" shouted Flavio.

"Grazie," was all I could softly verbalize as I pulled my eyes away from Luciano's and thought, thank goodness for Flavio's exuberance to distract everyone from my reaction to Luciano's words!

The meal was delightful. We ate and ate. Between mouthfuls, we filled Patricia in on some of the details Flavio might have missed about the day of our mountain hike up north. Details like the fact that Flavio did not hike to the summit. So after many corrected versions of the day, I had the opportunity to relay the invitation from Zia Margarita and Zio Josefa for Patricia, Flavio, and Susanna to join us for dinner tomorrow.

Patricia smiled broadly. "I would love to," she said. "I will bring some of my olives."

"Oh, yum!" I responded, as she made a special olive brine for which she was famous in the area. After we all cleaned up the kitchen, Luciano and I said our good-byes. It had been a good but long day.

The ride home was unlike our ride to Flavio's. The sky was now a deep navy blue with the brightest of stars. There was a new moon over by the eastern horizon. The smell now in the absence of the sun had more moisture and was heavily scented by the roadside flowers and plant leaves. It was as if they didn't have to protect themselves from the sun's heat, and could open to the night's darkness and freely emit their scent.

When we got back to the courtyard, Luciano put the scooter and our helmets in the shed. I lay on the low courtyard wall and took in the night sky. Luciano came over and lay down on the wall in the opposite direction to me with the top of his head gently against mine.

Luciano said, "Francesca, I have something to tell you."

This was how Luciano began our old childhood game, so I responded, "I know, Luciano. I remember. You've told me a million times. The little dipper is over there in relation to the big dipper. See? I remember," I said as I pointed to the sky above us.

"I love you," Luciano said without acknowledgment of my big dipper and little dipper comment.

"Luciano, what did you say?" I exclaimed as I sat up on the wall.

Luciano swung his feet around, sat up, and placed himself close to me on the wall. He gently took my face in his hands and said again, "I love you."

My whole being was beyond excitement. I could not speak or move. My body felt like I had just received a swallow of fresh, cool spring water when all my cells were parched for thirst. I let his words sink in.

Then I turned and, with my arms now around his neck, looked into his soft brown eyes and said, "I love you too, Luciano."

He gently kissed me. Then I snuggled against his chest, as his left arm enveloped me. Hmmm, with the honest truth now between us, my life just took on a lot more texture and depth.

After some time, with my arm around his waist and his arm around my shoulder, we walked slowly towards the house. Luciano said, "You know Francesca, I told Josefa and Margarita about my feelings for you. I wanted to be sure there was no blood relation between them and my parents' family. They assured me there was none."

"Did you tell Papà about your feelings on the mountain hike?" I queried. "Because Papà looked a little like he had swallowed a canary when he joined the rest of us after your trek. I couldn't figure out why until now."

"Yes, I wanted to be sure that if you felt towards me as I did towards you, that he and Alessia would feel comfortable about it."

"And if they weren't comfortable?" I teased.

"Not an option," said Luciano as he smiled broadly.

"I know. Just teasing," I replied.

As we neared the front door, we instinctively we turned towards each other and kissed. We were about half a second into the kiss, or so it seemed in that timeless place, when the front door burst open and Zia Margarita, Zio Josefa, and my cugini Maximillian and Laura burst out towards us. They descended upon us with hugs and kisses.

Zio Josefa said, "Zia Margarita and I had wagers on you two since you were barely in your teens. We each guessed as to how long it would take you two to discover the special spark between you."

"Who won?" Luciano asked.

"He did, of course," said Zia Margarita. "I guessed age seventeen. Josefa said early to mid twenties. He was right. He argued that you needed a little more life under your belt than what age seventeen offered."

"What do you owe him, Mamma?" Luciano asked as he hugged her.

"He said that I owe him," then she looked straight at her kind husband and said, "to be at his side for the rest of our lives."

Luciano turned to me and said, "Let's also wager on something that you will lose."

"Such a copycat you are, Luciano," I retorted and dashed behind Maximillian for protection.

"I'll show you copycat," Luciano said as he grabbed me, and swung me around high in the air. I then gladly landed into his arms. Everyone laughed. Tired from our day we all headed to bed, but with lighthearted spirits. It took me a little while to settle into sleep as my heart was still in a fast spin. But, it felt good.

In the morning I went with Zia Margarita to market. For the last few years Zia Margarita has hired a younger woman to run the family's stall. She goes to market to pick up items for her family and only helps at the stall for a short while. Luciano went over some of the farm accounts with Maximillian, Angelo went out to the fields, and Laura to the library.

I have always loved the markets around Naples. Today, as usual, the market women sang praises of their wares in full voice. I have always enjoyed the song-shouts. Zia Margarita's booth did a constant trade. She let me assist at the booth for a while. I sang out about the produce and haggled with the customers like a Naples native. Zia Margarita and Bianca enjoyed my antics. They helped me out with the price barters and gave me a nod when I was at the final price. After some hours at the market, we loaded our produce on the motorbike and headed back to the farm.

Upon arrival at the farm, Zia Margarita and I began preparing the vegetables for the lamb stew. That evening we would feast on a large pot of lamb stew, greens, cheese, and focaccia bread. The stew was to cook on a solar burner on the patio to capture the outdoor flavors. Zia Margarita and I drank some hot herb tea with lemon, and ate some figs, orange, cheese, and hard crust bread to fortify ourselves while we chopped the vegetables. In no time we had the vegetables chopped and in the water of the large pot. We cut some herbs from the garden and sautéed the marinated lamb chunks for a moment. Then we placed the herbs and the lamb with its sautéed juices into the pot. The pot was covered and left to do its own magic on the solar burner for the next few hours.

Zia Margarita went to take a nap and I sat with my feet up on another chair on the patio. I must have dozed off because when I opened my eyes there was Luciano standing at my feet with a grin on his face.

"I see you and Mamma Margarita got the stew on. Beautiful. Want to take a walk, or do you want to catch some more zzz's?" Luciano asked.

"No. Let's go! I'll just get a glass of water first. Do you want one?"

"Yes, thanks."

Well hydrated, we headed among the grape vines first and then to the small orange orchard.

Luciano said, "I got some news today from Piedmont's agriculture commission."

"Really?" I said a little surprised. "What kind of news?" I added trying to keep myself calm.

Luciano's eyes filled with excitement as he said, "They have asked me to take over the directorship of Piedmont's agriculture commission and to chair the coordination committee of the northern provinces."

I could hardly contain myself. I jumped up and spun around while I repeatedly shouted, "Wahoo, wahoo, wahoo!"

"You will be up north! Yes!" I said emphatically as I threw my arms around his neck and planted a kiss on his welcome lips.

Luciano returned my kiss. There we were, two folks among the orange trees who did not want to separate their lips. After many leaps of my heart, or trembles of the earth, it was really hard to tell which these days, we at last parted and returned to our walk in the orchard. Luciano said, "Francesca, I want us to be together. I mean to live together. No more long trips to each other and no more long nights alone. I want to walk with you not just through this orchard, but through life." Then he knelt down in the shade of the orange orchard, took my hands, and said, "Francesca, my dear Francesca, will you marry me?"

This felt so dramatic and romantic to me. It far exceeded any performance we did as kids at my house in Turino. This was the real drama of my own life. I was definitely going for this scenario!

I knelt down in front of him, kissed his hands, looked into his wonderful trustworthy eyes, and said, "Yes! In a heartbeat!"

Then we lay down side by side under the orange tree and took in the smell of the ripened oranges, looked at the sky and at each other, and just rode the soft breeze of joy.

"I love this orchard," I said to divert us from what we both wanted to do. After all we were in clear vision of the farm kitchen.

"And I love you! It feels so great to say it at last!" Luciano responded as he turned towards me.

I stood up and held out my hand to him.

"Come on Luciano, let's head back to the house before I just go up in flames of passi…uh…joy."

He sprang up and said, "Race ya!"

"Okay, if you want to lose," I said while I trailed after him.

Halfway he stopped, waited, and grabbed me into an incredible embrace. We walked the rest of the way in what felt like a new dimension of life created by the energy of our love. We decided to tell the family of our engagement on Sunday before I left for Turino. Today was for Flavio and Susanna.

And so it was. Flavio, Susanna, and Patricia arrived for dinner with big smiles that literally radiated. Patricia shared her olives and also brought beautiful cut flowers from her garden.

"Oh, how beautiful!" exclaimed Zia Margarita when she was handed the flowers. "I have always wanted to be able to grow such beauties."

Margarita and Patricia chatted amicably. They talked of the market, the crops, and the positive changes around Naples over the years. Then Patricia disclosed that she was so happy that Flavio had found such a lovely young lady.

"I have really enjoyed my time with Susanna," she said. "She mastered our southern technique of fresh pasta in one short afternoon," said Patricia happily. "But more than that, I enjoy her pleasant, quiet nature. She is a good person. What more could a mother want for her son?"

"I know exactly what you mean," said Margarita as she glanced at me. Patricia caught her subtlety and they gave each other a knowing glance.

With our bowls in hand, we all gathered informally at the big pot of lamb stew on the patio. Maximillian volunteered to fill everyone's bowl. Then we settled down at the big patio table to toast and eat. Josefa stood up and said, "Flavio, I believe you have a toast you would like to make!"

Flavio stood up and raised his glass. "Yes, I do, Zio Josefa. I would like to toast Susanna, the beautiful woman that sits beside me and is soon to be my wife!"

Everyone cheered and clinked glasses while Flavio and Susanna, of course, kissed. They kiss at every excuse, as they should.

Flavio took a sip from his glass of wine to ready himself to share the next exciting news. As the family knew, Flavio had worked on an engineering project to fix the infrastructure issues in the Naples area. The project oversaw waterless toilets in new construction and coordinated that with fertilization for the farm co-ops. It also worked on the increase of rails and decrease of cars in the city limits. In addition, the project expanded the trash recycling project. It relieved the city of the trash problem and opened up a huge waste-less trash process enterprise that provided thousands of jobs.

So now Flavio said, "The work of the infrastructure engineering project for Naples has been so successful that Genoa decided to implement one of their own. They also want to have a multitask committee with political support that coordinates these green activities with the various city departments." Flavio then took a deep breath and continued, "Anyway, the bottom line is that they submitted my name for the Genoa project and I agreed. The contract will be ready in a week or so."

"Oh, this is so exciting! You will be close by!" I blurted out.

"Yes, we plan to marry very soon, before the weather gets cold. Everyone here is invited!" Susanna said happily.

Zio Josefa said, "We will be there for sure!"

Everyone joined in with enthusiastic shouts of support while they clinked their glasses in joy. It was quite emotional. I blew a kiss to Susanna. Flavio and Luciano stood up and slapped each other's palms. Then we all dug in to the sumptuous stew. There was so much happiness that the air molecules seemed to burst out their oxygen to us in an energetic whirl. This fed our fire all the more.

After dinner, Zio Josefa pulled out his accordion and began to play. As the evening continued, some of Laura's friends and Maximillian's girlfriend, Julianna, arrived. While they helped themselves to the stew, we all began to dance. After a few songs, Zio Josefa played through one of my parents' love ballads. Luciano knew that I knew them all by heart, but usually avoided solos. So he came over at Josefa's nod and asked if I would sing it with him. I looked at Luciano in shock. I had no idea that he sang—no, that's not true. We always sang at family gatherings and he was always there with a great baritone. I just never paid it much attention, as everyone always sang in our families. There was never much fuss about it. That was one of the reasons my parents were able to handle their notoriety so well. They considered themselves a public version of what had always been a family thing. They never felt apart from family with their gift. Anyway, by the time my surprise calmed down, Josefa had played through the melody once again. I took Luciano's hand, smiled, and said, "Of course. Let's go!"

For this ballad, Luciano began and then in a couple of phrases I came in alone but for only one phrase before his voice joined mine. We wound and spiraled through the song. At the end of the song I felt like a blossom that had just found the sun and opened. We kissed. We had to. There was nothing else to do after such a time in song together.

The family went nuts with catcalls and laughter and to get the heat off us, Zio Josefa put the accordion down and plugged in the electronic device with ballads, tango, and salsa ready to blast out. We all danced like families dance when they celebrate the kind of love that keeps family in expansion.

Flavio, Susanna, and Patricia did not stay late. Flavio planned to take both Susanna and Patricia down to Positano the next morning for a stroll and lunch. So they left around ten o'clock. Patricia promised to come by next weekend as a new friendship had blossomed between her and Zia Margarita.

The next morning Luciano and I sat at breakfast with Zio Josefa and Zia Margarita.

"So," Zio Josefa said, "I watched both of you take your first steps on this farm. So, I know the determination that both of you possess. What do you two have planned for your future?" he asked.

Luciano said matter-of-factly, "We plan to marry soon. Yesterday, I asked this beautiful lady by my side if she would marry me."

I excitedly interjected, "And I said yes!" We all laughed.

Then Luciano continued, "But nothing set, yet. I go into Turino in two weeks to sign the contract for my new post there. I will know then the start date. How will this timing affect you and Maximillian at the farm?"

"Luciano, you've taught Maximillian well. We'll be fine, as long as these little quakes don't upset our Vesuvius too much," Zio added with a wink. "No, seriously, Luciano, continue on with your career. You've given us hints of possible work in the north for a few months now. Maximillian may give you an occasional call, but I think he's ready and I know he's excited to take over the farm management. I am proud of both of you. And as far as a wedding goes, whenever that is, it will be a joyous day for us as we love both of you so much!" Zio Josefa concluded.

"Papà, you and Mamma have been the best papà and mamma ever," Luciano responded. "I cannot image the life I would have had without you both. I will miss you terribly. I will make sure that we will see each other often."

"What did I do that you call my name so early in the morning, Luciano?" said sleepy Maximillian as he stumbled into the kitchen.

"Nothing to worry about on a Sunday morning," Luciano said to Maximillian jokingly. "Don't worry," he added in his big brother voice, "Francesca and I will be only a few hours away by rail and instantly here by phone. We'll always be close if you need anything."

"Francesca and you, huh?" said Maximillian in his little brother voice as he darted out the kitchen door.

"Don't tease about my lady," Luciano shouted as he sprung from his chair and out the kitchen door to catch Maximilian and wrestle him to the ground.

My zia and zio and I just shook our heads and drank our coffee.

After breakfast, Luciano and I struck out for Vesuvius for a short hike up to the top. From there we could not only enjoy the countryside of Naples, but also the Mediterranean. What a sight! There were a few scattered clouds, but the view was clear to the sea. I had done that hike many times since childhood. Today Vesuvius had a different vibe that I couldn't quite put my finger on. Maybe it was the way the steam lifted from its summit. The mountain seemed unsettled. Maybe what I sensed was just about myself as so much had happened recently in my life. Or maybe it was both the mountain and myself that held elevated energy. Perhaps the predictions about our Vesuvius were right.

Later in the afternoon Flavio arrived with Susanna on his scooter. Luciano secured my satchel to the back of his scooter. Zia Margarita sent cheese and hard wheat flour with me for our family in Turino. I hugged Zia Margarita and Zio Josefa hard before we departed. They had given me so much in my life. Now, as an adult, it continued. I was grateful.

We took off for the station. I held Luciano's torso and felt secure. Hopefully I would be honored to hug his strong chest for a very long time.

It was hard for me to leave Luciano at the station. But both he and Flavio would be in Turino in two weeks, so that made the departure for Susanna and me a little easier. As we mounted the stairs into the station, I glanced back at the street and thought I noticed that Luciano and Flavio had their chests pumped out as they sped away in the traffic. But then again, maybe it was the wind that billowed their shirts.

On the train, my head spun with things I wanted to do. First of all, there was the conversation with my folks. Of course I called my mamma when we got back to the house from the orchard walk. This woman had so generously shared her love, energy, and wisdom with me since before my birth. I could speak of anything and get the truth from her. Our spirits were always close. Therefore, of course, not much time could pass before I shared with her the great news of my engagement to Luciano! And of course she immediately told Papà. Actually, neither was surprised. But, I looked forward to sitting down with my parents face to face to share the news again.

Of course I also needed to tell Nonna Tizianna and Nonno Angelo, as well as Nonna Mikaela and Nonno Robert in Genoa. They all would have heard the news from my mamma and papà, as it was not secret. But, they would expect a full report from me! Then, there would be the solidification of the plans of my move onto the farm.

OUR DOUBLE WEDDING

Soon exhaustion took over, my thoughts quieted, and both Susanna and I slept until the Turino station call. Papà met us at the station. Susanna and I were both all smiles as we brought greetings to him from Zia Margarita and Zio Josefa. Of course Papà could not resist teasing Susanna and said, "Wow, Susanna. Since Flavio has been in your life I don't know who smiles more, our Italian sunshine or you. It's good to see!"

Susanna blushed and I said, "Well, guess what, Papà? You will see Susanna's smile from now on as she and Flavio are engaged!"

"Congratulations!" Papà said. "Both of you engaged! Tell me, what is in the water you ladies are drinking?"

We all laughed and then Papà got a serious face and said, "Both of you can be grown up and everything. But, be sure and understand that I don't get any older!"

"Got it, Papà," I laughed.

"Got it, Signore Dominico," Susanna said with one of her now permanent smiles as she exited our car at her apartment building. Her papà and Catrina rose to greet Susanna from the front bench where they sat in the warm evening air. They waved to Papà and me as they helped Susanna with her satchels. Susanna blew us a kiss as she entered the building's courtyard. "See you tomorrow," she shouted.

"See you tomorrow," I answered.

As we approached our house, there was Mamma coming down our block with her pizza carry bags. As she spotted the car, she shouted, "Hey, Francesca!"

"Mamma!" I shouted back.

She had been to the community brick oven to bake two pizzas for my homecoming this weekend. After we parked, I ran to meet her and threw my arms around her neck with a big kiss on her cheek. She kissed my cheek and held me close. I took one of the pizza bags and we were soon at our front door. Papà stood just inside by my satchels, with his left arm extended, opening the front door wide for us.

"Come in, come in, ladies of my heart," Papà said.

I unpacked my satchels while Mamma and Papà set the steaming hot pizza out on the patio. I brought the flour, cheese, and olives from Zia Margarita into the kitchen. This cheese is perfect to grate on the pizza, I thought. I brought some cheese, a small grater, and a small dish of olives to the table.

We three sat down to a late supper together. Our space together had always been sacred to us. My mamma and papà have loved each other a long time and both shared their love with me after my birth. Tonight we honored that bond. Also, we would celebrate the addition, in absentia, of Luciano to our mix. He was an addition that had been a part of us in other roles for many years. Now it would be as my husband and as their son-in-law.

"Mmm, Mamma," I exclaimed, "This is the best pizza ever. Naples can't top this pizza. How did you do it as a northerner? No wait, as an American and a northerner. Two strikes against you, yet you were triumphant!" We three just laughed and laughed until our sides hurt.

Then I told them about the great fun at Flavio's dinner. I also told them how when Luciano and I arrived back at the farm, he declared his love for me in the guise of a casual comment while we relaxed on the courtyard wall.

"That sounds like Luciano," Papà chuckled.

I was once again animated at the remembrance. "Yes, but, Zia Margarita and Zio Josefa do not share his subtle ways of understatement. When we approached the house, Zia Margarita, Zio Josefa, Maximillian, and Laura burst out of their front door and applauded during our kiss!"

My parents both lost it in laughter. "I can just see Josefa. He loves the dramatic," Papà managed to say despite his laughter.

"You better believe it. Wait until I tell you what he did on Saturday night. Well, that dinner was a celebration of Flavio and Susanna's engagement and of life in general. Luciano and I did not speak of our engagement to everyone, as yet. We were going to wait until Sunday to first tell Zia Margarita and Zio Josefa and then the others. But, you know how Josefa loves to communicate in maybe an indirect but clear way?"

"Yes, we know," my parents agreed.

"Well during his accordion music and the dancing after the lamb stew dinner he played one of your ballads."

"Really!" exclaimed Mamma.

"Yes," I answered. "He then nodded to Luciano who came over and took my hand and asked if I would join him in the duet.

"Mamma and Papà, I could just stare for a moment. From the family gatherings, I knew that Luciano could sing. But, I didn't know that he had memorized your ballads as well. I trusted the man, so I stood up and joined him at Zio Josefa's side. Luciano opened the duet properly, I came in when you do, Mamma, and it went on beautifully from there. It was quite an experience to do that with him. I am still amazed by the feel of it."

"Wow," said Papà. "So Luciano and I share not only the love of a mountain hike, but the muse of music as well. Quite a fiancé you've found, Francesca."

"I know. A good guy," I concurred. "It was a good weekend. What were you two up to?" I queried.

"It was a quiet weekend. I took your mother to a café and the movies to celebrate our league's soccer win on Saturday afternoon. A win that she witnessed, by the way!" Papà said.

"Congratulations, Papà!" I commented. "I would have loved to see your win."

We went to bed early as Monday morning awaited, with students for my parents and plans for the move to the farm for me.

Early Monday morning after Mamma's speed walk and our breakfast, Papà went to his piano with some tune in his head that he wanted to hammer out. Mamma began to dig around her plants and harvest some herbs to dry. And I just sat with some tea in quiet contemplation.

"It's a lot to work out, isn't it?" Mamma offered.

"Yes, it is." I concurred. "It seems that everything has happened so fast. But not too fast. Things are at an energetic peak, but still in an orderly progression. Pretty cool," I concluded.

"It is good to see you so happy, Francesca. By the way, have you and Luciano decided when you want to marry?" Mamma asked.

"We haven't really had time to firm it up. We have no reason to wait, however. We'll talk about it in two weeks when he's here." I responded.

"Well, there are at least eight more weeks of nice weather for a country wedding," Mamma said thoughtfully.

"Mamma, Susanna and Flavio plan to marry soon. What do you think of a double wedding at Nonno Angelo and Nonna Tizianna's?"

"That's a great idea! See what Susanna thinks."

"I will!" I said excitedly.

That morning I went by Susanna's. She was in her apartment reviewing her moves for her audition on Thursday with the Genoa Ballet Co.

"Francesca!" she exclaimed as she threw the door open. "Come in! Here, sit down. Let me show you what I have worked out."

The small room had the couch, small chair, coffee table, plant, side table, and table with the TV pushed aside. I sat cross-legged on the couch. It was bright green and decorated on the arms and back with Catrina's lovely embroidered doilies.

Susanna began her routine with grace, precision, and emotion. She chose a piece that exhibited her skills beautifully. Susanna had the ability to perform the complex with ease. It was clear to me she would nail the audition, if the judges had any sense.

"Bravo!" I exclaimed when she finished. "You've got it, my dear friend. Can I help put the furniture back?"

"Thanks. Then, let's go for a walk and get some coffee."

"Great. I have an idea I want to talk over with you," I stated.

"Oh, mystery topic. I love it!" Susanna exclaimed as she and I pushed the furniture back into place.

We quickly had the living area in order. With light feet we descended the second story open stone stairs into the building's courtyard and then through an iron gate to the street's stone walkway.

"Well, this is what I'm thinking," I said as we walked arm in arm towards the piazza.

"Okay, now my suspense is really up. What is it?"

"What would you and Flavio think if we had a double wedding?"

Susanna raised her arms in the air and spun around. "That would be the best! I'll talk it over with Flavio by phone tonight. Then we can all talk about it in two weeks when the guys are here," she said as we settled back into our arm-in-arm gait after her spin.

We situated ourselves at a small café table with our coffees and watched the people as they gathered into or passed through the piazza.

"Francesca," Susanna asked, "Would you cover my dance class on Thursday?"

"Susanna, wouldn't you rather that I come with you to the audition?"

"Yes, of course, but…"

"Susanna, what about Matilde? She's a great teacher and always looks for more hours," I suggested.

"Okay. I'll ask her. Hopefully she'll agree."

"I'm sure she will," I reassured.

We then chatted for a while about some of our favorite moments of the past weekend in the way that only good friends can give them commemoration.

After our coffee we set off down the road to return to our preparations for our upcoming dance classes.

That afternoon I took the scooter to Nonna Tizianna's. When I arrived she had garden greens in the sink with salt and water. The chicken was in a pot that released its succulent flavor into the broth while the broth's seasonings flavored the chicken even more. The polenta was prepared and laid out in a circular dish to cool.

I took up some of the greens and began to clean them with her.

"So, I heard you had an eventful weekend." Nonna Tizianna was not one to wait if there was an urgent matter on her mind. True, she was a woman of patience, but neither did she waste time.

"Ohh, Nonna Tizianna, maybe we had better sit down with some tea so I can tell you the specifics."

"Oh, my," she said. "Let me get these greens on this cloth to dry so we can sit."

"Okay, I'll run out and cut some peppermint for the tea," I said.

I put on the water and went out to the warm sun and the garden to cut the peppermint. Back in the kitchen, I washed the peppermint, tore it up into small pieces, and placed them in the teapot.

As the tea brewed on the kitchen table, Nonna Tizianna and I sat down with our mugs and I began the story.

"Well, Nonna Tizianna, a couple of weeks ago I was honest with myself and knew that I had fallen love with Luciano. My intuition was that he felt the same way. But, I needed him to have enough commitment to come out with it without any prompts on my part."

Nonna nodded and smiled. She then said, "Good job, Francesca."

"Well," I continued, "Friday evening in the farm courtyard he did just that. He told me that he loved me in his usual casual way. It caught me off guard, but I quickly got with the program. He is very romantic, Nonna. Anyway, he proposed. He said he didn't want to be apart. I don't either, Nonna. We will probably marry soon. It's not like we need a long engagement to get to know each other! As fate would have it, Luciano received a promotion, which is up here in Piedmont. So he will soon start full-time work in Turino!"

"Oh, Francesca, I am so happy for the both of you. I know that you had planned to move here on the farm. Both of you are welcome here, if you and Luciano would like. Both Nonno Angelo and I are very fond of Luciano. We have noticed the beautiful affection between you two and the ease in each other's company. We had hoped it would blossom into this."

I got up and, with great enthusiasm, hugged and kissed Nonna Tizianna. We then sat together with our cups of aromatic fresh mint tea. I sipped the delicious tea and enjoyed Nonna Tizianna's dynamic presence.

"How is Susanna?" asked Nonna Tizianna into my silence.

"She is filled with emotion right now as her audition is on Thursday in Genoa."

"This is an exciting week! Are you going?"

"Yes, if she finds another sub for her dance class, I will go. We'll have an opportunity after her audition to see Nonna Mikaela, but Nonno Roberto will probably be down on the fisherman's beach with his buddies, so we might not catch him."

But there's more news," I continued. "Susanna and Flavio are also engaged. And Flavio has a new position in Genoa."

"I am amazed at the coincidence of such good friends to have work in the north. Do Susanna and Flavio plan to marry soon, as well?" asked Nonna.

"Yes. Very soon."

"Have you two considered a double wedding?"

"Actually, we have."

"Well, then, why not here? Nonno Angelo and I would love it!" concluded Nonna Tizianna.

"That would be wonderful, Nonna! The guys will be here in two weeks so we can firm up the plans then. I think they would love to have the wedding here."

By this point the chicken smelled amazing with the hint of caramelized onion, garlic, and well-seasoned chicken juices. We rose and I set the table on the patio as Nonna put the greens, now dry, in the salad bowl. She seasoned them with a dressing of fresh vinegar, olive oil, and spices.

Nonno Angelo appeared on the patio as if on cue with the explanation, "The delicious scents from my Tizianna's kitchen pulled me from the vineyard."

He kissed Nonna and me on the cheek and went to wash up. As we three sat at the patio table with the delicious chicken, salad, and polenta, we caught Nonno up with the family news. He just smiled and said, "This wedding will be grand! This is why we have the patio!"

That Thursday, Susanna and I walked arm in arm through the streets of Genoa from the train to the arts center. We found the room where she was to report and then went out to rest at a nearby café until her audition. Half an hour before her appointment we returned to the arts center. Susanna prefers to speak little and mentally go over her moves before an audition. So, we sat in meditative silence until we heard, "Susanna Valli!"

About half an hour later, Susanna re-entered the hallway with a smile on her face. "I did my best. We'll see. They said I'll know in two days as the auditions finish tomorrow at noon."

We met Nonna Mikaela at a small café near her apartment. There she sat, well into her eighties, with a beauty that seemed to become more intense as she aged. Her golden brown skin was without a wrinkle and her salt and pepper hair splayed out like a crown behind a colorful ribbon. She raised her arm when she caught sight of us so we could locate her, as if her regal presence didn't stand out!

As we all enjoyed a bowl of pasta and fish, Susanna and I caught Nonna Mikaela up on our news. She glowed in joy from our happiness. Nonna Mikaela exuded a wisdom and peace that struck all who were graced by her conversation. Susanna and I have always cherished our talks with her.

Nonna Mikaela urged Susanna to contact her if she needed anything during her life in Genoa. After many hugs and much encouragement from Nonna Mikaela, we parted. Susanna and I headed back to the train station.

The next afternoon Susanna heard that she'd been accepted into the dance company. Her papà and Catrina cooked a special dinner for her of her favorite white fish. Later that evening she and I celebrated together at a nearby café in the piazza. With less than a week until the arrival of Luciano and Flavio, and with the news of Susanna's new career, we were particularly animated. The people at the piazza and the sound of the water as it ran off the fountain tiers seemed to emit sparkles that accentuated our joy.

Thursday of the next week Flavio and Luciano arrived. They went directly from the train station to their jobs as they had work appointments. Flavio, Luciano, Susanna, Daniele, and Catrina were all to have dinner with us that evening. Susanna arrived a little early and assisted us in the kitchen. Mamma baked a fresh fish Papà had bought off his fisherman soccer buddy that morning. She used a fennel stuffing. The smell was warm and almost sweet. We had rice that I must say was cooked to perfection in spices and vegetable broth by yours truly. It was a perfect flavorful companion for the fish and greens. I was beside myself in anticipation to see Luciano. When both men walked through the door, Susanna and I were like two young comets in flying ecstasy towards their magnetic pull.

In a few minutes Daniele and Catrina arrived with fresh succulent figs. The incredible food fueled our conversation about the day and about our futures. After the meal, the men, led by Papà, did the kitchen cleanup. Papà made his coffee and I made tea. Susanna and Mamma put out some fruit.

As Luciano and Flavio arrived back at the patio table, they announced, "We want a double wedding."

We all laughed at these silly wonderful men. Susanna and I had presented the idea to them separately by phone. They both had positive responses, but said they would speak with us more on the weekend. This was such a fun way for the guys to acknowledge their decision. Our double wedding was on!

Soon, after our hot drinks, Daniele, Catrina, Flavio, and Susanna said their goodnights. Each couple left arm in arm for their own slow romantic walk towards Daniele's flat. Flavio would return eventually and sleep here. Luciano and I decided on a short ride to the river on the scooter. Mamma and Papà sat down to a movie.

At the river we parked the scooter and sat on a stone bench nearby. "Francesca," began Luciano, "the time frame when I begin up here is short. They want me to start in two weeks," he said as he turned his torso, laid his head in my lap, kissed my hand, and held it to his chest.

"Wow, that's fast. What do you think?" I queried.

He sat up, but kept my hand.

"Well, I would like to marry soon. The double wedding is fine as long as it is soon," Luciano clarified.

"Okay. How about a wedding in four weeks and a request for two days off after the wedding? We could do the day and night after the wedding at the sea. Then we could go to a mountain cabin for the next two days and night. What do you think?"

"I think it sounds great."

"You know that Nonna Tizianna and Nonno Angelo said that we are welcome to live at the farm. We can go out there this weekend so you can hear it from them yourself," I said.

"Can't wait," Luciano said as he took my face in his hands and brought his lips onto mine. The sound of a passing boat brought us back to our public location and we rose to return home for some rest.

The double wedding happened in four weeks as planned on a Saturday afternoon at Nonna Tizianna's farm. Nearby family and friends piled in with freshly cooked food and happy faces. The crowd from Genoa was Nonna Mikaela, Nonno Robert, Cugino Duccinio with his second wife and his son Tommaso with his family, Zio Pasquale, and Zia Andrea. Zia Margarita, Zio Josefa, Cugino Maximillian with his girlfriend, and Cugina Laura came from Naples along with Flavio's mamma, Patricia. Laura's boyfriend, now in Turino, also arrived. The Marcellis from Orvieto, of course, were there. The Allegrettis were not able to make it as they were on a visit to Roma to see grandchildren. From Barcelona came our American cousin Samuel and his family, as well as our cugino

Alfredo with his partner Antonio. The other family and friends in the States couldn't make it as international travel was expensive and required many arrangements. They sent us mountains of love by Skype.

There was a simple but large spread of food. We had solar roasted lamb, compliments of Zio Josefa, pasta with red sauce, salad, cheeses, and fruit. The fresh bread and the beautiful lemon wedding cake were ordered from the bakery. There was also bubbly mineral water, and, of course, the wonderful southern and northern wines. We hired two people to assist with the setup, food, and cleanup. Music was not an issue with us. We put on the recorded music but only after we had heard the beautiful accordion artistry of Nonna Tizianna.

A good friend of ours who was a priest came to bless our marriages. We had the marriage papers from the city court already. Mamma and Papà sang my favorite love ballad during our brief ceremony. It was right after our promises to each other. Lovely. The wedding continued with great levity. People danced and ate and visited and laughed. It was a good time.

Rather than remain at the party, as wonderful as it was to be with everyone, Luciano and I, as well as Flavio and Susanna, had other things on our minds. So, a couple of hours after sunset we changed into our casual clothes, kissed everyone good-bye, and headed for Genoa's coast. Flavio and Susanna planned to spend the next three days there, while Luciano and I would head up to the mountains the next day.

We stayed in a small family hotel at the sea. The view from our room of the night sea could not capture us for long. To me, Luciano was an incredible lover. He was energetic, patient, and creative. May I just say that I was in heaven that night as I lay with Luciano in the room by the sea.

The days at the sea and the mountain cabin gave us time to walk, talk, and dream our intentions into a shared reality. We savored each other and gently embraced each other's dreams. The beauty of those days has nestled into my heart forever. I can't justify by pen the depth of my loving and expansive feelings for Luciano, myself, and our future.

BACK TO LUCIANO AND I AS PREGNANT MAN AND WIFE

So now you know, dear reader, how Luciano and I came to be man and wife and live on this beautiful farm. I had known Luciano all my life. Who knew that it would blossom into this? Certainly not me, consciously.

As I sat this evening on the patio, I became aware of a tremor that actually moved the tree's soft branches. I looked towards the stone shed that had a soft light on at the window.

I guess Luciano found his paints after he did the evening chores, I mused.

Just then, Luciano marched across from the shed to the patio and extended his hand to me, "Francesca, come and see my latest project!"

I laughed and jumped up from my memories as I extended my hand to his. And off we stepped towards the shed.

COUSIN ANDREW'S VISIT TO TURINO

Later that week I stopped by my folks' after my two mid-week classes at the dance school. The Sunday before, Luciano and I cooked for Mamma, Papà, Nonno Angelo, Nonna Tizianna, Nonno Robert, and Nonna Mikaela. Mamma and Papà had picked my nonni up at the train from Genoa that morning. It was not an unusual pattern for them to go back and forth to each other's houses. My nonni enjoyed each other. So we were able to have our usual Sunday meal together with the three generations of both my parents. Luciano and I served chicken in a savory sauce over rice. Olives and bread with olive oil were on the side. Then we told them our great news of our pregnancy. As one can imagine, the kitchen exploded with joy, glasses chimed in toasts, and both Luciano and I were hugged, kissed, and patted on the cheeks. We felt special and like we were a part of something very old and unbroken.

So, when I arrived at my Mamma's mid-week, it was no surprise that she greeted me from the patio with, "So how's Italy's most beautiful mamma?"

"Tired, but good, Mamma," I responded as I blew her a kiss.

Mamma then continued to arrange potted herbs and dust the wind chimes on the patio. Nonna Mikaela was there for the day and busy with the seasoning of her famous chili. Nonno Robert had stayed on the farm to help Nonno Angelo with the post-harvest machinery repairs. I think that's where I get my love of tinkering with machines. Anyway, back to my visit at my Mamma's house.

I approached Nonna Mikaela, kissed her cheek, and said, "What's going on with Mamma? Usually she relaxes after her students."

"Well, I think it has to do with a visitor tonight," she responded while she stirred the delicious chili.

Papà closed the front door on his last student for the day, approached the kitchen and said, "Hey Francesca, how is my expectant figila?"

"A little tired, but happy, Papà," I responded without hesitation.

"Mmmm, that smells so good, Mamma Mikaela," Papà said as he peered into the pot with his hand lightly on Nonna Mikaela's shoulder.

"It really does smell fabulous," I added.

"Well, your papà requested this meal, but I don't think he will mind if I give you a little now to give you strength for the bike ride home," my nonna offered.

"The cook's the boss," Papà retorted as Nonna dished up a bowl of steaming hot chili over some rice for me.

Mamma came in from the patio. She hugged me around the neck and kissed my cheek.

"I got sidetracked with this delicious chili. But, what is this about a guest soon?" I queried.

"Your cousin Andrew was in Barcelona at your cousin Samuel's this past week while he attended and presented at a conference. Samuel had spoken to your papà about this visit, but it was a surprise for me until this morning. Now, he's on his way here!"

"Oh, Mamma, I'm so happy! It's been a long time since you were together, right?"

"Yes, over five years. The last time we were together was when I took you to the States when you were seventeen."

"I could never forget that great trip! Is Beverly coming?" I asked. "I really liked her."

"Yes, she is," Mamma replied.

"Papà, have you met Beverly?"

"Yes, over ten years ago when they were in Barcelona," Papà responded. "It was the first time I met them. The trip was short for them as it was for business only. Andrew presented at a conference. However, we had a great couple of days with them at Samuel's. This time they'll be here for over a week, so they have time for us to show them around this part of Italy," Papà added.

"Where was I during their first visit?" I queried.

"You were at the farm in Naples for a two-week, early summer vacation trip," Mamma responded.

"Oh, yes, I remember that vacation. Great fun as Zio Josefa sheared his sheep then."

Then Mamma said, "Come over tomorrow night, Francesca, with Luciano and your nonni."

"Absolutely. Thanks. I wouldn't miss their visit for the world. Mamma, why don't I come early and help you and Papà with the dinner?" I offered. "Luciano can bring the nonni," I added.

"Okay. Thanks. See you then," Mamma said as she smiled at me.

"See you tomorrow," I said as I kissed everyone good-bye."

"Well, I'm off to the train station to pick up Andrew and Beverly!" said Papà.

We left out the front door together.

As I got on my scooter I said, "Greet all of them for me, Papà. Until tomorrow!"

"Soon, then, Francesca," he said as he waved and got into the car.

Dear reader, please forgive this pause before we go back to the festivities with my cousin Andrew and Beverly. But, I am excited to tell you about my trip to America at age seventeen where I met and visited them and Uncle Mark for the first time. There I heard amazing stories about my mamma's people in America. I am so proud to let you in on the secrets of these valiant people. And I want you to know about them before we celebrate together in Turino at my mamma and papà's.

MY TRIP TO AMERICA AT SEVENTEEN

"Do you have everything, ladies?" my papà asked as he packed some hot tea for us to have at the airport and some coffee for himself for the fairly short drive to the airport. We were flying to Madrid, and then directly to Atlanta. I was now seventeen and had completed my exams successfully for the university. This was a trip promised me as long as I can remember. Actually I was beyond excitement, as this America seemed a place bigger than life and a little scary.

"Yes, Papà," I answered. "I will miss you so much!" I said as I planted a big kiss on his cheek. One couldn't help but miss this man who was like a quiet rock to my mamma and me.

After many hugs and kisses with my papà we headed towards security and then boarded the plane to Madrid. The connection out of Madrid was on time so the layover was only one hour. I settled into a seat between my mamma and a stranger. My emotions were high. The jet could hardly move fast enough across the ocean for me. Despite my impatience, the flight went quickly and land we did, in America!

It was a hot southern day in Atlanta when we arrived. This was the home of my mamma's cousin Andrew and his family. His wife, Beverly, picked us up at the airport. Beverly was then in her fifties as were my mamma and Andrew. Her complexion was clear and a honey brown color. Beverly wore her dark brown hair in long twists that piled beautifully on her head. She was tall, but had substance to her long curvaceous figure. Her form was much like mine, my mamma's, and Nonna Mikaela's, only taller. Beverly had a quiet manner. But as a professional, she didn't hesitate to maintain her authority as teacher in her classroom of fourth graders. She also stood her ground as the only female of her household. During our visit, I admired the peaceful smoothness with which she organized herself and her household.

On the car ride from the airport, which was about forty minutes in city traffic, she asked about Mamma's students and also about Mamma's thoughts on the European distribution modalities of her music. She also asked about my career goals. In addition, Beverly entertained us with funny stories about her students. I enjoyed her graciousness.

On American soil for less than two hours, I already felt at home in this busy, almost out of control energy that oozed from the American streets.

As we emerged from the car with our bags, Andrew came out onto the front porch. Before he could descend the porch stairs, Mamma was before him. She kissed his cheeks and they held foreheads together for a few moments. Then he opened his arms to me.

"Come here, little Francesca, now a grown woman!" Andrew exclaimed as he embraced me.

"Let's go inside," said Andrew, "and get under the cool fans while we have some lemonade."

We filed inside. I never forgot the peacefulness in Andrew's eyes. His eyes seemed to say, "Whatever goes on, there is always a place for peace." He stood six feet tall, which is average for the men in my great-uncle Mark's family. His long limbs and thin but muscular frame gave the illusion of even greater height. Andrew had very dark and even-toned black skin that shouted out royalty. At seventeen, I was totally in awe of his handsomeness.

We settled on the couch and chairs with our lemonade. Mamma began, "I owe both of you so much. Our abuelita Temia was at peace her last couple of years here. When her Alanzo was gone, you folks were here to take her in. It made it feasible for my mom and Uncle Mark to get to her in her last days. I know it meant a lot to her to be surrounded by your love."

"It meant a lot to us, too," said Andrew.

"Besides," said Beverly, "I think she liked the hint of tropical here, given her love for Jamaica."

"Her what?" I interjected.

My mamma said, "Your great-abuelita Temia was in her upper forties when she went to Jamaica for the first time. She fell in love with the country and convinced herself she was in love also with a man she met. Her children were grown and had their own lives. Temia felt lonely. She had tired of big city life, and also of the tunnel vision demonstrated by her beloved medical profession regarding their pharmaceutical and corporate insurance arrangements. So, at that time, this man and Jamaica seemed to be for her a good life."

Mamma continued. "Well, it didn't turn out how she imagined it would. She got her medical license there, sold all her belongings stateside, and with her children in attendance, married her new lover in Jamaica. Soon she got her Jamaican citizenship and did her best to settle into life as a Jamaican. She loved many of the people she met, the culture, the air, the food, the water, and the plants. She was committed to her island life. But, the marriage soon fell apart as Temia's husband was committed only to his ability to have many women. Yet, he was possessive of Temia, so she had to escape rather than openly leave. She returned to the states, divorced, and began life anew. For a short time she did hospital medicine, but then chose to teach in a community college. She loved the students at the college. She also maintained her connection with Jamaica through her Jamaican friends. Those relationships blessed her for her entire life."

"Over a decade later, our abuelita Temia went on to find love in the desert and its mountains. Only death stopped her earthly quest to live each day in love and balance," Mamma concluded.

"Oh, so the desert was not her only big move," I surmised.

"That is so true," said Andrew. "Francesca, would you like to hear about Abuelita Temia's family?"

"Cousin Andrew tells them the best, as he has remembered the details," added my mamma.

"Let's continue on!" I exclaimed excitedly, as I settled under the fan with my lemonade. I want to hear all about my American people.

TWO AMERICAN PATRIARCHS' JOURNEYS

Andrew began, "Your great-great-great-grandfathers underwent incredibly long journeys. They were journeys of distance and emotion. One of those great-grandfathers on your grandma Mikaela's side named Jake walked away from his life as a sharecropper on the same land his parents had worked as slaves. His family had been free in the continent of Africa but then enslaved in America under the most inhumane inter-generational slavery known to man. It lasted for nine generations. He was the first generation free.

"Although it was not slavery, Jake lived in the brutal post-slavery soci-etal caste of sharecroppers. He had a big risk of being hung if he left the land on which he sharecropped. He planned and waited for the right time and then left one night. Many of Jake's relations during slavery had attempted to run away from the plantation. Some had been successful and many had been tortured or brutally killed in their attempt. Jake was determined to make it away from the south and his confinement in the sharecropper system.

"He did not leave alone. He took with him his wife and two small children. It was more difficult for him to run with his family, but he could not risk a return trip. Clan vigilantes would be looking for him to return if his family was left. Jake was successful in his escape from his servitude. He and his family made it up north thanks to his brilliance and the help of friends and family along the way. He worked as a fish vendor and eventu-ally set up a little fish shop in the northern city of his freedom.

"The details of Jakes trip north were never passed down because it would have put the people who had helped in danger. Sometimes, dear Francesca, the silence that we carry within us is more powerful than the story."

My eyes were big as I realized what memories were packed into my bones.

Then Andrew continued, "I was told more details of the journey of another of your great-great-great-grandfathers. His journey was one of danger, but every step was not wrought with the possibility of death as was Jake's. His name was Michael and he began his journey around 1893. This is how Abuelita Temia told the story."

The air smelled of the soil pregnant with sprouted seeds. The sun was warm on Michael's back as he set off down the road towards town. The northern Midwest fields were covered with the fresh green of new plants. Michael saw the beauty, but his focus was ahead. In town he was to meet the Duffy family. He was to assist them with their move to a large northern town two days away by horse and cart. He was strong and reliable and had only himself with a small satchel of belongings. Mr. Duffy needed another man's assistance on the roads. Michael would provide that assistance, as the roads were rough with both occasional washouts and occasional thieves.

Michael was grateful to get a ride to the city where he would attach himself to any work team that headed west. He left his mother and three sisters on the farm. They would be fine. Together they had finished the spring planting. Shortly they would have fresh food. Already there were wild greens to cook. And the chickens were laying many eggs in the warm spring weather. They would be without him, he hoped, for only a few months. He would find a place of steady work out west and send for them. Michael was a man at eighteen and with a clear head about his responsibility.

As a youth, Michael had walked into town from the farm every day to attend school. He had completed all the school levels available to him there. He read avidly.

With equal enthusiasm, he worked the farm every minute that there was daylight before and after school.

His father had walked away a few years before Michael turned eighteen. Michael never knew why or to where. Michael came home one day from classes and his father was gone. His sister told him that he had just left. Michael had never felt attached to him. His books, farm chores, mother, and sisters gave Michael satisfaction with life. His father seemed to always sit in a shadow or work in another section of the field. Then when Michael was fifteen, his father just walked away from the family.

Over the next couple of years, Michael saw that the farm could barely feed them. He wanted more security for his mother, sisters, and himself. Thus, with a great sense of responsibility and adventure, Michael set off westward.

The Duffy family and Michael reached the northern city safely. Michael said his good-byes to the Duffy family.

Michael had an open but confident way about him that allowed him to easily win the respect of people. His smile was warm and his eyes firm but kind. He stood an eighth of an inch short of six feet. He had black hair and black eyebrows. His nose was arched and his complexion olive. Very handsome. He was called Blackie by the men he met on his travels. Michael was an intense listener and a man of few but well placed words.

Soon he learned from other men in the city that there was work as phone linemen. They were moving the lines westward. So, immediately Michael presented himself for lineman work. Michael loved the challenge of work at great heights. He worked with precision and ease at the top of the poles. The work fascinated him. Michael moved west as the line work moved west. He saved every penny of his pay that was not needed for food or a night's cot. Every few weeks he wired some of this money to his mom and sisters.

The line work soon brought him to the foothills of the great Rocky Mountains. There the work stopped. The winds began to cool as winter approached in the mountains. Michael reasoned that if he stayed in the town at the foothills of the mountain range, he would spend all his earnings to survive the winter. Michael had heard of the routes to the Native American bands in the mountains. He headed up to those routes. He watched for members of the tribe as he continued to move along the trails. He knew they would soon approach him. In a couple of days, as he cooked over a small fire the fish he had speared moments ago, he was approached. Michael shared his meal with the three men. They then welcomed him to winter camp with their band.

Michael felt at home with the band. He did his part on the hunts, but always followed their lead. Michael respected the long years of training of the other men and followed carefully their maneuvers. He had two grandparents from tribes further east. Some of their ways to pray, socialize, hunt, and prepare the food were similar to this band's. But, there were differences. And he lacked their depth of information. So with mutual respect, Michael and the other men did the work of winter survival for the band.

The women he met amazed Michael. They had the strength and fortitude that he admired in his mother and sisters. Michael was attracted to a daughter of one of the elders. She was, to him, exquisitely beautiful with her gentle eyes and long black neatly braided hair. She moved swiftly and with grace. She always took opportunities to laugh and be happy. Sometimes they would speak together as a stew cooked or as people gathered in the warm dwellings to share stories at the end of the day.

She explained her obligation to continue with the band northward when the spring thaw arrived. Michael understood. He would have joined her, but for his obligation to his family. She also understood his obligation to continue west to provide for his mother and sisters. The band members noticed the envelope of love that surrounded the young couple. But they said nothing.

Despite the strength of their feelings, Michael and the elder's daughter never consummated their love. Neither could justify that with a known separation soon. This increased the respect of the band towards Michael, as a baby to feed would be another burden for the band.

As spring arrived, the band moved north and Michael west. He left some of his money with the band and lots of his heart.

When Michael arrived at the western border of the Rocky Mountains, he came across a lumber camp and took up work with them. His strength, accuracy, and comfort with heights enabled him to master the job of topping the trees before their major fall. Once again he worked hard and saved his money. He continued to move west as he was told of other lumber camps westward in need of more labor.

In a couple of months he thought he had found a community near a large river that would socially support his mother and sisters and financially support him. Its logging business thrived. There was a coach route between the town and the city near his mom and sisters. Thus, he sent word for his mother and sisters to come out by stagecoach. He wired their tickets and in mid-summer his family arrived.

He settled them into a small log house above the spring floods of the river. His eldest sister found a husband and the younger sister found work. Michael's mother found peace of mind.

Unfortunately, the nearby lumber camps were soon not able to support the financial needs of Michael and his family. Michael heard that there was work on the west coast docks that paid well. So, he rode his newly acquired horse on the trail through the Cascade mountain range to the coast. It took a few days, but they passed without incident. Mountain survival was an integral part of his set of skills. Upon arrival at the coast, he found work on the docks immediately. Within a year, he bought a small house not far from the docks in Seattle. He sent for his mom and one unmarried sister to join him in the house. They were excited to arrive at the coast and settled easily into the little house.

Michael felt that his mother was settled. His sister would also soon be settled as she had fallen in love and would marry within the month. Her husband was from a neighboring tribe and she went happily to live with him on a nearby island.

So, now Michael was open to find love again. And find it he did. But this time, rather than in the mountains, it was near the sea. He fell in love with a beautiful but opinionated waitress down by the docks. She was as light as he was dark. She was as short as he was tall. She was as stubborn as he was convicted. And, she was engaged to another. But that was no obstacle to Michael. He convinced her to marry him instead. That was the last time he was able to change a direction she had set her mind to. That did not matter to Michael. He remained happy in their life together.

"And that's one story of your great-great-great-grandfather Michael," concluded Andrew.

"Oh, please, just one more, please!"

"Okay, a short story about your great-great-great-grandparents Bill and May," agreed Andrew. Michael was Abuelita Temia's paternal grandfather and Bill and May were Abuelita Temia's maternal grandparents.

LIFE ALONE

During the lives of Bill and May, it was a big feat for them to grab even a morsel of love for themselves. But they did. Here is what happened.

Bill met May for the first time at a small midwestern town dance. She had shown up late. Her dress was plain. But the way she moved her delicious hips to the music made the plain dress unimportant to Bill. Her dark, thick, wavy, long hair and her beautiful, full lips added to Bill's total absorption with her presence. Bill was usually focused on his own survival and didn't find time to pay much attention to women. But this young lady pulled him out of his worries. Soon he developed his courage and with quiet confidence, he strode his tall, strong frame over to May. She stood among three other young women. He held out his hand directly to her and said, "May I have this dance?"

May looked up in surprise and said, "Just one."

"I'm not greedy," Bill replied.

But he was and he asked for a second dance. During the second dance May said, "I have to go."

"Hopefully, I'll see you next Saturday, if I'm home from a run," Bill responded.

Bill worked as a fireman on a steam engine that ran through town. He doubted he would see May again. It didn't seem to him that she got to the dances often. But he couldn't keep this feisty, beautiful, and maybe a little mean, young woman out of his mind as he sat in the coal bin by the engine fire.

In a few weeks, they did meet at the dance again. Bill blurted out during their first dance, "Let's take a short walk."

He felt driven to get to know May a little more and hopefully answer some of the mystery about her person.

They walked along the river nearby. Bill found out that May did not live with her family. Her mother and stepfather had given her to a well-to-do family when she was seven, and she'd been their unpaid servant since then. She did their housework, laundry, and meals. She also worked their garden. She had food and a small bed in an alcove off the kitchen.

Bill suspected that her stepfather had received a payment, but who knew?

Bill went to the dance whenever he could and felt disappointed if May was not there. When May was there, they danced, walked around outside, and talked. May could only risk an hour away from her alcove at night before it might be discovered that she was gone. So their time together was short, which increased its intensity.

May liked Bill. He worked. He was quiet. May wanted to be close with Bill. She wanted to feel a flesh and bones presence of someone who really cared for her.

At home, if one could use such a term, May's human contact was in the form of loud orders by the woman of the house. The teenage boys of the house added their particular attention to May. It was mostly with their hands as they groped under her dress between her legs as she stood washing the dishes. These encounters filled May with anger and panic. She stood motionless, almost frozen, as their hands groped. One day, she promised herself, she would grab a dish from the dishpan and break it over their heads. But, she never did.

As the weather warmed, Bill and May were able to linger longer outside of the dance. Bill knew a grassy spot hidden by some bushes near the river down from the church cemetery. This became their oasis. By mid-summer, May was pregnant. Bill, five years her senior, married her and took her away to another spot on the railroad line. May, now fifteen, was as free as her life could offer.

Bill was glad to have a family. They moved into a small house a short walk to the railroad station.

May knew how to make four walls into a cozy home. But sadly, despite his pride in having a family, Bill didn't quite know how to embrace the domestic lifestyle. As a youth, he had never known his parents and never had a permanent home. He was told that he was Indian and Irish and had been abandoned. He remembers short stays with various families. By his early teens he struck out on his own and did odd jobs for money, food, and a temporary place to lay his head. He supplemented his diet with fish from streams and "stray" chickens.

Now at twenty, he had a railroad job. He could provide for himself and May. But, his time at home was awkward for him. It felt odd to have one place as home. The irregular hours and many days away on the railroad didn't help his adjustment to a home life. Bill adapted as best he could. He would listen to ball games, grow a garden, and fuss with May when he was home. Unfortunately, he didn't have the skills to support the romance part of their relationship.

For that matter, neither did May. Their relationship was challenged further by the stillbirth of their baby girl. Neither of them were able to heal their grief. They just stuffed it down into their hearts next to countless other pains already accumulated in their young lives. This left little space for their love to grow.

But they still related physically. They also held a semblance of respect for each other. Soon they had a boy. He was strong and healthy. Then, some years later, they had a girl.

Andrew took a break from telling the story. "Francesca, that was your great-great-grandmother. We actually knew her before she passed on," Andrew said while he looked at Alessia. Then he continued with the story.

Bill was dedicated to his railroad job. He worked himself up to engineer over the years. He was proud to have a regular paycheck. In addition, he made bootleg in the basement to supplement the family finances. Guests would show up and soak the floors and furniture with their drunken whiskey fights. Bill stopped the moonshine business because of the chaos it attracted.

When he arrived home on payday, Bill would cook huge pots of food over a fire in the back yard of the house. He fed all those in the area who showed up with a bowl or a pot. Not having known any of his people, Bill would say, "One of them might be my family." So to care for his possible extended family, Bill cooked for many.

As the children grew, Bill and May were no longer intimate. It was the result of a gradual process. In the early years of their marriage, Bill would invite her to have sex. But May had become disinterested. They moved into separate bedrooms. Bill occasionally demanded sex. Soon, however, he stopped the demanded encounters. Their once youthful love had morphed into their own version of domestic tolerance.

May worked hard in the house. She took in laundry and sewed for others. She sewed for her family. May was most famous for her delicious food and her love to gossip. It made her feel important to tell the business of others. Unfortunately, it also made her feel important to fuss with Bill and ridicule and beat her beautiful daughter.

Most of Bill's time was spent on the railroad. Eventually, he met a woman further down the railroad line. He loved the ease and peace he felt in her presence. But he chose not to leave his family. He knew he was the only buffer his daughter had against her mother. No one knew how often he visited his love further down the railroad line. But visit he did.

Bill had a heart attack one day. He was in his early sixties. The ambulance took him to the hospital and there he died.

Bill had a deep part of him where he felt lost. But Bill's empty spaces did not impede what love he had to be present for his children and grandchildren, so the next generations could propel forward.

BACK TO MY TRIP TO AMERICA

"Well, there you have it, Francesca, some American stories."

"Thanks, Cousin Andrew. I hope there is time for more this visit," I added.

"I am sure there will be," Andrew assured.

"Tell me, Andrew," Mamma asked, "how are Uncle Mark and Aunt Natalie? Are they settled in Louisiana?"

"Well, Dad is still in his country spot in Louisiana. Once in a while Dad and Mom leave the countryside and go into New Orleans for the restaurants and music. There is a train they can catch into the city now. But, even that is getting laborious for them. Dad loves the quiet of fishing in his pond and the success of his Rib Shack off the expressway. However, I think we have them convinced to move by us here. Mom would love the social life here in the Atlanta area. And we do have a well-stocked fishpond close."

"What about Uncle Mark's famous love for the kitchen? And his lack of love to clean up his dirty pots and pans afterward!" Mamma asked.

Mamma and Andrew laughed.

"Ah, you remember well, Alessia! Well, he has mellowed a bit and does clean up better at the end. He had no choice if he wanted Mom off his case!"

"Later in the day when it's cooler, I would love to show you the spot we have in mind for them. There is a group of single-level townhouses in this neighborhood. We've had our bid accepted on one that was for sale. It will give them their own space, but we are close to socialize together. We've got plenty of room here for both our visitors and theirs to stay," said Andrew.

"Oh! This sounds great! How soon do you think they will come here?" Mamma queried.

"I hope within the next four months. It's hard for Dad to leave the Rib Shack. It's expanded to roasted corn, peppers, squash, and sweet and Irish potatoes. They also keep a big pot of beans, and greens on the side grill that shares space with the tortillas and toasted French bread. His business is very busy. This is a dream come true for him.

"Remember, Alessia, how many years he worked that county job for the financial stability of our family? He enjoyed the work in the community, but the county politics were rough. Sometimes he was grumpy after a long day, but he never complained. He carried it as an honor to take care of his family," Andrew continued thoughtfully.

"Remember the great meals we had off his smoker in the back yard?" asked Alessia?

"And remember when as a little kid he gave you the big job to carry the burgers on the plate from the smoker to the table and they slipped off into the grass?" continued Alessia.

Both Alessia and Andrew broke out into another long bout of laughter.

"Yes! I lost points towards my male right-of-passage that day!" said Andrew through his tears of laughter. "Well," he continued, "it's understandable why Dad slows at the thought of leaving his business. But, as you know, he's a realist. He's soon eighty and Mom's not far behind. He wants a little more down time. So, he'll sell the Rib Shack soon. He has kept his prices down and still has made a profit. The business has an excellent reputation not only for the food, but also for the management style. He'll sell the business easily and will make a profit from the sale."

"That's good news. By the way, where's Martin?" Mamma asked.

Both Beverly and Andrew laughed. "One guess! He's out at his grandfather's for the summer. He works at the Rib Shack. In the fall he'll be back here for his final year at the university," answered Beverly.

"Great!" I interjected. "I'll get to see him when we visit Uncle Mark!"

"Absolutely," said Mamma as she turned to me and smiled.

"It is hard for me to imagine that he's in his final year at the university. What does he plan to do?" Mamma asked.

Andrew and Beverly responded in unison, "Music, music, and music!"

"I'm glad. He was always attached to some instrument or other every time I saw him on my visits. Let's see. He was with either a flute, or the piano, or the drum, or with his own vocal cords," Mamma remembered.

"Speaking of musicians, how is Dominico and all the family?" asked Andrew.

"While they continue to catch up, would you like to see the garden?" Beverly quietly offered to me.

How did she recognize a fellow lover of the earth? I mused to myself.

"Yes!" I responded as I rose to stretch my legs. Her garden had both some curved border beds and a planted center circular garden. The plants burst forth with beautiful colors much like our flower and vegetable gardens in Italy. She interspersed her flowers, herbs, and vegetables together.

"I love your companion planting," I commented.

"Ah, you noticed. Thanks for that. Many people don't know about companion planting and think that maybe some of the seeds came up by mistake!"

We both laughed.

"What would you like to pick for dinner? Your cousin will grill us some free-range turkey burgers. He has a trick to keep them moist. What do you want with them?" Beverly asked.

"I love your yellow tomatoes, zucchini squash, and onions. Oh! And your greens are lovely!" I commented.

"Andrew loves to grill the squash and onions. Like his dad, he loves the grill. We'll toss some greens with the yellow tomatoes, green onions, garlic, and fresh farm cheese. We'll dress it with olive oil and fresh squeezed lemon. How does that sound, Francesca?"

"Delicious!"

"Then I think we have dinner planned," concluded Beverly.

We retrieved a basket from a nearby cement bench and harvested the dinner.

"Let's go in and see if they've caught up enough to think food!" Beverly said as we mounted the stairs onto the back porch that led into the sitting room-kitchen combination space.

We put the basket on the counter and followed the voices of Andrew and Alessia. They were in Andrew and Beverly's study that was adjacent to the sitting area. It had large windows that overlooked the back garden on one side and a row of pines on the other. Their property was concise and beautifully landscaped.

Beverly's desk was filled with lesson plans. Andrew's desk and drawing table were laden with sketches for highly energy efficient renovations of structures that already existed. He was particularly skilled at the transformation of buildings to accommodate the needs of the present community. In addition, he was known for his ability to offer his clients three or four different options to make their present building more energy efficient and green in its structure. His creativity, frugalness, and the appropriateness of his plans won him great respect.

He was able to support his family despite the fact that he turned down many lucrative jobs that would not have supported the earth's sustainability. For Andrew, the decision to protect the planet was a no-brainer for his brilliant, calm, and sensitive mind.

When Beverly and I entered the study, they had just decided to go out to the shed to the right of the garden. We shared a look that said, "We'll hold our appetites a few more minutes." So all four of us trotted off to the shed. It was mostly glass on three sides. Inside there were a few bold yet soft in line abstract wooden statues of great beauty. They were only about two feet at the most.

"These are made entirely of scrap woods," Andrew explained.

They had a curve and tuck that brought both rest and joy to the beholder.

"These are beautiful, Cousin Andrew!" I exclaimed. "I just love them."

"Good," he said as he placed a beautiful piece in my hands, "I've made one just for you."

"These are his passion," Beverly added. "If ever I wonder where he has disappeared to, I just need to look out here."

"It's a beautiful passion," I said. "This is lovely. Thank you so much, Cousin Andrew. I am thrilled to have a piece of your work. How special," I added softly as I held and gazed upon my precious gift.

"Come, let's get this food on!" said Andrew as he put his arm around my shoulders.

I reached up and planted a kiss on his cheek. Then we all went inside to prepare the vegetables and patties for the grill. Andrew suggested the type of cut for the vegetables before he went to work on the sauce for the turkey patties.

"So what are your plans for the rest of your visit in the States?" asked Beverly as she turned her head to me while we worked at the counter.

"Well, we plan to see Great-Uncle Mark, and of course, Martin. The last time I saw Uncle Mark was when I was thirteen and he came to Barcelona to visit Samuel, Claudia, and their daughter Teresa."

"You are a lovely lady. Uncle Mark will be excited to see you so grown up!" said Beverly.

"After that we will stop in Philadelphia," added Mamma. "We'll spend a couple of days with my friend Perla and her family. They moved to Philadelphia from Chicago about fifteen years ago."

"Beverly," my mamma added. "I would love for you and Andrew to visit us. Any architectural meetings in our neck of the woods coming up? An Italian vacation awaits you at our place anytime."

"Thanks. I'm sure something will happen to send us there, and I hope it's soon!" said Beverly.

"I hope so too," said Mamma as she smiled at Beverly.

We ate in the late afternoon on the outside patio in the shade. The meal was sumptuous. The breeze kept away the bugs and gave a reprieve from the humid southern heat. We ate, sipped ginger beer, and talked amicably. We talked of family, art, education, and more family. As the sun set we went inside and cleaned up the kitchen together. When we had put away the last clean dish, Andrew made some popcorn and went outside to light the citronella lanterns. We sat on lounge chairs with our bowls of popcorn and, in the flickering light of the lanterns, my mamma told the family stories, as I had requested. These are the Temia stories that my mamma and Andrew told until our yawns replaced the dialogue and we shuffled off to bed for a sound sleep.

My mamma began, "Temia, called Abuelita, was the shared abuelita of myself, Andrew, and Samuel. Our abuelita has told us many American family stories over the years."

"Mamma, I remember Abuelita from our Skypes with her. She made me laugh because when I tried to teach her Italian phrases she said them with a Spanish accent."

"Yes, Francesca, that's our Abuelita Temia."

"Mamma, I remember she had salt and pepper curly hair and green eyes. She was the color of the desert where she lived her later and happiest years. Her limbs were long and thin. She had a smile of great excitement whenever we Skyped and was always happy. I miss her now that she's gone."

"We all do," added Beverly.

"Well, here's the story of Temia's early years and what happened to her family members during that time," my mamma continued.

ABUELITA TEMIA STORIES

Temia was born by the great mountains. They were not rounded, calm, aged mountains. Rather, they were peaked, young mountains that gave off amazing energy and demanded awe from all who gathered at their base. They were much like our mountains near Turino. They embodied confidence as they poked at the Creator's heavens. But, they also offered the comfort of deep green shadows as the sun played over their pines.

Temia's birth home was on the plain that ran to the base of the mountains, as did her heart from the moment the mountains were in her consciousness. She was born of an unsettled yet strong mother (Mildred) who knew none of her father's (Bill) people and few of her mother's (May). Temia's mom had no idea what features her first child would possess. She would pray that they would somehow be acceptable to this Swedish-American church for which her husband was preacher. Temia's birth was not easy and as an infant she cried incessantly. To be held in the arms of her dancing mother or on the ample chest of her grandmother seemed to comfort her.

Temia remembered none of her agitation. Her first memories were as a toddler. They were of the musical howls of the wolves at night as they stood in the shadows on the great mountains. They soothed Temia. Nightly, she welcomed the wolves' song to lull her to sleep. As Temia grew, the mountains' strength nurtured her, as did the music of the wolves. She held these things in her soul forever.

It was to Temia's delight to imitate the wolf cries. By age three she was quite good at crooning with her distant night companions. Her ancestors had done this form of shape-shifting for centuries. Temia bonded with the wolf qualities of family, loyalty, and communication. These qualities became a part of her consciousness and helped her later with her adult decisions and challenges. But that was as close as she got to her indigenous heritage as a child.

As her father was a protestant pastor, Temia went to church regularly. She and her younger sister learned the church songs and crooned together as only a two- and a four-year-old can do. Temia felt a little awkward at first, but soon enjoyed the attention of singing in front of the small congregation. Temia would come off of her seat on a congregation bench in the front and carefully climb to the second step that led to the altar. That was as close as she was allowed to get to the altar. The altar was far too holy to stand any closer.

And there Temia would sing, "Jesus loves me this I know, for the bible tells me so. Little ones to Him belong. They are weak but He is strong."

She liked to sing because the sounds made the air seem sweet to her. The words themselves, however, held some confusion for Temia. She thought it strange that Jesus, who was God's Son, would consider her weak. She was of the mountains and knew that she was strong. God's Spirit was in the mountains, the pine trees, the rocks, the wolves, and IN HER! How could Jesus, who knew everything, see her as weak? Thus began Temia's spiritual unrest with official church dogma.

Because of the war and her father's obligation to it, Temia was forced to leave her mountains. She carried her mountains in her heart during all of her subsequent journeys.

Just a few months after she began to sing in church, Temia's family left the congregation and moved to a desert military camp. Her dad had been summoned to active duty from reserve status. Within six months of their move to the camp, her dad was then ordered to depart to Korea from a coastal base. He left the next morning to the coastal base. That afternoon Temia's mom put their belongings in a few boxes. She then drove Temia and her sister Maria to her in-laws' house in a large city on the northwest coast. They arrived late in the evening to this rainy city. Granma Lily and Granpa Michael had waited up for them. They hurried out of the house to the car as it pulled up in the dirt driveway along the small house. Granpa carried Maria and her mom led Temia by the hand into the house and up some narrow stairs to a small second floor room that housed an end table with a lamp and a double bed neatly made with white sheets. The girls were tucked under the sheets and went fast asleep.

The next night they did not go to bed at their usual time. Instead, their mom drove them to a very dark place by the foggy sea.

Their father was there. He got into the front seat of the car. He turned to the back seat and hugged both Temia and Maria and then held their mom a long while. Temia asked him if he wanted to go to the war. He said he wanted to serve his country. This did not make sense to Temia. How could her dad want to leave for any reason, she wondered? Maybe he wanted to leave because of her weakness that they sang about in church.

She felt confused about this war and she felt confused about her place in her dad's life. A bruise appeared on Temia's soul. That bruise was the first of many to guide her alchemy that became her redemption.

IT IS ALL IN HOW YOU LOOK AT IT

Temia's dad, Martin, left his children maybe four to seven times too many depending on when you were born. He left his wife, Mildred, according to her, uncountable times too many. Yet, no one spoke of it in that way. Except maybe Mildred, in the confines of the family house or apartment, when she was in a frustrated and dramatic mood.

Martin was driven by many things. Among them were compassion, creativity, and dedication to the Church, God, and those in need. There was no apparent order of importance to this list, but of course, if asked, it would be God. And since he believed that God was the source of everything, then I guess he was right that it would be God. Thus, this humble man became a man of frequent and long absences from his family that spread his presence over four continents.

But at this first of his many departures, this young family was cognizant only of this first difficult separation. They had to believe real hard that he would return. Well, the grown-ups did most of the belief work. Temia was just angry that he had left, and Maria's two-year-old mind was uncertain about it all.

Martin left at dawn the morning after their good-byes in the car. He sailed away in the Army vessel as a Chaplain Major to participate in the "Korean conflict." He was resolved to go. Martin wrapped himself in the cloak of duty and inhaled deeply the comfort of his deep faith in God. He did not allow himself to think of his desire to stay with his family. Martin focused on his presence with his fellow soldiers.

It would be years before he would be able to sail in the opposite direction towards home. He would bring back on that future sail a very thin body filled with unspeakable memories. Martin would also bring back a heart filled with love for the Korean people he met and for the soldiers, both alive and dead, to whom he had become a brother.

Upon his arrival in Korea, Martin was assigned to a base platoon of twenty-four men. It moved fluidly, as did many platoons, between the North Korean mountains and the DMZ line. This fluid movement was not then called guerilla warfare. It was called work behind enemy lines.

In addition to his base platoon, Martin served as Chaplain to many platoons. He would often leave to travel alone in the mountains to these various platoons.

Martin knew well the personalities of hundreds of men. He was vigilant as to when a man was on the verge of a mental break due to battle fatigue. The military did not then use sleep or mood alteration drugs to the extent that they would in later years. Rather, the mental health of the men was part of Martin's duty as Chaplain. His fellow soldiers gained strength from his visits. He listened to them with sincere presence. They knew that he understood their situation.

Martin was concerned about James in the platoon that he ventured towards on this certain day. He followed the narrow snowy mountain roads that were declared clear by the last intelligence reports. When he arrived at James's platoon he found the men exhausted from a recent successful ten-mile push through some uphill terrain. They reported to Martin signs of recent North Korean soldier camps in the area, but they had encountered none inhabited. Martin was relieved to find James stable but concerned about his daughter's hospitalization a couple of months ago for pneumonia. He had had no further word of his daughter's condition. Martin agreed to carry a letter from James to his family to be mailed when Martin next crossed the DMZ. Martin not only carried personal letters across the DMZ, but also messages to his superiors that were best not transmitted over the air.

Martin spent the night with James's platoon. Then in the morning's first light he ventured back towards his base platoon. He made it through the roads without incident. However, when he arrived to his home platoon, there was no life. All of his twenty-four fellow platoon comrades lay dead in the snow. Their bodies were filled with bullet holes, and covered with frozen blood. Martin immediately radioed for reinforcements. His emotions did not register his great loss immediately. It was beyond his comprehension the incessant need for humans to hunt and kill each other in these snow-filled frozen mountains, or anywhere for that matter.

Martin was familiar with violence. His ancestors were from the Moors of Southern Spain, Ireland, Scandinavia, and two different Native American tribes. He knew of the conflicts and cooperation between these people in general and his family members in particular that cohabited his body's genetics. But, his father had taught him by example to relate with respect to himself and to others of all ethnicities and socio-economic status.

The only violence acceptable to Martin's father was to hunt animals, only when necessary to eat and only with respect for the animal sought. It was a perspective Martin longed for in this present war culture of human slaughter. As a youth when the salmon ran he took his spear and agilely climbed up to the higher streams to hunt for his family's salmon. As taught by his father, he knew how to look out for the mountain cats in trees or on rocks. He knew how to share the stream with the bears. He knew how to take his fair share for his family and no more. He knew how to go home quickly so as not to attract predators to himself.

But now Martin found himself in a situation where he was bathed in human violence. His environment of intense loss of human life demanded Martin to feel and see it clearly. He fled into his faith to cope with his loss of twenty-four of his closest friends in the war. He prayed for his friends that lay dead before him. He prayed for the hundreds of people in the families of these twenty-four men whose lives would now be changed forever. And he prayed for himself. Within an hour reinforcements arrived and soon heavily armed vehicles headed down the mountains towards the DMZ with the bodies. Martin followed in his jeep. Soon he would again return up to the mountain platoons.

Many of the mountain roads Martin traveled between his assigned platoons were now being used by families fleeing southward from the North Korean soldiers, and Martin began encountering ill children left behind.

The first children he encountered were an ill four-year-old boy, a blind seven-year-old girl, and an eight-year-old girl with a deformed leg. He gathered the children into his jeep, fed them his rations, and took off for the DMZ line. There they were housed by Korean families who worked to help the US soldiers in the crude military outposts. More and more Martin heard from those arriving at the DMZ of other children left behind. He would immediately venture north upon hearing such reports. Somehow he made it past the lines of conflict to those locations and brought the children back in his jeep.

If the snow was too high he would hide the jeep under brush and snow and continue on foot to the reported location of the children. One such day he pushed through the snow to return to his hidden jeep from a location where he had found four children. In his arms he carried a thin two-year-old and three exhausted children trudged along close by his legs. Towards dusk they came upon a small abandoned building. Martin knew they would not be able to continue without some rest and food. It was now sunset. Fortunately the snow came down hard so their tracks were untraceable by any North Korean soldier brigades. Martin brought the children to the second floor of an abandoned building for safety from forest animals. The children ate some of his rations and they all drank some water. Then they all huddled together under Martin's blanket to use their body warmth to prevent frostbite.

But they did not rest alone. The immediate danger was not from animals or from the cold that night. Shortly after they snuggled under the blanket, a unit of North Korean soldiers entered the building. They bunked down on the first floor. Martin put his finger to his lips to signal the children not to make a sound. They did not. Shortly before dawn the North Korean soldiers moved out and onward. Martin and the children moved out at dawn when the soldiers were out of sight.

They reached Martin's jeep within an hour. As providence would have it, a US platoon was on the same road. They helped him release his jeep from the snow mound. Martin informed the platoon the movement direction of the North Korean soldiers. The platoon in turn informed Martin as to the best route to the DMZ. Martin and the children made it across the DMZ to the outpost safely that day.

The children were taken in by local families, fed, and bedded down on the warm charcoal heated floors. As the number of children Martin rescued grew, the local town people and the soldiers built a house for the many children that Martin brought across the DMZ. Eventually, they had to build three such small houses. Martin was able to transport over forty children to safety.

One of the children, called Jeannie, followed Martin everywhere in the compound. He enjoyed her persistent personality. Martin was deeply moved by this seven-year-old girl. After the war had ended and he received his orders to return to the States, she asked him to take her with him. Martin could not find the words to explain that one day she would regret the abandonment of her rich culture. He told her he would always remember her in his heart and would always keep her in his prayers. Somehow he felt his words and his departure did not meet the needs of this young child that would stay in Korea. Likewise he had known that his words and his departure to Korea had not met the needs of his two young daughters in the States.

"Mamma, what did happen to Martin's daughters back here in the States?" I asked.

Mamma continued.

MEANWHILE, MARTIN'S DAUGHTERS BACK IN THE STATES

Temia and Maria depended on each other for comfort during the war. Temia loved the steady companionship of Maria. Sometimes at night as they lay in bed, Temia would tell Maria stories in the dark. They always had happy endings. Usually Maria fell asleep before the end of the story. But, no matter. Temia knew she heard it in her dreams.

During the day they would be at each other's elbows for most of the time when Temia was not in school. Maria wasn't chatty like Temia. Temia was chatty even to grown-ups. She frequently got her mouth washed out with soap. That didn't look like fun to Maria. So, Maria avoided saying many things. However, one day in their grandparents' house Maria left a loud message. While Temia was at school, her granma (Lily) at the market, and her mom engaged in sorrowful thoughts, Maria made her move. She quietly opened a small carton of crayons and chose the orange one. She then toddled her two-year-old self up to Granma's precious, pale-pink flowered wallpaper in the dining room. At about the level of her two-year-old shoulders, Maria lifted up her small crayon-filled hand and drew a bright orange line from the junction of the sitting room along the dining room wall to the kitchen door. Maria left a message more permanent and louder than any voice in that house that harbored the three generations abandoned by the war. As she grew, Maria continued to be an artist, to be tuned in to her older sister, and to avoid verbalization of many things.

However, Abuelita Temia assured me when she spoke of her childhood that all was not sad during the war. There was food! The succulent food of Temia's family kept the family grounded, nourished, and appreciative. Temia loved to sit at the kitchen table and smell the aromas from her west-coast granma's stove. She remembered the transition from the wood burning to the electric stove that took place before the war. Both stoves were in the same spot and the kitchen table was under the window on the adjacent wall. She missed the smell of the wood, but the food produced on the electric stove was consistently as wonderful as the food off the woodstove.

The fried mush was the best breakfast ever. It was always made after the day they had mush with milk, cinnamon, and sugar. Here is how her Granma Lily would make it. After the mush breakfast, her granma would take some bacon grease and wipe the bottom and sides of a rectangle tin pan. Then she would press down the leftover cornmeal, wheat, or buckwheat mush into the greased pan. This would set in a cool spot until the next morning. Then the magic began. Granma Lily would cut the mush up in squares. After she fried some bacon, she would place the squares in the hot bacon grease and fry them on both sides. The outsides would brown and crisp up. The insides would be firm and warm. She would set the fried mush squares alongside the two pieces of allotted bacon on each plate. Then she poured molasses over the fried mush. The crisp of the squares and bacon with the sweet of the molasses was heavenly. Temia would dream of these tastes in her mouth in anticipation of breakfast on the nights of leftover mush.

LEARNING TO READ

Temia loved to read almost as much as she loved savory food. She was grateful all her life to her Granpa Michael for her love of books as he taught her to read. She learned to read during the war when she lived with Granpa Michael and Granma Lily. Every Sunday after Sunday dinner, Temia's Granpa Michael would sit in his chair with the tightly woven tapestry cloth cover. It had thick upholstered arms. The back of the chair went up almost to Granpa Michael's neck. There was not a position that you could sit in that chair that wasn't comfortable. It was always described as a wonderful chair. Granpa would settle in the chair, open the newspaper in front of him and begin to read. Temia would pretend she was interested in something in the small sitting room. Maybe it was something near the tall skinny window or maybe something on the precious hand-swept rug. Because soon, oh yes, very soon, Granpa's thick black eyebrows and loving sea-green eyes would peer over the newspaper. Then he would say, "Shall we see what they're doing in the funny papers today?"

Temia would, in a flash, scramble up onto his lap, snuggle against his chest, under his Sunday shaved chin, and listen. As he softly read the comic stories, Temia watched the movement of his olive-toned left pointer finger. Its placement matched the words from his mouth perfectly. In this way, Temia learned to read. Temia loved the peacefulness of these moments with this patient man. Her Granpa Michael, who worked as a laborer all his life, taught Temia to read. Temia continued to read and love the written word from that time on. She would also say that these peaceful moments with her granpa brought calm to her tumultuous heart. It was in these moments that she felt the absence of her father less acutely.

"Abuelita Temia was a person of action, even as a child. And sometimes the consequences of her energetic ways of expressing her emotions backfired on her. Temia would always relate this story to me with much regret, as she had not wanted her actions to lead to her family's departure from her grandparents. But, it seemed they did," Mamma said as she began her next Temia story.

GOOD-BYES: MOVING AGAIN

Temia didn't want to leave this house with the wooden swing and trapeze that her Granpa Michael made out of wood scraps and big thick rope. There was a huge tree in the small backyard. The swing hung from a low branch that was on the house side of the rocky dirt driveway that ran along the side of the house to the large shed. There was also a trapeze that hung from another low branch on the other side of the driveway. Temia and Maria would spend hours on the swing and trapeze, respectively. Temia thrilled at the sight of her feet so high that it looked like they were more connected to the sky than the earth. Maria loved to hook her short two-year-old legs on the trapeze and hang there for very long times. Then she'd holler for Temia to help her down. They both enjoyed this ritual they had between them. Temia felt important to be there for Maria, and Maria felt cared for.

Temia didn't want to leave this yard that held adventures with Maria. She didn't want to leave her Granma Lily who cooked delicious fried mush and her Granpa Michael who read her the funnies on Sunday. These losses did not enter Temia's mind the weekday afternoon that she ran.

It was a usual day at kindergarten for Temia. Maybe she felt a little bit frustrated, but no more than usual. She exited the school and while in the schoolyard she saw her faithful grandfather in the distance. He walked dutifully to the school daily to walk Temia home. For some reason the sight of his frame, not unlike her father's, triggered the following thought: Where is MY DAD? Why do people think it is okay for someone else to be here instead of him? I will show them that this is not right!

Before her grandfather caught sight of her, Temia turned and ran in the opposite direction of his approach. Her five-year-old legs continued to run until dusk. Then, when she was all run out, she turned and found her way home. Her mother was beside herself. Her grandfather stated that Temia should not be punished. He understood Temia and her feisty need to run from abandonment. He had done the same years ago. Albeit he had left the family farm with a plan that was couched in a mission of responsibility. And, he was eighteen and Temia only five. Nevertheless, he could identify with her emotions.

Temia's mom sent her to bed after she made an apology to her grand-father. From then on, Temia wanted to prove how much she loved her granpa. Temia wanted to prove that she could be good. But, there was no time.

Temia's mom, Mildred, found a factory job near where her parents lived in the Midwest. It seemed that Temia's run was the straw that broke the camel's back for Mildred. There was also the constant rain, the lack of her own money, the feeling of her imposition on her in-laws, as well as many, many, other unknown things that led to Mildred's decision to leave.

Mildred, Temia, and Maria left the old house that had offered them love and shelter in the rain drenched Pacific Northwest. These three females exited together, but with their own separate spheres of sadness that none could articulate.

FRITTERS AND OTHER DELIGHTS

Temia loved the food of her other grandmother as well. Her Granma May was short with a strong roundness. She bustled between the sink and the stove for many hours during the day. Granma May's food made sure that Temia and Maria felt welcome and loved. She would also sew and wash for them. But it was her food into which she put her heart and soul. It was the kind of food that when one took a bite the flavor radiated through one's entire body.

Temia loved to stand and watch her Granma May make the corn fritters. Granma May wouldn't exactly let Temia watch. Temia was assigned
her own duties. She, along with Maria, had to first shuck the corn and
snap the beans or hull the peas before Temia could try to catch some of
the fritter preparation secrets. So as Temia set the table, she would cut her
eyes over to the counter by the stove and watch Granma beat the batter
with fresh corn from the ears Temia and Maria had just shucked. Then,
spoonful by spoonful, the round dough plops would be lowered into the
hot lard. They spat and sang as they encountered the grease. Abuelita
Temia would say that it was emotional to her as she watched them become
golden and slightly irregular in shape with some corn kernels poking out
of their crispy outer surface. At the right point of golden richness they
were fetched from the pot and placed onto a large plate. Yum!

Then all would sit down to fritters, stewed chicken, and potatoes
mashed or in with the green beans. There was always lots of rich gravy
heavily seasoned with black pepper. There was also some of any of the
following: turnips with their green tops seasoned with bacon grease,
swiss chard and spinach, beans with bacon, peas, carrots, beets, and
succotash seasoned with bacon grease. Granma May didn't know about
seasonings other than salt, black pepper, peppers, onions, oregano, and
bacon grease. But, no matter. Everyone felt healthy and strong when they
ate Granma May's food. And, even though her green beans were always
tough, they all felt like they were in heaven when they sat down at her
table to eat.

WHEN THE DEVIL GETS TOO CLOSE

In Temia's Granma May's house, she and Maria slept with their
granma or on a small cot in their mother's room. The third possible sleep
location was in a dark little house that their mother rented not too far
away. This little house gave Mildred reprieve on the weekends and some
weeknights from the age-old rocky relationship with her mom.

For Temia and Maria, it was hard to know which spot was their
favorite place to sleep. Granma May with her short stocky build kept
the small double bed warm. On the other hand, the small cot gave them
reprieve from her snoring. The benefit of the dark little house was that
they had their own room and their own small beds. Their room was

weakly lit with one window that viewed the alley. Despite the paucity of light, it was their own room. It allowed them space to be together and also to just be.

The house was a rundown little wooden place with signs that it had been painted at some point in its existence. In the front there were six steps that held little anticipation. Too often the house would fill with their mother's tears over a letter long overdue from their father. It invariably said he didn't know when he would be home.

One Saturday afternoon not too long after such a letter, Temia decided to take matters into her own hands and dig a tunnel through the earth to Korea. She would bring her father back through the earth tunnel and they could be a family once again. Temia found an old garden spade by a tuft of grass in this mostly dirt yard and began to dig. It was fall and the day a little cool. As she dug she could feel the earth change to a warmer temperature. When she felt the warmth, fear began to creep through Temia's young body and she slowed down her dig. Maybe they were right in Sunday school. Maybe there was hell under the ground. After all, she felt the warmth of its radiation through the soil with her very own hands!

It took all the control her six-year-old body could muster to be able to stay there and put the dirt back in the hole and pack it down. She hid the spade near the house so no one would dig in the yard again. Then Temia ran into the kitchen and announced to her mother that hell was very close to their back yard and she shouldn't go there. Her mother smiled in a perplexed sort of way as she often did with Temia and continued to fry the chicken.

Ah, yes. A fried chicken supper would heal the shadows of this dark little house and erase any thoughts of hell. Temia set the table with three dishes and three forks and then went to join Maria who sat on her bed with her crayons and tablet. She worked intently on her drawing. Temia didn't think it was necessary to bother Maria with the news of the hell close by because Temia would always be with her outside.

THE BIZARRE CORRELATION WITH SKIN TONE AND FAIRNESS

Down the street from this dark little house, set back from the street behind two big willow trees was a big yellow house. In the driveway sat a large brown-skinned lady in the presence of two young white-skinned children. Temia had seen different skin tones in her family and other families. But there was something unusual here that bothered Temia's six-year-old sensibilities. Temia was curious. So she walked up the walkway and asked the lady if they were her children.

"No," the lady answered. "Mine are home."

Temia asked, "Then who takes care of your children?"

The lady answered, "They are bigger and know how to care for themselves."

Determined to solve this strange arrangement, Temia asked, "What about this idea? How about you bring your children here so all the children can play together?"

"The lady of the house wouldn't like that," the brown-skinned lady answered.

Well, this made no sense to Temia. This seemed like a strange kind of local war that forced a mother to abandon her children for other children.

Temia marched home and got her dark brown-skinned baby doll and brought it down the street. She gave it to the lady. She said, "Take her home and give her to your children. This doll can keep your children company all day long until you get home."

The lady thanked Temia and looked at her with some puzzlement.

Temia noticed that after a short time she did not see the brown lady there with the white children any longer. She hoped that this silent local war was over and that the brown lady could be home with her own children. She hoped also that her father could leave his war and be home with her.

Years later, Temia would have to leave her own children alone for thirty-six-hour stretches at a time while she cared for other people's sick children in the hospital. Her children, she hoped at that time, would be able to "care for themselves." But, deep down, she knew better.

BACK FROM THE WAR AND SQUIRTS OF WHIPPED CREAM

The years of waiting for their dad to come home at last came to an end. Temia and Maria wondered if they would recognize him. So, after weeks of ocean voyage and then train travel, Martin did arrive back to his family from the war in a skinny body. Martin was full of smiles and hugs and kisses for everyone. Temia could feel the strength of his happiness, but she also felt that his heart shared space with many unspoken feelings about the people and events in Korea.

At the first dinner together since Martin's return, the family was gathered around the big kitchen table in Granma May's kitchen. The dinner was Granma May's usual Sunday dinner. It included pot roast with onions, potatoes, carrots, and turnips. There was a bowl of her consistently tough green beans and some hominy cooked in some of the meat's grease. The rest of the grease was used to make wonderful brown gravy. But the best item on the table was the golden corn fritters with pineapple sauce. And then there were, of course, biscuits with gravy or honey. Her rich molasses Indian pudding was the superb finale to the meal.

So, at this scrumptious feast when it was time for the Indian pudding, the whipped cream can was placed in the middle of the table. It was a modern replacement of the beaten cream from the top of the milk bottle. Granma May was sure to be up to date for this celebration! Martin saw the metal bottle with red and white decorations in front of him. It had whipped cream written in blue across it. Everyone was pleased that Martin thought this very fancy. He thought it would be the perfect fantastic topping for the Indian pudding. Martin took the bottle, held it horizontally and pressed the plastic nozzle at the top. Temia, who sat at his left, got the fancy whipped cream all over her surprised face. Temia couldn't help her laughter as her dad tried to clear the cream from her face with a napkin. The sweet cream that landed in Temia's mouth tasted yummy. Martin laughed too, as everyone did. But Temia could tell that her dad was a little embarrassed.

ONWARD TO VILLAGE LIFE

In a couple of days, the reunited family left for their new life in a little village in the Midwest where Martin would work as a pastor for a village church. The church provided him with a small salary and housing for his family. During the week Martin would attend the university two hours away to pursue his doctorate degree. This was the closest to the university that he could find such an arrangement. At this time, he was convinced that his doctorate degree was a peaceful and needed next step for him after the war. The first night there, Martin, Mildred, Temia, and Maria tried to get some sleep while they lay huddled together on and under blankets on the floor in the drafty, two-story, wooden-frame house. A boisterous rainstorm had blown in. The lightning was bright, bold, close, and frequent. Many bolts hit the earth just outside the windowpane. They were accompanied by loud thunder booms. Temia and Maria were convinced that a bolt would reach into the living room and do something terrible to them. All they felt was fear in the face of this incessant noise and light.

It was a knee jerk reaction for Martin to comfort the girls with reassurances that the lightning and noise would not harm them. This was the self-talk he had mastered over the past years in Korea. He had used it during manmade noise and light storms. This storm did pass and the family was able to get a little sleep just before dawn.

The next day the furniture arrived from the forlorn little house near Mildred's parents. But, there was an addition to the old gray couch, with its matched comfy chair, Mom's bed and dresser, and a vinyl kitchen table with big shiny metal legs. The small cot-beds of Temia and Maria had been left behind. Now instead there was a brand new twin bed set for Temia and Maria. Mildred had bought it with the money she earned at the feed factory during the war. Temia and Maria were in ecstasy. The moving truck soon departed. Martin and Mildred busied themselves outside with the decision of where the vegetable garden would get the most sun. Temia and Maria had waited for the moment when their parents would be preoccupied so they could celebrate their new beds. They jumped and jumped and jumped on the new beds and giggled with delight. Mildred shouted up at the window, "You're not jumping on those new beds are you?"

They immediately landed on the floor and answered in unison, "No, Mom."

Within a day Martin left for the university. So while Martin began his studies at the university, his family finished settling into the aged, airy, almost breathing-with-nature parsonage. There was always fresh air moving through the family's dwelling despite closed windows and doors. One of the house's good points, however, was that it kept out the rain—as was proven by the family's experience the first night within its wooden walls.

It was also a house of movement. Strong winds tended to shake it. However, the biggest movement resulted not from the wind, but from the freight train lumbering by on the tracks about three houses to the west. It passed by to pick up a haul at the food cannery at the end of street. This occurred either once or twice a day. Its frequency depended on the day of the week. The house would shake and the furniture would vibrate. Some of the furniture did more than vibrate. Temia and Maria never tired of the fast dash to their room to move their precious beds, with the bureau and small bookcase to match, back against the wall.

Martin put himself up during the week at the university with a family of five that lived in the graduate student housing. The housing was row upon row of military-style Quonset huts. Martin had a small corner in this family's Quonset hut where there was an extra couch. It had a small table next to it. That was it. His fellow graduate student and family made him welcome. He enjoyed the evening meals with the family. Then, back he went to the library until very late. In the morning he was out early for eight o'clock class.

Mildred found a few hours work as switchboard operator at the food cannery. The switchboard was housed in a small building at the railroad tracks. It was easy for Temia and Maria to find her, if need be.

What Temia and Maria enjoyed most was to play house. They lugged their baby dolls with their little beds onto the wooden porch off of the kitchen door. They created the rest of their imagined house with boxes. There they role-played and chatted away, although Temia did most of the chatting, for hours.

During hot summer days, Temia also ran a Kool-Aid stand in front of the house. Despite Temia's efforts to convince her otherwise, Maria didn't like the Kool-Aid stand much. She preferred to draw or play with the dolls. But Temia persisted with the Kool-Aid stand until it financed her first bike from the secondhand bike shop. It was a wonderful, strong, sturdy, black bike with silver handlebars. She rode it up and down the sidewalk to the railroad tracks while the baby dolls napped.

These young sisters loved also their mom's hot cooked food. This joy was not attached to their mealtime chores, however. It was okay to put the plates, spoons, forks and knives on the table. It was not fun to take the trash out to the burn barrel. And they shuddered at their duty to shuck the corn. There always seemed to be mountains of it to shuck.

They ate a corn-based diet. For that matter, they lived a corn-based life. To stay warm in the winter, Mildred burned dried husks in the furnace. But back to Mildred's great magic with cooked corn. There was roasted corn, popped corn, boiled corn, succotash (corn with beans), fried corn-meal (fritters), hominy grits, hominy in meat grease, corn pudding, corn-meal mush, fried cornmeal mush, flat corn cakes, and cornbread served hot with butter and honey, or with a white or brown gravy.

Many an afternoon Temia and Maria sat in contemplation at the pile of corn before them. Then they grabbed an ear and began. And sure enough, there it appeared. The dreaded fat worm. Temia and Maria never knew which husk when peeled back would reveal those ugly intruders. The revulsive creatures could appear when the leaves were lowered barely an inch. Or, perhaps when the girls thought they might be home free of the disgustingly juicy worm, there it would be at the base of the cob, just like it owned the place.

Mildred made all of these worm encounters tolerable with not only her corn delights at mealtime but with her other culinary yummies that accompanied the corn. The best in this succulent adjunct category to the corn dishes was Mildred's fried chicken. It was tasty, juicy, and had a flavorful crisp crust. She got the crispness from the marriage of the hot oil and the flour and milk dipped skin. Somehow her coating and skin became one as they clung to the chicken meat, itself. Her season-ings were warm, rich, and awakening. In short, the taste was incredible. Mildred's fried chicken gave Temia's taste buds a gift that Temia claimed was never repeated after childhood. Family picnics, train travel, or car travel were always accompanied by Mildred's fried chicken. For travel or outings, Mildred fried it as usual and then let it cool. She then wrapped it in wax paper. The bundles of chicken were chilled for a couple of hours and then placed in clean shoeboxes. The shoeboxes were securely closed by a tied cotton string. Those special boxes accompanied family picnics, car trips, and train rides across country. The chicken was incred-ible! Maybe there was a special quality that the shoeboxes with the string tie brought to the chicken. It's hard to say.

Martin completed his course work for his doctorate degree in little over a year. During that same time, he also raised funds for the little church to build on a small gathering hall with a kitchen and a couple of small classrooms. He also began work on his thesis. However, at this time, inside Martin there began to rise up a restlessness and discontent. He felt himself disengage from academia. He tired of its static inertia. He felt disenchanted with weeknights sleeping alone on a couch. He also felt disenchanted with his meals away from his family.

Thus Martin, with his thesis unfinished, moved himself and his family away from the rural community. They moved to a big city on the East Coast where Martin took on the pastor position of a large church in the inner city near an Ivy League campus. The church offices were housed on the first floor of an old mansion. Martin's family lived in an apartment made up of part of the second and third floors of the old mansion. This old mansion had a large, and to Temia and Maria, romantic wide wooden staircase up to their apartment's front door. The girls loved to play house on the terraced gardens off the mansion's first floor. Their parents allowed them to do this much to the chagrin of the mousey, gray haired, tightlipped church secretary, Miss Archson. The cold stares of Miss Archson didn't bother little Temia and Maria. What was important to them was that their dad was home every night. No cold stare could diminish that joy. And anyway, their dad's permission to play there trumped Miss Archson's claim to power.

NEW HOME AND BROKEN TEA CUPS

In their new home, Temia and Maria tried to be helpful in their room upstairs and take care of their own things. They even tried to move big pieces of furniture around to improve its arrangement. After all, they were expert at it from when they lived by the railroad tracks. So when the opportunity emerged to move a piece of furniture in their new bedroom, it seemed natural to attempt it. But their attempt had some rough edges to it.

Temia and Maria played house not only on the terraced gardens, but also, on rainy and cold days, in their third floor bedroom in the mansion. There were lots of windows so the room was bright. One day they decided to move a wooden bookcase across the room to act like a divider. That way their beds would be on one side of the room and their special pretend house would be on the other. They could make their own perfect world in their pretend house on the other side of the wooden bookcase.

They were very excited as they placed their pretend kitchen stove, table, and baby bed in their new locations. Temia and Maria chatted happily back and forth with each other. They fussed over the perfect arrangement of their items so their imaginary world would be cozy. Then they began to push the bookcase from along the wall to its new divider location.

In their eagerness, they did not remove the special china tea set of a teapot, creamer, sugar bowl, and four little saucers and four little cups off the shelf. It was a beautiful china tea set in mostly yellow and white. Their mom had given it to them to be able to look at, as it was precious to her. But they were not to touch it.

Well, they didn't touch the tea set. They knew that maybe they could have carefully touched it to move it off the shelf. They knew that they just weren't supposed to play with it. But out of fear and excitement they held fast to the strict definition of touch and moved the shelf as a whole. So, with Temia at one end of the small three-shelf bookcase and Maria at the other, they began to push and pull it the few feet needed to get it into place. On the third push, when it was almost in place, the bookcase hit a slight irregularity in the wooden floor and every piece of the tea set crashed onto the floor. The girls looked at each other in horror. By three anxious breaths, Temia and Maria heard their mom's voice from down the stairs, "What's going on up there?"

Mom was at the bedroom door by their fourth breath and surveyed the broken china all over the floor. Mildred could not think. The tea set was the only intact thing that came out of her fractured childhood. She was able to bring this little china tea set from a household that never drank tea. She was able to bring this little china tea set from a household filled with her parents yelling. She was able to bring this little china tea set out of a house set in the back lots of the huge grain factory where the air was always heavy with the smell of mold and cooked grain. Mildred had been able to get the smell out of her mind, but it came back now. She was able to keep her mom's regular slaps and beatings out of her mind, but they came back now.

Mildred felt shaken to her spine. At first, her voice was gone. Then, in a stern, stiff voice she said, loudly, "Get this mess cleaned up. Both of you!"

With clenched fists and a fast heartbeat, Mildred turned and went back to the kitchen.

Both Temia and Maria worked at the cleanup. They felt lost now in how to make it right with their mom. It seemed to them that they could never enter her good graces again. Somehow, without intention, they felt they had inflicted pain on a grown-up. Their innocence was lost. In this predicament, Temia felt more angry and Maria more silent. They completed the creation of their pretend world. But it was not perfect.

MARTIN AND MILDRED EXPAND CHURCH AND FAMILY

Once again Martin raised the money to expand a church's space. A few classrooms and meeting hall expanded into a large church sanctuary with a full kitchen and large room on the lower floor. Martin and the congregation opened the church to the community. He began a daily lunch program for the hungry or lonely. Every day the large hall was filled with people and savory smells from the kitchen. In addition, there were church choirs, youth groups, ladies' groups, men's groups, and Bible studies. Community groups that needed meeting locations also used the space. Thus, human needs of fellowship, support, faith, food, and information were all addressed.

Martin asked Mildred to organize a preschool daycare. She had incredible organizational skills and a sharp mind that had been underutilized until then. So Mildred did a huge turnaround from solely a pastor's wife to the creator of a preschool daycare center at the church. She gathered a gifted staff of teachers and up-to-date educational equipment for the children. The preschool daycare was a huge success. It became a model preschool daycare in the city.

Mildred was proud, but a little disappointment scratched at her inside. It was a lot of work. There was no salary for this organizational feat. She could not teach in the preschool daycare as high school was as far as she had gone in school. Mildred decided that one day she would seek a teaching degree. Ten years later she did, and completed her bachelor's and master's with honors.

Temia and Maria saw their dad mostly for brief moments at a meal or if they went to the church. It was easy to get to church because it was downstairs and the new construction extended out from there. But, despite the spatial closeness, it wasn't easy to see him, because it would be an interruption to just show up. The best way to show up was to carry a message from the parsonage phone to him. They loved that mission as it was a legitimate and important reason to see him.

There was another great time with their dad that the girls loved. It occurred after the Sunday services when everyone had left, even those with last minute questions or problems. At that time, Martin would let out a soft but audible sigh, smile at his daughters, and walk together with them to his office. There he took off his stole and cassock. When they were properly put away he would take Temia's hand into one of his and Maria's hand in the other. Thus hand in hand, the three of them walked to the attached mansion and upstairs to the servant's quarters. There, Mildred would have ready the most wonderful roast and hominy dinner with lots of gravy.

Their family grew during the years at this parish. Despite five miscarriages and stillborn babies over the past few years, Martin and Mildred had faith somehow that this next baby would live. She did, as did a son two years later. Temia and Maria were so excited to have a baby sister and brother. They knew how to help because they had played with their babies in their pretend houses for years.

To have more children in the household was an easy adjustment for Temia and Maria. They had often shared their twin beds with other children that needed a place to stay for one reason or another. So a new sister and brother was an easy adaptation for Temia and Maria.

MARTIN ON THE MOVE AGAIN

Shortly after the birth of his son, Martin left for a few weeks. Mildred explained to the children that he would sponsor a church tour in East Germany. He sponsored a few of those tours over the next couple of years. Temia and Maria knew that their dad had extensive knowledge of church history, as he would often lecture at a nearby divinity school. So they thought nothing of these "church tours" to East Germany in the middle of the cold war.

During this same time frame, bishops from East Germany on special lecture leave would come to stay at their apartment parsonage for a couple of days before their return to East Germany. One day after they left and before her dad's last trip to East Germany, Temia remembers that she was drawn to the window by her dad. He parted the curtain slightly and said to Temia, "Do you see that car?"

"Yes," Temia answered softly.

"It is the KGB," her father said.

"Oh," was all Temia could say. She had learned in school what KGB stood for. She felt a little worried.

"Don't worry, Temia. They are just looking," her father reassured.

Temia sensed that her father had told her something that she should not discuss further. And they did not until Temia was grown and had her own children.

In a few months, Martin left for northern Europe. He was gone for over three months, but did return safely. Mildred told her children that he was doing speeches. When the children were grown and the cold war had calmed, Martin and Mildred sat down with their grown children and Mildred told them the whole story of their dad's European visits. They were told it was not to be spoken of until after the death of Martin, which occurred, unfortunately, a few years later. This is the story as related by Mildred.

Martin and Mildred had arrived at their hotel in East Germany. Martin put his finger to his lips as he knew the room was wired. He went into Mildred's underwear in the luggage and unwrapped a large sum of German money and placed it on his person. Mildred was in shock and a bit miffed that she had no knowledge of its presence in her underwear! Mildred liked more control than that. But she was clever enough to realize that it would have been unsafe for her to know. Still, part of her was not pleased. But the challenge of this trip trumped her passion for control.

She had known that there was to be a money delivery. The details would unfold; however, it would be easier for her psyche if there were no more surprises. Martin understood her personality. So they walked to the tour group in the open air away from the electronic devices. On this walk, Martin laid out the plan to Mildred. She agreed to participate.

At a certain point of the church tour excursion Martin and Mildred positioned themselves to the rear of the group. While the preoccupied group moved on, a CIA car arrived alongside Martin and Mildred. They got in. They were driven to a nearby church. They had fifteen minutes. They entered the church office area. The room was filled with four wooden desks with phones. At the sight of Martin, the office workers took the phones off the hooks and left the room. Martin and Mildred then went into the back room and Martin gave the money to the pastor. It was for the education of the children of the church. The East German government did not permit the education of children whose parents attended church. Martin and Mildred were then picked up by the same car and returned to the back of the church tour group. That afternoon they left the country.

The same thought went through both Temia and Maria's minds, "Sooo, dad had been smuggling money from the church in the United States for education of church children in East Germany. Not just once, but multiple times. This explains the KGB cars that cruised by our residence and the visits of the German bishops. Hmmm."

It seems that the KGB became uneasy with Martin's behavior, so he had to stop the money runs. But he went on to his lecture trip to Scandinavia. He lectured on freedom and God. Both topics irritated the KGB. One night after Martin had lectured and broadcast near the Russian border, some of Martin's "friends" came to him.

They said, "We have to get you over to Norway because the KGB plans to pick you up before dawn."

So he left with them and crossed three countries to safety. There he completed his talks.

In a couple of months Martin returned to the States. After that, he did not return to Europe to do any more talks.

However, in a few years, Martin was back in Europe. This time he was at the Vatican. He was on a delegation to discuss the possible unification of the Roman Catholic and Protestant churches. Martin was all about organizational efficiency. But sometimes efficiency is not what is most important to organizations. Sometimes keeping up appearances and financial superiority are more important to organizations.

While at the Vatican a cardinal escorted Martin through the Pope's private catacombs. As a church historian, the early church mosaics fascinated Martin. There he saw some from as early as the 12th century. In those mosaics there were men and women of all skin colors. They all were in bishop garb from that era and all had their heads at the same level. Of course Martin had to comment on the diversity of early church leadership. And of course, the cardinal informed him that it was the church's position that only the man with the white complexion was a bishop. So the discussion was closed and Martin simply basked in the obvious truth described by the colorful well-preserved mosaics.

After meetings of superficial pleasantries and no deep discussion of unification, Martin returned to the States. There he focused on the freedom of all Americans. Soon he found himself on a plane to Washington, DC, summoned by the president. He was asked by the President to serve on his civil rights advisory committee. Martin was unsure what information contributed to the president's decision. Maybe it was his recent win with other pastors in a civil rights court case. Maybe it was his civil rights work to organize clergy representation on the marches called by Dr. King. Maybe it was his transcultural work in the national church office. Whatever was the motivation for his choice on the committee, Martin was determined to give his best. He did so until the tragic assassination of the president.

Then, once again, Martin sought to move. He sought the quiet of the rural Midwest. This time it was not after a war. This time it was after the emotional and physical violence of American corporate and political life. Temia was now away from home at her university studies so the move did not affect her. Maria did not want to move from the East Coast, as she would miss her friends in high school. Mildred was tired of the moves, but rose to the occasion. The younger ones didn't care. Martin pastored a small town church that grew into a sanctuary for all those in need of fellowship, food, housing, and faith.

After only a couple of years with this rural parish, Martin moved his family again. He had accepted a seminary's administrative position in a large city in the Midwest. He was to raise the funds to build a large seminary campus. The family went along with minor complaints, hopeful that this might be the last move. Martin was out of town most days of the week for a couple of years to raise the majority of the funds. The seminary was built.

Mildred, now relieved of care of young children and church responsibilities of a pastor's wife, began and completed her education. Mildred became a lead teacher in their community.

About six years later, Martin, now in his sixties, decided to move again. This time it was to a small church in a rural northern community by a great lake. Mildred accepted his need for a rural lifestyle. But it was really difficult for her to leave the school where she taught. For the first time in her life she had a professional job that was independent of her husband's work. It felt like she had to pull herself from the embrace of a dear friend that she would never see again. She did it with only a few verbal barbs flung at Martin. Not bad, considering the depth of her emotion. But Mildred also knew that the corporate environment, church or not, was harmful to Martin's health.

Martin had plans for this move other than a less stressed life style. He knew that his retirement would be small. He wanted to leave a secure living environment for Mildred. So with the help of a friend, he put up a pre-fabricated cottage on a cement slab. It was on an acre of woods filled with firewood that overlooked a small lake inlet. He had a well dug. Thus, when he was gone to heaven, Mildred could have a dwelling, water, and warmth.

Martin worked in a small rural parish. There was adjacent land connected to the church. Since there was a paucity of affordable housing for seniors in town, Martin procured federal funds to build senior housing on the adjacent land. His full church schedule did not stop him from welcoming Temia's children for some weeks in the summer to give them a relief from their intense city life. Nor did it stop him from his maintenance of a freshly chopped woodpile to burn in the cottage's wood burner.

During this time, Martin was silent about the chest pains that would come and go as he chopped wood. He was silent about the occasional dizzy spell during a walk in the woods.

Eventually, when a dizzy spell occurred while he drove, Martin mentioned his symptoms to his physician. After tests he was scheduled for open-heart surgery. The night after the open-heart surgery Martin suffered a massive stroke and went into an unrecoverable coma.

Mildred, his children, and grandchildren gathered around his hospital bed. They thanked him quietly for how he had blessed them. They read him Psalms. Mildred struggled with when she should let the doctors disconnect the respirator. In a couple of days she granted them permission. Martin's heart beat for only a few more hours. But his spirit lived on. Temia saw its beautiful light rise up from the room. Quietly the infectious disease doctor sided up to Temia and asked, "Where has your father been? We can't identify some of the organisms that grew out of his sputum and blood!"

Temia looked at the man and said softly, as her voice was enveloped with sadness, "Many places, but the most important place is forever in my heart."

"And that's the story of Temia's family in which she grew up."

"Hmm, Mamma, I didn't realize there was so much going on in Abuelita Temia's family," I said doing my best to encompass it all.

"A lot goes on in all families. We just talk about it," my mamma said with a twinkle in her eye.

"I'm glad you do," said Beverly. "This is the first I heard the stories in such details. Interesting people in your family, Andrew," Beverly added as she rose and kissed Andrew on the cheek.

The night was warm, filled with the evening cricket sounds. But, we were ready to leave the stories and the night to rest. We hugged each other goodnight with anticipation for another day together.

As we walked towards the house, Beverly asked, "Alessia would you mind telling more of your mom and Andrew's dad's early years tomorrow?"

"Of course. We have time and I love to go over those old stories."

I slept well and dreamed of dark nights and hopeful days.

In the morning we three women brought a blanket, tea, and tacos with us down to the fishpond. Andrew stayed in the house to catch up on some work.

We settled under a tree on the blanket near the pond. We had shade, water nearby, a sunny sky, and lunch. As we began to munch on our tacos, Mamma said, "Some of Abuelita Temia's stories have a lot of emotion in them. Are you ready Francesca?"

"Rights of passage stuff. I'm ready!" I responded.

Beverly laughed and my mamma began.

TEMIA'S VOYAGE AS A GROWN WOMAN

As a university student Temia worked for an organization funded to improve the neighborhood in which she lived. She enjoyed the cooperation and dedication between people of various skills and ethnic backgrounds. Temia also enjoyed the presence of a particular draftsman who worked there in the day and as a musician in the evenings. Soon Temia fell head over heels in love with this handsome man. They shared both a love for their community and for music. While John played his music in clubs in the evenings, Temia drummed, taught dance to a group of young girls at a local church, and studied. For the first time, Temia was excited about her life.

Both she and her newfound love had something else in common. It was something that they never discussed and personally tried not to think about. They both were sexually molested in their younger years. Temia thought in later years, "How is it that two people with unknown-to-each-other histories of sexual molestation can look across a room, see each other, feel attracted, and fall in love?"

Well that's what happened. Temia was molested by a church janitor from age seven to eight and John was molested by a neighborhood grocer at age five. Since neither had addressed these issues, they were both awkward with intimacy. But they were in love and began to live together.

However, to compound their difficulties, the community organization for which they worked was in failure. Well, the organization did not fail. In fact, it was too successful. It had made many positive changes in the community. This disturbed the powers that be and thus, through complicated means, they cut off the community organization's funds.

With the closure of the community project, John not only lost his job, but also watched his community to go back to its prior state of deprivation. This hurt his soul. He lost the strength to be positive about himself as a man. He had desperately wanted to contribute to the relief of centuries of horrific treatment by the greater society towards his people. John felt he had failed himself and his community. He became more and more saddened and drank more frequently and intensely. Temia's continued fight for a bright future annoyed him. He began to strike her when drunk. This shocked Temia. She thought, How could he do this? We love each other, and I am kind to him always and he was kind to me. He will certainly change, she reasoned, once he can feel my love down to his bones. But, he continued to attack Temia when drunk. And he continued to drink often.

Temia painted the picture in her mind that he would again adore her, find another job, and they would live happily ever after. But, it did not happen and Temia felt trapped.

At this time, Temia's family had discontinued communication with her. Mildred's pain from Temia's choice to live with a man while unmarried was insurmountable. In addition he was of African heritage. For many decades Mildred had fought to be acceptable to the greater dominant society. She was beautiful, she had married a preacher, she had gotten her education, and she had safely tucked her ancestral people of color into unspoken question marks. But now, here it was in her family again, and right in her face! She could not manage it. Martin stood by his wife, as he knew that she would work it out within herself. It took some years, but she did.

Temia wanted to stay with John to prove to her family that she was not a sinful woman, but rather good and wise. She was determined to make their relationship work. After all, according to her religious beliefs, no other man would have her, as she was no longer a virgin.

"What a failure I would be if I left him," Temia mused to herself. "Also," continued Temia in her worries, "if I return home it would involve multiple confessions of my wickedness and once again I would be required to hide parts of who I am. Not worth it!"

Thus continued the slippery slope of her thoughts that led her to stay and endure the abuse. Temia had completed her education and then worked as a nurse until she delivered her daughter. She married John, who had procured a job. After her daughter's birth, Temia stayed at home to care for her daughter. She did not want her daughter out of her sight, as she feared possible erratic behavior from her husband. Fortunately he did not hurt his daughter.

But it seemed to Temia that no matter how good she would be, God would not protect her from John's blows. So, she let go of prayers and relied on her wit to keep herself and her baby safe. After the loss of her hearing on one side, John stopped the strikes. However, he still verbally threatened Temia and occasionally pushed her around.

Despite her estrangement from her parents, Temia had called them to inform them that they were grandparents. They couldn't resist the pull of their new granddaughter. Thus, under the pretense of a visit in order to baptize Mikaela they came for a visit. Though guarded, communication was once again open between Temia and her parents.

Within eighteen months of her daughter's birth, Temia birthed her son, Mark. But the births of the two children did not change John's daily drink as Temia had hoped. With continual verbal assaults and frequent pushes, Temia decided to leave. So, filled with fear, and a broken heart, Temia carefully planned her escape. She had to be very clever in her arrangements because if caught, she would be in great physical danger.

Temia decided to call upon her family's assistance to leave. The prospect of her family's judgments against her was not pleasant. But, that would be a small price to pay for the safety of her children.

Temia hated her labels of fornicator, abused wife, single mother, and future divorcee. Temia felt they put her on a tight rope across an abyss without a safety net. But an ancient, deep strength visited her. It was the same strength that was present during her labor and delivery of her children. This time the strength came to her to safely leave and to walk the tight rope of society's critics. She would not fall.

Despite her lack of faith in God at this point, Temia called her pastor for a sort of spiritual clearance to leave. Her pastor gently said, "God wants us safe."

Now with the echo of those words in her brain, and strength in her heart, Temia moved ahead with her plan. First, she asked her father to wire a ticket to the airport. Temia promised to pay back the ticket money from her first paychecks when moved. He wired the ticket immediately to the airport.

Temia then called an acquaintance from outside the immediate neighborhood who had agreed to be her transporter to the airport. Temia left a note for her husband that said she would raise his children with respect for him and that she would leave him to his freedom. To avoid the possibility of any word reaching John about her move, she and the children left their home without a word to John's family nor Temia's friends. With a small satchel of a few clothes, the three of them left one large city for another hundreds of miles away. For the reason of safety alone, they left people that loved them and whom Temia deeply loved.

Temia immediately found a position as an instructor for a nursing program. She paid her parents for the airline ticket and a little rent, and she saved for an apartment. Within a few weeks, she rented an apartment two blocks from work and continued her life there with her children.

APPEARANCES OF TEMIA'S ANGELS

Temia was not yet close to the healing of her broken soul. Her energy commitment was to her children and her ability to provide for them. It seemed to her that this left her little energy to tend to herself. She didn't realize that it would have been a great gift for her children for her to have healed her broken heart. But at this point she honestly did not know how. So she busied herself with work and her children.

In time Temia began to embrace a sense of safety. She was now a long physical distance away from her prior domestic danger. At first the sensation of it seemed to cling to her body like sticky glue. Little by little, however, the fear let go of its grasp. After a few months it waved over her only in occasional little wisps.

A year later, Temia was forced to resign from her job. Ah, Temia! She had criticized the racial unfairness of certain hospital policies during their founder's day speech. The maladies were fixed, but to save face the hospital asked Temia to resign. Now, forced into the reality of no job, she realized that domestic violence was not the only thing to avoid. Unemployment was another. So she promised herself, as best she could, to keep her mouth closed so as not to threaten her children's economic security.

Temia heard about a graduate program in nursing. She spoke to the director of the program who arranged a scholarship, small loan, and an evening clinic job for her.

It was during those years of study and work that spirituality crept back into Temia's psyche.

How else, she thought, without the strength from something greater, could she have gathered the strength to escape from John, leave his family and her friends, face her family, survive the turnover of many babysitters, and handle long waits in the icy cold for the bus after evening clinic, late night hours of study, and far too much time away from her children? Could all this have been endured by sheer will power? No way. She had help from a power outside herself. She just knew it.

Soon Temia and her young family had an experience that slammed the presence of the Creator into her consciousness. This is what happened.

One dark winter day there was a terrible snowstorm that hit the city. This big midwestern city had big snowstorms. But this was the king of all storms. It was a blizzard of cold winds and incessant snowfall. And it hit in full force by late afternoon.

Temia had taken the children, now four and five years old, by local train with her that morning to the clinic where she worked as a nurse practitioner. The preschool was closed in anticipation of the storm, but the clinic director refused to close the clinic. So she had to go, as there would be patients and she could not afford to lose the pay. Remember that now Temia was of the mindset to avoid any situation with an employer where she might lose her job. So she went with her children to the clinic.

The storm began to increase in intensity about mid-day. Yet, the clinic director refused to close the clinic early. Sadly, it was later discovered he had a brain tumor that occluded his thinking. Thus when the clinic closed at five o'clock, the snow was high and the wind fierce. Temia and the children fought the wind and the cold snow the two blocks to the train stop. Temia huddled with her children in the little wooden train stop shack. The children were cold and hungry. Temia's mind struggled to think of other possibilities to get to shelter. The clinic was locked and she knew no one in the neighborhood. And, since no cars could travel, to wait for the train seemed not only her best, but her only, option to get home to warmth and food. There were five others in the shack, and everyone sat close together to share body warmth.

Six hours later, at eleven o'clock at night, a train was able to get to the stop where they waited. About forty minutes later they arrived at their stop near their apartment, which was part of a hospital complex. But here there was a serious dilemma. The tracks ran along the bottom of a hill and the hospital complex parking lot was at the top of the hill. Temia's apartment building was near the parking lot. There was only one path from the train platform to the parking lot above. It was an open metal walkway over the tracks and the hill's slope to the flat parking lot. There was only a thin metal horizontal railing that ran the length of the walkway. The stairs up and the elevated, open metal walkway was icy, windswept, and totally unsafe. The children and Temia would have been swept off the bridge to the tracks twenty feet below. The only alternative was to climb off of the wooden platform, cross the tracks, and climb the hill of snow drifts that were taller than her children and above Temia's waist.

Temia safely navigated the children over the tracks. The recent train had blown enough snow off of that area. But as she stood at the foot of the hill, it was evident that the snow stood a foot over the head of the children. It would be hard for her to push through with both the children in her arms. With willed courage that came from some ancient female survival source outside of herself, Temia supported her four-year-old son against her torso with her left arm, and with her right hand, held her daughter's hand to guide her in the path cleared by Temia's body. She had taken but two steps when she saw two apartment complex and hospital security men run out of a security car and plow down the hill to her. They each grabbed one of her children and plowed up the hill with her children in their arms. Temia followed in their wake. She was convinced that angels had sent them. There was no other explanation.

They placed the children into the security car and then helped Temia into the warm security car.

When everyone had caught their breath and had settled into the security car, the officers explained that this was not their assigned route for this time of the night. They did not know what prompted them to drive in this direction.

"We were so shocked to see you and the little children on that hill," exclaimed one of the officers. "We have never encountered such a situation before."

"We are so grateful. What a blessing. Thank you both so much. I can't imagine what would have happened to us otherwise. Thank you. Thank you. Thank you," said Temia.

"We're just glad you're safe. This is frostbite weather. Now let's get you to your warm apartment. Which building is yours?"

The plows had been working for hours to keep the streets around the hospital passable for the ambulances. So it was a short and easy drive home. After more thanks to these kind officers, Temia lead the children into the warm building.

Once in their apartment, Temia, Mikaela, and Mark drank some water and fell into their warm beds. In the morning Temia cooked for her little family a huge breakfast of pancakes and sausage.

Mikaela and Mark waved and smiled at all the security guards in their cars from then on.

Temia's angels returned on another cold night. Once again, she found herself in a snowstorm. But that's all it was. It was a cold night with lots of snow, but not a blizzard. This incident happened after work as well. This time her children were safe at home, sound asleep with a nursing student babysitting them.

Two evenings a week Temia worked at an evening clinic. It was busy this particular evening so the staff got out late. Temia had to take the L train and then a bus to her apartment. It was about ten o'clock and the storm caused the buses to run slow. All of a sudden, amongst the snowflakes, an older guy about Temia's height appeared at her side. He waved a gun in her face and asked for her money. His speech was slurred. By this point in her life, Temia knew when she could push a drunk and when she couldn't. Him you could push. So she said, "I'm on my way home to my babies after work. They need every penny that I have for their milk and food."

He then waved the gun around, looked at her, and then at the ground. Then he said, "Okay, okay. Go on. This late the bus stops over there," he slurred as he waved his gun towards a spot a few feet away.

Temia was in such a spot that the driver would not have seen her. She was cold and thus grateful to this probably cold man as well.

"Thanks," said Temia. "Take care of yourself," she added. Then she walked over to the late night bus stop.

Temia completed the graduate nursing program and then taught in the program for a year. The following year she entered medical school to pursue the dream of her ideal clinic. She wanted to exemplify for her children that dreams are to be pursued. In addition, she understood herself enough by then to realize that a profession like medicine could accommodate her independent personality, but nursing could not. Therefore, it would be more secure for herself and her children.

However, it took her an entire journey with medicine to learn that dreams and independence manifest from within and are not given by a profession. During that time and afterwards, her children became some of her strongest teachers.

"How did her children become her strongest teachers? I'm really curious. Have I been a teacher for you, Mamma?" I asked.

"Yes, many times. Like now. As I tell the stories they take on a different depth of meaning. I might not have received that new understanding if I wasn't able to relate the story to you. Are you ready to hear some tales about Uncle Mark?" Mamma asked.

"Ready!" Beverly and I responded.

"Well, okay, then!"

PASTA BROUGHT UP TO A NEW LEVEL

Uncle Mark was born with deep awareness of food. As an infant he demanded to be fed often. When he was weaned he turned his culinary sensitivities to table food. He ate with enthusiasm and opinions on flavors. Mark was strong, energetic, and smart. By age five he prepared scrambled eggs. They were seasoned perfectly with black pepper and a little salt. He often cooked them for Temia when she came home from the 36-hour shifts as a medical student. When Temia was a medical resident with 110-hour workweeks, Mark was eight and held the responsibility of the main family cook and food shopper.

Mark and his sister, Mikaela, cared for themselves at far too early of an age due to Temia's hospital responsibilities. But they did it well. Mark knew how to take the grocery cart, Temia's list, and the fifty dollars in small bills hidden carefully in his pockets to the grocery store three busy city blocks away. There he spent this weekly allotment for his family's food supply. When he arrived home, Mikaela helped him put away the groceries.

Mark's dinner specialty was pasta! Of course he had perfected tacos, rice, and refried beans. But his pasta meal had a special dramatic twist. Maybe that's what made it his specialty.

First he would boil and salt a pot of water. Then, he added the pasta when the water was at a boil. Meanwhile he would heat up the tomato sauce seasoned with ground beef and onions that Temia had left in the refrigerator the night before. He tasted it and added the right amount of black pepper, Italian seasoning, garlic powder and salt to his liking. When he thought the pasta was almost done, he would dip in the ladle and pull out a pasta strand. Mark then tossed it up to the low ceiling. If it stuck, he would use the ladle to move the pasta into a bowl, so as to not burn himself by handling a pot of boiling water. Then he would add just the right amount of sauce. Voila! Dinner! Generous amounts of parmesan cheese from a round cardboard container would be sprinkled on top as the final touch. Eagerly, he and his sister would eat their fill.

This was how Uncle Mark initiated himself into the culinary arts. This is how Nonna Mikaela first ate pasta. And this is how the basement apartment kitchen ceiling became decorated with dry spaghetti strands.

MANNING THE PHONES

During Temia's residency, every day after school Mikaela, now age ten, would go to the community recreation center until dinner time. Her younger brother didn't like how some of the young male counselors treated him at the center so he never joined any of their programs. Rather, Mark often hopped on his little bike and zoomed around the neighborhood sidewalks. Sometimes he'd show up at the community center to watch the activities and maybe greet Mikaela. Often in the later afternoon he'd watch TV in their basement apartment down the street from the community center. He never cooked until his sister got home.

But today Mikaela had not seen her brother on the sidewalk by the community center. When she lowered herself down the six stairs under a private home to their basement apartment, the TV was not on and her brother was not there. This was highly unusual. Something was not right.

Mikaela figured that Mark would show up or there would be a call. So she dragged the phone on its long cord to the center of the cool linoleum floor, and sat down next to it. She crossed her strong brown legs in their red shorts and sat and sat and waited and waited. Within what seemed like far too long a time, the phone rang. It was the ER of the nearby hospital. The nurse asked for the mother of Mark. Mikaela gave her the hospital number where her mother worked as a medical resident. Mikaela then put her chin in her hands and waited and waited. The shadows seemed to gain a lot of length outside by the time her mother called. But Mikaela knew it was just a short time. Temia said that she was on her way to pick her up. Then they would go to the nearby hospital where Mark waited. Temia reassured Mikaela that the doctor said that Mark was all right. Mikaela resolved herself to the long wait for her mother.

When Temia arrived home after her forty-five minute drive from her residency hospital, she found Mikaela on the floor with her legs crossed and the phone beside her. Temia's emotion at the sight of her patient young daughter during the family crisis was more than Temia could hold in. She hugged and kissed Mikaela profusely, then grabbed her hand as they rushed out the door. They quickly moved down the walkway to the back alley, hand in hand, towards the old blue car with holes in the flooring under the mats.

Temia blurted out, "Mikaela, how did you know to do that? How incredible! I mean, how did you know to sit by the phone? You are amazing!"

Mikaela had no answer.

In five minutes they were at the hospital and there was Mark in the ER bed with the white sheet pulled up to his neck. The ER doctor quickly told Temia how brave he had been during the past two hours. She said the x-rays were negative for fractures and there were no signs of internal injuries so he could be discharged for home. The doctor also related what the police report said.

Evidently, as Mark rode his bike across the street an elderly lady ran the red light and knocked him off his bike. As he flew off his little bike onto the sidewalk, the pale-skinned, white-haired lady in the driver's seat sped off. Passersby on the corner talked to him kindly and told him not to move. They could see no cuts or any blood on his strong but young nine-year-old body. They called the ambulance and Mark was taken away.

Temia kissed and kissed her brave son. Then she introduced Mikaela to the ER doctor as Mark's ten-year-old sister who had coordinated the phone calls. The doctor complimented Mikaela's wise presence of mind.

As Temia walked hand in hand with her children out of the ER to their car on the warm asphalt of the nearby parking lot, she felt big thankfulness for her children's health and great respect for their strength. She also felt shame for her long hours away from them, but she had committed to this medical path and she owed too much payment in service to the government to turn back now.

In these same moments, Mark struggled with his own set of mixed feelings while he held his mother's hand. He was glad to be holding his mom's hand and he was glad that he was brave at the hospital. But he felt ashamed that when he was hit by the car, he was on the way to buy candy, which was not allowed.

Mikaela felt glad they were all together and somehow had known they would all be safe in the end.

"Uncle Mark kept his courage also as an adult. There is an incident that happened to him, Aunt Natalie, Cousin Andrew, and Cousin Samuel when they were a young family. Do you know which one I'm thinking of, Beverly?" Mamma said.

"I think so, but go ahead and refresh my memory."

"Okay. Here goes!" said Mamma as she took a swig of water.

WHEN THE RISK OF DEATH IS WORTH THE PRICE

Uncle Mark always had a sixth sense for danger. Some theorize that it's in the DNA of a people who have been terrorized for generations. Such is Uncle Mark's inheritance as a grandson of a sharecropper and a great-grandson of a slave. One Sunday afternoon his two young boys, Andrew, then age five, and Samuel, age three, were out for a walk with their mother, Aunt Natalie. It was to be a short walk, just around the block of this residential area of the city. Uncle Mark had just placed the ribs on the grill in the back yard when he sensed that he should go out to the front steps to check on his family. At that moment Andrew ran around the corner to their driveway. His movement triggered the attention of a pit bull until then unnoticed by Uncle Mark. The dog bounded off the front porch of the house across the street. The dog immediately bounded towards Andrew.

Uncle Mark sprang across his front yard into the middle of the street in the direct path of the pit bull. He shouted, "Andrew don't move!"

Uncle Mark, who was totally unarmed, then screamed at the man on the porch previously shared by the pit bull, "Call your dog or I'll kill him!"

Uncle Mark continued to shout, "Call your dog or I'll kill him!" as he bulked his muscular six foot one inch, 225-pound presence in front of the pit bull. The pit bull stopped dead in his tracks and paced back and forth in front of Uncle Mark. He kept his gaze on Uncle Mark. But Uncle Mark kept his stance and continued to shout, "Call your dog or I'll kill him!"

The man on the porch was too drugged to respond. But, with Uncle Mark's aggressive stance before him, the pit bull began to take a step backwards.

At that sign of hope, Andrew started to run towards the front door. But his movement again triggered the pit bull to move forward towards him. Andrew froze. Once again Uncle Mark moved to be directly in front of the large pit bull. He shouted repeatedly, "Call your dog or I'll kill him!"

Then, an elderly man, obviously drunk but aware of the situation, came through the front door onto the dog's porch. He shoved himself past the drugged young man and called the pit bull to him. Upon his command, the pit bull turned and left the street. The dog moved past the two mind-altered men into his house.

After that, Uncle Mark's family never went on walks. They kept the driveway wire gate closed to the back yard. Uncle Mark and his family moved away a short time later.

"Oh my, Mamma. I have to ask Cousin Andrew when we go back to the house if he remembers that! Although, I imagine he does. Who could forget something like that?"

"That's the truth!" responded both Mamma and Beverly.

"Tell me more about Andrew's dad's early years, Alessia, if you can," requested Beverly.

"I know one story about how a friend of Abuelita Temia became a lifelong supportive friend to Mark. This is how it happened," Mamma said as she took in a deep breath and began the story.

APPEARANCES OF A FRIEND

As a child of nine, Mark stood in the outfield of the softball field. He was a strong, muscular kid with golden brown skin. He wore his hair in a short natural, as that was all Temia had time to cut. When he smiled, he sported two adorable dimples. But at this moment, his face didn't have a smile. He made an attempt to concentrate on the game, but it was too slow for his fast moving mind. Rather, the different shapes of the clouds attracted his attention, as did the rustle of the red maple's branches at the edge of the field. He then checked out the front row of the bleachers. Yup, there he was. At the end of the row, nearest to the field possible, stood Thomas. Mark didn't really like softball. But he liked that Thomas showed up at his games.

In prior years, Thomas had pitched balls to Mark in the small green area between the medical school dorms and the hospital. He also tossed the football to Mark. The football passes are what Mark really loved. Tom, that's what he wanted Mark to call him, would, on occasion, have Mark and Mikaela to his apartment for dinner so Temia could have time to study. When Temia thanked him profusely, he always laughed with his deep chuckle and said, "I get a kick out of these kids."

Mark and Mikaela looked forward to their time with Tom, but especially Mark. Often in the early evening after supper, Mark would stand under Tom's apartment window and shout up in his young but deep, loud voice, "Tom can you come out and play?" Often Tom did, even if just for a few minutes.

These special encounters stopped after four years. For by then, both Temia and Tom had graduated from medical school and had entered medical residency programs at different institutions. Tom told Temia to call him when Mark had a sport event. He said he wanted to attend them. So, Temia called Tom with Mark's sport schedule. Her schedule and commute distance to the hospital prevented her attendance at the softball games. But Tom's schedule and commute didn't, so he was there.

Mark really liked Tom. He had a frequent laugh that seemed to rise out of the bottom of his belly. When Mark heard the laugh and saw the smile in Tom's eyes, it helped Mark to feel calm. Mark felt anxious about himself most of the time these days. He felt anxious during his 'mis-performances' of reading and math at school. He felt anxious during his mom's long day and night hours at the hospital as a medical resident in training.

Unlike Mark, Mikaela coped with her mom's absence by participating in the community center's activities until it closed in the late afternoon. She developed a close friendship with one of the girls there. That anchored her. When the community center closed for the day, she returned to the lonely basement apartment. Mark was usually there or nearby on his bike.

Mark passed the time after school on his bicycle or in the basement apartment until Mikaela got home. Then, Mark always cooked a great spaghetti, hamburger, taco, or tostada dinner for the two of them.

Despite Mikaela's company in the evening, Mark felt a pervasive loneliness in his strong but young heart. Temia would call from the hospital to check that they were safely in the apartment by five o'clock. He'd hear her say, "How was your day? Have you finished your homework? I love you and will call you at bedtime again. Be sure and go to the neighbors if you need anything." Then he'd hear her beeper go off, and she'd say "I have to go. I love you."

She'd call again at bedtime and say, "I love you. Sleep tight. I'll see you tomorrow evening. I miss you. Crawl in my bed if you can't sleep. I love you."

She seemed so far away to Mark. Her calls seemed to accentuate her lack of presence in the apartment. Thus, they offered little comfort to Mark.

Not only did he miss his mom, but Mark also felt at a loss of how to place himself in this community. He pedaled his bike around the neighborhood in a detached whirl. This adjacent suburb to the city attempted to avoid solid areas of only black residents so they dispersed some black family apartment dwellers into the predominantly white part of town. Mark's family was one of those designated to be dispersed.

This well-meant policy came with a price for Mark and his family. Far too often groups of white boys would jump on Mark. Mark would fight back, but his assailants were older and bigger. On those nights, Mark and Mikaela would go to the neighbors. Their kind neighbors would treat Mark's bruises and call Temia at the hospital to say that the children would be with them for the night. Mark and Mikaela would sleep in their sleeping bags on the neighbors' living room floor.

For Mark, school was an experience of failure. His failure to read easily, write clearly, and successfully perform math computations shamed and confused Mark. He understood all the concepts. His memory was impeccable. Yet, he couldn't make sense of the order of the letters he saw on the page. Nor could he make sense of the order of the numbers on the math assignments. When Mark wrote, the order of the words made sense in his head, but somehow his pen wrote them in a jumbled up order. Mark felt very frustrated.

Temia asked for academic testing for her son. Eventually her request was honored. The testing showed that Mark's brain read from right to left and not from left to right. His brain processed sequences in a different way. It also showed that his intelligence was in the genius range. They gave him a label of a type of dyslexia and a teacher gave him thirty minutes a day of assistance with math and reading. This was a little helpful. But, basically Mark had to use his intelligence to retrain his brain to focus and process information differently. It took years, but he plowed through the frustrations and did it.

In this era of Mark's academic abyss, he enjoyed music. His ear clearly heard tones, tunes, and rhythms. Later he would teach himself guitar, drums, and piano. Although his mind had not yet made clear to him the worlds of numbers and words, it guided him to the ability to see overt and hidden relationships of shapes and objects. He became an excellent artist and often sought solace with a pencil and paper. He drew cartoon characters and any shape he saw or imagined. Much later he would carve faces, animals, and designs into wooden walking sticks. But for now it was pencil and paper.

His mom's positive comments about his school efforts, music, art, or athletics seemed almost meaningless to Mark in these years of academic failures and loneliness. He needed more of her. It seemed she was always at the hospital. And furthermore, she was a girl. A grown-up girl, but still a girl.

But, there was Tom. Tom continued to check in with Mark by phone between Mark's games. Tom encouraged his academic efforts as much as possible.

When an opportunity to play flag football arrived, Mark was very excited. With his mom's encouragement, Mark began to play.

Tom attended his games. He paced the sidelines and watched every move Mark made. After the game, Mark liked that Tom would put his hand on his shoulder, smile at him and say, "You did a good job today, Mark. I was proud of ya'."

Tom knew that he had never experienced the complex difficulty of Mark's academic challenges and his social challenges as African American. But Tom believed in this stubborn kid and just plain liked him. He would stand up for him always, without question.

Mark knew that this man with blonde hair and the bluest of eyes was not his father. Part of him ached that he would never hear the phrase that echoed in his teammates' ears, after the game, "Come on son, let's go home."

But Mark knew he could count on Tom's appearances at his games. He knew Tom would call occasionally. He knew Tom honestly enjoyed him. Mark hung onto this strong cord given to him by Tom. It gave him strength for his uphill climb towards manhood.

At the end of his mom's residency, when Mark was twelve, they moved north to another state. There, Temia had a Public Health Corps obligation. Tom also moved. However, he moved farther south than Mark's family moved north. During his residency, Tom had fallen in love with an irresistible nurse. They married. Tom went into practice and began to raise his family.

Mark's grandfather lived near Mark's new rural small town home. Mark looked forward to being close to his Granpa Martin. On visits to his grandparents, Granpa Martin would often secretly take Mark and Mikaela on drives to the Dairy Queen for an ice cream. The three of them enjoyed these little clandestine trips, which Granma Mildred knew nothing about. Now that Mark lived close to his granpa, he thought they could continue these fun escapes. He looked forward to settling into a secure relationship with his Granpa Martin.

However, a few months after his arrival, Mark found himself, at age thirteen, walking in step with three other men with the back right corner of Granpa Martin's casket on his left shoulder. Mark's usually active mind was blank except for the repeated phrase, "What now? What now? What now?"

In his new rural location, Mark faced typical US small town harassment of people of color. There were little things like name calling with the N word, coaches that removed his running back yardage in football games, visits by the police to the house for undocumented reasons, etcetera. When faced with these tired old American rituals towards young African American men, Mark threw himself strongly into his football. He greatly excelled as a running back. Eventually the coaches no longer subtracted his yardage. He had become too valuable to them.

As he matured during adolescence, Mark understood more and more how his brain worked. He applied himself to his schoolwork. He confronted his failures in the classroom and gradually improved academically.

Tom, now with his own family of three girls, called regularly to speak with Mark. His loyal encouragement towards Mark of sports and school never wavered. They talked about little things that strengthened the big bond they had for each other. The phone calls lightened Mark's spirit.

Temia finished her obligation with the Public Health Corps and moved her family from the rural town to a nearby larger city. Now in high school, Mark continued to love football and to do his best at his studies. By his senior year, Mark was one of the leading high school running backs in the state. His handsome statuesque presence of over six feet shone with pride and ambition. Mark saw himself in college on a football scholarship. He believed that despite all of his past academic struggles, he would be able to complete his college degree. And regardless of the precarious American attitude towards his color, Mark felt that he had a place in American manhood.

At the beginning of his high school senior year, under a new inexperienced coach, there was a night game. The sky was a gray-green black. The field lights seemed weak in the night's presence. In the first quarter of the game, Mark received a pass and ran to a make the touchdown. His team's defensive coverage was not there. Mark ran the ball while two opposing players clung to his leg. As a result, his knee was severely damaged. Mark's young mind was shocked with the pain in his knee. "I just have to walk it off," he told himself. He began to pace, but couldn't due to the severe pain. He knew his life was about to change, but he did not want to imagine the details.

Mark believed he had to forge on. He fought back the dark shadows of doubts. His football dream still had to happen. He moved ahead. First he had the surgery, then he completed the rehabilitation. Unfortunately, by then his senior year was over. The scouts with offers of free tuition to their colleges had disappeared.

One large university near Tom's home accepted Mark as a student and football team member. Mark knew that he could show the coach how much they needed him. But the opportunity never happened. The coach was not his advocate. The tutor program mixed up Mark's work with another African American student's. Mark's frustration mounted. His circumstances seemed to not match his vision for his future. He was unsure how to turn things around. He became edgy and less able to focus on his studies.

During this difficult time, one day, in the dorm one of the students hurled a foul insult at Mark. This infuriated Mark. He planned a fight between himself and that student with baseball bats. At that very moment, Tom happened to call Mark's room. Tom sensed something very wrong in how Mark answered the phone. He said firmly, "Mark. Wait. Stay there. I'm on my way."

Mark had been a fighter. No one, since he was ten years old, had ever beaten him in a fight. He was known in junior high as the protector of the smaller boys against the bullies. In high school he was known for his ability, when challenged, to take on as many as four men at a time and be victorious. The combination of his fight skills and strength made him a fearsome opponent. For years now, Mark had no fear of anyone or of any consequences. Now, his late adolescent hormones were pumped and the frustrations of the past years compressed into this moment. Mark was ready both physically and emotionally for battle.

Tom appeared at the dorm room door red in the face and breathing heavily, but not out of breath, after the three-flight sprint upstairs. Mark stood by his bed with a bat in his hand. A buddy, who had clearly failed to calm him, stood by Mark. Tom walked right up to Mark and asked what was going on. There was too much strong positive history between them for Mark to dismiss him. Tom and Mark talked. As Mark calmed, they sat down on the bed and talked some more. By the end of the long conversation, Mark had lost his anger. He was ready to cope with and to ignore crazy insults. Tom took the bat home. Mark did not fight then, and he did not fight physically again. However, Mark continued to have no fear of anyone, nor did he fear death.

At the end of a year of poor grades, Mark left that university that could not keep promises nor connect his name with his face. Temia picked him up, and they headed back up north.

Temia, with strong faith in her son, struck a deal with Mark. He would attend a junior college a couple of hours from where Temia lived. She would pay tuition and books. Mark would work and cover his living expenses. He would get C and above grades. Then, in one year, she would support his transfer to a university that also accepted him as a football player. Mark agreed.

He signed up for daytime classes and got a job loading trucks at night. Tom called occasionally and Mark stayed focused.

A historically black college in the south accepted Mark after that year. After his try-outs he was also accepted on the football team. Often Mark would stop to visit Tom on his way back home for holidays. Tom checked in with him at the university by phone. Mark thrived at this university. His grades reflected his hard work and comfort in the environment. He loved the positive culture of debate. For the first time, Mark saw himself as a scholar as well as an athlete.

Mark continued to love football. Mark was concerned that he would not get enough first string time his senior year for his personal satisfaction, as he loved the action of the game. Thus, he quit the college team in the beginning of his senior year. Because this school knew the names of the faces, the coach paid him a personal visit in his dorm room. He asked him if he was sure about his decision. The coach was aware of Mark's deep love for the game. He told this incredible coach that he was sure.

Mark joined the southern football league. He got full support from Tom by phone in his decision. He played every other weekend and practiced on the off weekends. This gave him plenty of time for his studies during the week as opposed to daily practice with the college team. Mark loved the weekend travel with the league. The team would chug around the south in an old school bus. At times it would break down on the back roads. The country people would come out and help them with the repairs and onward the bus would chug. At last, Mark felt a part of a bigger community. This community gave him sincere respect just to be who he was. He held onto this sensation his whole life.

Mark played defense now because of his knee. At these weekend games, he got frequent attention from NFL scouts. Mark couldn't help but reach his visions into this realm.

At the end of his senior year there was a big game in a nearby state. It would be heavily attended by scouts. This was Mark's last game with the team. This game meant a lot to Mark. It might be the last football game he would ever play. His Mom now worked at two different clinics to keep him and Mikaela in college. She couldn't travel the thirteen hours to the game. But Tom did. He drove the six hours from his home and stood on the sidelines just as he did back in Mark's flag football days.

Mark played linebacker position on defense. He was fast and strong, as he had been as a high school running back. But he was now more secure in himself. As fate would have it, there was a key play by Mark that turned the tide of the game for his team. Mark was in his linebacker special team position at a kick-off. Immediately as the ball fell in the hands of the receiver, Mark flew down field. His mind that easily saw patterns was able to maneuver fast through the blocks. His blend of strategy and strength landed him on top of the receiver before his opponent made it to the 20-yard line. As he stood up from the solo tackle he shot his eyes over to where Tom was standing. Tom was there with a huge smile on his face. Both men knew that Mark had nailed that one.

Shortly thereafter, Mark graduated. Tom stood at the ceremony with loud applause for Mark. Mark did not go to the NFL. He was courted by one of the teams whose coach really wanted him. But, in the end his knee was too much of an issue.

So Mark headed back up north and worked with youth in trouble. Mark would talk occasionally on the phone with Tom. His spirit would feel a little lighter after their talk, but the ache of not playing football was really deep.

The next few years were socially intense for Mark. At work he met a beautiful and smart woman with whom he fell madly in love. Soon they were engaged. His future wife had a young daughter. Mark took her daughter into his heart as his own.

During the engagement period, with the help of Temia, Mark found his dad. This opened for Mark emotions of regret, resentment, anger, sadness, forgiveness, and acceptance. The order and intensity of these emotions mixed around for many years. But in a couple of years he had settled these feelings about his parents enough to marry. He was convinced that he could—unlike his parents, but like Tom—do this successfully. The wedding was in a beautiful garden of a former country club. After the ceremony everyone went inside the big white building surrounded by brick verandas to an upstairs banquet hall to celebrate. The beautiful hall had wood floors, white wood trimmed doorways and ceilings, and many large chandeliers. All of this opulence opened onto a balcony that overlooked the garden. There were copious amounts of food, drink, music, dance, and joy. Mark was constantly grinning. His dad's family, his mom's family, and his bride's family were all there. Tom and his wife were also there. At one point, Tom stood beside the wedding table with the mike in his hand. He then gave a great toast of support to Mark while he flashed Mark that familiar grin.

Mark and his wife went on to have two sons. Mark let go of his youthful definition of manhood as a football star. He lived his adult definition as a dedicated husband and father. Unlike his childhood experience, his sons grew in the presence of constant support from their father. He walked them to school. He went to their school conferences. He played with them at night. He went to their sports events on the weekend. He cooked many weeknight dinners, weekend breakfasts, and barbequed meats for their birthdays and other huge holiday family gatherings. He loved his family.

Mark was dedicated to excellence in his work with the youth. He faced the many dangers of the inner city streets with a calm ease. When the gangs were at war, he flattened himself behind a wall until the bullets stopped their evil pop. When his clients challenged him with their unchained pit bulls at their side, Mark remained calm. One night as he stood at a youth's door a pit bull leapt out of the dark towards his neck. Fast, Mark grabbed his baton. As the dog was midair Mark came down with big strength onto the dog's head. The dog dropped dead. For Mark, it was especially sweet that night to walk through the door of his home to the presence of his family.

Mark's challenges as a youth served him well on his job. His intuition was superb with his clients. He knew when and how to push the boundaries. The tight discipline he needed to succeed at the academic work of his past served to make his court reports concise and accurate.

Slowly Mark's spirit began to acknowledge the man he had become.

When his stepdaughter, Veronica went off to college, he drove her, her mom, brothers, and all her belongings to the university. They were all very excited and proud of her. Mark's family's spirits were high on this trip. On the way back home Mark, his wife, and boys stopped to visit Tom and his family.

Tom laughed and laughed while he and Mark played with Mark's young sons. Mark laughed and laughed, too. He realized that he laughed and smiled at his sons like Tom had at him over the years. Then, on that wonderful warm day on the grassy yard of his friend Tom, Mark also smiled at himself. It felt like sunshine to his spirit. Those old aches and wants? Yes, they happened. That's all. They happened. Friends like Tom helped get him through. Now, Mark could be his own friend. Mark appeared for himself.

"Wow, Mamma. I am very excited to meet Uncle Mark tomorrow. You know, to be an adult always looked so awesome to me. But as I listened, it seemed that adulthood happened as Uncle Mark kept one foot in front of the other. I can identify with his intensity. I will always remember how he kept going forward. So glad I heard this whole story," I commented. "But, what happened to Cousin Veronica?"

"She was a strong young lady. Your Nonna Mikaela told me this story about Veronica."

THE NEGOTIATOR

Veronica began her negotiations with herself before the age of five. She decided in her head that her mother's new boyfriend would leave and then her real dad would come back. But, this new boyfriend, called Mark, stayed. In fact, to make it worse, her mother married him. And then, of all things, her mother became pregnant by him. Not once, but twice!

Veronica's father began to visit her when he saw that there was a step-dad in the picture. Sometimes he would take Veronica out with him. But on these outings he would negotiate with Veronica to lie to his multiple girlfriends about his loyalty. Veronica thought that maybe if she could do enough favors for her dad, he would come back home. But, that never played out.

Veronica's dad would negotiate time with her when he needed her for something. He would also show up at the wrong place and at the wrong time, or he wouldn't show up at all. Like the time he negotiated with Veronica to take her out for her birthday. Even though he hadn't shown up for the prior two birthdays, she dutifully awaited his arrival for the third year in a row. He did show up. But he took her to a relative's and left her for a few hours because he had to make a quick run that lasted all day. But, Veronica reasoned, at least she could breathe the air of the same house where her dad lived.

When Veronica turned sixteen and had her driver's license, her father negotiated with her for rides in Veronica's family car. Gradually it became clear to Veronica that this was not negotiation. Rather, he held her hostage by her dreams of what the relationship could be.

Veronica realized that the relationship she fantasized was not the real relationship her dad offered. Veronica saw that, sadly, there was no magic that would change her dad.

Thus, little by little, Veronica let the fantasy she had built around her dad fall away. She began to see her life as it was. She saw that it was her step-dad and mom that came for her when she was stranded somewhere by her dad. It was her step-dad, mom, and two younger brothers that took her out for Chinese food when her dad didn't show up for her birthdays. She also saw that her step-dad always respected the space of her relationship with her mom that had established itself before he was in the picture. She saw how he and her mom consistently provided for her.

None of these things filled the void she felt. She had to fill it. So, Veronica accepted her disappointments and moved on. She began to turn her negotiation skills towards herself. She negotiated with herself how to get good grades and was accepted into a big university.

Veronica studied hard at the university. She negotiated scholarships and part-time jobs for herself. She negotiated a loving relationship full of respect with a young man at college. At home, Veronica negotiated a pleasant relationship with her family.

Veronica was happy. She moved on to a prestigious graduate school on the east coast. In Washington, DC, she built up a reputation as a superb negotiator. Veronica was clear about the difference between fantasy and realistic negotiation offers. She was clear about the difference between manipulation and compromise. Veronica was also able to clarify the difference for others at the negotiation table. In this arena, she had the magic to bring opposing forces to a resolution.

She loved her life in DC. After she established her career, she married a young lawyer in the State Department that understood, loved, and appreciated Veronica. I would be remiss to not mention that he was also smitten by her beauty. Veronica had the elegant height of royalty. Her tall, lithe, dark skinned figure caused heads to turn when she entered a room. Her smile was always warm and gracious. She remembered now, with the years of anguish about her father long gone, to cast that beautiful smile on herself first as she prepared for her day.

Finished now with Veronica's story, my mamma laid down on the blanket. Beverly and I did the same. We watched the gently moving branches of the tree above with the blue sky in its empty spaces. We heard the ripples of the fishing hole and the chirp of birds. And with the stories of our family members in our hearts, we fell asleep and dreamed these stories into our depths.

Later on that evening as we sat on the patio by the lit citronella lanterns we finished the Abuelita Temia stories. My mamma started out the stories, and as Beverly had spent many hours by Abuelita Temia's side during her last weeks, she told us the last story.

WHEN KNOWLEDGE FROM SOMEONE ELSE HELPS US TO HEAL

Temia worked as a public health physician in a small rural town for a few years after medical residency. This was a required four-year assignment because the US government had paid her medical school expenses. Temia and her children lived in a clean pre-fabricated house near the hospital. She would drive the ten miles out to the country clinic daily. Between the clinic and the hospital, she worked the same 110 hours a week that she had done during medical residency. Her children were now in junior high.

Temia decided that she had to be stronger on the inside to continue more years of this huge demand on her body and mind. She sought out emotional support from a social worker, who turned out to be of great assistance. They spoke of the present and of the past. One annoyance to Temia for as long as she could remember was the call of her name in her head every time she entered a basement. She dismissed it as just something about her and basements. But the social worker figured out that it was more than that. This is the story the social worker heard that gave her the answer.

When Temia was seven years old, it was her chore to take out the family trash from their parsonage apartment on the second and third floor of the old mansion. Temia hated to do it. The trash had to be dumped in the lower level incinerator room of the large new Sunday school and pre-school building attached between the old mansion and the large church. So to take out the trash involved many stairs, darkness, and an unwanted game.

Daily Temia gathered the trash from the two bathrooms and placed it into the medium-sized, round, metal trashcan in the kitchen. Then, she would make her way down the dark curved narrow wooden stairs from their kitchen to the main hallway on the first floor of the mansion that housed the church offices and church kitchen. A few feet to her right was an additional door that went down larger, dark red painted stairs to a small landing and then turned sharply to the left to the hallway that led to the lower level of the Sunday school building.

If one glanced one's eyes to the right from the platform, one would see the darkness of this old basement room. The light from the stairway cast scary forms into this dark room. Temia avoided anything more than a quick cut of her eyes to the right. She hated to do even that much. But she feared worse the possibility that she would not detect that he was there to surprise her as he had many times. He would always call her name to herald his approach, but still it was the shock of it all to hear her name coming out of that dark old basement room.

Most often, however, he would show up in one of two other places. One was in the gray linoleum passageway at the bottom of the stairs that led past the lower level classrooms. The other was in the boiler room itself. The gray boiler room door was just past the daycare preschool classroom with its small chairs, blocks, and worm farms. It was Temia's goal each day to get to the boiler room, dump the trash, and make it out before he showed up.

He was gray-haired Gunther. Gunther liked to play the tickle game. He would corner Temia and tickle her under her skirt, over her panties between her legs, and under her panties to her lower belly, and over her private parts. He would always ask Temia if she liked to be tickled. Temia always answered, no. Gunther would laugh and that was the end of it, for the moment. Temia felt afraid but wasn't sure of what. After all, this was Gunther, the nice church janitor. And she felt confused as to how a tickle game could feel scary.

One day he was at the entrance to his workshop, which was near the bottom of the red stairs in the hallway that lead to the classrooms. He asked Temia to come inside because he had something he wanted to show her. Temia went inside and he said, "How about the tickle game?"

He then started tickling Tamia on her ribs first, then his hand moved quickly into her panties. He moved a finger into the middle of her opening while he held her private parts with his hand. Gunther then reached behind him and slammed the door closed and locked. Tamia didn't like the force of the lock that clicked into place. Tamia didn't like the feel of his finger in her opening. All she could then feel was the need to escape. She puffed up her strength and spun behind him. She then slammed herself against the door while she pulled the lock back, and then she flung open the door in the face of stunned Gunther. Temia ran as fast as she could up the red stairs. She flew past the landing and pounded up the stairs to the mansion hallway, and then, with hardly a breath inhaled, she ran up the curved narrow back stairs to the family's kitchen. She slammed and locked the kitchen door and looked for her mom.

The trashcan was left in the basement with Gunther. After she told her mom, Temia didn't have to take the trash out anymore. Gunther was not the church janitor anymore, either. But there was total silence to Temia about the incidents. That's what happened in those days after such a thing. Silence. The noise that was left was Temia's name called out in the shadows of her mind whenever she entered a basement alone.

After Temia related these experiences with Gunther to the kind social worker, the social worker explained to Temia that these experiences and the subsequent silence about them had led to the noise in her head of her name as called by Gunther when she entered dark basements. She explained that this was a common aftermath of molestation. Temia understood and it made good sense to her. From that day forward, Temia never again heard her name called when she entered a basement. She was most grateful.

"It's beautiful when we can heal from such a thing, Mamma."

"Yes, it is," my mamma continued. "She also worked to heal her spirituality. She wanted to resolve her childhood experience of dogmatic religious rituals with her personal belief of a loving Creator of all things.

"In addition, she wanted to resolve the divisions of her multiple ethnicities. She wanted to embrace all of her North African, Native American, Spanish, Romero Gypsy, Irish, and Scandinavian ancestry.

"She was actually able to do it. In her Public Health Corps assignment she loved the work in the rural Hispanic community. She felt peace of mind to be in the culture and to speak Spanish. This, and the love of and from her children, nourished her tired body during the long work hours.

"Temia was also given another precious cultural and spiritual gift in her last year of her rural Public Health Corps obligation. Here it is."

SECRET PRAYERS

Temia drove a long distance into the woods after she exited the small rural town where she lived with her children for almost three years. With the long hours at the rural clinic and hospital, her body was chronically tired. But two days ago she had received an invitation from a group of Ojibwe women to join them in their full-moon prayers. She really wanted to connect to this part of her culture. Her whole being tingled with anticipation. Temia left her fatigue back at the edge of town. She seemed to travel with the intent of a message bird towards a long sought destination. The dirt roads were the darkest of dark as the large tree branches loomed over the car. She continued on, grateful for an occasional burst of moonlight between the branches. After a certain turn that had been described to her, on the left was a wooden gate that gaped almost completely open. It led to another dirt road with deep gouges and scattered large rocks. Carefully, she maneuvered her old Chevy along this large path and descended to a small open space in which a few cars stood along a stream. She saw a small cabin a few feet downstream and a small house across the stream beyond a small field. There was also the frame of the long house used for ceremonies on the north side of the cabin. Behind the cabin there was the muffled sound of men's voices as they built the prayer fire for the women. That was their job as Ojibwe men, to support the spirituality of the women.

Temia entered the cabin quietly. There she saw about twelve women busy with their medicine bundles in their laps. She recognized some of the women. Temia was introduced and invited to sit down and work on her medicine bundle. As they worked, they softly exchanged the latest stories of their families and of the people in the community. Their bundles were made of four herbs that represented the spiritual qualities of the four sacred directions. The women placed in their bundles the balance of qualities necessary for them this lunar cycle. Temia knew the medicines and quickly made her bundle. Then the leader began with the talking stick. As the talking stick was passed, each person spoke in turn when holding the talking stick. They shared many secrets of their hearts. The circle was completed only when everyone had said all that was to be said. When the women were about halfway finished with the talking stick, the leader raised a candle in the cabin window to signal the men that had gathered at the house to come and light the fire at the back of the cabin.

The men came across the field to light the fire. Then they retreated to the house to wait for the women to complete their prayers before they would monitor the sacred fire again. Now that it was legal to practice Native American beliefs, the men could relax during the prayers. Only a few years ago, they had to post themselves out by the roads to be vigilant for the police, because such gatherings were often raided. But no longer.

The women entered the fire circle from the east and stood in a circle around the fire. They carefully smudged each other. Then the prayers began. The prayer was always for others. There was no need to pray for themselves. Their nourishment was in the medicines of their bundles. So, one by one, the women prayed to the feminine aspect of the Great Spirit. One by one, they put their energy from their heart towards the needs of others and then dropped their bundle into the fire.

Temia loved to watch the smoke and sparks from each bundle reach upwards towards the heavens. She loved the way the bundles flamed on the coals in their own individual pattern. She loved the visual energy transformation from the medicines to the energy in the smoke. The woody herb smell was like the embodiment of peace. Temia's body welcomed the smell into her core as it nourished her life energy.

After the prayers, the women filed away from the fire in the western direction. They went back to the cabin and briefly feasted on some strawberries. Then Temia and some of the women went to the house to let the men know the fire was ready to be tended and to tease them about their fire building. It was now late.

Temia did not stay long. She had at least an hour drive home and an early morning clinic. Temia enjoyed the movement of herself in the car through the night. Balance and joy were the words that came to her.

Temia returned every subsequent full moon. When she eventually moved back to the large city in the Midwest, the Pipe Carrier asked her to continue to do the ceremony for the women in the city. He would tell Temia, "Always create sacred spaces. We must always be with sacred spaces. We must not be dependent on sacred spaces that are no more. Because some people and some authorities attack sacred spaces, we must create them again and again. Continually, if necessary."

Temia took his advice to heart and did just that. The first sacred space that she acknowledged was her own body and soul.

Temia began to let go of her passion to force her environment to be okay. She focused on her heart to be okay. She recognized in a small, soft way the presence of peace in her. She no longer required a big external event to convince her of the presence of the Great Spirit within her. She had returned to the Great Spirit despite the long distance from her mountain of origin. Ah Ho.

"Mamma, now I get on another level why you burn the sage by the candles on the patio."

"She continued to burn her sage when she lived with us," added Beverly. "The story Abuelita Temia told me was how she came to live out in the desert. It includes both Temia and your Nonna Mikaela in this one, Francesca."

"Lay it on me," I said as I laid back in the lounger.

VOYAGE TO THE DESERT

Temia sat at her kitchen table in her second floor rear chilly flat in the cold northern city. It was December and the temperature outside was fifteen below zero. She felt tired. Temia could see the gray sky above the rooftops from the window a couple of feet away. Temia decided that she needed some hot tea. She looked at the teapot on the stove. Then she looked at the filtered water container on the counter between the stove and sink. Carefully she counted the steps from the table to the water faucet and then to the stove. It seemed overwhelming to her to take those four steps. At that point it clicked in her head what she needed to do. It was something other than to make tea.

For many days she had tried rest and different home remedies for her cough, headache, and fatigue. She went out briefly only for a few groceries. She didn't admit to herself that she could not move an adequate amount of air in and out of her lungs. After all, she didn't hear or didn't want to hear the wheeze as she breathed. Today she felt cold, tired, and isolated in the back of this brick building of five flats.

Temia had lacked her usual joy for a few weeks before her illness. She had recently retired, a year earlier than planned, from a college professorship that she loved. The faculty contract negotiations made it imperative for those near retirement to leave or risk loss of money. So she left. Post-retirement, she taught part-time at another institution of higher learning. The students were dedicated, but the institution had many fiscal challenges. Temia had to work hard for little money. She rejected the unreasonableness of this at this point in her life. She left the position.

Now, with no distractions from herself, it was time to create her present by her own dictates.

And, at this moment, on this gray evening, Temia felt that she had to make a change for herself. She was now in touch with the weakness of her body and probably her soul at this moment. She could feel that her lungs barely inflated as she breathed. Temia decided to change her situation. She rose, put on her hat, put on many scarves around her face, neck, and chest, and put on her coat, gloves, and boots. She left the apartment. Carefully she made it down one and a half flights of the old gray curved stairs of the inside porch to the brown back door. She opened it and walked on the couple inches of snow the few feet to her car parked at the alley's edge. Away she drove to what she thought was a nearby medical center. But, it was not nearby. It took over thirty minutes. Temia knew how to force her body to make a destination. From her years in medicine, she knew how, in times of extreme fatigue, to have her body keep a focus until the task was accomplished.

She made it to the medical center. It was warm and brightly but gently lit. The receptionist smiled with both her mouth and eyes. Temia knew she was in the right place. She sat down to wait after completion of the basic forms and immediately fell asleep. Temia was soon awakened and escorted back to the nurse practitioner. The nurse practitioner listened to

Temia's lungs and said, "You are not moving air well at all."

Of course, Temia thought. The cough. The fatigue. How could she have missed it? Here in the room with the nurse practitioner her wheeze seemed to echo off the small room's gray walls.

Temia received a breathing treatment, oral steroids, antibiotics, and inhalers. She felt so much better after the treatment that she had no concerns about the drive to the pharmacy and home. Temia assured the clinic staff, "I'll be fine."

The nurse practitioner informed her of the nearest hospitals on her path home. "Please go there if you are short of breath on the drive home," the nurse practitioner encouraged.

Temia picked up her meds and arrived to her alley park safely. Temia climbed the old gray stairs in the back to the second floor. She took her meds, went to her bed, and threw the warm wool blankets over her.

The high dose steroids gave her dreams of purple people. But, she breathed much better during the subsequent days and nights. She no longer counted her steps from one location to another in her apartment. The clinic called to check on her daily. They reminded her to keep her inhaler with her at all times. She rested and completed her medications. After a few weeks, Temia thought that she would be just great. But, every time she stepped out into the frigid winter air, her lung's bronchioles squeezed down and she lost her air.

As the universe would have it, Temia was forced to consider another location that would be better for herself. She rationalized that certainly a debilitated Temia was no good to herself, nor to her children and grandchildren. She would have to let go proximity to her grandchildren if she chose the ability to breathe. Temia allowed herself to open her mind to big possibilities.

"Just maybe," she allowed herself to think, "I could find a place with warm air, affordable housing, uncrowded open spaces, social opportunities, and, if need be, income opportunities."

Temia decided to leave the city, and the Midwest. She would move to the Southwest desert. She became excited about the prospect. She mused in her happy thoughts, "There are native people and Hispanic people there. Rejoice ancestors! Good. My sister, Maria, who was my dear childhood companion, is there. Good. There are open spaces for plenty of adventures. Good. It was full of sun and warmth. Good. I think

I've found my spot!"

Temia decided to move after her grandchildren's birthdays in the summer. Thus, the family and Temia had the spring to adjust to the idea of her big change. Her children were a little shocked, but got used to the new Temia over time. Her furniture and smaller items sold in forty-eight hours after she sent an e-mail out to friends. She easily found apartment options in the Southwest online.

Temia became ecstatic about her move. It had many aspects of a return to home. Born in the west by mountains, she now returned to the west among mountains. Her bones longed for heat. It had not been in her destiny to remain in tropical warm Jamaica where she had spent three years of her life. It was the desert heat that was her destiny! Now Temia could feel her heart sing in such a way that surprised her with the intensity of its joy. Temia lost her retired, pale, drawn face. She had a face of light now. Even her hair that was always a little springy had more springs.

Yes, yes, she would return north for visits in warm seasons. She would write, Skype, and call. She would purchase a sleeper couch and encourage family to come for visits. Her love for her family would swarm generously over the miles to their hearts from hers. But, Temia was out of the city and onto a new life!

So after a brief visit with Maria and her husband in the early summer to solidify an apartment for herself, she returned to Chicago to pack up. A few days after the grandchildren's birthdays, Temia rented a small truck. Her son Mark and her sister's son, John, packed it perfectly. Mikaela had offered to drive the truck with Temia. Mikaela took precious vacation time from her job and from her young family to do this.

Thus, on a hot summer afternoon, after many hugs to Mark, John, Robert (Mikaela's husband), and a tearful seven-year-old Alessia, Temia and Mikaela drove out of the city.

After a couple of hours, as the truck driven by Mikaela passed green country fields, the two women seemed to take on a transformative energy. The strength of these two women united by fate since Mikaela's conception gave power to this big change for Temia and to subtler changes for Mikaela.

The miles passed. As they continued over the next bluff, a wide irregular body of water appeared below them. This mighty river that controlled the environment for hundreds of miles lay below them in a deceptively unassuming presence. The bridge was quickly traversed. The sky turned into a purple gray after arrival at the river's other tree-lined shore. As they went on, the fields deepened into warm browns and dark greens. Mikaela and Temia drank in the beauty around them. Their view was a relief from the cars, trucks, and potholes that filled the city streets.

They softly chatted of the latest family news. They marveled how fast Mikaela's and Mark's children had grown. They mused proudly over their latest feats, or cute antics. They talked of the cousins, in-laws, and great-grandparents. After the conversation was exhausted, Temia offered to drive. Mikaela said she felt fine to drive and would let Temia know if she tired. They decided to only do a few hours and stop before nightfall. As navigator, it was Temia's role to find the motel for the night. She found a great motel just off the highway with its own restaurant.

When their bags were deposited in their room, they walked directly with their empty stomachs to the restaurant on the lower level of the motel. Cleverly, this lower area was decorated in a medieval motif. Mikaela and Temia seated themselves in one of the heavily wooded nooks with its small wooden table. They opened the low wooden gate to enter. The table benches had a comfortable wide width with wooden backs to the low ceiling.

As they received their menus, Mikaela announced, "This dinner is on me as a celebration for your new life's adventure, Mom. So order whatever you want!"

Soon Mikaela's glass of white wine and Temia's cup of hot tea arrived. Both women were giddy with the emotion of their escape from the big city. Temia's escape was permanent and Mikaela's only for a few days. The two women laughed and giggled through every bite of food and through every bit of their conversation.

Before they left the table, Mikaela called her family on her cell phone. Alessia told her about her fun afternoon at the park with her dad. Mikaela listened with a peaceful heart. Mikaela and her family blew kisses over the phone and sent "abrazos grandes" over the airwaves. Thus the young family said goodnight.

"Come, Mom. Let's go get into the hot tub before bed!"

"Great idea," responded Temia.

They soaked and smiled at each other and soaked some more. Temia loved the soft brown wide eyes of her daughter. Her dark eyebrows and thick dark eyelashes framed them beautifully.

The next morning as they loaded the truck with their overnight satchels, Mikaela said, "Mom, I just want you to know that I intend to do all the driving."

"But," Temia tried to interject.

"No, I really want to. If I get too fatigued, I'll let you know."

This both relieved and surprised Temia. She was really anxious about how she would manage the little square truck on the road, but had resolved herself to it. Now she wouldn't have to. Hooray! Temia also felt a little guilty. She knew that Mikaela did not enjoy driving. She knew that Mikaela was still tired from her job's long hours. But all Temia could do was say, "Well, okay, but if ever you are too tired, let me know."

"I will, Mom. I like the activity of driving as opposed to just sitting for so many miles. It's really okay." And that was that.

Now that she didn't have to face the idea of time in the driver's seat, Temia found herself more relaxed. Mikaela could see it in her face and laughed. Temia laughed, too.

Temia settled into her seat comfortably. With the truck's smooth movement, she began to self-reflect. She admitted to herself that she had seen life as full off obstacles to climb over, fight through, or cleverly avoid. And, of course, to complete this desperate picture, she admitted that she saw herself as alone in these situations.

What an exhausting way to live life, Temia mused to herself. After all, was I really alone? No, not really, she decided.

The two women chugged along in a companionable silence surrounded by green fields and the expansive bright blue sky of the prairie.

Temia continued in her self-talk. Actually, I was never alone. The Creator was always here. Furthermore, there were always people there for me. Maybe not who or in the way I had expected, but there nevertheless. What a great revelation with which to begin my southwest adventure!

Temia dozed off for a short time. Then she opened her eyes and looked at her daughter. Mikaela sat with a strong posture in the driver's seat. Mikaela was one of those women that looked beautiful in any setting. Her golden brown skin, short curly natural hair, and slightly arched nose made an awesome profile of feminine beauty.

Within her beauty she housed a courageous spirit. Temia always admired her daughter for it. Mikaela had let go of the anxiety of the lonely childhood nights when Temia was gone on hospital call. She had let go of the anger in her heart from the N word shouted in her ears while she walked to middle school in the rural community where Temia did her Public Health Corps assignment. Mikaela chose faith and love in herself over anxiety and anger.

Mikaela worked these choices now as a wife and mother. Her husband, Robert, had been unemployed for the past two years due to a corporate takeover. Mikaela continued to work long hours as well as be an emotional anchor for her family. During those years she spoke only positive encouragement to her husband. She believed in his sense of family and his ability to find work. By the end of this journey with Temia to the desert, he had found work.

Mikaela and Temia continued to chug on in the truck. They passed along flat lands for most of the day. Then they entered more rolling green hills scattered with cattle that lowered their heads to the grass. The fields were also dotted with tall wind columbines. As they passed over more hills the columbines were a part of the landscape for as far as they could see. They were very dramatic with their long, slow turning blades. Despite their danger to the occasional bird, they seemed to herald an American future of less pollution and, consequently, fewer deaths.

Mikaela turned to her mother and said. "I'm proud of you making this move for yourself. I will miss you a lot. But, I'm happy about your new life."

Then she reiterated her mantra to Temia, "Keep faith that everything will work out and enjoy yourself, Mom."

So Temia, in the presence of her kind daughter in this little truck, could only embrace this beautiful mantra and consciously let it grow.

At dusk, the women did their ritual stop at a motel with a nearby restaurant. They also repeated the hot tub soak and enjoyed its warm comfort. Both mother and adult daughter slept well all night.

In a few days they arrived at Temia's new home. Mikaela flew home to her family, glad of her mother's desert choice.

In the desert Temia grew in health and joy. She loved the dramatic storms with the earthy smell given off by the desert governadora plants afterward. She loved the unapologetic heat of the desert. She loved the cacti that she grilled and put in her stews and smoothies. She loved the evening walks with the vast array of stars almost at her fingertips. She loved the slower paced lifestyle and the people that walked it.

Temia opened herself to every moment and every part of her life in the desert. Temia had many adventures there.

TEMIA'S MOUNTAIN FOUND

By the time of this story, Temia had lived in the Southwest for a few years. One of Temia's favorite activities was to hike up what she called "her" mountain. It was very near her apartment, so she conveniently did the hike several times a week. It was one of the many quartz and slate mountains of the area. The desert foliage of governadora, sage, saguaro, cholla, fishhook, barrel, nopalito, and ocotillo grew all over the mountainside. There was even palo verde in the washes.

Temia believed that the mountain with its quartz base gave her strength. The pieces of quartz that washed to the surface after a monsoon were her favorite kind of eye candy.

Temia was well known by the other habitual hikers and them to her. She was easy to spot on the trails with her trail shoes, jeans, t-shirt, cloth backpack, Mexican cowboy hat, dark glasses, and carved ironwood cane from Jamaica.

One particular day on the mountain, the sunny blue sky had its famous clarity. Temia bathed herself in its brightness as she made the climb. It was late afternoon. She chose a trail that would finish about two hours before sunset. Temia preferred to leave the mountain by nightfall to respect the coyotes' night hunts.

At one saddle of the trail one could see far in all directions. The mountain ranges that scattered this ancient oceanic floor, offered her a vision of endurance and beauty. The scattered boulders at the saddle provided a great support to sit on or lean against for weary hikers. Temia loved to lean against one of them while she took in some water and drank in the view. On this day, Temia stood there with her thermos in her hand and her eyes filled with distant mountains when she heard a pleasant voice greet her, "The view is magnificent, isn't it!"

"Yes, it is," Temia answered as she smiled at this pleasant man. I'll never tire of it."

"My name is Alanzo," he stated as he held out his hand.

Temia shook his hand and liked his intelligent soft brown eyes.

She answered, "I'm Temia."

"Good to meet you," Alanzo said, and then added, "Do you hike this mountain often?"

"Yes, I love it. And you?"

"This is my first time. I just moved here from California."

"What brought you here?" asked Temia.

"I've always loved this area and thought it would be a good place to retire. I was a professor of Spanish literature in the state's college system. What about yourself?" Alanzo asked. "What brought you to this part of the world?"

They talked and talked and then were awestruck by the light show display of the sun's descent behind the mountains in the far west. Temia suggested they begin their descent while there was still some light.

When they were almost to the flat desert trail that lead to the car lot, the land plunged into darkness. The new moon cast enough light to carefully make out the trail. As the darkness enveloped the desert, the air immediately became cool and all the small leaves on the governadora bushes and palo verde trees responded with an unseen rapid movement. They opened and released their moisture, oxygen gas, and desert musk scent into the air. It filled Temia's and Alanzo's nostrils with a rush of energy.

"What a treat to inhale this sweet air!" exclaimed Temia.

"Yes, this is fantastic!" responded Alanzo.

While Temia and Alanzo enjoyed their moisture laden oxygen bath, the coyotes began their night calls to organize the hunt. Temia and Alanzo hurried along the flat trail towards their cars. But it was just to avoid a problem. It was not out of fear. They both felt honored to be there in the dark and to witness the desert's nightly ritual of opening to its night.

Temia and Alanzo continued to share hikes, and soon they decided to share their daily lives, as well.

"Thanks, Beverly, for that," said my mamma. "Temia and Alanzo were so in love for the rest of their lives together."

"Yes, when she was here she spoke of countless happy memories with him," added Beverly.

"I would have liked to know both of them better, but at least we did have some talks on FaceTime that I remember as a little girl," I reminisced.

MY VISIT TO UNCLE MARK IN AMERICA

The next day we were off to Uncle Mark's. It was hard for me to leave this gracious couple who were family to me. And, it was really hard for my mamma. She and Cousin Andrew had been close since her birth. When she was an infant he would go up to her, as he was almost a year older, and place his forehead gently on hers. They seemed to take strength from each other to face this precarious world. This closeness has continued all their lives. Fortunately the distance did not weaken their support for one another. But, still... to say good-bye... and feel the distance...

Upon arrival at the Louisiana airport, we called Aunt Natalie. Mamma knew her uncle and his sporadic response to his phone, which is why she called Aunt Natalie, who answered immediately. She suggested that we go to the Rib Shack directly to surprise Uncle Mark. Aunt Natalie gave us clear directions. We settled into our rental car with its GPS and headed for the Rib Shack. Within forty minutes we had arrived.

As we exited the highway, the GPS was unnecessary. Our nostrils had filled with the aromatic smoked scent from Uncle Mark's Rib Shack. That sweet aroma became our GPS. We were guided to the shack not half a mile from the exit. It was nestled in a grove of trees. The small building was constructed with walls of thick wooden slats. The sign above the front window was a wooden board freshly painted white with bold letters in red that said Rib Shack.

There were five picnic tables painted bright red scattered around the grove of trees at the side of the Rib Shack. The cars parked on the other side, where there was ample space for the cars and the steady flow of people. Some of the tables were filled, but it seemed that most of the people did carryout. At the back of the building three huge smokers and grills puffed away. They emitted the most amazing aroma from spices, corn, meats, onions, and sweet potato. Since I first inhaled the smoky aroma at Cousin Andrew's, I was sold on the American art of bar-be-que. But now at the Rib Shack, as the spiced sweet smoke caressed my olfactory senses, I knew I was on sacred ground of a master.

We entered the shack and saw Martin at the front counter. His face shone with delight at the sight of my mamma and me. He quickly rounded the counter to greet us with many kisses and hugs. Another worker took his place at the counter. Uncle Mark, back at the grills, sensed a change in the flow of things and looked up. He lowered the lid with the request to his assistant to "take out the chickens in five more minutes." He then wiped his hands on his apron and strode to the front of the shack.

There he was with his usual charismatic self. "My, my, look at you two," he said as he encircled my mamma and me in his strong arms. "My Italian nieces have come for this good bar-be-que!"

"And there you are, Uncle Mark, bending over the grill just like when I was a little girl," Mamma said. "You look handsome as ever," she added.

Martin and I strode over to one of the picnic tables anxious to talk as previously we had only communicated by Skype. We knew of each other's love of the arts. It was great to be together in person and talk about our plans with our art.

"This is a great summer with Granpa Mark and Granma Natalie. I've learned a lot of blues guitar from Granpa as well as a lot of bar-be-que secrets," Martin said.

"Treasures for life," I said.

"Right," he responded.

Uncle Mark came towards the table with his assistant, Vincent. They carried trays that were laden with his chicken and sauces. One sauce was gentle and slightly sweet with a hint of mango. It was for the vegetables. The other one was smoky with warm spices and peppers. In addition they laid before us ribs, corn, sweet potato, squash, toasted French bread, and tortillas. Then we all sat down and feasted.

Uncle Mark ran pretty much a waste-free establishment. We ate on banana leaves. The drinks were glass bottles of ginger beer and mineral water. The silverware was washed and reused.

"This is incredible, Uncle Mark!" I said as chewed this tasty, aromatic food. I felt truly nurtured, Uncle Mark style!

"When you finish your food, I'll take you back to see the smokers and tell you a secret or two," Uncle Mark offered.

"Great!"

"How long are you staying?" Uncle Mark asked. "I'd love to have you join me and Martin at the fishpond tomorrow morning."

"We have a couple of days before our flight to Philadelphia," Mamma said. "You have plenty of time to show your grandniece the fishing hole."

"Alright. It's a date then. We'll set off at six tomorrow morning! Just kidding," he quickly added. "We can go at seven-thirty and have plenty of time for a good catch."

Aunt Natalie arrived and, after big hugs, grabbed a piece of chicken. She wrapped it in a napkin and said, "I have to run you guys. There's a meeting of my professional ladies local branch in about half an hour. See you all at the house in a couple of hours. Just make yourselves at home." Aunt Natalie kissed Mark and waved at everyone with the one hand that grasped her chicken as she answered her most recent text with the other. Then off she drove.

After Aunt Natalie's departure, we all settled back to the last precious bites of our meal and our ginger beer.

"So, Uncle Mark," Mamma started, "Your son and daughter-in-law await you. Are you ready to leave the Rib Shack?"

Uncle Mark laughed. "Alessia, you always were direct. Yes, I am ready. I have done my dream. Now I have other dreams. I still want to work a smoker, but it can be at Andrew's or at my new spot. Now I'm ready for more time to fish and play my music.

"What makes it easier is that Vincent, whom you met earlier, really wants to buy the Rib Shack. He has the finances ready, and I know that he'll run it well. So, I'm ready to move on. Not just me, but your Aunt Natalie would be happier in a little more populated area where she can easily meet up with her professional groups and fellow speed walkers.

"Andrew has sent me some pictures of the inside of the single-level townhouses in his neighborhood. We've seen the outside. Natalie and I both think the layout inside the townhouse with the small, private back yard will be ideal. I think the next phase of my life will be just fine. Anyway, it is closer to the Atlantic and a shorter ride across the puddle to you guys," Uncle Mark concluded with a twinkle in his eye.

"I'm going to hold you to that," Mamma said. "It is beautiful around Andrew and Beverly's. I'm glad that you and Aunt Natalie will have such a beautiful spot," she added.

"I agree. It is beautiful. We'll be fine there." Uncle Mark continued, "As you know most of the family has left Chicago. The earthquakes there were a little more frequent and a little stronger. It seems the fracking destabilized the geologic layers. And with the water issues from the still-used old nuclear reactor on the lake, it is a city to be avoided, for now.

"So here we are in the south. We find more environmental stability here. The folks around Andrew seem to be focused on sustainability of our earth as well. It's funny, Alessia, as a people we had to run from the slavers and then from the Clan in the south to the north. Now we run from the north. Go figure. Life goes on, dear Alessia," Uncle Mark concluded with a deep look of appreciation at my mamma.

"I understand Uncle Mark. And, I love you for your tenacity," Mamma added.

As I listened to this conversation I gained even more respect for my uncle, the country of my mamma, and the people in it. I recognized them as a people of humble strength. I am surrounded by such folks in Italy and now I and surrounded by them here. It is no wonder that my parents found each other.

LAST PART OF MY TRIP TO AMERICA AND BACK HOME TO ITALY

So after my great fishing expedition and a lot of good bar-be-que, we left for Philadelphia to spend a day with Perla, mom's lifelong friend. Perla and her family were delightful. The day went too fast, but I was also ready for home. The next day we caught a direct flight to Roma and a fast train home.

It was so good to see my papà at the train station with his tall welcoming frame. Both my mamma and I folded into his arms. He then grabbed our bags and we piled into the car. When we arrived home he had a big salad, bowl of oyster pasta, olives, grapes, and wine ready for our consumption.

We told him all the news from our family visits that included Uncle Mark's eminent move to Cousin Andrew's neighborhood. He told us that everyone was well on the farm and his soccer team had its second win this season. He told me, also, that Marco had asked that morning when I would return.

That, dear reader, was my first and only trip to America. That was now more than four years ago. The relationships and knowledge from that trip became a part of me. Thus, in the present, I understood how my mamma could have a fearless attitude towards our increased earth tremors and the troublesome predictions about Vesuvius. It was because she came from a strong, fearless family legacy. I understood why my mamma and papà were attracted to each other. They both came from families filled on the inside with courageous character.

BACK TO COUSIN ANDREW AND BEVERLY'S VISIT TO TURINO

So now, dear reader, that you have met Cousins Andrew and Beverly in the context of their home country, we'll continue with their visit here in Turino. Needless to say, I am ecstatic about their visit.

The day after their arrival I was at the house in the mid-afternoon, as promised, to help with the dinner. However, I did not ride alone. My Nonna Tizianna was too excited to come later so she rode with me on the back of my scooter. Nonna Tizianna brought some of her beautiful pesto sauce to go with Mamma's fresh pasta. She also brought some fresh salad greens, tomatoes, and onions as well as fresh goat cheese.

As we came in, we spotted Beverly and Mamma in the kitchen. It was so good to see Beverly again. I will never forget how gracious she was to me during my visit to America. Here she is in Turino, as regal as ever.

Nonna Mikaela was at the kitchen counter chatting with them as she sipped her hot mint tea. After many hugs and kisses all around I asked, "Where's Papà, Cousin Andrew, and Nonno Robert?"

"They have gone for fresh, hard crust bread at the bakery," Mamma answered.

Beverly and Mamma had just put the pasta dough aside for a moment to rest before it was to be rolled out. Andrew and Papà had rubbed enthusiastically the rack of lamb with its simple marinade that morning. They both agreed, despite their culinary traditions an ocean apart, that the marinade should be simple. It was salt, pepper, and a garlic paste in fresh lemon juice. I guess that their conversation about it in the morning was quite entertaining. I heard from the women that they talked as if the decision weighed in importance equal to the proper tempo of a song Papà would write, or the line of a building roof Cousin Andrew would design. The conversation had all the components of artist's sensibilities focused on a rack of lamb ribs! Nonna Mikaela had the red sauce accented with finely diced onions, garlic, and peppers. The aroma from her additional herbs and spices was similar to Mamma's. It was savory with a hint of warmth.

I cleaned and dried the salad greens, and added onion, tomato, black olives, and some crumbled goat cheese. I also put out a bowl of marinated olives to serve with dinner, and arranged a plate of cheese for during the meal and a plate of fruit for later.

When Papà, Nonno Robert, and Cousin Andrew returned from the bakery, Cousin Andrew was introduced to Nonna Tizianna. She took an immediate liking to him. Nonna Tizianna asked, "Do you by chance play the accordion?"

"No, but I play a mean harmonica, which I happen to have with me," Andrew responded with a smile.

"Nonna, it sounds like I need to call Luciano and tell him to bring your accordion," I interjected.

"Nonna Tizianna," Andrew said, "It would be an honor to hear you play and I will do my best to accompany you."

Nonna Tizianna just beamed.

Within a couple of hours, Nonno Angelo and Luciano arrived. I ran to the door. I was so proud to introduce both of them to Cousin Andrew and Beverly.

"Cousin Andrew and Beverly, this is my Nonno Angelo and my marito, Luciano."

Both Andrew and Beverly came over and embraced them. Luciano couldn't help but to say, "Wow. My moglie comes from a beautiful family from both sides of the ocean."

"Thank you," Andrew said. "It seems that Francesca has made a fine choice. She talks about you nonstop if she is here when her mamma Skypes us."

Luciano looked at me and smiled. I love his smile, I thought to myself.

"I am really interested in the work that you do in modern green restoration architecture and you, Beverly, in your sustainable garden," Luciano said.

And so, the conversation began. As Papà poured the huge pasta pot over the strainer, Nonno Angelo and Cousin Andrew talked green technology. As the lamb rack came off the grill, Cousin Andrew and Papà talked mountain climbing. As the salad was served, Luciano and Beverly talked produce gardens. As the pasta was enjoyed with the lamb, bread, and olive oil, we all talked music.

As the delicious food warmed our whole body, we enjoyed the

intimacy of family presence while we sipped the wine and ate the fruit. Gradually our conversation drifted to family. Everyone touched on some of their dreams for the future. But the main content was in the present.

Papà raised his wine glass and said, "It is incredible, and a blessing, that our journeys led us to each other. A toast to these great moments together!"

Andrew followed the toast immediately with a hopeful look in his eyes as he said, "Dominico, speaking of great moments, I have a request. For a very long time, I have wanted to hear live one of your ballad duets with Alessia."

"Alessia, what do you say? Should we indulge your cousin?"

Mamma rose and touched Andrew's shoulder and said with a shrug of her shoulders, and a twinkle in her eye towards her husband, "How could I refuse?"

They sang one of their compositions, called "Mi Amore."

What emotion I felt to hear them sing. Their voices spun the powerful love in their hearts for each other and all of us. The incredible beauty of their sound filled the room and enveloped us with its fullness. All of us in the room knew that the love we felt now was the same love that had brought us from so many cultures to be a family. My eyes filled with tears during this incredible moment.

When they finished, everyone was still for a moment. After a short while, Beverly slowly rose with her tall grace and approached my parents, held out her arms and embraced them both gently. "Thank you," she whispered.

Beverly knew it would take a little more time for the rest of the family to unwind themselves from the journey of my parents' song.

Then Andrew stood, clapped, and said, "Bravo, Bravo."

Everyone else stood, hugged, clapped, and wiped their tears away. In a few minutes, Luciano brought out the accordion.

Nonna Tizianna embraced her accordion and drove out of it a lively number that allowed people to awaken from their emotional depths and to begin to dance. Andrew pulled out his harmonica and accompanied Nonna Tizianna with a rhythmic haunt that embellished Nonna's artistry beautifully.

"Nonna Tizianna, we need to go on the road!" Andrew exclaimed.

"Yes, we do. Angelo, pack our bags! Let's go with Andrew!" Nonna retorted with a big smile.

Everyone laughed, and as they began their next ballad, my family danced. Luciano danced with Nonna Mikaela. Angelo danced with Beverly. Nonno Robert danced with Mamma. Papà set out the coffee cups as his fantastic coffee brewed. Then Papà tapped on Luciano's shoulder and danced with Nonna Mikaela while Luciano grabbed me. He held me close. I was, as always with him, in heaven.

"I love you and I love your family," he whispered into my ear.

"I love you and your family, too," I responded.

"Shall we tell my cousins that the family is about to expand?" I asked Luciano quietly in his ear.

"Do you want to?" Luciano replied.

"Ah-uh," I whispered.

As the dance ended, Luciano clanged a glass and said proudly with his chest fully expanded and a big smile on his face, "I have an announcement for our cousins! We are going to be parents in...in..."

"In seven months," I added.

Andrew and Beverly were ecstatic!

"This calls for hazelnut chocolates and coffee!" Papà shouts. Our family loves any excuse for a celebration on a celebration.

The men slapped Luciano on the back and the women hugged me. I lapped up the love and thought, "Just what I need to continue with this adventure. Family love!"

The next day we all planned to show Andrew and Beverly the national forest at the mountains. Nonna Mikaela and Nonno Robert decided to stay with Nonna Tizianna and Nonno Angelo on the farm. So, it was just the six of us. My parents, Beverly, and I, at Luciano's insistence because of the distance, rode in my parents' small car. Andrew enthusiastically rode the scooter with Luciano. When we arrived, Mamma, Beverly, and I decided to meet the men up at the creek in the valley. This afforded us a pleasant, less than two-hour walk. The men could get in a good two-hour climb and then cross over onto a forty-minute descent trail to the creek. So off the men went with their water, some bandages, and cell phones in their light packs.

We put the bread, cheese, fruit, olives, and mineral water in our backpacks along with a couple of blankets. We meandered along the path towards the valley. After a short time, the valley opened up before us.

We crossed it and, not too far from the stream, spread our blankets by a large boulder that cast an area of shade for our comfort. There we rested, talked, ate, and drank the mineral water. I enjoyed the food immensely. It seemed to quell the slight sense of nausea that was my companion for this last month.

"It is beautiful here," said Beverly as she stretched out and gazed up to the blue sky pierced by the mountain peaks. "I see why you stayed, Alessia. And Dominico is great. I guess it was destiny for you here."

"It has felt that way from my first encounter with Italy. That feeling was solidified when I looked into Dominico's eyes for the first time. I don't begin to understand how that sort of attraction works. But, it is powerful," Mamma added.

"I know. When I looked into your cousin's eyes for the first time, I knew I had encountered my destiny. The depth, peace, and intelligence of his eyes were profound for me. I had yet to get to know his person. I didn't know if we would be colleagues, great friends, or lifelong lovers. But, I knew it would be something strong and over all time," concluded Beverly.

Mamma laughed. "I'm glad it was you that came along, Beverly. You have the ability to respect Andrew's calm ways. I will never forget the Skype when Andrew first met you. He was so excited. His eyes shone. He just went on and on about how he met this beautiful, creative, lively, intelligent, and kind woman. I had never seen him so animated. Then in a couple of months I heard that you guys were engaged. Andrew continues to be so happy. I can tell."

"It's been twenty-five good years and still counting!" Beverly said.

I sat up against the boulder with my face to the sun and listened to the women. The voice of family. They chatted away in a stream of connection that transcended the distance between their homes. Their gentle voices nurtured me and my baby within. I drifted off into a sun-filled sleep.

I awakened to the sound of the men's voices as they strode across the valley towards us. Their sound was filled with energy from their climb. I readied myself, as did the other women, for their stories of adventure and, of course, exaggerated successes against the mountainous dangers.

My papà said loudly as he approached, "Well, guys, have you ever seen three more beautiful women?"

"Can't say that I have," said Andrew as he bent down to kiss his wife.

"Translation, ladies, is, 'I hope there is some bread, cheese, and olives left because we are starving!'" said Mamma.

We all laughed as Mamma pulled out the packages of bread, cheese, and olives from the backpacks.

Luciano grabbed a couple of mineral waters, some bread, and cheese. He then sat down next to me and offered me one of the mineral waters.

"Are you and the baby thirsty?" he asked with a big grin on his face. Luciano made no attempt to hide his excitement about this pregnancy.

"Yes, I think so," I responded as I took the bottle. He kissed me on the cheek and then enjoyed a couple of swigs of his mineral water.

The water tasted great after my rest in the sun. Both Luciano and I listened quietly to the stories that the prior generation began to spin. We munched on our food and enjoyed our closeness as we listened.

A small tremor then hit the valley. My papà caught my look. He then said, "I know a story about Liaco and Rosa who were my Mamma Tizianna's great-nonni. They were also pregnant during uncertain times."

"Please tell the story, Papà," I said. The others echoed the request.

LIFE AND FAMILY ABOVE CULTURE

Liaco loved the land around Turino. His family had been here since the 1500s when they and many other Jews were ousted from France. Every morning he rose with the sun to the smell of rich soil in his nostrils. He went directly to stand outside, before his prayers, to fill his eyes with the early morning sun and the row upon row of expertly trimmed grape vines. He knew the touch, smell, and taste of the perfectly ripened grape. Flawlessly he began the harvest at the precise moment of the optimal wine grape maturity. Today, however, his thoughts were focused and open to another type of decision. He wrapped his prayer shawl around his shoulders, and retreated to the front room of the house. He seated himself and began to recite the call to prayer in Hebrew. He repeated the call a number of times until his mind soothed into his favorite psalm. Then he sat and rocked for an untold amount of time in a state of peace and honor to God. In a few moments, he was ready to think through the hardest decision of his life.

His meditative mind opened to one thought after another. He was a Jew. He would always be a Jew. The order of the rituals, dietary health rules, and roles of family members gave him identity and peace. His wife was now pregnant with their first child. If the child was a son there would be, according to custom, a circumcision within two weeks. The child would be forever marked as a Jew. Was this the best action to be taken now?

Liaco was a man that held tradition in great respect. However, he held human life at an even higher level. The story of Abram who was ordered by God to spare the life of his son filled his consciousness.

Liaco decided that he would also spare the life of his son. There would be no circumcision!

Liaco was an intuitive observer. He was aware that central Europe was in a horrific war with the Nazi regime as aggressor. He had heard rumors of the deaths of many Jews. As the world power alliances shifted, Liaco foresaw the advancement of the German armies into Italy. He viewed this likelihood as a threat to the lives of himself and his family. Thus he decided that if this child was a boy, he would not be circumcised, but rather baptized. In fact, he and his wife would be baptized as well. Thus, Liaco made the painful but clear choice for him of love for his family over tradition.

Rosa had busied herself in the kitchen with the stew while her husband took an inordinately long time at his prayers. She sensed that after his prayers there would be a change for them all. But, she did not know the depth of the changes.

As Rosa peeled the vegetables for the stew, her mind drifted back to her childhood and her first sensations of fear based solely on her Jewishness. Because Rosa's papà was a gentile, she and her mamma couldn't go to synagogue. She learned about her Jewish culture from her maternal nonni and from the practices followed by her mamma in their home. She loved the breads, and the prayer ceremonies with candles. She thought it odd that she couldn't go to the synagogue but rarely gave it thought. Her papà was a man of great faith in God, but usually side-stepped the whole idea of religion. Rosa remembered fondly some of the Jewish holidays at her mamma's parents' and she remembered the Christian holidays at her papà's family. She enjoyed both celebrations and felt comfortable with her intimate connections to both Jewish and Christian cultures.

However, a group of girls whom Rosa had to pass by on her way home from school were not comfortable with a peaceful relationship between the two cultures. They thought that Rosa's Jewishness was some sort of an issue. They would whisper nasty comments under their breath as Rosa and her friend Elena walked by. It seemed that they felt it an insult that her father, a gentile, had chosen to love a Jewish woman. But, with Elena, a gentile, by her side and both of them usually engaged in their own banter, the effect of these girls was minimal on Rosa.

But one particular fall day her friend Elena was not with her. Elena was home with a stomachache. She, like Rosa, lived above her father's shop. He had a carpenter shop that was next door to Rosa's father's tailor shop.

Alone, Rosa walked quickly towards home. She saw the girls at their usual corner two blocks from the school. She just had to make it one block past the girls. Then she would be at her papà's shop. She felt their eyes bore into her as she passed them on the other side of the street. She especially felt the eyes of the taller girl with the big hands and the pronounced chin. Rosa heard the loud whispers of, "Ugly mixed breed," and other stupid phrases.

Rosa knew these girls were confused, but that didn't quell her fear as a ten-year-old. She began to run. At the same time the tall girl picked up a stone and hurled it at Rosa. It hit her left leg. Elena's papà had, by chance, glanced out his shop window when the rock struck Rosa's leg. He saw her look of panic as she sped down the street with blood running down her leg. He immediately ran out of his shop and yelled at the girls to go home. Rosa thanked him as she grabbed her leg and quickly entered her papà's shop.

Her papà was at the door by then as he had heard his friend's loud voice. He lifted Rosa up onto the cutting table and examined her leg. She had a big red area on her calf with a half-inch opening that was bleeding profusely. He immediately took off his shirt and applied pressure to her wound. Rosa's mamma rushed down the stairs when she heard the yelling. Elena's papà related the story. Rosa explained that they would always make comments, but had never thrown stones before.

Her papà carried Rosa upstairs to their apartment. Her mama bathed her leg in rosemary water and put a rosemary poultice over her wound and secured it with a cloth bandage. Rosa remembered how soothing it felt. She also remembered the protection she felt on her walks to and from school from her papà and Elena's papà.

So now, comforted by her memories of protection, Rosa awaited her husband's emergence from his prayers. She was able to complete both the stew and polenta preparations before he entered the kitchen. He kissed Rosa on the forehead, patted her belly, and then sat down at the table. Rosa placed a hot cup of coffee on the table before him that he then cradled in his hands. Rosa sat opposite him with her hot cup of coffee as well. He raised his eyes to hers. Then Liaco began in his usual kind way to relate to her his decision.

"Rosa, my decision may cost us the loss of some of our Jewish friends and our wine business to Jewish merchants. But, if this child is a boy, we will not circumcise him. However, we will continue to pray in private and to teach the prayers to our children when it is safe to do so," Liaco began.

Rosa waited patiently for him to finish. Rosa knew that this was very hard for him, yet the right decision for their family.

Rosa stood up and went to the open kitchen door and looked out onto the fields. She couldn't stop the tears that poured down her face. She wept and wept. She knew this would be harder than some unkind school children. She knew this would be harder than their loss of citizenship a couple of years back. But she also knew this would not be harder than the Nazi capture.

Rosa turned towards her husband, approached their kitchen table and placed her hands on the table. Then the following words came out from between her clenched teeth, "You are right, Liaco, what you have decided. I may have to give up the spiritual rituals that have been a comfort to me all my life to survive these fools. But, my spirituality can never be touched by them and its light for me will only get stronger!"

Liaco rose up and took his wife in his arms and they wept until their grief had softened.

Rosa and Liaco had a son named Carlo. Carlo was not circumcised. Rather, Carlo as well as Rosa and Liaco were baptized. Liaco and Rosa continued some of their practices in secret and after the war taught their son. Rosa taught Carlo to find peace with both cultures.

After the baptisms, Rosa and Liaco went on to lose some Jewish friends but also to keep many steadfast Jewish and Catholic friends. During the German occupation of Northern Italy, the Germans did round up, as Liaco had predicted, a few thousand Jews and sent them on to the camps. But the round-up was sloppily done and many Jews were able to escape. Liaco was able to hide some adults in a friend's merchant ship to Naples. It was a dangerous voyage. So to avoid the dangers of the sea, two of the families requested that Liaco keep their younger female children. He and Rosa took in the three youngest girls of ages that could have been their own. The sloppiness of state records due to the loss of citizenship was in their favor. The adults and older children did survive the voyage. After the war they returned to their community in Turino. They were eternally grateful to Rosa and Liaco, for they found that their daughters were loved and well cared for. The bonds between these children and Liaco's family that grew over the three years that they stayed with them continued after their return to their families.

MORE OF COUSIN ANDREW AND BEVERLY'S VISIT TO TURINO

"Thanks, Dominico," said Luciano. "Thanks," he repeated softly.

"Thanks, Papà," I also said softly.

"Thanks, Dominico, for that powerful story. Their spiritual strength has continued down the generations, it seems to me. I will enjoy telling it to more of the family when I return home," said Andrew.

Dear reader, in my thoughts, I agreed with Andrew. I made a pact with myself to draw on that strength more mindfully as my future unfolds.

All of us sat with our thoughts for the next few minutes. But with the arrival of another tremor and with the sunlight's movement towards the mountains' peaks as well, we decided it was time to leave the mountains. Together everyone walked through the valley. My feet walked in rhythm with Luciano's. We strolled behind our family. The grass felt like a soft cushion above the firm earth. What a beautiful place.

When we arrived home, Nonna Mikaela called and said she and Nonno Robert planned to stay the night on the farm. Mamma offered dinner to Luciano and myself before our bike ride to the farm. That sounded good to me, as I was tired. We all showered. Then, Mamma heated up the sauce. She shredded cooked chicken into it. As it bubbled she tasted it for a good blend of spices. Meanwhile, Papà made polenta. We all settled down to the simple but delicious meal accompanied by wine—and, for me, mineral water.

This was the last evening Andrew and Beverly had with my folks. They were leaving the next day late in the afternoon, so we planned a departure dinner for them at the farm around noon.

Andrew, with his consistent heart of concern, asked, "What adjustments have you folks had to make with the increase in earthquakes the last couple of years?"

"We've had to make some changes at the farm that you'll see tomorrow. We reinforced the second floor and built a couple more bedrooms on the first floor. Also, we replaced the windows with shatter resistant plexi-glass. Luciano has made some crucial alterations in our vegetable crop and also in some of our soil care in the vineyard and the fig grove," said Papà.

"Luciano and I have put our heads together with my papà to make the farm as safe and sustainable as possible. We've tapped out on our ideas. So we'd love to hear any suggestions you might have tomorrow on the building structures," Papà added.

"Yes, cous', more ideas would be great," said Luciano.

"I'll be glad to look. The older construction here is so solid that I'm sure you've done the most that can be done. Your house here, Dominico, looks very tremor resistant, by the way, with the changes you've already made."

Andrew continued, "We've had issues with more earthquakes in the States as well. They have intensified around areas of heavy fracking such as along the fault in the Midwest. All I have seen clear to do as father, husband, and architect has been to live away from these areas and argue for the rehabilitation of the infrastructure.

"But, whatever tomorrow brings, it brings." Andrew continued as he raised his wine glass, "Thanks to you, Dominico and Alessia, for today and for our entire visit. It has all been incredible. Thanks to you also, Luciano and Francesca. Love to you both. I am so excited about our new family addition on the way."

Luciano stood up. "Cousins Andrew and Beverly, I have enjoyed you so much. And those mountain passes will never be the same in the absence of us three brave mountaineers!"

Everyone laughed. Luciano continued, "Fortunately we have some time together tomorrow on the family farm. And speaking of the farm, it seems that if I read the face of my wife correctly, I need to get her home to rest."

I smiled at my husband in appreciation for his sensitivity.

We kissed and hugged everyone goodnight and headed out on the scooter. With shouts of, "See you tomorrow! Thanks everyone! Love you all!" we sped off.

Once again I was able to rest against Luciano's back with my arms around his chest. I felt safe.

The next morning I found both Nonna Tizianna and Nonna Mikaela at the kitchen table with their hot morning drinks. I kissed them good morning. Nonna Mikaela said, "The mint tea in the teapot is still hot, if you want some."

"Thanks, Nonna," I said as I poured myself a cup. "Where's Luciano?" I added.

"He's off with both your nonni. There was something in the vineyard and the vegetable garden that Angelo wanted him to check out," answered Nonna Tizianna.

"Well, that figures. He and Nonno Angelo love an excuse to dig in the dirt, and Nonno Robert wouldn't want to miss anything," I responded with a shake of my head.

"How was the mountain, yesterday?" asked Nonna Mikaela.

"It was lovely. Only a few clouds. Plenty of sun. The men loved their hike and we women enjoyed the stream in the valley and ate and talked. Well, actually, I slept while they talked. Papà told the story of Liaco and Rosa. It was great."

"So," I continued, "What did you two masterminds plan for the dinner today?"

"Well, we have perch, rice, zucchini, olives, figs, bread, cheese, and fresh salad greens. We'll grill the zucchini and the perch," offered Nonna Tizianna.

"Mmm, yum! Okay. I'll marinade the perch."

"Done, Francesca," said Nonna Tizianna.

"Okay, I'll go pick the greens."

"Your husband will bring them before he comes in from the garden," informed Nonna Mikaela. "And before you offer," she added, "I've got the rice covered."

"Eat some breakfast and take care of yourself, my dear. You need to gather lots of energy for the next few months and for long into the future," kidded Nonna Tizianna.

"Okay, okay, I get it," I responded as both elders smiled knowingly.

"Just one thing more, when you speak to your mamma this morning, please remind her to pick up the bread at the bakery. The baker will have it ready," added Nonna Tizianna.

"Sure thing," I said as I peeled an orange while my cornmeal porridge bubbled.

Luciano entered the kitchen laden with fresh salad greens, tomatoes, basil, and cucumbers. Angelo and Robert were out on the patio. They had moved the tables together to accommodate everyone.

"Ah, she has awakened," said Luciano as he kissed me on my neck.

"Some porridge Luciano?"

"Looks good. Yes, indeed!" said Luciano as he put the greens in a huge bowl to wash.

"Nonne? Porridge?" I offered.

"No, amore," they said in unison. "We've munched quite a few of these succulent figs," said Nonna Mikaela.

"Nonni, porridge?" I shouted out the kitchen door towards Angelo and Robert.

"Don't mind if I do," each quickly answered.

Luciano washed up and then made more coffee while the greens soaked in the salted water.

The four of us made short work of the porridge. Everyone munched on the figs and also on the slab of cheese, fresh from our neighbor, that Nonno Angelo placed on the table.

Then the six of us went to work on the meal for Andrew and Beverly. Nonna Mikaela rinsed and put the rice on with her special spices. Luciano built two salads. The first one was of greens, slivered red onions, olives, and small pieces of goat cheese. The second one was of tomato, soft cow milk cheese, and basil. Nonno Robert assisted Nonno Angelo organizing the solar grill for the fish and zucchini. Nonna Tizianna sliced the zucchini.

I set out the cheeses and olives. Then I went to change out of my nightdress and call Mamma.

It wasn't too long before everyone arrived. Andrew stood a moment in the courtyard and gazed at our family farm. I could tell that he was moved by the beauty of the old farmhouse and how it gently accepted the new addition that was also made of stone. After our usual enthusiastic greetings, people began their comments of how beautiful the farm was and how delicious the food smelled.

Everyone moved to the patio behind the kitchen and helped themselves to the mineral water set out. The nonni eased the fish and zucchini off the grill, seasoned with a little fresh olive oil, oregano, black pepper, sea salt, and a squeeze of lemon. Then my family sat down to the sumptuous meal.

It was fun to watch my mamma's interaction with her American cousins. Nonna Mikaela seemed amused when her eyes cast on Alessia and Andrew. They spoke intensely with each other as they had done as children. Meanwhile, Beverly was engaged in a conversation with Luciano about zucchini. Robert and Angelo complimented themselves on the perfectly cooked perch. Papà winked at me, ate, and took it all in.

The air was pristinely fresh on the patio, the food a slice of heaven, and our enjoyment of each other sublime. We ate in a leisurely fashion. The mid-day warmth relaxed us. But also, the desire to keep each other's company motivated our behavior to attempt a time warp into a slowed pace. As we finished off our after-dinner coffee or garden-fresh herb tea, we all decided to take a walk through the vineyard and orchard. The kitchen cleanup was fast with so many hands. Then we women donned our sun hats, the men their field hats, and everyone took off for a tour of the vineyards, fig grove, garden, and chicken coop.

Angelo, Robert, and Luciano were in the lead followed by Dominico and Andrew. I walked between the two nonne while Beverly and Alessia were arm in arm behind us. Such a parade we were. Of course Beverly loved the conversation about the plants. She was able to ask Luciano about some of her issues in her garden, as the climates were similar.

When we returned to the farmhouse, the men went on alone. They pointed at ceilings, walls, windows, and plumbing. We women retreated to the patio shade with some fresh lemonade. We could hear the lower calm voice of Andrew make a comment followed by a loud "Great idea!" on the part of the other men.

All the men came out beaming from their interchange. Andrew has always been respectful with his suggestions. And Angelo, Dominico, and Luciano were great listeners. Must have been the years of listening to the family stories that trained their ears to be open.

The day had passed all too quickly and it was time for Papà and Mamma to take Andrew and Beverly to the evening train that would take them to the rail along the coast to Barcelona. So with food packed in a satchel by the nonne that would last them more than the ride to Barcelona, they bid their good-byes. Even after many hugs and kisses to everyone, it was hard to say good-bye. But eventually they got into Mamma and Papà's car. Nonno Robert and Nona Mikaela left with them as well. They would stay at my mamma and papà's until their return to Genoa in a couple of days.

Angelo and Tizianna walked arm in arm into the house followed by Luciano and myself. Angelo and Tizianna had settled into their reading chairs. Luciano and I made some lemonade for them and then took ours to the patio. We shared our lemonade together before Luciano headed to the shed to work on his paintings and I headed upstairs to write, dream, and plan my dance classes for next week.

The late fall and winter weeks of my pregnancy passed smoothly. Well, dear reader, smoothly is not the right word. The tremors had increased to multiple times a day and the government had announced that it was not a matter of if but when in the near future Vesuvius would erupt. So, Luciano, my papà, and Nonno Angelo worked diligently to secure the structure of the farmhouse and the house in Turino. But, this weekend there was a rest from the almost completed work because, I am excited to say, our dear friends, Flavio and Susanna were to visit us from Genoa.

Chapter Three

CHANGE AND PREPARATIONS

That Saturday morning, Luciano and I sat out on the patio in the early spring warmth. We cradled our hot beverages in our hands, sipped their rich warm liquid, and rested back in our chairs to inhale the sweet spring air and feel the warm sun's caress on our faces.

"It will be good to see Flavio and Susanna," I said.

"Yes, it will. When I spoke with Flavio last week, he was concerned about his mamma in the house alone. He wants her to live with them. But, so far, she doesn't want to leave her house."

"I have a feeling that she will be up here soon. She just needs to have it in her mind a while. It's hard for everyone around Vesuvius to decide what to do with the more frequent tremors," I suggested. "What are Aunt Margarita and Uncle Josefa's plans?"

"Uncle Josefa has begun to sell his sheep. But other than that, I am not sure. Your papà and I were talking about going down to see what they want to do about the farm. They are in the government's yellow zone. The government has offered to buy the land of the people in red and yellow zones to encourage relocation out of the area around Vesuvius."

"Has the government offered to purchase Uncle Josefa's farm?" I asked, a little unsettled.

"It seems to be in process," Luciano answered.

"Wow," I said with a rub over my now greatly expanded belly. It seemed hard to imagine that our child would not be able to run around the Naples farm.

Luciano kissed me on the cheek and departed for the vineyards until the arrival of our friends. I went to the kitchen to join Nonna Tizianna. We chatted as I put together a medium-sized pot of rice and chicken soup for the noon meal. Nonna put together her fabulous red sauce with sausage for the evening meal. We intermittently sipped our tea or coffee, as our preferences dictated, chopped, and happily seasoned away our pots. Our spices echoed of Africa, Italy, and the Americas. To me it was a sublime blend. Maybe my child will not run around the Naples farm fields, but these aromas will stay for my baby to smell.

Out the window I could see Luciano and Nonno Angelo in the

vineyard. Here, inside, I had the company of my Nonna Tizianna, my unborn child, and these delicious smells that arose from our pots.

I asked Nonna Tizianna, "How did you meet Nonno Angelo?"

Nonna responded, "It was shortly after my graduation from university."

TIZIANNA AND ANGELO

I enjoyed my years at university. During the last two years I was involved with a young man named Fabrizio. But even though he was kind and smart, he did not move decisively towards marriage so I had to let him go. I wasn't into casual affairs. After graduation I busied myself with my students, accordion wedding engagements, friends, and the farm chores. I was happy. Little did I know that I would meet someone who woud make my life even happier.

One weekend my brother brought home his good friend, Angelo, from the school of engineering. They planned to study for their final written exams on the farm, as it was quiet and my Mamma Cecilia's pasta sauces were incredible!

Angelo was three years older than Pasquale and had completed his master's cycle. Pasquale had completed his bachelor's. But, they were scheduled to sit for their exams at the same time and their camaraderie encouraged one another to focus on their studies.

I enjoyed Angelo's lively conversations at the dinner table during their study breaks. He was excited about the research in the experimental lab. The lab had adapted an idea from an Indian engineer of small wind energy generators. He explained that their low five-foot height avoided harm to flying birds and yet they were efficient. Angelo was excited that it would soon be implemented in Italy along with an extensive solar energy plan. Also he talked excitedly about the solar plate technology for bikes, cars, ferries, boats, and farm equipment that he would be working on in his promised job at the Fiat research division.

After about three weeks, Angelo and Pasquale had completed their exam preparations. Angelo had spent most of those three weeks at the farm. After they sat for their exams, I missed Angelo's presence at the dinner table.

But, his absence did not last long. Every Saturday or Sunday after the exams, Angelo was at the farm to supposedly visit Pasquale. However, he spent more and more time during his visits in conversations with me. He told me later that he was fascinated with my classroom stories, my songs on the accordion, and with how I moved around. He described my walk as a lighthearted dance. Angelo's visits continued.

I enjoyed his levelheaded conversation, and besides, I thought he was cute. But I sensed that perhaps Angelo needed a direct indication that I liked him. So, one Saturday when Pasquale was not at home and I heard Angelo's motorbike in the courtyard, I put my students' papers aside and went out to greet him.

"Angelo! How about some fresh coffee? Pasquale just left, but come on in and have a coffee!" I said.

Angelo emerged off his bike, kissed my cheeks, and said, "That's a great idea."

So I boiled the coffee and put some fruit and cheese on a plate. I then poured the coffee into small cups. As I handed Angelo his cup I suggested that we sit in the shade on the patio.

Angelo opened the kitchen door while I transported the plate of food and my coffee cup.

We sat at the table and talked and sipped coffee and talked some more. Our conversation came easy. We then headed out for a walk through the vineyard and fig grove.

As we moved our way through the vineyard, Angelo blurted out, "How did you learn to move with such grace and emotion?"

I could tell he was embarrassed, and I was surprised at the outburst from the mostly serious Angelo. But, I played it off in a cool way and just said, "Didn't learn it. Just how I am, Angelo."

Angelo raised his chest, took in air, and then let out a big sigh, "Ahh, natural beauty. I get it." I thought that Angelo felt a little embarrassed at the intensity of his praise.

I remember that I laughed and took his hand. "Come on. Let me show you my favorite fig tree to climb. You can see down to the river from one of its branches."

Off we went down the first row of grape vines, then past the end of the five rows to the fig grove. There in the middle of the grove stood the queen of all fig trees.

Well, I climbed up to the lookout point on the thick branch that reaches east. Then I quickly got down so he could climb up as we didn't want to stress the tree.

Angelo shouted down to me, "This is a great spot! Wow! I can see where the river makes that bend towards the rice patties!"

Angelo lowered himself down from the tree branch. "Okay. After that beautiful view, the least I can do is to offer you one that I have found," Angelo said.

"Really? Where?" I questioned.

"In the Grand Paradise National Park by the mountains," Angelo replied.

I love the mountains so this was one more point in Angelo's favor.

That next Sunday he arrived a little early to our agreed eight o'clock time. Another good sign, I thought. I will never forget that my engineer amore came with, of course, a small portable water purification system for us to use on the hike. I loved it!

I had packed water, some olives, figs, cheese, bread, and smoked fish for the outing. My Papà Ario made his great coffee and put it in two thermoses to warm us on our early morning ride. I took that as a paternal blessing for the relationship.

We had a great day in the mountains. And he did show me some fantastic locations that I had not been to before. But it was Angelo that I appreciated most. Underneath his serious aspect he was thoughtful and had a relaxed way about him that cushioned my intensity. I think I really fell in love with him on that mountain hike.

He told me a little about his papà and mamma on that day. He explained that his papà was an engineer, but that his mamma never went to university. She was raised in a rural region near Alba. They grew hazelnuts but at that time the region was poor and of little economic interest. But his mamma observed that the people in her area were well fed when they shared with one another and when they were wise with their resources. She believed that these common sense principles could be applied to our planet to return it to its intended sustainable state. Angelo explained that her beliefs influenced him greatly in the development of his green orientation to the field of engineering.

After our day on the mountain, Angelo and I got together every weekend and at least once during the week. Soon I met his mamma and papà. We joined them for dinner at their flat frequently. I found his papà and mamma as delightful as he had described.

In a couple of months, Angelo surprised me one Saturday as we finished up the dishes while Papà Ario and Mamma Cecilia sipped on their coffee at the patio table. Angelo said, "Tizianna, I don't want to be apart from you. When I ride the scooter home I think, why leave wonderful Tizianna at all? I think about you every day between my visits. I love you, Tizianna. There you have it. I love you."

It was so unromantic I almost giggled. But, I didn't as I knew that was how mi amore Angelo thought. So, I just looked at him with the dish and dishtowel in my hand and said, "I love you too, Angelo."

Then, he took the dish and towel out of my hands and placed them on the counter. He took my hands in his, kissed them, and said as he held on to my hands, "Tizianna, I have a solution to my lonely scooter rides home. I really hope you like my solution!"

"Okay, Angelo, my scientist, what is your solution?" I said as I tried to be serious, but I couldn't hide the sparkle in my eyes.

He then gently touched my cheek and looked deeply into my eyes and said, "Please say you will marry me!"

"Angelo, yes! I will marry you," I said, my eyes filled with happiness.

My serious Angelo broke out in the shout, "Wahoo!" as he grabbed me and spun me around while he held my torso close to his. As he slowed the spin, we wrapped our bodies around each other and lost all sense of time in a deep kiss. As we slowly emerged from our embrace, Mamma Cecilia and Papà Ario had piled into the kitchen to see what all the commotion was about. They were so ecstatic with the news that they joined in the excitement with hugs and kisses.

We called Angelo's Papà Carlos and Mamma Susanna and gave them the news, as well as my brother, Pasquale, who had relocated to Genoa for his work.

One month later, Angelo and I married on my family farm. It was a beautiful fall day. We then drove to Positano for a few romantic days. We had decided, upon my Papà Ario and Mamma Cecilia's invitation, to live on this farm with them. It was a convenient commute for me to my classroom and for Angelo to Fiat's research division. Angelo was, in fact, hired by the research division of Fiat. This division was abuzz with excitement in green energy research. He was on the team that worked out the kinks of the new, shorter, wind turbine as well as those of the vehicle solar plates.

I continued to teach at the nearby school. Our evenings were filled with lively discussions of our day. Ario and Cecilia were not to be outdone and added their own tales to the dinner table conversation. Soon the conversation dwindled off into a song while one of us played the accordion.

My Angelo loved the farm life. He became adept at the harvest of the grapes, figs, corn and vegetables. Early in the morning before work, he also loved to seek the eggs laid the previous evening. It was hard to tell after a while which Angelo loved more, his time on the farm or his green energy research. As if life wasn't sweet enough, we also visited the mountains and Angelo's parents often. However, gradually it became a ritual for his parents to come out to the farm on Sundays. They arrived with their arms full of cooked rice, meat sauces, wine, and hazelnuts. When your papà was born our life took on a bigger dimension as only children can give.

And that's the story of how your nonno and I met. His parents also have a fun story of how they met. One day I will tell it to you.

"Nonna, your beautiful history with Nonno Angelo reminded me that it is the people that make a location special and sacred. That will help me with the probable loss of the Naples farm."

"Oh, yes, Francesca, our Naples farm! Some things seem to disappear so fast! I have said good-bye to places, things, and people before, but am never short of blessings. Today you are here, Luciano is here, and my dear Angelo is here. Not to mention the fact that soon Flavio and Susanna arrive. I love you, soon-to-be-mamma Francesca," Nonna said as she embraced me.

Nonna can always tell when I need a hug. And I hugged back my generous-hearted Nonna.

Our sauces now demanded our attention. We turned them down to a low simmer.

VISIT OF FLAVIO AND SUSANNA

A little before noon, Flavio and Susanna arrived. I was so excited that I could hardly contain myself. Her father now had a motorbike and they borrowed it to travel out to the country. Susanna barely got off the bike when we grabbed each other in the biggest most fantastic hug. Luciano saw their arrival from the vineyard and sprinted down to the courtyard.

"Papà!" Flavio shouted as he embraced Luciano. They both slapped each other's back and laughed.

Susanna and I tried our best to ignore them.

"Susanna you look so great," I exclaimed. "Life must be good to you!" I continued.

"Well, life is life, but Flavio gives it a new twist! And I like the twist," Susanna said as she glanced towards her husband at her side. "But, Francesca, pregnancy suits you well!" Susanna added.

"Susanna, how does it suit me?" Flavio said as he stuffed a travel pack under his shirt like he had a baby in his "stomach."

Susanna and I just shook our heads, and before we could come up with a clever response, Flavio exclaimed, "Mamma!" as he kissed and hugged me in greeting.

I laughed and said, "Well, come in, because this mamma and papà have some cold lemonade and hot soup for you."

At that moment Nonno Angelo and Nonna Tizianna came out of the house and warmly embraced Flavio and Susanna. Tizianna said, "Since you two have to travel back tomorrow we have invited Susanna's papà and Catrina for dinner tonight. Alessia and Dominico will be here as well."

"Thank you so much," said Susanna warmly.

"You young people just enjoy yourselves. We older folks have got the dinner covered," Tizianna added. "Your mamma went to market this morning so we have fresh bread, cheese, olives, pasta, and citrus on the way. The red sauce is on the stove. So all we need tonight are some big appetites."

I could only kiss my nonna's cheek in response.

Susanna, Flavio, Luciano, and I headed into the kitchen where we loaded ourselves up with lemonade, hot soup, and sliced polenta. We settled our provisions on one of the patio tables in the shade. Then, Luciano and Flavio took lemonade out to Tizianna and Angelo. They had settled themselves under a tree in the courtyard. There they busily cracked a bag of hazelnuts.

Susanna took advantage of our moment alone and asked, "How have you been feeling? Are you all right?"

"Oh, yes. My stomach has been more settled than earlier in the pregnancy. Luciano is a patient guy and lets me get my rest. This pregnancy really came fast. I'm glad we knew each other all our lives. It makes it easier to navigate the fast changes that pregnancy brings. And I'm really glad I chose to live in this gorgeous countryside. With my family and best friends close, what more can a pregnant woman need?"

"It does make things better," my dear friend responded.

"Susanna, I also think about our country and the world more now, too. I wonder what would our child need to live in our world now? What could Luciano and I teach him or her to help? Luciano and I have talked a lot about that," I mused.

"Well, for starters, my friend, this child will have a huge reservoir of love. That's the main thing, right, my dear?" said Susanna as she squeezed my hand.

"Of course. That's the most important," I added, grateful to be out of my heady thoughts.

Just then we heard Flavio announce loudly as he and Luciano came around the side of the house, "Well, have you ladies missed us terribly?"

"Of course we did," Susanna and I said in unison as we playfully fluttered our eyelashes.

The two of them settled down at the table with us.

"So, Flavio, what adventures do you have to relate to us about the renovation of Genoa's plumbing infrastructure?" I teased.

"Well, I'm here to tell you that the south does not have a monopoly on creative complexity of patterns of the pipe runs," Flavio said with a laugh.

"Okay. Good. I knew that the north and south were more alike than different in our fair country," I added.

We all laughed as we knew there still were some challenges in this regard, but that the statement was more true than false.

"Flavio says that your travel schedule can be pretty intense," said Luciano looking at Susanna. "How do you manage?"

"Well, I love to perform. I also love my colleagues and our director. It has been good in many ways. I could not have done it without the support of Flavio. But, for me, it is too much time away from Flavio. You see, I really like your energetic friend," Susanna said with a twinkle in her eye. Then Susanna continued, "I'm tired of sleeping on planes and trains. I just want to be in my own bed with Flavio."

"Well, I guess that's clear! So, what are you going to do?" asked Luciano.

"I'm going to enjoy the five months left on my contract. Fortunately there will be little travel in these last months of the contract. I have negotiated to rent space in a studio near our flat. I will have access to it in two months so that will give me time to slowly begin teaching students before my dance company contract is up. It will be a better lifestyle," Susanna concluded.

"I can't wait for her to be free from the travel," said Flavio. "I'm on the lookout for a space to purchase near our flat. That will give her a more stable location."

"After all," said Susanna, "when we do have our family, I do not want to leave our child. Our child will be a dance studio child!"

"I would do the same in your shoes," I said.

"Well," Flavio interjected, "before the next generation gets here and entices our attentions, I'd love to head over to the shed and see your latest work, Luciano."

"Me too," said Susanna.

"Great! Let's go," said Luciano.

So we paraded over to the shed with Susanna and I arm in arm, and the guys a few steps ahead. Luciano spoke animatedly about his present art project. He explained it as follows, "The work on the easel is the second of a series of three paintings. The first was a sunrise from behind the farmhouse in Naples. It includes Mt. Vesuvius in the background as it is now."

"The second," he continued, "is a sunset behind your house, Flavio, on the ridge at Positano. That one is for you, Flavio."

Just then we arrived at the shed. As Flavio entered the shed, he saw the painting of his house on the easel near the far wall by the window. For the first time since I have known Flavio, he had no words. He stood quietly and looked at the house in which he had spent his entire youth. His shoulders dropped and his eyes welled up with tears. He saw the warmth of his mamma's love transformed into this painting. It was a beautiful sunlit house on the ridge. The main colors were yellows and blues. The yellows were light, bright shades near the sun and the house. Then the yellows deepened as they neared the earth. The blues appeared in the sky, sea water down from the ridge, and in some wildflowers along the ridge.

Overcome with emotion, Flavio turned, kissed his friend on the cheek, and then double slapped his back with a big hug.

Susanna and I didn't know what was more exciting, the reaction of Flavio or the artwork itself.

After a deep breath, Flavio asked "What's the third one like?"

"Well, the theme of all three is change. They are all paintings of locations of love that will never be as they were this year. I will begin the third one this week.

"So what is the subject of the third one, Luciano?" I queried with a repeat of Flavio's question.

"My wife with child," said Luciano tenderly.

"Oh, dear. I walked into that one!" I said softly.

"Well, sort of," Luciano said as he smiled at me.

We all laughed and I suggested, "Let's head up to the lookout tree and check out the river."

Everyone agreed. I grabbed a cloth from the patio. We took the slow way up along the vineyard and around its far end to the fig tree grove.

The day was a perfect early spring day with lots of sun and cool temperatures. The river had let go of its early day mist and shone brilliantly from our vantage point. Luciano and I spread out the cloth under the tree. Flavio and Luciano leaned against the tree's generous trunk and Susanna and I leaned against them.

Settled into our comfortable positions, Flavio reported, "At last, yesterday we got my mamma's agreement to move up north. She called me in the morning before I left for work."

"That's great, Flavio. How soon will her move happen?" asked Luciano.

"Probably in about a month," Flavio replied.

"Actually," said Susanna, "it was my papà's idea that wooed her up here. Catrina has moved in with my papà," Susanna went on. "So, her apartment in the courtyard level was vacant. Papà and Catrina then started their little campaign to get Patricia to agree to move into Catrina's old apartment. Papà offered to build a growing box for Patricia's herbs in the courtyard just outside the apartment. Catrina told Patricia that it would mean a lot to her if they could be neighbors. That was it! Patricia decided to move north!" Susanna concluded.

"Because of the changes in the region," added Flavio, "many of her friends have left. I think she was lonely, but didn't want to give up her independence and live with us. This arrangement is perfect. She has her friends Catrina and Daniele in the same building. She has her plants to fuss over and the nearby market to explore. Actually she is quite excited about her move."

"Great solution!" I exclaimed. "She will be close to famiglia again!"

"What have you decided to do about the house, Flavio?" Luciano asked.

"We still have to figure that out. How about your folks? What have they decided about the farm and the farmhouse?" questioned Flavio.

"I hope to know more after next weekend. Dominico and I are going down by train to talk things over with them. Is there anything that you need us to carry to your mamma?" asked Luciano.

"No, not that I can think of. Can you think of anything?" Flavio asked as he looked into Susanna's eyes.

"No, the papers are signed for her apartment. We're all set."

"Well okay, then," I responded as I stretched out on the blanket and laid my head on Luciano's strong thighs, "things are coming into place!" As he gently stroked my hair, I fell into a deep sleep.

Susanna lay down as well. Tired from her travels and its constant physical push on her body, sleep came instantly to her as well.

While Susanna and I slept, the men discussed different options for Luciano's family property and for Flavio's house. They agreed that there would be more clarity after Luciano's trip next weekend. As if to herald the timeliness of their conversation we felt a slight tremor that shook some of the blossoms off the trees and awakened Susanna and I. We were accustomed to the more frequent tremors, but the tremor did motivate us to make our way towards the farmhouse. By now it was late in the afternoon. Susanna and I felt rested after our nap so we challenged the men to a game of bocce ball. Nonno kept the bocce court in good order in the courtyard.

"Same distance on the court, right?" said the men.

"Of course not. We get a shorter distance as women!" we said in unison.

"We're equal in rights, not muscle power," Susanna added.

"Well, okay. Shortened distance it is for the ladies!" said Luciano.

Nonna Tizianna and Nonno Angelo had fallen asleep in their court-yard chairs under the tree. Thankfully, Nonna had turned off the sauce before she settled into her chair in the warmth of the afternoon. This was a favorite nap spot for the two of them. But now, due to the noise of our discussion, they gradually awakened. Nonna decided to mix it up a bit and cheer for the men. Thus, Nonno was the very loud supporter of Susanna and I.

After the men won the game, narrowly, may I proudly add, my folks arrived with Daniele and Catrina. Daniele looked healthier than ever. His complexion was radiant and his black hair shone in the sunlight. Catrina was filled with smiles and was obviously very happy.

After many joyous hugs and kisses we all headed to the kitchen with the food that had been securely packed in the car trunk.

With the food safely deposited in the kitchen, Susanna and her papà went off for a short walk together towards the vineyards. Dominico, Flavio, Angelo, and Luciano gathered around another table with hot coffee to continue their discussions about family in the Naples area.

Nonna Tizianna guided Catrina to the kitchen. She poured some lemonade for the both of them and said, "Come, Catrina, let's take our lemonade to the patio, as I'd love to hear of your latest embroidery project. Also, I have always wanted you to tell me how you do your risotto, as it is the best I've ever tasted."

"Okay, I'll tell you my secret!" said Catrina as they settled at a table near the kitchen. "I use some pulverized pine nuts in the sauce with the cheese. It enriches it and lightens it at the same time," Catrina explained. "I'll make it for you our next time together."

"Oh, that would be wonderful! Thanks, Catrina," Nonna said.

Mamma and I took advantage of this time together as we busied ourselves in the kitchen. We put on the water for the pasta, and while we waited for it to come to a boil, we set out the dishes on the patio table.

"I'm feeling really good, Mamma," I said. "Did you feel as well with me?"

"Yes, I did. I loved being pregnant. I loved to feel your kicks, except for those at night! And as much biology as I studied in my youth, it still seemed like a miracle that the kicks I felt inside were from a person that would soon be in my arms. The pregnancy not only caused physical and emotional changes for me, but changes in my work as well. My music compositions during that time seemed more spiritual and universal in their themes."

Mamma stopped for a moment in her memories. Then she proceeded.

"Your delivery was orderly with evenly spaced contractions and your exit was easy with a few pushes. You cried loudly and went directly to my breast. After you ate you fell asleep, as did I.

"When I awakened I felt amazement when I saw you asleep in your papà's arms. I looked at my flattened stomach and there was a touch of sadness. That type of intimacy between us, of your development in my body, would never be a part of our relationship again. I realized then that your growth would continue and one day the infancy would also be a memory. The powerful impact of motherhood with its gains and losses has become a part of my non-erasable existence."

Mamma continued, "Now it is an honor for me to be around as you enter your life of motherhood."

"I love you, Mamma," I said as I gave her waist a squeeze. But the squeeze was short lived, as I saw the pasta water.

"Oh, we have our water bubbling!" I exclaimed.

Mamma threw in a generous portion of sea salt, and I the pasta. She brought fresh pasta so it would be a short cook. I signaled to Luciano from the kitchen door and he arrived.

"Luciano, you know you are my favorite pasta pot pourer," I said.

"I know," he said as he smiled, lifted the pot, and poured the contents into the large strainer in the sink.

I then tossed the pasta into a large bowl and gently mixed in a little of the sauce.

Luciano brought the plates out to the patio. With that as their signal, the rest of the men came in to carry out the mineral water, wine, sauce, pasta, olives, bread, cheese, figs, grapes, and oranges.

We sat down to feast, laugh, and enjoy the early evening air together.

During the course of the conversation, Luciano had offered to go down to Naples with Flavio to help move his mamma's things. They decided to rent a small truck so she could bring all she needed for her apartment. They settled on the weekend in three weeks.

The next morning Flavio and Susanna left early to breakfast at her folks and hop the train back to Genoa.

LUCIANO'S AND FLAVIO'S FAMILIES ON THE MOVE

The next Friday, Luciano and my papà planned to take a late afternoon train to Naples. Early that morning, Luciano held me in his arms in the courtyard. He planted a big kiss on my lips. Then, only when satisfied with many promises from me that I would take good care of myself, he left on his motorbike for my folks' house. He would leave his motorbike there, take the bus to work, and later that afternoon, meet my papà at the station.

Later I wrote the story of their journey as Luciano had described it to me. I wrote the following.

Luciano and Dominico sat together on the train. They ate the food Dominico had packed for them and settled into a long nap. Both men were tired from the week's work. But, they also were tired with the emotional work they had to do inside to be ready for the trip.

They both awakened and looked at the beautiful sunset in the direction of the sea.

"This will work out. There will be a direction for the famiglia by the end of the weekend," said Dominico.

"Yes, I think there will be," answered Luciano. "I'm not quite sure how Margarita will feel about the eminent changes. But, Josefa is a wanderer. He will be fine as long as he can move around out in fields."

"And my cugini, Laura and Maximillian?" asked Dominico.

"Laura and Mariano are still in love. He's continuing his medical work in Turino and Laura wants to study in Turino," offered Luciano.

"Oh, that sounds good," answered Dominico. "And Maximillian?"

"He really loves the land. I'm not sure what he is going to say."

"I guess we will see how it all works out," said Dominico.

"Yes, we will," said Luciano grateful that he had an ally in this situation.

Luciano looked out of the train window as the hilly countryside sped past him. The terrain took on a drier topography as they neared the outskirts of Naples. Luciano felt its dramatic beauty go straight to his heart. As he contemplated the changes this land would experience with the predicted eruption of Vesuvius, it struck Luciano how much his physical environment had changed in his life. Only the mountains and the deeper part of the sea held a hint of constancy. He wondered what changes his child would see in his or her life and how best to prepare him or her. It seemed to him that Josefa and Margarita had given him not only skills of country life, but also a deep sense of self-confidence to face any situation in life. He decided that he would teach as much as he could to his child.

But most importantly he would love his child as Josefa and Margarita had loved him in order to catapult his child, as they had him, into his or her own realm of self-confidence.

"Now there's a contemplative face if ever I saw one," said Dominico.

"Yes, just considering how to be a papà in this world of fast changes."

"You'll be great," assured Dominico. "You make good choices. You married my figlia, didn't you?"

They both laughed and gathered their satchels as they pulled into the station. Maximillian was on the platform with his arm raised so they could see him.

Luciano was struck how mature and strong his younger brother looked. Maximillian embraced both men. They climbed into the small car nearby and Maximillian drove them to the farm. Both Luciano and Dominico were struck by the change in the countryside on the way. It was nothing that a stranger would notice. But both men, especially Luciano, had detailed memories of the types of crops that grew in each field and of the colorful curtains in the windows of the farmhouses. They remembered the pattern of stone walls around the courtyards and the fields. Some of the walls had fallen into disrepair or were built up in a certain upwind position. Some houses were without curtains and the plantings had changed to more tuber crops that would be less damaged by volcanic ash.

"Lot of changes, my fratello," said Luciano.

"Yes, many," answered Maximillian. "The visible landscape changes are from some of the many plans the government has put in place. These plans are based on a high degree of probabilities. But we have had to prepare the farmers for many scenarios. It's the best thing we can do. Nothing is certain when it comes to the moods of Vesuvius."

"Who would have thought that what you trained for would be so crucial for the entire Naples area?" mused Luciano.

"Well, we'll see. It has been a challenge for me both professionally and personally. I still haven't completely come to grips with the fact that we will lose the farm. But, I will. Our famiglia survived before the landowner bequeathed them our piece of land. Our famiglia will survive now and help others to do so as well," continued Maximillian.

"Do you think that Margarita and Josefa would consider following Great-Nonna Sophia's steps and come up north?" Dominico queried.

"Josefa is in serious consideration of the government's offer for the farm. We are in the borderline area for the expected lava flow and ash fallout. In those areas the government has presented a purchase document to the landowners. The land will continue to be farmed for now, but by a locally run government farm organization. The church has actually contributed a huge amount of money to this government purchase fund. So far, all of the farmers have been relocated out of the red zone area, and now the government has moved to address the yellow zone farms like ours. For those in the yellow zone there may be an opportunity, many years in the future, for farmers to purchase the land back from the government. But all that is speculation."

"What do you think, Maximillian, is it a fair offer they have made?" interrupted Dominico.

"Yes, I think it is, but we can look at the figures together," offered Maximillian.

The skies were into their evening darkness as they approached the farm. But despite the hour, Margarita and Josefa were in the courtyard ready to greet them.

They welcomed the three men with hugs and kisses. It didn't matter that they had seen Maximillian earlier that day. He was given a hero's welcome as well. That's just how Josefa and Margarita were—generous with their feelings.

Margarita ordered all the men to wash up and come to the kitchen for hot fish soup. They did so gladly. Then they ate voraciously. When the last drop of soup had been slurped or wiped up from their bowls with Margarita's fresh bread, the men cleared their dishes and took their hot coffee out to the patio for a short evening chat before bed.

Margarita quickly cleaned their bowls and laid them on a clean white cloth to dry. She then joined the men on the patio. They all knew that this was the last time all of them would be on this land as a family. This land had nurtured all of those present and many more. But now, it was time to move on.

The next morning after breakfast Margarita, Josefa, Laura, Maximillian, Dominico, and Luciano sat down to decide the future of both the farm and themselves.

After consideration of the money offered by the government for the land, Laura's plan to study in Turino, Maximillian's desire to stay in the Naples area, and Margarita and Josefa's desire to decrease their workload but still live a rural life, the following plan was devised.

Laura would live on the farm outside of Turino with Luciano, Francesca, Tizianna, and Angelo while she studied.

Maximillian would stay in the Naples area. One possibility was to stay in Flavio's mother's house. The government had expanded Maximillian's job description to run the farms that they had bought. Therefore, he would be able to manage his old farm. The present farm workers would be able to maintain their positions. They would be housed in this farmhouse.

Margarita and Josefa would accept the Marellis' offer to buy two acres of their land near Orvieto in central Italy. It was less than four hours from Turino. It had a small house, well, and land to garden or graze. The money left over from the relocation would be put in a trust divided between Maximillian, Luciano, and Laura.

Margarita and Josefa would be ready to move in three weeks. Luciano and Dominico would return to Naples then to drive the truck with their belongings. Josefa, Dominico, Luciano, and Maximillian decided to rent a car and go up to Orvieto early the next day to see what renovations might be necessary on the house before the move. Josefa promised to send photos to Margarita for suggestions while they met with the contractor.

Thus the plans were made. None of Aatif and Sophia's family would be covered in ash!

The rest of the day, the men assisted Josefa in deciding which tools to take and which to leave. Laura and Margarita packed family mementos.

The next morning, with ample food provisions and written requests from Margarita for the contractor, the men took off for Orvieto. There the men discussed some minor changes to the house with the contractor. Margarita agreed by phone to the changes. Then Maximillian drove Dominico and Luciano to the train.

Maximillian returned to the new family land to check on his papà's progress with the paperwork between himself, the contractor, and the Marellis. All was in good order. And the Marellis had invited him and Josefa for supper.

With peaceful hearts, Maximillian and Josefa joined the Marellis on their veranda for a delightful supper.

"We apologize for this early departure," said Maximillian after supper, "but we need to return to Naples tonight."

"We understand," said both Liliana and Giberto Marelli.

"We look forward to the day soon when you and Margarita are up here permanently," said Giberto while Liliana nodded in agreement.

After many heartfelt hugs, Maximillian and Josefa began their drive back to the Naples farm that had been in the family for generations. Maximillian drove and his father soon fell into a calm sleep.

Both Mamma and I were at the station in the Turino suburb to meet Dominico and Luciano. For me, Luciano's absence seemed far too long. He folded me in his arms and I knew by his touch that he felt a positive resolve about the trip. He and Papà described the family plan while we drove back to the house. Mamma had hot bean soup with fresh bread and cheese ready for us. Luciano and I ate as though we had forgotten to eat during each other's absence. Mamma and Papà just giggled at us. We started to help with the meal cleanup, but Papà and Mamma shooed us off to the farm.

"Get home safely, both of you," Mamma said as we climbed on the bike.

We tiptoed into the house so as not to awaken Nonno Angelo and Nonna Tizianna. But, of course, Nonna awakened with the door closure, heard our familiar footsteps, felt reassured, and promptly went back to her dreams.

Luciano and I fell asleep in each other's arms with dreams filled of family on the move, children born, and the unpredictability of nature.

In two weeks, Flavio and Luciano rented a small truck and drove directly to Flavio's family house. Once again the trip is written as narrated to me by Luciano.

Flavio's Mamma Patricia, welcomed them with seafood soup, fresh bread, and wine. She had her marvelous olives on the side. Flavio glanced around as they ate.

"It looks like you're ready for this move, Mamma," Flavio offered to his mamma.

"Yes, Flavio. This house will stand. I just have a feeling that it will. But, the area will change. Many of my friends have joined their families in other parts of Italy. Your folks will be leaving soon, Luciano. It is time for me to go up and be closer to you, Flavio. Who knows what's next? But for now, I'm content to relocate to Turino. I have everything that I need in those boxes…except, of course, a winter coat!"

"You are amazing with your organization, Mamma," Flavio said.

"I took my time, as it does take time to say good-bye. What do you guys think? Will what I have put aside fit into the truck? It is those boxes, two of my favorite flowerpots that are outside at the front of the house, my bed, the small dresser, this table and chairs, and the small loveseat."

"Oh, yes, Mamma. We can make this work. Right, Luciano?"

"Absolutely, Zia Patricia. We got you covered. I think we can do anything after this great fish stew. "

"Yes, it was great," concurred Flavio.

Patricia laughed. She looked up and saw through the window that Maximillian had pulled up on his motorbike. She went to the door to welcome him, and then went to retrieve another bowl for his soup.

Luciano and Flavio stood up and greeted Maximillian with hugs as he came in. Maximillian then sat down to the steaming hot bowl of soup that Patricia placed in front of him.

"I hope that you have left some of your cooking skill in these walls Zia Patricia. I will really have to step up to the plate with you and my mamma gone."

"You'll do just fine," said Patricia. "I have left some of my pots and some of my dishes for you, Maximillian. Your mamma will probably use hers as she will still be in the countryside. But, I won't. I have all that I need in those boxes. Flavio and Susanna have all they need so, please, Maximillian, use them. Also, I do not need the second bed. So, it's yours if you want it. Please use it. My new spot is a one bedroom. Eventually, I will get some sort of sleeping arrangement in the front room for guests. But, I want to be there before I figure that out."

Then Patricia reached into her apron pocket and pulled out a key for the house front and back door and the key for the shed. "Here are your keys, Maximillian," Patricia said. "I still have a spare set so we can lock up tomorrow when we pull out." Patricia smiled contentedly now that her preparations were completed.

"How are your folks doing in their move?" Patricia asked.

"Well, they've almost completed their box packing. They'll leave quite a bit of the furniture for the workers to use. The government bought their heavy equipment. So basically they'll move two beds, two dressers, the kitchen dishes and pots, table and chairs, and their two favorite sitting chairs and a small couch for the front room. Laura has taken what she needs from her bedroom and has taken the kitchen items precious to her.

I have all that I want to keep in a couple of boxes. I also have a couple boxes of tools and some fishing poles. Papà will help me get my bed and boxes over here tomorrow afternoon. So, your house will have me here to keep watch right away."

"Thanks, Maximillian," said Flavio. "But why don't we run over to the farm with the truck after supper. It won't take us but a minute to load up your few boxes, bed, bureau, your bookcase and table with chairs. Why try to figure out how to transport it by car and cart?"

"I'm in," said Luciano.

"Go on ahead so you fellas get some rest tonight. Don't worry with the dishes," said Patricia as the young men carried their bowls to the sink.

"If by any chance I'm asleep when you get back," Patricia added, "just put Maximilian's things against the far wall."

The young men kissed her cheeks and went off into the night with a departure shout, "We'll be back soon!"

And they were. Patricia had just nestled between her sheets when she heard the young men in the front room. They tried to speak in hushed tones, but their grunts from the weight of the boxes were clearly audible. Patricia softly fell asleep. She was happy to be cared for by such great young people. She felt happy to soon be in the same building with Catrina and Daniele. She loved their company and looked forward to fewer hours alone. This house in which she now slept for the last time, had served her well. But, that time was over.

Everyone had awakened by six in the morning. Luciano and Flavio made the cornmeal porridge and ham while Patricia put their sheets and towels in the washer. They were on the line in the sun and gentle breeze within the half hour. At six-thirty the three voyagers settled down to their hot morning beverages, cornmeal porridge, and ham.

"Nice breakfast, gentlemen," Patricia complimented.

"Thanks," they responded together.

"Well, I guess it's time that we demonstrated our excellent truck packing skills," said Luciano as he and Flavio rose from the table.

"And excellent they are," said Flavio as he went outside to open the truck back doors and bring in the dolly.

As the young men loaded the boxes into the truck, Patricia efficiently washed and dried the dishes and placed them in the cupboard. She then packed up lemon water in thermoses, oranges, grapes, olives, cheese, and bread for the drive.

After the boxes were tightly packed in, Luciano and Flavio tied the few pieces of furniture into place against the boxes. Next, they securely cushioned the big flowerpots and lastly placed their overnight satchels near the pots to add extra cushion. The food was placed in a small cold chest and placed in the back as well. Patricia kept the lemon water and grapes in the cab for energy on the road. The sheets, now dry, were taken off the line, folded, and put in a plastic bag that was then placed in the back of the truck and used as even more cushion for the pots.

Maximillian arrived on his scooter to see them off. Thus, Patricia was able to give him her second set of keys. It gave Patricia a secure feeling to see him in the house's doorway, ready to care for the house.

All three of them fit snugly and fairly comfortably in the front of the cab. They waved and shouted at Maximillian as they drove off. They hit the highway for the north a little before eight o'clock. The traffic moved well. The sky was blue with a few scattered clouds. The countryside was in full spring bloom. The farm fields had the special tender hue of green that glowed from young plants eager to grow and give their nutrition to the world.

In a couple of hours they stopped, stretched their legs, drank some water, munched on some grapes, and then drove onward. For lunch they pulled off the highway to a side road where they sat under a small tree and ate their mid-day provisions.

"This is a nice spot. I'll have to remember it for next weekend," said Luciano.

Patricia chuckled, "You are quite the road runner lately."

"It's true, but I'm glad family is settling closer to us and farther away from Vesuvius," responded Luciano as he smiled at Patricia.

"Speaking of changes, Flavio, how much more travel does Susanna have?" asked Patricia.

It was Luciano's shift at the wheel now. As they all climbed back into the cab, Flavio said, "Only four months now, and only a couple of short trips. We're both looking forward to a more settled schedule. She's glad that she has had the performance experience and needed to experience it to realize that the travel was not her cup of tea. We've missed each other. Glad it will be over."

"Both of you are very lucky," Patricia replied, and then asked, "When do Daniele and Catrina expect us?"

"Thanks for reminding me. I'll give Daniele a call now. We're about three hours from Turino. We should get there between five and six o'clock.

It was shortly after five when they pulled up in front of Daniele and Catrina's building. Daniele and Catrina were on the front bench awaiting their arrival. With hugs and kisses, they welcomed everyone. Catrina took Patricia by the arm and ushered her through the courtyard alive with spring blooms into Patricia's new apartment.

"Oh, my," said Patricia as her eyes sparkled. She noted the planters that awaited her own plantings at the front door. And as she walked in the front door she noted how cheerful and bright the rooms were. The front room had wide windows onto the courtyard, but also wide windows on the wall that faced the southeast and overlooked a neighborhood soccer field. She could see the tall wall that stood about ten feet from the building, and within that space grew tomatoes, herbs, and greens in large pots. She noted the laundry lines that ran from the wall to the side of the building.

"The apartment walls seem freshly painted," said Patricia as she turned from the window and looked around the front room that flowed into a kitchen on the far side.

"Daniele and I did it," said Catrina. "We thought that these old walls needed a boost to welcome you."

"It's beautiful. How did you know that I love the bright creams everywhere, but soft blue in the bedroom?" Patricia said softly, as her eyes filled with tears and her throat lost its volume.

Patricia kissed Catrina and Daniele in great gratitude as well as Flavio and Luciano. She felt she could have lit the room with her joy alone.

Catrina said, "We have some good pasta for everyone. Come upstairs with me, Patricia, and rest yourself."

"Mamma, Luciano and I will unload the truck now before we eat. Then we can relax together before I head back to Genoa," Flavio explained.

"I'll help unload the truck. You ladies go ahead," said Daniele.

The two women ascended the stairs together while the men went to work.

"We have the guest room here made up for you for the night. Then we can, if you would like, help you to unpack tomorrow."

"Is that a rhetorical question?" said Patricia.

Both women laughed.

Within half an hour the men were upstairs and everyone sat down to pasta with sausage in red sauce, bread, olive oil, and a big spring salad with vinegar and olive oil dressing.

Flavio got a text message that Susanna had arrived safely home from Milan. Flavio grinned a wide grin as he read the text.

"Well, my friend, I think we need to get you to the station for that eight o'clock commute into Genoa," said Luciano. "Francesca will meet me at the truck drop-off with the scooter, so I can first take you to the train in the truck. She's at her parents now with the scooter."

"Can she still ride the scooter, okay?" asked Patricia.

"Not for much longer, truth be told. She has less than a couple of months until the baby comes."

"I'm glad that I'm close enough to see the baby soon after arrival," said Patricia.

Flavio left his mother in a more relaxed and happy state than he had seen her in a long time. Now, he could relax a bit more as well.

"Your mamma's in a good place," said Luciano as they rode in the truck cab.

"I think so too," said Flavio. "Thanks for the weekend," he added.

"My pleasure, my fratello," responded Luciano.

The men hugged and slapped each other's back as Flavio left the truck. The men were silent. There were no words that could cradle the depth of their trust and gratitude for each other. They simply quietly acknowledged its strength that had continually given them great security in their lives since they were youths.

I met Luciano at the truck drop-off location He felt tired after the weekend events and was ready to go home.

"Hmm, I missed you so much!" said Luciano as he enfolded me and my expanded belly in his arms.

"I missed you too," I responded. "Glad you're back. Let's get home."

Once again I held Luciano's chest and felt secure as we rode in the night towards the farm.

"For me, the week went entirely too quickly," I said to my mamma at the market on the next Saturday. Both Luciano and my papà left on the late train the day before to Naples.

"I understand. Everyone will get settled soon. How are you feeling?" Mamma asked.

"Good, Mamma. Really good. Ready for this little one in a few weeks."

"You look good, Francesca," said Mamma with a special "mamma" smile. "Do you want to stop at the house and have some lunch before you head home?"

"I'd love to. Why didn't Nonna Mikaela come to market?"

Nonna Mikaela and Nonno Robert were in town for their monthly visit.

"Nonna Mikaela wanted to do her magic with the rice while I was at market so there would be some hot food upon our return," explained Mamma.

"Sounds like just what this pregnant woman needs!" I responded.

At my folks', it was just as Mamma had said. Nonna had done magic with the rice. I sat down and ate and ate and ate.

"So, you folks are coming to the farm tomorrow for the noon dinner?"

"Absolutely. Wouldn't miss it," said Nonna Mikaela.

"Laura will arrive with her things by late in the afternoon today," I added. "Her boyfriend from the medical college, Mariano, left yesterday to move her up here, as he has a car."

"Good, I haven't seen them since the wedding. Are she and Mariano serious? It sort of sounds like it," commented Nonna Mikaela.

"I think so, Nonna. They have been a couple since shortly before my wedding. She seems happy. He's in specialty training for internal medicine. He's dedicated to public health issues. I like him," I added.

"I remember him from the wedding. Very cordial. He's a little older than Laura, I imagine. That can be good," said Nonna Mikaela.

"Yes it can," I said with a grin. Nonna winked at me.

Then, as I looked around at the windows, I said, "It looks like Papà finished the caulking around the windows and doors. Looks good. We're almost finished at the farmhouse, too. The doors are done. We still have the windows in two more rooms to do, and then that's it!"

"Bravo," said Mamma. "Did Luciano say if there were tremors down near Naples last weekend?"

"He said at night they were strong enough to awaken him, but the furniture did not move."

"So, it really is as they say," Mamma mused.

"Yes, it seems so," I answered.

At that point of the conversation, Mamma's phone rang.

"Ciao, mi amore," the caller said. It was papà.

"Ciao, mi amore" Mamma said. "Francesca is here. She has just finished a plateful of Nonna Mikaela's rice!"

"Sounds like a good thing for a pregnant woman to do!" Papà responded.

Papà continued, "Luciano heard me say 'pregnant woman' so he blurted out 'I love you, Francesca' just in case you didn't hear him. Tell Francesca her husband is driving a pretty good sized truck right now, or I'd turn the phone over to him."

"She says she loves him, too. Well, other than sitting in a truck with a man that misses his pregnant wife, how are things going?" Mamma mused.

"Very well. We're over halfway to Orvieto. Josefa was organized. The truck was rented and ready to load first thing this morning. We left by ten o'clock. We'll be able to have the truck unloaded by supper. The Marellis have been great. Not only did they monitor the contractor's work so the house would be ready, but they invited all of us to stay in their guest rooms tonight and supper with them."

"That's great amore," Mamma responded.

"Yes, it is," Papà agreed. "Right now," he continued, "Margarita and Josefa are right behind us in their family car. So we have a mini-caravan. In the car, Margarita packed the items they'll need right away, before everything else is unpacked. She also packed up olives, cheese, tomatoes, olive oil, flour, salt, spices, dried herbs, and fruit to set up her kitchen. She has a lot of seeds from her garden plants. The Marellis have invited them to eat with them until they're settled. What can I say? They'll be fine! Luciano and I want to stay tomorrow to get the furniture placed where they want it and to get all the boxes opened and most of them unpacked. That won't take more than half the day. We plan to be on the two o'clock train up to Turino. We'll call you when we're on the train."

"We'll meet you. Love you."

"Love you too, mi amore. Ciao," and Papà hung up.

We felt a little tremor and then after big hugs for Nonna Mikaela, Nonno Robert, and Mamma, I took off on the scooter with our market provisions the few miles to the farm.

When I arrived at the farm, Nonna Tizianna and Nonno Angelo were in their favorite chairs under the tree in the courtyard. Nonno Angelo was dozing and Nonna Tizianna quietly hulled beans for tonight's soup. I greeted her and went in to put the vegetables and fruit away. Laura was on the patio in the back with her books spread out before her on one of the tables. I made a pot of hot mint tea and offered some to Laura. She gratefully accepted it.

"How is it going?" I asked the energetic student.

"Well," she said, "I love this economic theory class. But, I'm still clear that I want a career in accounting. I just love numbers and how they relate."

I laughed and said, "I guess you're right. They do relate. How wonderful for people like you to enable people like me to see their relationships. Laura, I'm so glad you're here. Let me know if you need anything to feel more at home."

"I already feel at home, Francesca."

"Good. And when do we see again the famous Mariano?" I said in a tease.

Laura laughed and broke into a big grin that confirmed her strong feelings for him.

I kissed my cugina on the cheek and said as I went into the house for a rest, "I'll leave you to your books."

I dreamt of mountains, earth movements, Luciano's arms around me, baby's kicks, and clear air.

The next afternoon I went to the station with Mamma to pick up Papà and Luciano. Nonna Mikaela and Nonno Robert were visiting Danielle, Catrina, and Patricia for the evening. Since we were in my parents' family car, she drove Luciano and me back to the farm first. Both men were obviously tired. One could tell by their slightly rounded shoulders. But their faces showed contentment with their accomplished task and contentment to be home.

At the farm, Nonna Tizianna had a large pot of lamb stew with some fresh focaccia bread ready for us.

"Come in and eat," said Nonna Tizianna as she greeted us at the car. "Then, Dominico and Alessia, you can just go home and relax."

"Thanks, Mamma Tizianna. That sounds just great! What do you think Domi…."

My mamma had no time to finish her sentence, for the men were out of the car, kissed Nonna Tizianna, and headed straight to the kitchen.

As we enjoyed Nonna's succulent stew, Nonno Angelo asked, "How did Margarita and Josefa settle in so far?"

"Actually, they really like the house and both are relieved to have less responsibility with the land. Josefa will plow his small field next week to put in his spring crops. Margarita will plant the spring house garden at the same time. So, basically, they felt right at home," said Dominico.

"It will be good to have them closer. We'll be able to visit each other more often. And, they'll be able to see the baby frequently," added Luciano as he gave me a squeeze and gently stroked my stomach.

We all shooed my papà and mamma off to home to rest after the meal. In a matter of minutes, my nonni and I had the kitchen cleaned up. Meanwhile, Luciano unpacked his satchel. My nonni soon settled under their favorite tree in the courtyard to crack hazelnuts.

Luciano and I embarked on an early evening hand-in-hand stroll in the vineyard rows and the fig tree grove. We talked softly without any urgency. It was pleasant to hear each other's voices. We retired early and I dreamed of peaceful skies that reflected a peaceful earth.

LUCIANO AND SICILY

It was a couple weeks later that Luciano arrived home from work with a new look on his face. I wouldn't describe his look as unsettled, rather it was a look of surprise, curiosity, and maybe a little sadness.

"What's going on, Luciano?" I asked as I greeted him at the door.

"I'm not sure," he said as he kissed me hello. "Let me show you something," he added.

"Okay," I said, ready for a mystery. "I'll grab us a mineral water."

We headed out onto the patio. Nonno Angelo waved from over among the vegetables. Nonna Tizianna could be seen in the distance in the fig grove. She loved the grove for her late afternoon stroll. She also kept a look out for early growth of next season's fruit during these walks.

Luciano pulled out a copy of an e-mail he received at work today. He handed it to me. It read as follows:

My name is Girolermo Vento. I also work in the Department of Agriculture but in the Messina, Sicily office. Recently I came across your name in one of the publications of the projects up there in Piedmont. Here in Sicily, we have much respect for your work and have implemented some of your ideas.

But the point of this e-mail is more personal than professional. I wonder if we might be cugini. Although our last name is common, it is noteworthy that we have the same last name. In addition, there is a family story that a couple years before your birth, Cologero and Serafina Vento left Sicily to work the fields in the region of Naples. I know this is a long shot, but I wonder if they were your folks? My papà, who also left the Sicilian countryside in search of work, had a fratello named Cologero. My papà was killed in a shipyard accident a few years after I was born, so I never really knew him. My mamma remarried a shopkeeper in Messina. My mamma and I did not return to the countryside.

I hope I have not offended you with this information. If I have, please disregard this e-mail, and I look forward to your professional colleagueship in the future.

Sincerely yours,
Girolermo Vento

"Luciano! What a surprise! What do you think?" I asked quietly.

"I feel a little odd and at the same time a little hopeful. It would be nice if it turns out he is my cugino. But you know Margarita and Josefa had my parents' deaths published in the major newspapers including those of Sicily. It was mentioned that they had a child. For my safety they gave no details of my age or sex. Still, my parents' names were listed and no one responded.

Out of respect for my parents, whom they loved, when Margarita and Josefa adopted me they kept my last name as Vento. So my name does represent my blood ties. But, I am suspect if this man is a relation because of no response to the newspaper posting," Luciano explained.

"It could have been that no family member read the reports, and this man was too young to have read them," I reasoned.

"True. He wrote his e-mail as if my parents were alive. Hmmm. This opens up a lot of questions for me. I have to sit with this for a while. I've lived with one concept of family, and now it may have taken on a new expansion," Luciano concluded.

"Whatever you decide to do or not do, I love you," I said as I rose. I kissed Luciano on the cheek and went into the kitchen to make the rice for supper.

I watched out the kitchen window as Luciano strode out into the vineyards. He would decide his next move once he got his feet moving over the ground. In a while, Nonna Tizianna came in with some fresh early spring greens for the salad. Luciano strode back to the house with Nonno Angelo. They were in an animated conversation on the early spring evaluation of the grapevines.

Luciano is the type of person that works things out in his mind in an orderly fashion. He avoids crooked side roads in his thought patterns. Then he stays at peace with his decision. He glanced at me as he went to wash up for supper. I knew by his look that he had made his decision.

I had steamed the perch in olive leaves, with a squeeze of lemon and black pepper. I had made Nonna Mikaela's rice dish. Nonna would first sauté finely diced vegetables like onion, garlic, and red and green peppers in olive oil with the well rinsed rice. Her favorite spices were added to this mixture. She then added water, brought it to a boil, and lastly turned the heat down to steam the rice mixture 'til cooked. I always followed her format. Tonight, the meal was topped off with Nonna Tizianna's fresh green salad, bread, last fall's olive oil, and our vineyard's red wine, with mineral water for me, of course. Thus completed our beautiful meal.

While we ate, Luciano spoke of his e-mail. He had already shown it to Nonno Angelo out in the field. Nonna Tizianna was surprised.

"After so many years, family possibly emerges," she commented.

"What do you think is best to do about the e-mail? Or is it too early for you to say?" questioned Nonna Tizianna.

"Well," Luciano began as he took my hand, "I'm going to see what the e-mail means. Tomorrow I'll e-mail Girolermo and arrange a visit to Messina."

"Take someone with you, Luciano. Maybe Flavio or Dominico," Nonno Angelo said. "If it doesn't work out for them, then I will go with you."

"You're right, Nonno Angelo. I am sure that Flavio will go with me,"

Luciano responded.

"What about meeting him here in Turino?" I offered, concerned for my husband's safety.

"Francesca, I want to see who he is before he comes on our turf," Luciano explained.

"That makes sense," I said very aware of the many ramifications of this meeting.

"Also, I think it best if I go sooner than later. It's only a few more weeks before the baby. This is something that I would like to get sorted out before the birth," concluded Luciano.

"I agree," I concurred.

That evening Luciano called Flavio. Flavio definitely wanted to go with him. The next day Luciano checked the database of the Department of Agriculture and sure enough there was a Girolermo Vento that worked in the Department of Agriculture in Messina. He also asked around the office if anyone had been at any meeting with a Girolermo Vento from the Messina office. No one had.

However, when Girolermo told his supervisor that Luciano Vento was to be in Messina, his supervisor sent Luciano an e-mail with a request to meet about their interprovincial work. Luciano agreed. Girolermo would be at the meeting as well. Luciano felt comfortable with a professional setting as his first encounter with Girolermo.

In two weeks Luciano and Flavio were on the overnight train to Reggio and then took the ferry across the strait to Messina. They checked into a small hotel near the Department of Agriculture offices and then headed to the nearest café. Luciano had two hours until the meeting.

"No, Luciano, I won't be bored at the Department of Agriculture. I brought a book and my laptop. Anyway, I want to see how he reacts to you. If he is your blood, I'm sure he's great, but all of this is unknown," said Flavio.

"All right, my friend, let's go."

The receptionist announced their arrival to both the supervisor and Girolermo Vento. Girolermo Vento came quickly out of his office. He smiled and extended his hand out to Luciano. Luciano smiled and extended his hand out as well.

"This is my friend Flavio Martoni. He is the engineer director of Genoa's infrastructure renewal project."

"Oh, yes, Signore Flavio Martoni. We have many of the same issues here with the fault and surrounded by the sea. We are in admiration of your work in Naples and Genoa," said Girolermo.

"Good to meet you," said Flavio. "I'll sit over here and do some work while you meet."

"Please help yourself to the office water and make yourself at home," Girolermo said.

"Thank you," said Flavio as he turned and seated himself in a nearby chair.

"Come, let us get to the meeting. I have so many questions for you, Luciano, after the meeting," said Girolermo.

"And I for you," said Luciano as he smiled at his gracious new acquaintance. He quickly processed the fact that this man could be his cousin. Girolermo was basically a shorter and darker version of himself. They had the same shape head, nose, and cheekbones. Luciano's eyes were rounder and his lips slightly fuller. But it was clear to Luciano that they could be family. Well, at any rate, he was a pleasant fellow, he mused to himself. Then Luciano re-oriented his mind to the business meeting.

The meeting was efficient and completed in an hour. Girolermo then invited both Luciano and Flavio to meet him and his wife at the same café where Luciano and Flavio had lunched. They agreed to meet at seven o'clock.

"What do you think?" Flavio asked Luciano as they headed back to their hotel room.

"I think he's probably my cugino, is what I think. What was your take?"

Flavio laughed. "Well, if it's a matter of looks, he definitely could be your cugino, or your fratello, even."

"I know!" said Luciano as he laughed, too.

Luciano called me after his meeting with his positive first impressions. We chatted a few moments and then when we were ready to hang up, Luciano said, "Take care of yourself, Francesca. Know that all is good here. I'll give you a call in the morning, as our dinner conversation tonight may get a little late."

"That's a good idea," I said, "I seem to be jealous of my sleep these days. Love you."

"Love you too, Francesca."

Exhausted from the night train and the emotion of anticipation, both Luciano and Flavio sprawled across their beds in their hotel room. They told each other that they would rest a short minute. Immediately they fell asleep and didn't awaken for an hour.

Refreshed, Luciano said, "Well, Flavio, let's go out and see the part of the world my papà and mamma chose to leave."

"Let's! I'm up for the adventure!"

Luciano and Flavio walked along the rebuilt streets and the ocean-front. Luciano felt a connection and enjoyed the city. But, he did not feel attached.

Luciano and Flavio met Girolermo and his wife, Teresa, at the café at seven o'clock. Teresa was a pleasant woman. She smiled warmly at her new acquaintances as well as at her husband during the conversation. She was a nurse at the municipal hospital in Messina. Girolermo and Teresa had met in the hospital when Girolermo had an appendicitis attack two years ago.

"She didn't want to give me her phone number at first. So I gave her mine," Girolermo teased as he looked fondly at his wife.

"I thought about him for a couple of weeks before I called him," Teresa admitted. "It was his smile and the kind look in his eyes that convinced me this man was different from my previous boyfriends. So I called. And here I am two years later, married and happy. It was a good move for me to make that phone call."

They all laughed. Her lighthearted way and her ease with the story broke the ice between all of them.

Giolermo went on to explain, "When my mamma married the shop-keeper, the few members of my papà's family that had not left Sicily ignored me. Or, maybe they just forgot me, as their lives were hard.

"All of my nonni had died when I was a child. The farm laborer life was hard and shortened many people's lives. My zii and zie had moved on to other countries to find harvest work. Some were lost in route, but of those that landed, none returned. There were only a few distant cugini left here," Girolermo concluded.

Luciano looked at Flavio and then at Girolermo again. "Girolermo, please go on," Luciano said.

"Our famiglia did not own land here. I can show you the general rural area where our nonni and papàs lived, if you'd like. It's not far into the country from here."

"Thanks. I'd like that."

"But, Luciano, tell me. What happened to your folks? Did they find work in the harvest?"

"Yes, they did. They worked a farm near Naples and Vesuvius that same year. The owners of the farm loved my papà and mamma and asked them to stay on as permanent farm workers. They did and soon I was born. My papà and mamma walked the road between their small house and the fields. One day, on this road, they were killed by a car that took a fast turn. I was two at the time. I was at the farm with Margarita and Josefa, my future adoptive parents. I remember vaguely a lot of sadness, but have a sketchy memory of my papà and mamma.

"Despite announcements sent by Margarita and Josefa to several Sicilian newspapers, no one responded to grieve my papà and mamma's deaths. So Margarita and Josefa buried them and adopted me. They kept my original last name out of respect for my papà and mamma. I love Margarita and Josefa as my famiglia. Later they had two children of their own, who are like my sorella and fratello."

"And Flavio?" Girolermo asked, "Are you a cugino?"

"No, Flavio is my fratello of fratelli, a very good friend. Who else would come with me to find my long lost cugino?" Luciano asked.

Everyone laughed. Then Luciano and Flavio showed Girolermo and Teresa pictures of their wives. They both said that they were both beautiful. What else could they say? But, it was the truth.

Luciano took a picture of Girolermo and Teresa together. Then Teresa took a picture of the three men together. With the arrival of the pasta the conversation slowed. Now at ease with each other, they savored the food and planned the country escapade tomorrow.

The next morning, Girolermo took them up into the hills. They were rugged and many were covered with vineyards. They stopped at a farm that served travelers a noontime meal. The conversation moved easily between family stories and professional projects. Luciano and Flavio liked Girolermo and Teresa a lot. After the meal they strolled for a while along the vineyard of the hill. Its beauty was an intoxicant to Luciano. But he understood why his parents left. There was no room for the landless here.

On the way back to Messina, Luciano invited Girolermo and Teresa to visit Turino. They agreed and promised to keep in touch by e-mail and phone. Luciano and Flavio were dropped off at the hotel so they could check out. They then were invited to Girolermo and Teresa's for coffee before their ferry departure.

Soon, the four of them sat at Teresa's cheerful kitchen table with their cups of Teresa's rich coffee. Luciano felt at home with his newfound cugino and his wife. Like Luciano, Girolermo was one of the few in this generation from their family's past. Luciano felt grateful to Girolermo to have told him of his family. The courage of his parents was now a huge reality for Luciano.

"Girolermo, if you hadn't reached out to me with the e-mail, I would not have known about my papà and mamma's origin and their necessity to leave it. I would have never been able to feel their tremendous courage. Thank you."

"I'm so glad to meet you. Here let me show you some photos." Girolermo then went to a drawer and pulled out some photos.

"This is a photo of my mamma and padrigno. And here is the only photo she had of my papà. And here is the only photo of him with his fratello Cologero before everyone split up."

Luciano just stared at the photo. Then he said slowly, "My papà with your papà!"

"Yes. I had a copy made for you. This is yours."

Luciano gave Girolemo the biggest of hugs, kissed his cheek, and showed the photo to Flavio, "My papà, Flavio, my papà!"

When Luciano and Flavio arrived back in Turino, both Susanna and I were at the station to welcome them. It was early morning when the train got in. For me the separation had seemed longer than it was. Maybe because I knew that Luciano had found many years of missed information. Maybe also because I felt the heaviness of my child and a sensation that he or she would soon begin the exit from my body. But now, Luciano was here! And in this beautiful moment I am in his strong embrace.

We all got into my parents' car. The men were a little quieter than usual, especially Flavio. Flavio may be the kind of guy that jokes around a lot, but feelings run deep with him. It was a powerful experience for him to share this voyage to meet Luciano's family's past.

This morning Susanna and Flavio had planned to go to their parents' building for a few hours of visit. Then they would take the short train ride home to Genoa.

"Catrina, Patricia, and Daniele were up early this morning and pre-pared a large early mid-day meal," she told Flavio. "They have become a famiglia. They chased me out of the kitchen and told me to just get ready to greet my marito!" Susanna added.

We left Flavio and Susanna at Susanna's childhood building amidst hugs and thanks. Luciano and I went directly to the farm. My mamma and papà were there with a large pot of chicken, bean, and pasta soup, to be served with polenta, hard crust bread and cheese. They had lent me their car, as the baby's position was too low for me to drive a scooter.

When we arrived in the courtyard, Alessia, Dominico, Tizianna, and Angelo all took their turn to give Luciano a big hug. He grinned from ear to ear as he pulled out the picture of his biologic papà. Dominico and Angelo slapped him on the back and commented that he came from a handsome people. My mamma and nonna patted Luciano's cheek and kissed it. Mamma, Nonna, and I left the men and went into the kitchen. Soon, with a light step, Luciano came through the kitchen, kissed me again, and went to shower. The day was already warm so the men placed the patio table in the shade. We brought out the food with wine and mineral water while we talked about Luciano's visit, the crops, and our preparations for a possible Vesuvius eruption.

My parents left in the early evening. Nonna Tizianna and Nonno Angelo sat with Luciano and I a little longer in the courtyard under the tree. The evening air was warm with only a slight breeze. It felt good on our faces. As the new moon moved across the night sky we left the courtyard and went to our beds with dreams of the movement of celestial bodies.

Chapter Four

VESUVIUS AND LUCIANA

Luciano wasn't home but one week when the government gave the two-week warning for the Vesuvius eruption. I met with my dance students and cancelled our classes until after the Vesuvius eruption was over. Then Nonna Tizianna and I gathered what tuber vegetables we could. We had bought rice at the market. We harvested and pickled some vegetables so they would last.

Luciano and Nonno Angelo finalized the seal of the windows and doors. They also gathered a few gallons of water from the well to store in the kitchen. There was a pump for the water transport to the house run on a solar battery. This was just a backup. Luciano made sure that all of our family and friends had the government issued masks.

"You don't think the ash will reach us, do you, Luciano?" I asked late one afternoon as he worked on the kitchen door seal bands.

"It shouldn't, but I'm not sure. The wind currents can double back and move north as they head east from the Naples area. It depends what happens with the air currents around the mountains."

"Well, we're about as ready as we can be, I guess," I answered.

"Yup, we'll be all right. Tomorrow after work I'll go by Susanna's folks and your folks to see if they need anything. Flavio checked on your Nonna Mikaela and Nonno Robert, and their place is sealed up, they have food and water stored, and they have their masks. Dominico contacted Cugini Duccinio and Pasquale by phone and they are prepared. He also contacted the Marellis and Zio Josefa and Zia Margarita in Orvieto. They're all fine. Maximillian has Flavio's house sealed up in Naples, as well as the farmhouse."

"Sounds like we've done all we can do. Still, I feel like a sitting duck and I don't like the feeling."

"Well, Francesca, you're not a duck, you're a beautiful woman about to give birth any day now. And furthermore you're standing by a man who adores you."

Luciano put down his caulk tube and took me in his arms and said, "I can't imagine how you feel now, but I will be at your side."

"Good! Because I will keep you busy when I go into labor!"

Luciano laughed his contagious laugh and I began to laugh. I laughed at my silliness because I had no idea what I would do with him when I went into labor. Who knows how I would feel towards him at that point? I laughed and laughed and held him in abandon. It felt so good to release into the laughter.

As we reluctantly loosened our embrace, I announced to Nonna Tizianna who was at the other end of the kitchen with some herb leaves that she had dried, "I love this man so much!"

"Yes, you do, my dear. That's a good thing!"

I approached her and took some of the dried herbs and asked, "Would you like a hot cup of herb tea with me, Nonna?"

"That would be lovely."

"Luciano, can I fix you a cup of coffee?"

"No, thanks, mi amore. I'm going out to the shed to do some more caulking."

"Nonna, the other day we didn't get to the love story of Nonno Angelo's parents, Carlos and Susanna. I would like a happy story today. I need to think about another time when Vesuvius was calm."

"Let's go out to the patio where we can put our feet up and I'll tell you their story."

I was ecstatic! Dear reader, I was ready to escape my reality if only for a few moments!

SUSANNA AND CARLOS

Nonna Tizianna and I settled ourselves on the patio and then Tizianna began after a sip of her hot tea.

Susanna is the name of Nonno Angelo's mamma. She rode her bicycle every day to her job at the hazelnut spread production plant. She lived nearby on her family's hazelnut and vegetable farm. They sold most of their hazelnuts to the plant. So today Susanna balanced a sack of hazelnuts on her bike as she rode to work.

Susanna had chosen to not sit for her university entry exams. Her parents were older. They needed Susanna's help on the farm and they needed her income from Valli's factory.

Susanna always loved books and read at every spare moment. She told me this satisfied her need for knowledge and exercised her imagination.

She had no regrets about her decision. It was far more important to her to care for her parents. Her teachers from the secondary level kept her supplied with books. Because she was always with a book, her co-workers and neighbors nicknamed her 'the little professor.'

Susanna blessed everyone with her peaceful constitution. It wasn't that she was shy or quiet. It was a deep peace. She took time to do her meditation prayers daily. Well, on this particular day Susanna was almost to the factory when she heard three loud motorbikes. They approached fast and the three young men on the bikes yelled, "Hey, country girl, out of the way or we'll do more than this to you!"

They then swerved their bikes towards her. As suddenly as they swerved towards her they drove away in a sound cloud of loud laughter. Susanna always peddled at the side of the road. Their approach forced her off the road and her front tire hit a small rock. The bike overturned onto the stubbly grass and dirt at the side of the road.

At the sound of the shouts, a certain young man named Carlos hurried around from the back of the factory to see what was going on. He was friends with the factory owner, Vincenzo Valli. They had met at the university. Carlos was junior to Vincenzo by a couple of years. As fate would have it, Vincenzo had asked Carlos to come out to the factory that day to evaluate some production issues from his engineering perspective. He had arrived early, as was his habit.

When he saw Susanna fall he tore into a run towards her. Susanna calmly raised herself up to a sitting position and evaluated her situation. She hardly had time to complete her self-assessment before Carlos was at her side. She had some bloody scrapes on her right arm and right leg. The right sleeve of her work blouse was torn, as was the right leg of her work pants. The hazelnuts were wrapped so tightly that the knot did not loosen, but a few had popped out of a tear in the side of the satchel.

"What a surprise that was!" said Susanna as Carlos squatted beside her.

"What jerks!" Carlos blurted out. "Are you all right? Well, of course you're not. There's blood on your arm and leg. Did you hit your head? Where is the worst pain?"

Susanna smiled at this earnest man and said, "No, I didn't hit my head. I let my arm take the brunt of it. I think it's just cut. It doesn't feel like anything is broken," she responded.

"What about your legs? How do your ankles feel?"

"Just sore. I think the right one has begun to swell."

"Okay then. Let's get you to the factory where we can clean these scrapes. I'll carry you there and then come back for your bike. Agreed?"

Susanna looked Carlos in the eyes deeply and said, "Agreed."

At the factory Carlos took off his clean shirt and tore it into strips. He found soap and water. Then with some of the strips soaked in soap and water, Carlos gently, but thoroughly, cleaned her cuts. Then he covered her cuts with the clean cloth strips from his shirt.

Susanna was overwhelmed by his kindness. She was also overwhelmed by the strength of his now shirtless torso. She thought that her feelings were due to the shock of how fast everything had happened. So she tried to focus her gaze on his face or somewhere other than his gorgeous chest. Carlos went to get the bike and the hazelnuts. He left the hazelnuts in the office with a note to Vincenzo that he would be back but had left to take Susanna home. He covered his torso with his jacket. Then Carlos carried Susanna to his motorbike and gently placed her behind his seat. As he slowly drove the two kilometers to the farm, he frequently asked her how she was doing. Carlos pulled up into the courtyard of the small farmhouse. A tidy hazelnut grove was behind the house. A small shed was on one side of the house and on the other side were long rows of greens, root vegetables, and corn. He lifted Susanna into his arms to carry her to the house at the same moment that her mother rushed out of the front door.

"I'm okay, Mamma. This kind gentleman helped me when my bike turned over," said Susanna.

"My name is Carlos Martoni. I am friends with Mr. Vincenzo Valli. I saw the accident and wanted to help."

"Thank you, Mr. Martoni. I am Rosa Gusberti. Thank you, again, so much. Please come this way."

Carlos carried Susanna into the small but cheerful house. There were two bedrooms off the kitchen-living area. He carried Susanna, as directed by her mother, to the smaller bedroom. After Rosa laid a clean cloth on the bed he laid her on the bed.

"Thank you," Susanna said to Carlos.

"Yes, thank you. Please, would you have some coffee?" asked Rosa.

"Thank you for your kind offer. Right now I must go back to the factory and finish my work. But, if it's all right, I would like to return this afternoon and check on Susanna." Carlos looked back and forth between the women.

"Of course," Susanna said as she smiled.

"Please come and have some coffee with us this afternoon," invited Rosa. "My husband will be back from fishing and will be glad to meet you," she added.

"Alright then, until later," Carlos said as he smiled at the two women.

As he rode back to the factory he could not get Susanna out of his mind. Her dark black wavy hair was stunning against her cream toned olive skin. He loved the way her almond shaped dark eyes danced with light as she smiled at him. There was a peacefulness about her that he wanted to be close to again. He smiled to himself at how fast his world had changed since he arrived at the factory this morning.

Carlos went to the office and explained to Vincenzo what had happened. He said that he planned to return to check on Susanna in the afternoon. Vincenzo smiled at his friend and said, "She is a lovely young lady."

Then Vincenzo added, "Here's a shirt for the factory tour," as he pulled a factory work shirt out of a cabinet drawer in the office. "You might want to cover up those great pecs, my friend."

The two men laughed. Vincenzo because he had never seen his friend so smitten, and Carlos because he was surprised at himself.

"I know you wanted to see the factory layout before the morning operations began," Vincenzo said, "but I think you'll see what you need in order to make your suggestions."

The two friends walked through the factory rows of busy machinery and then back to the office. Carlos gave some suggestions from his perspective and the meeting was concluded.

"Well, my friend," Vincenzo said, "Am I to expect you back at the house a little later?"

"I'll be back in a couple of hours," Carlos responded with a smile.

"See you then. Take your time," Vincenzo said as he slapped his friend on the back. "Please assure Susanna that she'll continue to receive her pay while her ankle heals. She's a good employee and deserves as much."

"I will," Carlos said as Vincenzo turned to return to his office. Carlos went to his motorbike, strapped Susanna's bike onto the back of it, and turned his bike towards Susanna's.

When he arrived at the Gusberti's courtyard, he removed Susanna's bike from his motorbike, intending to fix the misalignment of Susanna's front tire for her.

A man Carlos assumed to be Susanna's father stepped out of the small shed while he wiped his hands on a white cloth. He waved and said, "You must be Carlos Mantoni. Good to meet you. I'm Ignacio Gusberti. My wife and daughter told me of your tremendous help."

"Good to meet you, sir," said Carlos. "I'd like to straighten the wheel on Susanna's bike for her. May I borrow some tools?"

"Of course. Bring the bike into the shed," said Ignacio as he looked at this young man curiously. He wondered who he was and why he was at the factory. But there would be time for all of that a little later, he thought.

As Carlos worked on the bike, Ignacio said, "Did you see the accident?"

"Yes," Carlos responded.

"Tell me what you saw," Ignacio inquired with a serious tone in his voice and a concerned look in his eye.

"Well, I arrived at the factory early. I wanted to study the machine set-up before the first shift began. I came down a back road from the owner's house to the factory on my scooter. I had parked my scooter in the back. So, neither I nor my scooter was visible. With the young men's shouts I quickly rounded the corner of the factory that faces the main road. I saw three large motorbikes moving fast in the same direction as Susanna. The drivers headed towards Susanna and then swerved away. She was on the edge of the road, and their approach forced her off the road. Her front wheel seemed to hit a stone and that overturned the bike. It all happened so fast, just a matter of seconds from the men's appearance and aggression to her fall. Immediately I ran to help Susanna. Unfortunately, I wasn't able to get any license plate numbers off their bikes."

Carlos looked up from his work on the tire and saw Ignacio with his gaze fixed intently on him while he listened to the story.

Carlos continued, "Sorry about not getting plate numbers."

"No, no, no. You did the right thing to help Susanna first. I just want to say that the way you told the story, the way you talk—you have a lot of education, no?"

"I don't know about a lot, but I will finish this year at the university's school of engineering," Carlos responded in a matter of fact manner.

"Hmmm. Interesting mix. A scholar with kindness," said Ignacio.

Carlos shrugged. "I was fortunate and respected the opportunity to study. That's all," he explained.

"Tell me, Carlos, who were those guys on the bikes? I don't want Susanna to ride her bike to work if they might return."

"They looked to me like some young, well-off, secondary school students that had partied all night. They probably came from Alba and were headed back to Turino," Carlos said as he once again shrugged his shoulders.

"But, I can't be certain because I'm not from around here. I did describe them and their bikes to Vincenzo at the factory and he had no recollection of them in this area before."

"Just the same, I think that I'll ride her on the mare on the back roads. That would be safer. Other workers use the back roads as well," Ignacio mused.

"Susanna seems to have a very strong constitution. It must run in the family," consoled Carlos.

"Well, how about some fish? I caught them this morning!" said Ignacio as he smiled for the first time since their meeting.

"My pleasure," said Carlos as he tested the security of the tire position.

Ignacio handed him the white cloth now decorated with streaks of dirt and grease marks. He also handed him a clean, damp cloth dipped in vinegar. Carlos wiped his hands. The two men then headed for the house.

As they entered the front door, there was Susanna seated in a comfortable chair by the fireplace. She was not too far from the table and chairs in the kitchen area. The smell of delicious fried fish came off the stove. A large plate of hot polenta sat in the center of the table.

Susanna sat in a lovely, short sleeve, pale green dress. Her right arm and right leg and ankle were wrapped in mysterious herbal poultices, brewed by the expert hand of her mamma, Rosa. Rosa turned from the fish and said loudly, "Welcome, Carlos. Sit, sit. We will eat soon."

Ignacio said, "I have to bring in some greens for the salad. Here, take this chair." He pulled a chair from the table and placed it near Susanna, and then disappeared.

"Thank you, sir," said Carlos, unable to take his eyes off of Susanna and her beautiful smile.

"Susanna, you look better," Carlos said as he gently touched her left hand, as it was uninjured.

"I slept a long while and then was besieged by Mamma with her poultices and teas. I could only be better! Right?"

"Right!" Carlos responded.

"Did you get your work done at the factory?" Susanna asked.

"Yes, and by the way, Vincenzo sent a message to you. He said that your pay is covered while your ankle heals."

"I don't think it'll take more than a couple of days to be up on my ankle. Mamma is strict with my regimen and her herbs are incredible."

"Are you writing her potions down?" asked Carlos.

"No, actually. I watch. I think that I could reproduce many of them. But I like your suggestion. She modifies with the situation and the herbs available. So it could get involved. But it would be helpful for me to note down her healing magic," Susanna said.

"If you'd like, what you write down I can take and type up at the university study library," Carlos offered.

Surprised at this generous offer, Susanna was a little slow in her response. "Thank you, Carlos. How great," said Susanna as she studied Carlos's face.

"Okay, enough of you young people plotting to steal my remedies," said Rosa as she placed the fish on a platter next to the stove. Ignacio had put together a lovely salad of greens, tomatoes, onion, olives, and a sprinkle of cheese. He added olive oil and vinegar with salt and pepper.

"Now, Carlos, please assist Susanna to the table," said Rosa. "Don't worry. Her poultices are securely in place."

"Okay, Susanna, here we go. First I'll help you to stand up. Put your weight only on your left foot and lean on me as I help raise you up. Okay. We got it! Now here we go!"

Carlos then carefully raised Susanna into his arms and carried her to the chair at the table with a padded bench in front of it. With much laughter on Susanna's part he lowered her onto the chair and gently raised her right leg onto the bench. He placed a pillow under her knee and then asked, "Comfortable?"

"For sure," she said a little embarrassed from the attention and because of her flushed face.

"Oh my, this looks and smells so delicious!" said Carlos as he eyed the well-seasoned fish on the blue plate and the greens in the terra cotta bowl. These dishes were also joined by the golden polenta in the large, flat, green dish. He was grateful for the distraction from his emotions that the beautiful display of food offered. For his emotions had over-whelmed him since he had held Susanna's sumptuous body in his arms just moments ago.

As they began eating, Ignacio entertained them with the heroic epic of his fishing adventure. Of course there were bears that came down from the mountains and tried to scare him from his favorite spot in the stream. But he bravely withstood their threats. Then there were the thieves and robbers on the road who tried to steal his fish. But he was able to trick them to leave him alone. Lastly there was the danger of his thirst and fatigue. But he made it home at last. Voila! This fabulous meal!

Everyone ate and laughed during Ignacio's rancorous tale.

"I don't know which is more fabulous, Rosa's food or Ignacio's amazing tale!" said Carlos.

After dinner, Susanna said, "Carlos would you please do that muscular feat again to land me back in the chair."

"Absolutely!" he said, and immediately he swung Susanna up into his arms.

Rosa and Ignacio cleaned up the dishes. It was a comfortable end of the day ritual for them. They chatted about which vegetables would be ready for market on Saturday. They chatted about how to get the rest of the hazelnuts to the factory while Susanna was home recovering.

Susanna turned her head to Carlos and said, "They treasure their time together. They take nothing for granted."

"Sounds like a wise philosophy," said Carlos.

"So what do you plan to do after graduation?" asked Susanna.

"I'll work in Turino at the iron ore plant. I have a connection for a job there. Just the hurdle of the exams awaits me," said Carlos.

"You'll do well," assured Susanna. "If your mind is as quick as your feet, they will go very well," Susanna added as they both laughed.

Rosa brought them both a cup of coffee. Ignacio left out the kitchen door and then reappeared a few moments later with an old cane in his hand.

"I forgot about this old cane, Susanna. It's been out in the shed. But it cleaned up just fine." Ignacio handed the cane to his figlia.

"This is will do the job, Papà. Thanks."

Susanna smiled at Carlos and added, "Although your air lifts, Carlos, had their advantages."

"Any time," Carlos quickly responded. Then, trying to refocus himself, he said, "But that is a terrific cane. Did you carve it, Ignacio?"

"Yes, I did. It was my way to celebrate the exit of the Germans from our land."

Carlos took the cane in his hands. "These carved shapes seem to evoke a presence of vegetation that can only grow in the sun of freedom," Carlos said as he slowly turned the cane in his hands and gazed upon the smooth shapes evoked from this hard piece of wood. "This is a beautiful piece of art, Ignacio."

Carlos then stood up and said, "I should leave now. Maybe tomorrow morning I could come by before I head back up to Turino? It would be good to see you on the mend, Susanna."

"I look forward to it," said Susanna as Carlos leaned down to kiss her cheeks.

He kissed Rosa on the cheeks, shook Ignacio's hand, and was off.

Carlos did return the next morning. It was curious that as he entered the house, Susanna's face broke into a huge smile. She couldn't help it. She thought it curious that his face did the same.

Carlos returned also the next Saturday and every Saturday after that for two months when he asked Susanna to marry him.

Susanna agreed immediately. Susanna was able to sense things about a person.

His presence gave her peace and she found his conversation interesting. She felt fortunate to have met such a compatible person. And then there was his touch. She had never felt that sensation with a touch before. It was warm with an intensity that moved through her heart. It gave her what felt like a thousand sunbursts throughout her body.

Soon after their engagement Carlos brought Susanna into Turino to meet his mamma and papà. They lived in a small workers' apartment near the plant. To celebrate Susanna's visit they had the apartment packed with every nearby relative who brought rice, pasta, sauces, olives, fruits, cheeses, mineral water, and wine. Susanna had a great time. When at last everyone's fatigue overcame them and the last person had left, Carlos's mamma created a comfortable bed for Susanna from a cot. She used colorful quilts and pillows. Susanna was exhausted and slept from the moment her head hit the pillow until the rays of sun entered the living room.

By the time Susanna awakened, Carlos's mamma, Nadia, was in the kitchen. Nadia had the coffee to a boil and the polenta bubbling. When she heard Susanna stir, she greeted Susanna warmly and, knowing her to be a modest woman, whispered "The men are still asleep. No one is in the washroom. Help yourself."

Susanna emerged from the washroom, folded her bedding and went into the kitchen. By then she could hear Carlos and his papà in and out of the washroom and their bedrooms. Susanna and Carlos's mamma sipped their coffee and laughed at the loudness the men seemed to create just with an entrance and exit from a room. Carlos entered the kitchen. He first kissed Susanna and his mamma good morning. Then he poured his coffee. He dipped out a bowl of corn porridge with cream for the two women and for himself.

As his papà entered the kitchen he asked, "Papà, porridge?"

"Thanks, figlio," he said as he poured himself some coffee. He kissed his wife good morning and asked, "Susanna, did you sleep well?"

"Yes, very. It was such a great day yesterday, how could I not?"

"Well, that was only the beginning. There will be many other good times," answered Nadia. "What do you two have planned for today?"

"We are going to check out an apartment near my work. It is in the same building as a friend from work. Even though it is an older building, it seems to withstand the earth tremors well. It is a few minutes by train to the plant and it is only a few blocks from the market. Hopefully it will work out."

That apartment did work out. It was a five-flat building with a court-yard that held potted plants and benches. There was an indoor space to wash and pully lines to hang laundry. The apartment itself opened into a large living area with an adjacent kitchen. Their balcony was over the street and off of the living area.

"Angelo told me that he loved to sit and watch the street activity from the balcony, but he preferred the quiet of the courtyard and looked forward with a passion to their frequent family trips out to his nonni's farm. But, back to Carlos and Susanna," Nonna Tizianna continued.

It was just under three months since they met when they married on the patio of Vincenzo's house. Carlos's relatives that had jammed into the small workers' apartment in Turino arrived. They brought with them delicious sauces, wine, ravioli, fried fish, rice, olives, breads, and polenta. How they stuffed the food and themselves in the few available vehicles was a sight to behold. Susanna's parents prepared a large stew of beans, garden vegetables, and lamb meat. Vincenzo's family provided a beautiful cake, wine, more pasta, breads, roasted lamb, and, of course, plenty of hazelnut spread. It was a great celebration.

"And that is the story how your Nonno Angelo's parents fell in love."

"It is a beautiful story, Nonna. Thanks. I wonder, did Susanna miss the country?" I asked.

"She never hinted at that. She always loved her books and that continued in the city. Eventually she began to write. At first her stories were not accepted, and then after about nine years of attempts, a literary magazine printed one of her stories. After that she had more work accepted than not."

"Ahh, Nonna, so are you saying that my love to write has a family history?"

MY LABOR BEGINS

"It seems so…Francesca…what's going on?"

"Nonna! That was a big cramp! Is that how it feels?"

"Could be," said Nonna. "Let me put my hand on your belly the next time."

"Okay."

We cleared our cups into the kitchen. We gathered some vegetables from the garden for a pot of vegetable soup and began to clean the vegetables.

"Okay, Nonna, here's another one!"

"Yup, Francesca, your belly gets tight! We should time them. Then we'll know if they're false labor or the real thing."

"Okay."

The rest of the afternoon my belly was quiet. Mamma dropped by to check on us. It was good to see my mamma. I told her about my false labor. Right now I wished Mamma and Papà could stay with us on the farm. That was pregnant Francesca thoughts because in reality they were only two kilometers away. When Mamma readied to leave, I held her long and hard. Nonna and I sent some of the vegetable soup home with her.

The next day, Luciano left for work at his usual time. I had settled into my morning when the alert went off on our phones. As long as I live I will never forget the time. It was 10:15 a.m. and Vesuvius had erupted. This was eleven days prior to the predictions. But, who are we to predict such a thing? Immediately I wanted Luciano home. I also wanted to be sure my papà and mamma were safe in their house and I wanted to be sure that Nonna Mikaela and Nonno Robert were safe in their apartment. I called Luciano. He was released from manning the government communications due to my pregnancy at term. He would be home soon. Nonna Tizianna called Nonna Mikaela who reassured us that they were in their apartment and fine. I called my mamma. She and Papà were in the house and fine. Laura called and said she would stay with Mariano at the hospital to help.

I needed to move around. I went out to help Nonno Angelo put tarp over the machinery in the shed and over the chicken coop. Then we covered the frame Nonno Angelo had built over the vegetable garden to protect the vegetables from any possible ash fall.

It seemed like hours, but in reality it was only one hour until Luciano was home. He quickly put the scooter in the shed and covered it.

He no sooner had one foot in the house when he greeted me with, "How are you?" as he took me in his arms.

"Where is Angelo?" he asked as he looked around. Nonna Tizianna was at the stove with her spoon in the beans.

"He just went out to check the solar batteries one last time and to secure their cover," Nonna Tizianna responded.

Just then Nonno Angelo came towards the patio, turned and gazed towards his beloved vineyard and fig trees, and then walked to the door. We had discussed at length if it would be feasible to cover the grapevines and fig trees. But, it was far too cumbersome and expensive a project. We could only hope that the winds that often move through Piedmont would blow any possible ash quickly off the trees and vines.

When he entered, Luciano said that the wind currents created by the explosion were easterly as predicted, but also northward. It seemed that the possibility of the mountain current interception was now a reality and a huge ash cloud would reach us in Turino in a couple of hours. We then heard our phones go off with the same alert.

My cramps had returned around the time that I helped with the tarps. But I was sure that it was just more false labor due to the excitement of the eruption news.

As we sat with our rice and beans, I had another cramp. Nonna saw the beads of sweat on my forehead and the small amount of food that I had eaten.

"How often are they, Francesca?" asked Nonna Tizianna.

"Not sure," I responded.

"How often is what?" asked Luciano.

"My cramps," I responded.

"Is that what labor is called now?" asked Luciano a little concerned at my state of denial.

"No, Luciano, it's that I'm not sure if this is the real thing. I have to time the distance between…"

"The cramps," Luciano helped to complete my sentence.

"Right!" I said.

"Okay, then let's time them. Let me know when they happen and I'll time the distance between the…"

"Cramps," I completed his sentence.

"Right!" Luciano responded.

Nonna and Nonno did their best to muffle their chuckles as they cleared the table and did the dishes.

"Do you want to lie down?" asked Luciano.

"No, I want to sit and then walk around a little when I feel like it."

"Okay, mi amore."

The sky had begun to prematurely darken.

Luciano jumped up and said, "I need to put some quilts over the windows in our bedroom. If the baby is born before the ash goes away I want to be sure that none gets through that window area. Nonna Tizianna will you time for me for a little while?"

"Of course. Go on, Luciano," said Nonna Tizianna.

"I'll help you with the quilts," said Nonno Angelo.

I just shook my head and smiled at Nonna Tizianna.

"Don't worry, amore. He'll settle down. Your pains have been pretty regular, right?"

"Yes, Nonna. About twenty minutes apart for the past couple of hours. But they aren't that bad."

"Good. Would you like some hot mint tea?"

"Yes, a little. But, Nonna, I would like the distraction of one of your stories."

"How about my Nonna Nora? She was a feisty little one since birth with bright red hair. Our remembrance of her will help us get through our time of darkness. She went through one of her own."

"I'm ready to hear about it, Nonna. Don't mind a frown or groan. Keep going. I'll tell you if you need to stop."

"Okay, then," Nonna reassured.

SONG IS THE VOICE FROM THE SOUL

The neighboring gentile farm of Riciotti and Stefano nestled along the fig grove of Rosa and Liaco's. Riciotti and Stefano remained steadfast friends with Rosa and Liaco during the pre-war, war, and post-WWII years. Riciotti and Stefano had a daughter named Nora. She was a playful redhead with green eyes. During the war most people's souls got pretty bruised up. Nora had a special gift that helped lessen the bruises and hurried their healing. When Nora was eight, during the German occupation, she found her grandfather's accordion wrapped carefully in a case in her parents' clothing cabinet. What a find for this little one that understood the connection between the songs in her head and the movement of her fingers on its keys and buttons. She began to play the songs from her head and any other that her mother would hum.

During the almost three years of German occupation she was, as most children were, kept close to the house. While most children felt confined, Nora felt huge spaces of freedom open before her as she pushed and pulled the sweet sounds out of her accordion while she ran her deft fingers over the accordion's buttons and keys. She had to play with a blanket over the accordion to muffle the sound and could play her beloved instrument only when there were no soldiers on the road. After the war she played whenever she wanted and without the blanket. She played at family birthday celebrations and in her early teens at country weddings around Turino.

Nora's family raised mostly peaches and figs. They sold them at the local markets, and after the war, up into Switzerland as well. After the war, Nora loved to go to market early Saturday morning with her mamma and their neighbor Rosa. Her father would take all of them and the produce in the bed of the farm truck. Nora loved this early morning truck ride. She inhaled deeply the early morning moist air of the river fog and then looked up at the distant mountains' emergence through the fog, as if in a magical dream.

At the market she worked to arrange the peaches, figs, tomatoes, and grapes in neat piles. After she finished her assistance with the setup, Nora wandered past the colorful produce and pungent cheeses set up on nearby tables. She made her ritualistic stroll brief as she knew that the market would soon be busy and her mamma, especially, but Rosa also would need her help.

I say especially her mamma, as the war left a scar on the soul of her mamma. Often soldiers on the road near the farm would demand peaches. Rosa would carry a basket of peaches to them at the road. One day near the end of the occupation, two soldiers threw her in the grass at the side of the road to rape her. They had torn off her blouse when another regimen passed and yelled at the soldiers to join them as they were ordered over to Milan. My nonna said that it was from that day onward her mamma acted like someone had punched the air out of her. Little by little she began to feel better. She was lucky compared to many women during that time. She was also lucky to have a daughter like Nora whose presence gave her strength to heal.

The Saturday market venders welcomed the presence of Nora. They called to this cheerful redhead as she passed by their stands and gifted her with pears or a slab of cheese to carry back to her mamma. The vendors also knew Nora from local summer weddings that she graced with her accordion music.

Liaco's and Stefano's family assisted each other with their harvests. Their produce was harvested at different times so this cooperation worked well. They also helped each other gradually restock their post-war goat herds as they had been confiscated by the German soldiers. During these cooperative work engagements, Carlo, Stefano's son, and Nora would work hard as well. Carlo would not hesitate to tease Nora and call her music notes or some other silly name that infatuated boys invent. Nora would laugh and smile and turn her green eyes right at Carlo, which made him nervous and brightened his heart at the same time.

By the time they were sixteen those looks didn't make him nervous, but his heart still brightened at her every glance. Nora always liked Carlo. She liked his straightforward nature couched in a lot of respect for himself and others.

Nora began to look forward to her work alongside Carlo in the fields with a sense of feminine excitement. His rhythm was steady and organized. She appreciated his respect for her fast picking fingers. She also noticed the moves of his shoulder and back muscles with the work. Their raw strength planted a robust song in her young but fully woman musical heart. Their love grew generously as if nourished by the same eternal energy that grew the crops with which they worked.

Nora and Carlo married when they were eighteen, in 1959. It took place on Nora's farm. The tables in the courtyard were graced with chicken stew, pasta, polenta, figs, grapes, cheeses, firm crusted breads, greens, olive oil, wine, and a beautiful lemon cake. Nora played the accordion for herself, her husband, and all of the family and guests. She played just a couple of songs because she and Carlo wanted to dance in each other's arms. Her cousin took over the accordion and the party continued.

Nora was excited to see the room that Carlo had built onto the farmhouse for them. Carlo wanted it to be a surprise for her, so he restricted her from entering until their wedding night. Of course, as soon as the moon rose, Carlo and Nora decided to check out the room. They left their families and friends to continue to celebrate. With music and laughter behind them, Nora and Carlo headed for their new home. Rosa and Riciotti smiled at each other as they watched Nora and Carlo scamper over the fields to Liaco's house. Needless to say, Nora and Carlo did not return to the festivities that night.

"What a delightful couple, Nonna Nora and Nonno Carlo!" I said.

MORE LABOR AND MORE LABOR

I stood up and looked out at the now complete darkness.

"I think I want to lie down for a while. I'll see if they are finished in the bedroom. After my rest can you tell me about the birth of your Mamma Cecilia?"

"Of course, dear."

Nonna then went to sit down in her favorite chair and, I imagine, fall asleep for a little nap as the men came bounding down the stairs.

"I'm heading up to bed to rest for a little while," I announced to Luciano and Nonno Angelo. "Thanks for the window cover."

"I'll come up with you," offered Luciano.

"I hope you both can catch some rest," said Nonno Angelo.

As I rested, the cramps came pretty regularly, but I was able to doze between and even through some of them.

But then, after a couple of hours, they came with greater strength and at shorter intervals. Now I felt uncomfortable during what I had mislabeled earlier as cramps. Oh, my God, this was really happening. It wasn't going away. I have to hang in until I have a son or daughter. I don't know how long it will take and I don't know how it will feel at each phase of the process. Also I don't know when this ash will stop burying the earth around me. Okay, okay, okay. Too many unknowns. Too much thinking.

Luciano had dozed off. Of course. I nudged him. He sat up quickly when he saw my sweat soaked face. I said, "I need you to help me focus on one pain at a time. I need to ride it like a wave and then rest between." I continued, "Get me out of these clothes. I need my cool nightgown on."

"Which one is your cool nightgown?"

"That one there, over the chair."

"Yes, mi amore, of course," said Luciano as he grabbed the nightgown off the chair.

Luciano got me out of my clothes and into my nightgown. He then said, "Let me get a cool cloth for your forehead and then call the midwife."

Nonna Tizianna heard us milling around and came up the stairs. She saw Luciano on the phone and my flushed face and went directly downstairs to bring up a basin of cool water and a washcloth.

Luciano said, "I can't get through to the clinic. The ash is too thick."

"Mi amore," I said, "we have an emergency childbirth kit the clinic gave to all women with due dates near the time of the expected eruption. My nonna delivered me. We'll be fine."

"Of course, we will!" said Luciano.

"Luciano, walk Francesca around here upstairs. It will help to make her time shorter. I'm going to boil water for a source of almost sterile water, get some herbs ready for her poultice afterwards, make some coffee, and bring some rice water for Francesca."

So Luciano and I walked around the bedrooms and the narrow hallway for what seemed like hours, but was only a couple of hours. I stopped every ten minutes and leaned on him during the contractions. He breathed with me during each contraction, which helped in a strange way. Then we took another step onward. I was centered. There was no choice to be otherwise. I saw in my mind each contraction opening my uterus so the baby could easily get out. I saw the baby exit with a strong cry and a healthy body. Another contraction and then another step forward. And then, oh, my Dio! There was water everywhere! That was followed by a very strong contraction.

Nonna actually heard the splash of the water downstairs. She calmly came upstairs with my rice water and Luciano's coffee. She placed it on the bedside. She then put down the rubber pads and clean white sheets on the bed. I was really tired now. Luciano helped me into bed and propped my upper body up onto pillows.

Nonno Angelo mopped the floor.

The little sips of the rice water actually helped my energy. Luciano and I continued to breathe together when I signaled him, which was now every seven minutes. He kept a cool cloth available for my forehead. I had joked during my pregnancy that I was going to keep him busy during my labor, and I really did!

BIRTH OF LUCIANA

The pains had become serious and were now every five minutes or so. That went on for a lifetime. I exaggerate. That's how long it felt. It really was just two and a half hours. There were some moments that I wanted to scream and escape, but I didn't. I continued my breath work. It was almost a relief when I felt this primordial urge to push as if my life depended on it. Luciano called Nonna Tizianna to come and see how far down the baby's head was.

Yes, the baby's head was close. She worked the opening gently to give it a little more stretch so I wouldn't tear. She instructed me to continue to push with the contractions. After a few more contractions the baby's head was at the opening. Nonna instructed me to stop pushing. So I, along with Luciano, panted during my contractions.

Then, I couldn't believe what happened next. This beautiful head emerged with an immediate loud cry as her—yes, a her—beautiful body slipped right out of me! Luciano and I had the biggest water-filled eyes and the biggest grins at the sight of her! Nonna Tizianna clamped her cord after it had drained, placed her on my chest and covered her with a clean white blanket. The placentae then slipped out with my next contraction. Yahoo! I was done!

Wow. There she was. Beautiful. And there I was. I had done childbirth with the incredible help from, of course, my baby girl, my Luciano, Nonna Tizianna, and Nonno Angelo who appeared at the door when he heard her strong cries. Nonna Tizianna cleaned me up below while I nursed my daughter up above. Then Nonna disappeared and brought back a warm cloth soaked in her herbal poultice. She placed it over my perineum. It truly felt like a comfort balm from the angels.

Luciano tried to reach my mamma and papà but the cell towers were too disabled by the huge amount of ash in our air.

Nevertheless, it felt good to have had so many of my loved ones around me during our daughter's birth. I fail at words to describe the depth of satisfaction it gave me. Despite the intense discomfort from the contractions of this huge muscle they call a womb, I could still sense the love of Luciano, Nonna Tizianna, Nonno Angelo, and even though not here, the love from my mamma, papà, Nonna Mikaela, and Nonno Robert. In addition, I could sense the presence of Guadalupe, Mother Mary, Pele, Grandmother Moon, and all of the other goddesses of women in childbirth. They were all here as well as the good wishes of all the female ancestors.

Dear reader, this is not post-delivery euphoria talking, I really felt their beautiful presence!

However, I missed my mamma's presence. I had planned for her to be there. But I heard her words in my head during the labor. I remembered her words of gratitude for the skill and presence of Nonna Tizianna at my birth, her words of assurance that all would be well, her words of confidence in me to be calm and focused through the process. I guess I did pretty well with the calm part. I felt a little unnerved when the close contractions seemed to go on so long. But, no matter, even with the life threatening ash accumulation outside, today was the blessing of my lifetime.

And, dear reader, I hope I can do my beautiful daughter justice when

I describe her. Because she is the most incredible baby girl ever! If only you could see her round brown eyes with dark eyelashes, her curly brown hair, and her beautifully shaped mouth. If only you could see her lovely earlobes that give a hint of her future skin color with their rich golden olive tone, and if only you could sense her grounded energy with a softness around its edges, I am sure you would agree with me that she is a worthy embodiment of the feminine life force!

Besides my fatigue, what I found a little disconcerting after my daughter's birth was the continued contractions that occurred, especially during breastfeeding. Intellectually I knew that they were important to contract the womb back down to its pre-baby size. But it still seemed unfair. Oh well, they weren't really contractions. They were more like cramps. And I do have my beautiful daughter to gaze at now.

There must be an unlimited supply of love in our universe because I feel so much love for her and no less love for Luciano, my nonni, my papà and mamma. Go figure!

Nonno Angelo asked, "What is her name?"

Luciano and I looked at each other. Then I clearly blurted out, "Luciana, Luciana Sole!"

Nonno smiled. Luciano's eyes teared up as he said, "It fits her! She is the sunlight in all this darkness!"

Then Luciano kissed me and our Luciana.

Nonna Tizianna came bustling in with a change of my poultice. She was pleased that my womb was firm and my bleeding negligible. She also brought me some more of the vegetable broth from our big pot of soup. I handed Luciana to Luciano, drank the broth, and fell into a deep sleep where I dreamed of sunny skies with peaceful clouds.

Luciana, who had slept in her papà's arms, awakened me at about two in the morning. Luciano changed her diaper while I tested my land legs. I was able to stand and not feel dizzy so I made my way to the washroom while Luciano comforted Luciana. I got back into bed and breastfed Luciana. She was a vigorous and efficient eater. I was grateful because I wanted to sleep again. I felt like I could have slept forever. Luciano was his usual patient self and eased Luciana back to sleep. He attempted to lay her in her small bassinet. It worked! She slept for the next three and a half hours! Both Luciano and I slept for the entire three and a half hours as well!

By then it was almost six in the morning and my nonni were up in the kitchen with their morning beverages. Nonna came to check on us. She had brought me some more broth and some water. I then fed Luciana, put her back in the bassinet, and fell asleep again.

After the next three hours of sleep, I think I was as hungry as Luciana. After she ate and was back in her bassinet, I left sleeping Luciano and Luciana in the bedroom and slowly made my way down the stairs to the kitchen.

"I'll go up and sit with little Luciana so you don't have to hurry back upstairs," offered Nonno Angelo.

"Thanks, Nonno. Luciano is sleeping so deeply, I am not sure he would hear her if she wakes up and I'd like to sit with Nonna a minute."

I dished up a bowl of cornmeal porridge with cream, poured a cup of mint tea, and sat down.

"Thank you, Nonna," I said as I reached across the table and grasped her hand. Your guidance got me through it all. I love you bigger than the big mountains that we cannot see at the moment."

I released her hand, sipped my wonderful tea, and began to eat the best tasting cornmeal porridge of my lifetime.

"Francesca, you were incredible. Continue to rest when she rests."

"I will. I'm going back up now. I will turn on the small lamp in the room during the day to give some sense of normal light. It is so depressing to see the darkness out there," I said as I glanced out the window at intense blackness where there used to be brightness and brilliant colors.

"It will pass, Francesca," said Nonna as she rose to put on a pot of beans.

"I hope, Nonna," I responded as I made it up the stairs.

When I got to the bedroom, the three of them were asleep. Luciana in her bassinet, Nonno Angelo in the chair at its side, and Luciano in the bed. I shook my head and decided to enjoy a shower before I nestled into the bed next to Luciano. Fortunately, I got a couple of hours of sleep before Luciana awakened all of us.

Luciana was ready to nurse. My milk wasn't in yet so I didn't expect her to go much longer than about three hours between feedings. The men left us to enjoy each other and went downstairs to drink some coffee and eat. What a beautiful child I held in my arms! If gratitude is heaven, I was in heaven.

Nonno Angelo and Luciano shooed Nonna Tizianna out of the kitchen as they took over the chef duties for the lunch and dinner meals. They told her to go put her feet up.

She had thawed and heated up a broth from greens for me. Her experience had taught her that this broth helps women to regain their strength after childbirth so she had some frozen for me. She came up to the bedroom with the broth.

"Nonna, this is great! I can feel my body slurp it up! Thanks," I said.

"You are welcome, mi amore."

I had placed Luciana in Nonna's arms to burp her so I could manage the hot liquid safely.

Luciana enjoyed Nonna's arms. She burped and needed a diaper change. Nonna cleaned up Luciana and settled her back into her arms as she sat and gazed at her great-granddaughter. Soon Luciana was asleep. Nonna placed her in her bassinet and went to her bedroom to rest a while.

The day passed quickly, marked by the awakenings of Luciana. We didn't want to take Luciana out of the bedroom yet since it was the most airtight room of the house due to the quilts at the windows. We didn't want any of those micro-sized ash particles falling in the air outside to find their way into her lungs. So someone was with Luciana in the bedroom if I went to the kitchen or the bathroom.

The air was still intensely black outside the kitchen windows. Late in the afternoon Luciano received a text on his government cell that there had been two eruptions of Vesuvius, about twelve hours apart. The report to him said that the cold mountain air drove the hot ash current to our town. It would continue to fall here over the next few hours.

I felt better knowing what had happened. But what would happen was unknown. Yet, I felt a profound sense of faith that just as my labor had ended with the presence of Luciana, this darkness would end with the presence of light. So I chose live moment to moment.

We decided to eat our supper in the bedroom, so we all took our plates of savory bean stew over rice there. Luciana slept through our meal. These were sounds of our family that she seemed to recognize. Luciano and Nonna Angelo took our plates to the kitchen to soak and brought Nonna her accordion. What a great idea! We listened to her sweet music, sang, and even laughed in this darkness. Luciana stirred, but slept on!

By early evening, Luciano was able to get through to my mamma and papà. It was so sweet to hear their voices! The reception wasn't great but they understood that it went well and that they have a healthy grand-daughter. We understood that as soon as travel is permitted they'd be here.

"Love you," I said as we disconnected. I don't know why, but as I hung up I burst into tears. It was a huge emotional release to be able to connect with my mamma now that I was a mamma. It felt good for me to be able to tell her that I was all right having gone through the same process that she went through to bring me here.

The phone call also had physical results for me as my milk came in. Wow! It felt like my chest was filled to full! Now I needed Luciana as much as she needed me!

With the nutrition of the milk on board, Luciana was able to sleep through the night in four to five hour intervals. Luciano did diaper changes during the night so I could go back to sleep after her feedings. Since I began to sleep by nine o'clock, with Luciano's help I was able to accumulate ten hours of sleep by nine in the morning. With the combination of my ability to sleep and Nonna's nutritious broths, I felt noticeably stronger by Luciana's second day of life.

On this day I could see from the kitchen windows a slight decrease in the darkness as it had gone from total black to a dark gray. This was some sort of progress I convinced myself.

When Luciana awakened around nine o'clock, I engaged her in a little sponge bath followed by an olive oil wipe down. She loved the stimulation and calmed with it. But then she remembered her hunger, so we settled in to a breastfeed.

I could hear the men downstairs in a boisterous game of mancala.

Nonna Tizianna came into the room to visit. "Nonna, I remember a little about Great-Nonna Cecilia and Great-Nonno Ario, but would you tell me more about your mamma and how she met Great-Nonno Ario?"

"Oh, yes, Francesca. I miss her so much and wish she could have met Luciana. I would love to pull her here with us through my memory," Nonna Tizianna enthusiastically answered.

CECILIA AND ARIO

Let me give you a little background, Francesca, on Ario, my papà. I am sure that you are familiar with the many family stories about his papà,

Aatif and Sophia.

I nodded my head in agreement.

Well, Aatif and Sophia were concerned because Ario was such a serious child. They thought that maybe it was because he was a child of love born in the war. Or they thought that maybe it was because of the social and political struggles in our Italy after the war. There were often noisy strikes and even bombings in the general area of Aatif's business and home. So they moved to the farm and always maintained a peaceful home. Nevertheless, my Papà Ario maintained a serious demeanor.

He was serious to learn his papà's trade and soon became his papà's first assistant on bike repairs. Ario was serious to also meet his academic obligations and did well in school. Ario had a great ability to focus on any task and thus he efficiently accomplished them.

Ario prayed with both his papà and mamma. He found no contradiction that the prayers were nurtured from different religious traditions. Neither did his parents.

He also loved horses and was in charge of the care of the two horses on the farm. His soul soared with freedom when he took the stallion bareback for a good run in the field. His father had taught him the ancient way of gently moving the bridle while he hugged the horse with his thighs and whispered firm but kind words in the horse's ear.

Ario received his mechanic certificate and continued to work in Aatif's shop. His work interested him and he was now thirty-one without any plans for marriage. He had had some infatuations, but no real love. Many of the young women in the area would find silly excuses to bring their motorbike to the shop to try and entice his attentions. He loved the attention. But he refused to let himself be drawn into marriage just to satisfy his body's cravings. He wanted someone with whom he could create the type of trust and love that his parents shared. He would not settle for anything less.

One Saturday, late into the fall, he was invited to the country wedding of his good friend Bernardo from the mechanic certificate program. They were great buddies, so Ario went to celebrate Bernardo's good fortune and enjoy the food, music, dance, and attention from the young ladies. The wedding celebration gave people a reprieve from the tense issues in the factories in Turino. Ario's friend's farm patio was filled with family, friends, roasted goat, sauces, breads, and pastas. Although a serious young man, Ario loved social gatherings and quickly made himself at home at the wedding celebration.

My future Papà Ario had known my future Mama Cecilia as the young daughter of his papà's good friend, Carlo, whom he called Zio. He viewed Cecilia the way an older cugino views a much younger cugina. She was ten years his junior. He had held her in that place mentally until this particular social gathering. For at this event his perspective did a 360-degree change!

Cecilia played the accordion. But tonight Ario heard her artistry with the emotion and depth of a grown woman. Cecilia was a teacher now. She had graduated from university. She possessed the multiple skill sets needed to foster the academic growth for many differently endowed children. She kept them encouraged and stimulated the entire school day. She also knew how to guide the children to safety under the tables when episodes of angry demonstrations erupted in the streets. Cecilia was, in every sense, a grown woman at twenty-two. She played her accordion with joy and wisdom in a manner that only a woman rich with life's experience can play. To say that Ario was fascinated would have been an understatement. Ario was awestruck. She had a warm smile, soft brown eyes, a gently arched nose, and brown curly hair that possessed a hint of red coloring. Her shape was curvaceous. Cecilia cast a light of graciousness around her that was even greater, if this could be possible, than the intensity of her beauty.

Ario now seriously worked his brain for a casual but definite way to approach her. After a few songs, Cecilia rested her accordion. When she turned around, Ario was there with a cool fruit and wine punch. Cecilia was grateful for the drink and for his company. She had always enjoyed the presence of the handsome and serious Ario. To her, his peacefulness was a welcome cushion for her exuberance. But she had also felt his discount due to her age. She did not feel that now. After Cecilia finished her next set, Ario asked if he could escort her home. She thanked Franco, the groom's father, for her payment and let him know that Ario would escort her home. Cecilia rode behind Ario on his motorbike with her accordion safely strapped to the cycle's back rack. Cecilia knew well the route home from this farm. Yet tonight, to her, the Piedmont hills were different. They took on a deep, brilliant warmth in the moonlight, as the motorbike took them up and down their topography.

Ario showed up the next day in the early evening to inquire if Cecilia would want to go for a ride. This time he had his horse. And this time she was in front. It was a ride they would enjoy many times together. In whatever activity, Ario and Cecilia felt strong and free when together. Their love happened fast, as it was a matter of recognition of a seed planted long ago that now burst into a great beauty.

Ario and Cecilia were married one month later in the year 1979 at the magistrate, which was the custom for adults not baptized in the church. They then celebrated the wedding at Cecilia's family farm. However, they decided to live on the farm with Aatif and Sophia. It was close to Cecilia's family and close to the school where she worked in the village.

Ario and Cecilia often rode the horse over to Cecilia's parents' on Sunday for dinner. Though often they would first ride to the favorite family spot by the river, a place often frequented by their families. There they dismounted and let the river's movement, with the powerful mountains in the background, strengthen and soothe their souls. Ario would glance at Cecilia and draw her close. How could he not have noticed this dynamic woman earlier? No matter. They were together now. Then, when ready, they would ride to Carlo and Nora's, where Aatif and Sophia had arrived earlier, laden with sauces, rice, and roasted vegetables.

Neither Ario nor Cecilia participated in a formal religious organization. They continued to follow sacred prayer customs of their families and grew in their spiritual relationship with the Creator.

Ario rose at daybreak, as was the custom of his father, to check on the fields and feed the animals before breakfast. After breakfast with Sophia and Cecilia, he and Aatif then left for the mechanic shop. Cecilia preferred to take the scooter to school. But if the weather was inclement, Cecilia tucked herself between the two men in the truck hub.

Within four months it was no surprise to anyone that Cecilia was pregnant.

"The rest is history, Francesca, because here I am," declared Nonna Tizianna. "Great-Nonna Cecilia's style of food preparation is still, for the most part, mine today. She was particularly good at spicy flavorful stews. She used onion, garlic, tomatoes, peppers, chickpeas, corn, carrots, and zucchini in her stews. They were flavored with a little goat meat and ladled over hot white rice. Cecilia knew how to combine the peppers, coriander, turmeric, cayenne, and cumin, with the herbs, oregano, mint, thyme, basil in a dish that made her sauces spectacular. Ario and his parents applauded her sauces. There was always some of Sophia's polenta or coarse heavily crusted bread and olive oil on the side. Our kitchen was a wonderful space!"

Nonna concluded, "We all flourished in the presence of my mamma. But I must also give my papà honor because, in addition to loving my mamma, he always respected her. She flourished in his presence."

IN THE FAMILY GROOVE WITH ASH ON GROUND BUT LIGHT IN SKY

Just then Luciano came to the door.

"Hmmm, Nonna, speaking of respectful men! Ciao, amore."

"Ciao, amore! Figs anyone?" Luciano asked as he placed the small bowl of figs down on the bedside table. He knew it was a rhetorical question.

Once again the day was paced for me with Luciana's awakenings. During the day, I encouraged her attention for a few moments before she ate to stretch out her social repertoire. But at nightfall, we just breastfed, changed her diapers, and settled her down. I hoped she would lengthen her sleep time at night this way and shorten it in the day. I think it helped a little. Who knows?

Towards evening it looked to us like the ash fall had decreased. It was difficult to know because of the natural darkness at that time, but it was what we truly wanted to believe.

Sure enough! By morning there was sun! Oh, Dio! I was ecstatic! The wonderful sun. It didn't matter that the ground was black with four inches of ash. We had the sun! All life was possible now!

Luciano's work cell phone rang and he was asked to report to a station about a kilometer away in about four hours to assist with the province's cleanup. He would have to walk, as the ash was too slippery to drive on.

I was grateful for two nights of assisted sleep from Luciano because now he would have big demands on his time from his job.

So, that morning, Luciano, with his mask, overalls, and long-sleeve shirt in place, shoveled a path to the nearby field and dug two deep holes. He placed our household waste in one hole as well as four wheelbarrows-full of dampened ash from the courtyard and back patio. He placed twelve more wheelbarrows-full of dampened ash in the second hole. After three hours of work at home, he made his way to work.

At home I called the clinic to report a good delivery. They said they'd send a midwife out to check on us when the roads were safe, but because all had gone well with Luciana's birth, we were not priority, so it would be a few days. That was fine with me.

Then I had a great talk with my mamma without mechanical static! I was able to give her the details of the labor and delivery. So great to share it with her! I was also able to reach Nonna Mikaela and Nonna Robert. The ash had bypassed them, so they were fine. As soon as possible they'd be on the train into Turino to meet their great-granddaughter!

Later that day, when I was sure that the ash had settled, I brought Luciana downstairs to be presented to the light for the first time. I'm sure she was impressed on some level, but she seemed to be more captivated with our animated faces. I am sure she saw in them our joy to be around the light.

Luciano worked long hours for the next couple of days to coordinate food for the provinces hit with the ash and to coordinate the ash management in order to save the crops. During his travel he was in contact with ash so he wore cap and mask as well as baggy pants and shirt that he literally stepped out of at the kitchen door and dropped into a bucket to soak.

Nonna Tizianna and I busied ourselves inside with the care of Luciana, food preparation, and the wash. We convinced Nonno Angelo to wait until Luciano shoveled the pathway to the chicken shed before he checked on them. He agreed reluctantly. On the second day of light Luciano got a path to the chicken shed cleared before work. Nonno was ecstatic to find most of the hens okay. A couple of the chicks were dead, probably because the little amount of micro ash that had entered their space was too much of a challenge for them. Nonno created another task for himself in the house. He cleverly mounted clotheslines in two of the spare bedrooms and became expert at the removal of the clean clothes from the washing machine and their placement on the clotheslines. But still, of course, he felt confined. In fact, all three of us felt confined. We loved to roam our fields. But that would have to wait. Luciano was the only one to be able to break the cabin fever.

Fortunately, in a couple of more days our spring rains arrived. This matted down the ash and made it easier to plow under and remove from streets and walkways. Most of it had blown off of roofs and trees, which we were grateful for. But, we needed the rain to wash it off the grape-vines. It didn't matter that the rain had once again darkened the sky. We loved it because it would bring our liberation from the house and it would bring a greater chance of life for our crops.

So on the fourth day of light we had rain. During one of Luciana's four-hour sleeps, I also slept well to the music of the rain on the tile roof. Early that evening when Luciano returned home, he smiled broadly and said, "Tomorrow the roads will be safe for travel by mid-day in the province!"

I hugged Luciano and immediately called my mamma and papà. That was the news they had waited for!

Luciana was now sleeping in five to six hour segments at night. She ate more frequently during the day, but that was fine with me. At about one o'clock that night Luciana awakened to eat. I put her on my breast and rested back against the pillow while she ate. The rain had stopped. Good. It was enough of a soak. Luciana burped and went back to sleep in her bassinet. I lay back down. Luciano turned and enveloped me in his arms. Our closeness brought back memories of the scooter rides when I held onto his chest. I nestled into his arms and went fast asleep.

By noon the next day my excited mamma and papà arrived to meet Luciana for the first time. Mamma brought one of her great sauces with white beans. She also had made a fresh focaccia. So we sat down to a wonderful meal and chatted about the welfare of our close friends and family. The cell phone usage had been spotty, especially southward. But, we were able to fit our separate bits and pieces together to form a col-lective picture. We chatted amicably, but urgently, like birds in the early morning after a dark night of heavy storms. Cugini Margarita and Josefa in Orvieto were not hit by the ash. Neither were Flavio and Susanna, the Allegrettis, and Cugini Duccinio and Tommy in Genoa. Cugina Laura and her fiancé, Mariano, were exhausted, but fine and still at the hos-pital in Turino, as there was a lot of work with those in respiratory dis-tress. Our close friends Patricia, Daniele, and Catrina in Turino were fine. Maximillian was the most difficult to reach, but I was able to relate to them that Luciano reached him at work on the government cell phone yesterday. Their conversation was something like this:

"Yes, Luciano, about one-fourth of the farm was covered with the lava mud, but no more than that. The men and I were safe in Flavio's house. My dear Julianna and her family in Naples are fine. When the eruption occurred, I felt as significant as an ant. And then with the second explosion, I almost couldn't compute it mentally or emotionally. I think and feel differently about life and the earth now. But I can't yet put into words how I am changed from all of this."

Then Maximillian continued, "You folks got more ash than we did here, actually. It was heat and gas here. The explosion and the wind pushed eastward. We only got about half an inch of ash here, which I know is nothing compared to how you got hit in Turino."

"Dear brother, I am glad you are alive and well and the men as well. Have you been able to reach Mamma and Papà in Orvieto?"

"Yes. They tried not to, but they did worry about me, so it felt good to all of us to hear each other's voices. I will go and see them when it calms down here a little. And Laura? I haven't been able to reach her," questioned Maximillian.

"She is tired, but good. She decided to stay and help at the hospital. So she is fine and with Mariano."

"Okay. Good. Tell her I'm okay."

"Absolutely, dear brother. Hey, by the way, you're a zio!"

"A what? What did you say? You mean Francesca…"

"Yup, that's exactly what I mean! We have a beautiful little girl named Luciana Sole!"

"Oh, wow! Great name! Congratulations! Everyone is all right?"

"Yes, everyone. Well, I'll call you again soon and come down to check on you as soon as we can travel out of our province."

"Okay, Luciano, that is if I don't get up there to see my wonderful new nipota, first!" Maximillian answered.

Luciana nestled in my mamma's arms while Nonno Angelo showed my papà his clothesline arrangement in the bedrooms. Papà loved it! I could hear the father and son joke with each other as they clambered down the stairs.

"Okay, okay, new nonna, my turn with our nipota!"

Papà sat down to receive Luciana in his arms. Nonno got himself a cup of coffee and sat down by his son. We women let the men have their moment with Luciana while we readied the pasta for the sauce and made our first green salad in quite some days. Nonno had gotten under the garden cover and harvested some fresh spring greens for us.

Luciana had awakened and enjoyed the men's company for a little while, but soon they were no compromise for her hunger. My family ate away while Luciana ate as well. Mamma and Papà wanted to hear the story of Luciana's birth in the darkness.

As you know, dear reader, I had told my mamma a lot of the details, but that was the daughter to mother rendition. Now it could be told in its entirety by my nonni and me. It was a drawn out process because, as you know, dear reader, my family loves the merger of food and story.

Therefore, the story with its three versions was interrupted with frequents comments of, "These greens are so sweet!" or "The flavor of this sauce is sensational!" or "To have focaccia again!"

It was also interrupted with frequent toasts to Luciana and all of us, including to Luciano, who was at work. I stuck with lemon water, with just a little sip of wine because of Luciana.

What better way to tell a story than to have it punctuated by food and wine! This story was now an official part of our family stories. It was now bigger than all of us.

This story became another pattern in our consciousness. It provided another plank in the scaffold on which we could frame our personal and collective perspectives. It was now available for comfort or courage. This was one of the first stories told in the presence of Luciana. She would hear many sound waves from many stories that she could weave into her dream space and give her a foundation from which to fly. For now, she had heard her first!

Dear reader, I don't know the big picture of what will happen next in my or my family's life. Vesuvius may erupt again, perhaps sooner than later. Who knows? Right now we have a lot of ash to till, cover, bury, or whatever in order to save our crops and secure a safe air environment. And we have each other and our larger community to care for right now.

I thank you, dear reader, for the comfort it has given me to share the stories of my family and myself with you during this particular phase of my life. Your patient presence gave me courage to embrace my pregnancy and now motherhood. I promise to continue to walk or dance, one foot in front of the other, to experience the energy of hope in whatever happens next.

ABOUT THE AUTHOR

Lois Collins, also called Loisa, Abuelita, Grandma, Lolo, and Doc, is a retired physician and tenured professor who is now a writer, balcony gardener, cook, dancer, drummer, grandmother, hiker, martial arts student, meditator, and human rights advocate in her community. She resides in Phoenix, Arizona.

45459448R00166

Made in the USA
Middletown, DE
04 July 2017